PIRATE'S TREASURE

Saber paused to stare at her thoughtfully. After a moment he murmured, "Why don't you do us both a favor and say what is on your mind?"

She drew in a deep breath. He seemed serious. Was it possible that he might have a touch of decency after all?

"Very well," she replied. "Emily and I cannot decide if you are monster or myth. We have heard so many stories that it is hard to separate fact from fiction. Are you what they say you are, Captain Saber?"

A slight smile tilted his mouth up at one corner. "And what do they say I am, Miss Angela? Murderer? I've killed men, though I can't say I've derived any satisfaction from it. Pirate? Quite true. Though at times, I've stolen things that belong to me, so I'm not quite certain what that does to my redoubtable reputation as a thief and scourge of the seven seas."

He took a step closer, his voice lowering to a husky timbre that sent chills chasing down her spine. One hand lifted to caress her cheek, then slid around to cup her neck in his palm. His fingers gently massaged her nape, and the breath caught in her throat at his ministrations. He smiled.

"What was it your Miss Emily spouted last night? That I am known as—let me see—*a defiler of damsels?* As for that reputation, I gladly plead. . . ." His hands shifted, fingers tightening in her hair to draw her head back. Angela's throat closed, and her heart beat so fast and hard she was certain he could hear it. Saber's voice was a husky whisper when he finished, ". . . guilty. I plead guilty, Miss Angela."

TODAY'S HOTTEST READS
ARE TOMORROW'S SUPERSTARS

VICTORY'S WOMAN   (4484, $4.50)
by Gretchen Genet
Andrew—the carefree soldier who sought glory on the battlefield,
and returned a shattered man . . . Niall—the legandary frontiers-
man and a former Shawnee captive, tormented by his past . . .
Roger—the troubled youth, who would rise up to claim a shocking legacy . . . and Clarice—the passionate beauty bound by one
man, and hopelessly in love with another. Set against the back-
drop of the American revolution, three men fight for their
heritage—and one woman is destined to change all their lives forever!

FORBIDDEN   (4488, $4.99)
by Jo Beverley
While fleeing from her brothers, who are attempting to sell her
into a loveless marriage, Serena Riverton accepts a carriage ride
from a stranger—who is the handsomest man she has ever seen.
Lord Middlethorpe, himself, is actually contemplating marriage
to a dull daughter of the aristocracy, when he encounters the
breathtaking Serena. She arouses him as no woman ever has. And
after a night of thrilling intimacy—a forbidden liaison—Serena
must choose between a lady's place and a woman's passion!

WINDS OF DESTINY   (4489, $4.99)
by Victoria Thompson
Becky Tate is a half-breed outcast—branded by her Comanche
heritage. Then she meets a rugged stranger who awakens her
heart to the magic and mystery of passion. Hiding a desperate
past, Texas Ranger Clint Masterson has ridden into cattle country
to bring peace to a divided land. But a greater battle rages inside
him when he dares to desire the beautiful Becky!

WILDEST HEART   (4456, $4.99)
by Virginia Brown
Maggie Malone had come to cattle country to forge her future as
a healer. Now she was faced by Devon Conrad, an outlaw
wounded body and soul by his shadowy past . . . whose eyes
blazed with fury even as his burning caress sent her spiraling with
desire. They came together in a Texas town about to explode in sin
and scandal. Danger was their destiny—and there was nothing
they wouldn't dare for love!

*Available wherever paperbacks are sold, or order direct from the
Publisher. Send cover price plus 50¢ per copy for mailing and
handling to Penguin USA, P.O. Box 999, c/o Dept. 17109,
Bergenfield, NJ 07621. Residents of New York and Tennessee
must include sales tax. DO NOT SEND CASH.*

VIRGINIA BROWN
CAPTURE THE WIND

ZEBRA BOOKS
KENSINGTON PUBLISHING CORP.

ZEBRA BOOKS are published by

Kensington Publishing Corp.
850 Third Avenue
New York, NY 10022

First Printing: December, 1994

Printed in the United States of America

To Laura Austin, one of the most important and appreciated people in my life. Thank you, Laura— I'd be lost without you.

And to Frances Teague, who has proven the value of a real friend. You're the best, Fran.

Prologue

London Docks, 1788

"Is that the ship, Charles?"

Elaine Davenport indicated a vessel docking at the Pool below London Bridge. Wind thick with the smell of foul water and rotting wood dislodged strands of her pale hair. Her gloved hand tucked the strays back into place, then pressed a scented handkerchief of Belgian lace to her nose. Her words were muffled. "I don't see a dark-haired child among those along the ship's rail."

David Charles Edward Sheridan, Fourth Duke of Tremayne and heir to the fortunes of Sheridan Shipping, frowned at the ship nosing into its berth against the broad stone quay. There was the sharp, sour smell of refuse and fish. A forest of masts swayed in the river: huge East Indiamen, galliots, whalers, and tea clippers. Raucous sea birds swooped and circled above quays teeming with activity.

Charles shrugged. "I don't see him either. Frankly, it's been so long, I might not recognize him. Ten years, you know. I suppose he's no longer a small child, as in the miniatures I've shown you. Christian would be . . . oh, he would be nearly seventeen now." Charles shook his

head. "The time has passed so swiftly. Plainly, we should
be looking for a youth instead of a small boy."

Elaine glanced around the dock. Her fingers curled
around Charles's arm, and she murmured disdainfully,
"Such riffraff gather here on the docks. It would have
been much better to have waited for Filbert to bring him
to the house, as I tried to tell you . . ."

Charles shot her a frown. "I was quite anxious to see
him and did not wish to wait. He's been gone so long,
and with pirates, for the love of God—I want to see for
myself that Christian is all right."

"Yes, so you said." Elaine released his arm to smooth
a hand over the folds of her immaculate brocade skirt.
"Well, I'm certain that once we are wed, I can help you
eradicate some of the taint that stains his character. Imagine. It took four of Sir Ramsey's men to coax him off
that ship. Pirates. Dear Lord, and he's been living among
them since . . ."

She halted when Charles gave her a pained glance. It
had taken him some time to accept his wife's death and
his small son's disappearance. Now that Christian was
finally coming home, his betrothed's reminder of those
painful years was a sharp jab. Elaine leaned close.

"If I've provoked uncomfortable memories, I apologize. It's just that I am so distressed for what you must
have suffered."

Charles's stare was level. "You should be more distressed for what poor Christian has suffered. To be kept
in the care of pirates sailing the Spanish Main cannot
have been pleasant. There is absolutely no way of knowing what he has been through in that time. Sir Ramsey's

letter mentioned that Christian was rather surly and distrustful."

"Yes, I can imagine." Elaine patted an offending curl of blond hair back into place and frowned daintily. "Still, it will take time and a great deal of discipline to remove the stain of years of piracy from the boy. You will have your hands full. Fortunately, my father has recommended an excellent school. It has only the best tutors for his education, and is known for the severity of its discipline when it comes to unruly, disobedient boys. I am certain it will do Christian a great deal of good to have the discipline he has certainly lacked in these past ten years."

"Unruly?" Charles shook his head. "Not Christian. He was always timid to the point of annoyance. Scared of his own shadow. I cannot imagine how he survived all those years with pirates."

"Can't you? I should think . . ."

Charles tensed. "Look. The ship is lowering its ramp."

Elaine's reply faded into the rising hubbub around them as Charles strained to catch the first sight of his son. Dray wagons rumbled by loudly, wheels clattering over rough stones. Long brick warehouses stretched behind the quays, and stacks of cargo waiting to be loaded rose like small buildings. Charles shifted impatiently, staring past Elaine to the lowered ramp nudging the stone quay. He frowned.

"Where the devil could he be? I was certain Filbert would be right at the rail with him, knowing how I've longed for this day."

Elaine tugged at the sleeve of his frock coat with a

decisive note of censure in her tone. "Do not appear overeager, Charles. It's unseemly in public."

He turned, brows lifting. "Unseemly? To want to see my son after so long? You overstep your boundaries, Elaine."

His reproof had the desired effect; she looked down, dark lashes lowering over remarkable green eyes. The soft bottom lip that so many men had gazed at with longing began to quiver slightly. Charles's voice softened.

"I appreciate your desire for proper etiquette, but I cannot think of a previous example for a man's son being returned to him after long years aboard a pirate ship in the Caribbean. There are no proper rules in this instance, I believe."

Her voice was distant and cool. "I am certain you are right, but I do believe we should maintain proprieties, even on so joyous an occasion."

"For God's sake, Elaine—" he began in an irritable tone, but was interrupted by a commotion on the deck of the ship.

They both turned, just in time to see a uniformed seaman go tumbling over the rail and into the narrow space between ship and quay. A loud splash sent up a geyser of water, but did not drown out the lurid string of curses that accompanied the man's fall.

These curses did not come from the sailor, however, but from the mouth of a youth being wrestled along the deck of the ship by no less than five men. Charles and Elaine watched in stunned horror. The knot of flailing arms and legs lurched closer, then balanced at the edge of the ramp leading to the quay below.

Ship passengers and those on the stones of the quay

gave a concerted gasp. The tangle of struggling combatants swayed precariously, threatening to tumble into the narrow ribbon of water below in the same manner as the unfortunate sailor. Above the grunts and curses that accompanied the tussle rose a shrieking litany.

"Slash 'im! Stick 'im! Belay, mates! Ship to starboard! Awwk!"

A flash of scarlet dipped above the heads of those involved in the conflict; the beat of wings snapped against the wind. Charles and Elaine exchanged glances of dawning horror. They moved forward to arrive at the bottom of the ramp leading from the ship just as the combatants lurched onto the quay.

Flushed faces were a blur, then a burst of curses and dark hair exploded from the center of the men onto the flat stones and landed in a half-crouch. Snarling with a ferocity that would have done a Bengal tiger proud, the panting youth shoved a brown fist into the air and shook it.

"Bloody buggers. If I 'ad my saber, I'd cut you inta too many pieces ta feed ta th' bloody sharks . . ."

A flash of scarlet squawked again and settled in a whir of wings onto the boy's shoulder. "Bloody buggers!" came the shriek, and the bird tilted its head to one side as if expecting confirmation. A brown hand stroked the wings, and then the boy turned in a whirl, eyes raking over Charles and Elaine with a hot blue gaze.

"Christian," Charles said in a strangled croak. "Are you Christian Sheridan?"

A harsh laugh cut the air, and the boy's lips curled in a sneer. "Not I, guv'nor. They calls me Tiger."

"How appropriate," Charles murmured in obvious relief. His gaze shifted to the breathless man limping forward. "Filbert," he said faintly. "You look—dreadful."

"Aye, Your Grace." Filbert shot the youth a baleful glare. "Lord Christian seemed to find it an inconvenient time to disembark. We tried to persuade him differently, but he was rather . . . firm . . . in his decision to remain aboard."

Charles slid a horrified gaze back to the boy. "This is Christian?"

As Filbert nodded morosely, the boy snarled, "Bloody 'ell! My name ain't Christian. It's Tiger. 'Ow many times do I have ta tell ya that, ya . . ."

He reeled off a list of colorful titles for the long-suffering Filbert, including several comments about the doubtful legitimacy of his parentage, while Charles listened in growing dismay and Elaine began to make gasping sounds of shock. As if just noticing her, the boy shot Elaine a raking stare.

" 'Ello, love. Ain't you a bit young ta be with this ole geezer? I can toss yer skirts for ya if ya need decent diddlin' . . ."

Charles stepped forward and clapped a hand over the boy's mouth. Reaction was swift. The youth turned in a savage whirl, a bare foot slamming into his father's middle as he jerked away. The Duke of Tremayne made a muffled sound and slipped to his knees, while the men who had wrestled Christian from the ship to shore grabbed him.

Above the chaos, the scarlet bird circled gracefully in a screeching frenzy. "Bloody hell! Bloody hell!"

With a low sigh, Elaine Davenport, the daughter of

the Earl of Southwild, slipped into a dead faint on the soiled stones of the quay.

Christian Sheridan stared at her with an expression of grim satisfaction, ignoring the clutching hands that held him still. A brisk breeze lifted his dark hair, stirring it against his bare shoulders and tugging at the bright red sash around his waist. Below the ragged knee-length trousers he wore, his legs and feet were bare. Sunlight glinted from the dark teak of tanned skin and immature muscle, and made the diamond earring in his left lobe glitter.

But it was his face that commanded the most attention, a caricature of youth with deep blue eyes that looked older than time. A faint scar ran from his left eyebrow to his cheek, and when he smiled, as he was now, he looked more like a dangerous predator than a boy of sixteen.

"Tiger! Tiger!" the bird screeched, and settled with a flap of its wings onto the torn shoulder of Filbert's once immaculate frock coat.

Filbert shuddered, and looked at the boy staring back at him with hot, resentful eyes. "Lord Christian, may I present your father to you, His Grace, the Duke of Tremayne."

Christian spat onto the stones. The Duke of Tremayne rose shakily to his feet and took a step forward. His voice was slightly unsteady.

"Welcome home, Christian."

"Go to hell," the boy snarled, and Tremayne turned.

"Bring him to our coach, Filbert. If that is possible. Oh, and someone bring Elaine 'round from her faint. It's time to go home."

* * *

Tension crackled in the wood-paneled library of Greystone Hall as if a towering blaze. The duke eyed his son with a mixture of frustration and trepidation. He leaned forward, knuckles gouging into the polished surface of his desk.

"What do you hope to gain by this display of rebellion? There is no reason for it that I can see."

"Aye, so ya keep saying," the boy flung at him. He sprawled his lean frame in a chair as if daring the duke to protest.

Charles held his tongue, though Filbert would have been beside himself at the insult. No one sat in the presence of a duke unless given express permission. And certainly not a wild-haired boy with a foul-tongued bird perched on his shoulder. The duke studied the bird, grimacing when the creature made a deposit upon the Flemish carpet.

"I would much prefer that you confine that nasty parrot to a cage," he said tautly.

Christian stroked the bird's feathers with a tender gesture. "He ain't no parrot. He's a lory."

"A what?"

The boy's lip curled with superior contempt. "A bloody lory. Cain't ya hear good—yer lordship?"

Charles stiffened. "Christian," he began, but was cut off by a rude oath and defiant glare.

"I told ya—my name is Tiger."

The duke's mouth tightened. "And I told you that I refuse to call you by that abhorrent name. Christian is the name your mother and I chose to call you, and—"

"Don't dare mention her to me!"

Lithe as the tiger of his adopted namesake, the boy surged to his feet in a fluid motion that made his father step back and the bird rise into the air with an indignant squawk. Christian vibrated with a rage that left Charles floundering for words.

"Whyever not?" Charles asked after a moment of smoldering silence. "Why should I not mention your mother?"

The lory settled back on Christian's shoulder, muttering several vile phrases that Charles ignored with only a slight tightening of his mouth to indicate he'd heard them.

Christian jerked around and began to prowl the room. His tattered trousers flapped around his knees. The only concession he'd yet made to conventional fashion was a loose white shirt with flowing sleeves. A red sash still circled his waist, and the diamond earring winked in gray light that streamed through tall windows lining an entire library wall.

With one hand clenched into a fist, Christian dragged it along a mahogany edge of the gleaming desk, then turned to face his father.

"You're not fit to have kissed the hem of her skirts."

Charles lifted a brow. "How did you arrive at this conclusion? Not that I argue the point, but I'm just curious."

Christian took a step toward him, eyes locked on his father's face. His diction was perfect, the ill-bred accent vanished.

"Do you really think a child of six is too young to understand what he hears? That he doesn't notice if his mother weeps into her pillow at night?" He dug a fist into his chest. "I noticed. And I noticed when you had those men follow us, too. I may have been young, but I'm not as stupid as you would like me to be."

Charles took a deep breath. His face was set, and his gaze did not waver. "I never thought you were stupid. Just too young to understand the implications behind my actions."

"Understand? What was there to understand?" Christian gave a harsh laugh. "You hired men to catch my mother when she left you. You didn't think I could recognize the difference between real pirates and men masquerading as pirates, did you? No, I can see by the look on your face that you didn't. But I did. Oh, not at first, true. But later, after my mother had been tossed overboard by your hired thugs and we sailed away on another ship, I discovered the deception. We were attacked and overtaken by real pirates, and I knew the difference." He looked away and took a deep breath. "Oh aye, I knew the difference well then."

"Christian—"

"No." Backing away, he shook his head. "You killed my mother as surely as if you had been the one to toss her over the rail without a thought."

"You're wrong."

"Am I? Can you stand there and look me in the eye and tell me that you did not send men after us? That you did not give them orders to take me and get rid of her?"

"I gave orders for her to be followed and you taken, yes, but I would never have given orders to throw her overboard. She could have gone on to meet the man she was fleeing to—or did you know that? Did you know she was leaving me for another man?"

Something froze in Christian's face, and he took an involuntary step back. "You're lying," he said in a hoarse whisper. "You're—"

"Am I?" Charles took a step forward. "I don't have to lie. If you say you remember so much, then try and recall the nights she left you alone in your cabin. Can you?" He took another step while Christian retreated backward, pain and denial on his youthful face. Charles continued grimly, "Do you remember her returning, all flustered smiles and whispers? You should, my boy. Because you and she were on her lover's ship."

"No." Christian halted at last, back to the bank of long windows. He stared up at his father's face where gray daylight picked out the bitter grooves on each side of his mouth. Denial strangled his voice until it came out only a faint husk of sound. "You're lying."

Charles's mouth twisted. "Oh no. Kill her? Why would I? She should have had to face her shame—and me. But Vivian St. Genevieve would never have done that." Charles put back his head and laughed, but it rang into the study with a harshness thick enough to be felt as well as heard. "She knew I would not give you up, and that is why she took you from me. I would have followed her to the end of the earth for you, and I damn near did. If you think to hear an apology for her loss, you're mistaken."

"You bastard . . ."

"Am I? Tell me, Christian—whatever makes you think your mother is dead?"

"I saw—"

"You saw what she meant you to see. Dead? Vivian?" The duke laughed harshly. "Oh no, my lad, not by half.

No, your precious mother is quite alive, more's the pity. She has just chosen to . . . absent herself from England, as well as from her husband and son."

"If she'd been alive, she would have come for me," Christian said tightly. "She would never have allowed me to be taken away like that."

Charles gave him a mocking stare. "You are so young and naive, my boy. And much too trusting in the gentle nature of women, it seems. Life has yet to teach you the realities of the fair sex, I see. A pity. Until you learn better, I fear you will suffer greatly."

For a long moment, Christian stood there. The bird on his shoulder muttered something obscene, then lapsed into silence as if sensing disaster. Without another word, the boy turned on his bare heel and stalked from the library.

Charles stared after him long after he'd gone. Shadows melted into night, and a fine drizzle coated the leaded glass panes of Greystone Hall before the Duke of Tremayne left his library.

One

Atlantic Ocean, 1802

"Don't be a goose, Emily. Whyever would pirates attack our ship?"

Angela Lindell gazed at her maid with fond amusement. Dear Emily, so addicted to fantasy instead of fact, even when it terrified her. It was one of her most endearing—and irritating—qualities, and Angela was frequently moved to tell her so.

Emily Carmichael glanced over her shoulder at the gray waves surrounding their ship, then shuddered nervously. She turned back to her mistress. "Oh, Miss Angela, it's said that pirates attack ships in these waters with no rational thought at all. Why, only last month, that horrible Captain Saber took three ships from these very same waters. Killed the crew, stole the goods, and"—her voice lowered dramatically—"and ravished the women."

"Did he. How energetic this Captain Saber must be." Angela curled her gloved hands over the side rail and leaned into the wind until it tugged her hair loose from beneath her hat. She caught at the pale strands whipping against her cheeks and murmured, "If I were to believe all the tales I hear about him from you and the *London Times,* the man is a veritable genius at being in two places at once." Tucking her hair back under the bands of her hat, she turned to smile at Emily when she made her expected protest.

"Emily, dear, you've been with me since I was twelve. I have considered you my boon companion for these past dozen years. I must confess, however, that I have noticed your tendency to ignore the disparate facts surrounding any romantic myth you stumble upon. While most of the time I find it quite entertaining, I admit that I am not very much entertained now. I am set on my course, and the *Scrutiny* has sailed, so you may stop trying to dissuade me."

Emily gave a half-sob and pressed her clenched hand to her mouth. Her brown eyes were wide and moist.

Angela sighed. "Are you going to be ill again?" she asked, but Emily shook her head.

Shiny brown curls whipped over Emily's pale cheeks. She mumbled through her lace handkerchief and fingers, "Whatever will your parents say when they discover that you and I are gone?"

"I'm well past the age for them to dictate my actions," Angela said after a moment's pause. "I realize they love me and want what's best for me, but we cannot seem to agree on just what that is." She managed a small smile of reassurance. "Once Papa resigns himself to my determination to wed Philippe and *not* that wretched Baron Von Gooseliver—"

"Gosden-Lear," Emily corrected faintly.

"I find Gooseliver more appropriate. At any rate, once Papa and Mama have become resigned to the realization that I will wed Philippe, they will come 'round. They always do."

"I think," Emily said in the same faint voice, "that you may have underestimated Mr. Lindell's determination to marry you into an excellent family. He seemed quite set on it, Miss Angela."

Angela tried to hide her impatience. "Papa has it in his head that Philippe's royal lineage is not enough to make a good marriage. Normally, I would agree. But Papa took an immediate dislike to Philippe, and never gave him a proper chance to prove himself. It was all over a ridiculous misunderstanding, and quite frustrating. If *I* deem Philippe a suitable husband, I do not see why my family will not trust my judgment. It's not as if I'm a chit barely out of the schoolroom, you know."

Emily looked down at her clenched hands. "But you hardly know him, except for his letters."

"Nonsense." Angela stifled a twinge of irritation. "One can truly come to know a man by his correspondence, and though Philippe and I may have been separated by miles, we are very close in a spiritual sense. He has written me almost daily for the past eight years, and I have come to know his soul."

Emily did not look up, her voice a low murmur. "Do you not think, Miss Angela, that Mr. Lindell may have a point when he said that Philippe du Plessis cannot support you properly?"

"I think it frivolous of Papa to decide that Philippe only cares for his money and my dowry. Though it is true that the du Plessis family was devastated by the ghastly revolution in Paris, and most of them foully murdered by the rabble, that does not mean that Philippe is bound to me only by necessity. We corresponded, remember, even before those terrible times."

Angela jerked irritably at her gloves, dislodging a tiny pearl button from one cuff. It pinged against the wooden deck and rolled through a scupper and into the sea below.

Emily bit her lower lip. "Yes, I remember your corresponding then. But you've seen him so rarely, Miss Angela, that perhaps you don't know him as well as you should."

"Nonsense. You haven't read his letters. The written sentiments of the heart can be more revealing than physical closeness. Papa is being unnecessarily suspicious. Though I do understand his concern, I do not share it. He seems more worried about his plump pockets than my feelings."

"Oh, that cannot be true," Emily protested. "Mr. Lindell sets great store by your slightest wish, Miss Angela."

"But not as much store as he sets by his senior partnership in City Bank, or his stock holdings in Sheridan Shipping, or all those sugar fields in the Caribbean, and tobacco plantations in the Americas—"

Angela halted abruptly. Emily's soft brown eyes had lowered, and her teeth dug into her bottom lip to still its quivering. Her voice was shaky when she said, "I do not think that I shall care very much for this place called Louisiana, Miss Angela. It is said to be filled with hostile savages, and lizards large enough to devour entire villages."

"More information from the *Times*, Emily?" Angela felt a surge of guilt at her maid's dismay and put a comforting hand upon the girl's shoulder. "I shan't allow anything bad to happen to you. Haven't I always been able to see us safe?"

"This is quite different than stealing away from Miss Hartsell's Academy and making a day in Hyde Park, Miss Angela." Emily drew in a deep breath. "Louisiana is far away from London, and far from Mr. Lindell's protection."

"True. But I'm quite capable in my own right." Angela gave her a last pat, then turned back to the rail to stare over the choppy waves that seemed to stretch forever. It was nearing dusk. England's shores had long since faded from the horizon, and she felt a swell of anticipation that bordered on excitement. A new world, a new life—and her beloved Philippe. What would he say when she arrived, and he realized what she had braved to join him? He would be overwhelmed, she was certain. This was, indeed, a drastic step for her to take, but it would be worth it when she saw his relief and joy.

She had several moments of pleasant reverie before Emily's distress once more penetrated her dreamy haze. She sighed at the girl's inability to envision their promising future and turned back to her.

"Emily, even Papa has always said that I am very resourceful. I beg of you not to distress yourself so. I have already written Philippe of our imminent arrival, so he will be expecting us. Once I am with him, Papa will be forced to recognize my determination and he will concede."

When Emily still did not seem convinced, Angela shook her head. "At any rate, once Philippe and I are wed, you can return to London if you're so very unhappy."

"Are you certain your Philippe is in Louisiana?"

"Quite certain." Angela's hand dropped to the reticule dangling from her arm. She could feel the folded sheaf of paper in the small velvet bag that held her last communication from him. "He went to relatives in New Orleans after Papa's abrupt dismissal of his suit. He was quite upset, you know."

"I daresay," Emily muttered.

Angela frowned. "You never have cared for him."

Emily shook her head. "No, Miss Angela. I cannot say I have. But then, I do not care very much for foreigners."

"That's what comes of being born and bred in Yorkshire, I suspect. You should broaden your horizons."

"Louisiana is broader than I should ever have wished to expand them," Emily said so wistfully that Angela felt another sharp twinge of guilt.

"Oh, do not look so glum, Emily. All will be well. Let us not dwell on things too much." She paused, then said, "I have honeyed dates below in my trunk, if you like. I know they are your favorite. Shall I fetch them?"

Even the promise of honeyed dates did not brighten Emily's round face, though she finally nodded when Angela said she was going below to fetch the tin. "As you will, Miss Angela. Though it won't help very much."

Along with the guilt came a surge of exasperation. Angela dutifully tamped it down as she turned away from the rail and made her way to the hatch leading below the main deck. Emily had become more a friend than a servant over the years, but there were times when her timidity was a great trial. If there had been a way for Angela to travel without her, she would have done so, but she dared not flout convention any more than she was already doing. Besides, it would not be long before they were all back in London.

Of course, Angela mused as she felt her way along the narrow, musty passageway toward their cabin, she had never dared so much before. And there was the nagging worry in the back of her mind that despite her assurances, Emily's fears might somehow prove true. However, nothing ventured, nothing gained, and she was convinced she was doing the right thing.

A thrust of pain at the memory of Philippe's stalwart expression when Papa had ordered him from their home in Mayfair made her flinch. Poor Philippe. He had looked so despairing and heartsick at the betrayal. None of her protests had swayed her father, who stood firm in his belief that Philippe du Plessis would never be his son-in-law.

Why was she the only one who could see behind Philippe's circumstances to the gentle, kind man he really was? She'd always considered her father more astute in his judgments. That he refused to reconsider his rash conclusion was painful.

After the scene in their parlor, Papa had arbitrarily announced his acceptance of Baron Von Gosden-Lear's proposal of marriage for her; it had fused her burgeoning desire to flout convention, and she had immediately declared her intention to wed Philippe without parental consent. It had, of course, been a disaster.

Papa had bellowed and blustered, and Mama had wept and implored Angela not to even suggest such a thing. The dreadful interview had ended with Angela's retreat to her room and nothing being settled. It had occurred to her as she lay sleepless in her bed, that her marriage to Philippe would be a very simple matter once it was a *fait accompli.* Papa would be forced to acknowledge Philippe as her husband, and Baron Gooseliver could slink off to propose marriage to some other young lady. She was made of sterner stuff than to meekly submit to something as important as marriage.

Angela pushed open the door to the tiny cabin she shared with Emily and lurched inside. Peeling off her gloves, she tried to keep her balance. The constant roll and pitch of the *Scrutiny* made her stumble about most clumsily. Really, you'd think that a shipping line as well known as Sheridan would offer better accommodations, though the purser at the main office had assured her that this was one of the best compartments available on a ship that did not normally carry passengers. Tucked into a corner of the 'tween-deck quarters occupied by the crew, the cabin had very little space, but did afford some privacy.

Angela eyed the narrow bunks with distaste and bent to fumble at the catch of her trunk. It had been stashed in a small space between bunk and wall; a tiny cupboard that held a washbowl and chamber pot was just above it. She tugged at the trunk, and succeeded in pulling it out enough to open the lid.

A sudden lurch of the ship slammed the lid shut, and she narrowly escaped having her fingers smashed. Without warning, the door to the cupboard slung open, and the washbowl and chamber pot tumbled out to roll across the dipping floor with a metallic clatter.

Mumbling to herself about the bleak comforts of a ship, Angela finally had them caught and stowed away again before she returned to her trunk. It took her a minute to find the tin of honeyed dates that she'd included at the last moment. A jumble of hastily packed clothes contended with gilt-framed miniatures of her family, hairbrushes, bottles of scent, and an assortment of odds and ends that seemed faintly ridiculous in retrospect. She smiled when she saw the porcelain music box she'd brought. Lifting it from the trunk, she turned the key to wind it. Light, tinkling tones were almost drowned out by the creaking and groaning of the ship, and she put the box to her ear and closed her eyes. Papa had given it to her for her tenth birthday. Scenes on the porcelain cover depicted unicorns and a maiden with long blond hair. Papa had said that he'd thought of her at once when he'd seen it, and had bought it for his own fair-haired maiden to enjoy.

A hot press of tears behind her closed lids made her sigh, and she opened her eyes and replaced the music box in the trunk. She could only hope Papa would understand and forgive her for worrying him. It had seemed like the only way to ensure her happiness with Philippe.

As she rose to her feet with the tin of comfits, the *Scrutiny* gave another heavy lurch to one side, then rolled so that she had to cling to the edge of a bunk to keep from falling to the floor. The rumble of pounding feet against the deck made her look up with a frown. She could hear the incessant piping of a whistle cut through the noise with annoying regularity. Why had she ever thought a ship would be relatively peaceful? It had seemed an idyllic interlude that would end with a joyous reunion with Philippe in New Orleans. She had quickly discovered that the ship was anything but quiet and idyllic, with piping whistles, the slap of canvas, humming lines, and roughly shouted orders.

Muttering to herself about shattered illusions, Angela made her way to the cabin door and threw it open. A shrill shriek gave her only an instant's warning before Emily barreled into the cabin. Her face was contorted with terror and her words were an incomprehensible babble.

"Emily." Angela gave her a slight shake by one arm that had no effect whatsoever. "Emily!"

"Oh . . . oh . . . oh Miss . . ."

Impatient with Emily's hiccoughing hysteria, Angela gave her arm a sharp pinch that brought the girl to a gasping halt.

"Tell me what has you so distraught," Angela demanded when Emily drew in a deep breath and seemed calmer. "Are you ill again? Why are you so hysterical?"

"P-p-pirates," Emily stuttered, brown eyes as wide as saucers and her face as pale as milk. She clutched Angela's arm. "Oh miss! We're being chased by pirates!"

"Nonsense." Angela's tart denial was more to convince herself than Emily. "We're barely two days out of England. Why would any self-respecting pirate be lurking practically in the English Channel?"

Emily moaned and closed her eyes. "I dunno, miss, I swear I dunno. I only knows that the c-cap'n told me to git below and s-s-stay here, as p-p-pirates are after us."

It was evident by Emily's descent into her broad Yorkshire dialect that she was beyond fear and bordering on mindless terror. Angela took pity on her, and gave her a gentle shove toward one of the bunks.

"Lie down, Emily. I shall go above deck and find out what is really going on."

As she sank down onto the hard comfort of a bunk and put the back of a hand over her eyes, Emily said in a pitiful moan, "Don't go up there, miss. Just the sight o' that pirate's black flag will give ye a fright. A saber. That's what their flag has on it—a saber drippin' with blood."

"You've gone too far, Emily." Angela tossed the tin of dates to the bunk and grabbed at the wall to support herself as the ship gave another lurch. "A dripping saber? It's too melodramatic."

Emily lifted her hand to peer at her with one eye. "Not this time. The Cap'n said it's Captain Saber, the most dreadful pirate to ever sail the open seas. Oh miss, when I think of all those articles about him and what he does to the captives he takes . . ."

Having heard enough, Angela fumbled her way out the door and into the dank, musty companionway. It was evident that something untoward was happening, as even from below she could hear the thunder of feet and male voices lifted in excitement.

Still, the scene that met her eyes when she pulled herself up the ladder and through the hatch was a shock. Men in various stages of panic scurried over the decks, hauling lines, loosing sails, and jettisoning heavy cargo. It was the last that shook her most, the confirmation that something bad was definitely about to happen.

She made her way to the captain, ignoring his irate glance and brusque demand to know why she was above deck.

"Captain Turnower, what is happening?"

He grasped her by the arm, shocking her as he whirled her around and gave her a shove toward the hatch. "I don't have time to stand here and explain anything to you. Get back below and stay there until you're told to come out."

Dazed, and fighting the rising fear that threatened to choke her, Angela fumbled for a steadying grip on the iron rail that edged the hatch. She looked up and past the decks. Her eyes fastened on the ship bearing down on them. Above the sails, fluttering in the wind, was the banner that Emily had seen. White against a black field, a curved saber dripped with a few scarlet drops of blood. The insignia amply identified the ship.

Captain Kit Saber. His name prompted a shudder, and she recalled news articles about him that she had always regarded as pure fantasy. Rumors about him abounded, from the ludicrous tale that he was the son of a duke, to the much more credible story that he was the illegitimate offspring of a wandering Englishman and a West Indian whore. As a pirate, Kit Saber struck terror into the hearts of seafaring men everywhere. He'd been said to take as many as six ships in a single day—though that was deemed improbable by most—and left behind no survivors to tell the tale of his depredations. Only a lucky few had escaped to whisper of his crimes against them, of his fierce, ruthless crew rumored to drink the blood of their victims before shoving them overboard at the points of their swords. Among his crew was a giant, with ebony skin and a tattooed face, and he and the captain were said to be in league with the devil.

Another shudder made her ache, and Angela stumbled back down the hatch to her cabin. Emily still lay moaning with terror on the bunk, and Angela ignored her as she moved to her trunk again. Somewhere . . . she had seen it in here just a few minutes before . . . ah, there it was.

Triumphant, she held up Papa's small pistol, which she'd tossed into her trunk. It held only two balls, but would at least be sufficient threat to hold a savage pirate at bay long enough to barter for their lives and freedom.

She looked up to see Emily watching her. Her grip tightened on the pistol. "Do what I tell you, Emily, and do not argue with me. There may be no time."

"Captain Saber."

Kit turned, sheathing his sword as he glanced down at his sailing master. "What is it, Mr. Buttons?"

Fading sunlight glinted in his pale hair as Mr. Buttons pointed toward a hatch that led below the *Scrutiny*'s top deck. "Trouble below, cap'n. Turk is there."

"Turk? If he's below, he's capable of handling any trouble himself. Captain Turnower and I have some negotiations to conduct concerning the surrender of his ship's cargo."

"But Captain . . ."

Kit had turned back to the white-faced Captain Turnower. Smoke hazed the air, burning his eyes and lungs, and Kit felt a wave of impatience to have this done with. The *Scrutiny* had yielded with the firing of only a few token shots, but some idiot aboard her had managed to set fire to a pile of tarred ropes. Normally, the transferral of ship's stores and cargo from one vessel to the other was quite satisfying, but the stench of smoldering rope was making his lungs ache.

Mr. Buttons loudly cleared his throat. Kit gave the sailing master a fierce glare that made him swallow hard, but he did not retreat.

"Captain, it was Turk who sent me to fetch you. He said it was 'most imperative' that you come at once."

A faint smile tugged at Kit's mouth at the awkward mimicry of Turk's speech. He nodded. "Very well, Mr. Buttons. Let me assure the captain that I have not forgotten him."

He slid his gaze back to Captain Turnower, who met it without flinching. No pleading or whining here, but a man's acceptance of defeat. It not only made matters go more smoothly, but always saved lives when the prey surrendered.

With a slight bow, Kit said, "Do be seated, Captain. My sailing master will see to your comfort until my return."

Turnower gave a short jerk of his head to acknowledge his agreement, though he could have done little else. His heavy-bottomed merchantman was too slow to outrun a ship much lighter in tonnage and built for speed. The *Scrutiny* was outmanned, outgunned, and outmaneuvered. Turnower had recognized that fact early enough to save the lives of his crew.

Grasping the edge of the hatch with one hand, Kit swung below in a single leap, landing on his feet in the dark passageway below. The lamps had gone out and it was gloomy. The air smelled of damp wood and lingering traces of spices from forgotten cargo. He walked down the passageway in long strides, moving toward a lantern outside an open door. He could see Turk's huge frame barring the doorway, and he stopped.

"What have you found that you cannot handle, Turk?"

Despite Kit's obvious amusement, Turk did not seem to share it. He barely turned his head; lantern light made the black skin of his bald crown gleam dully.

"This young lady desires to have a word with you, Captain. I exhorted her to defer it until later, but she seems a rather precipitate person, and insisted upon conversing with you immediately."

Turk's mellifluous tones rolled loudly in the dark, silent passageway, and Kit lifted his brow.

"A young lady? Aboard a Sheridan merchantman?"

"So it seems, Captain."

Kit eyed Turk's unusual rigidity and the way he stood in the doorway; and suddenly understood his stiffness. He stepped to the side to peer over Turk's shoulder.

A young woman stood in desperate determination, a pistol trained on Turk with fierce concentration. Kit stifled a laugh. How incongruous for the massive Turk to be held at bay by a slip of a girl with a tiny firearm no bigger than Turk's palm.

"Very well, Turk," he said after a brief assessment, "I will speak with her. Do move aside."

"Oh, no," came a voice from inside. "He doesn't move. If you would be so good, Captain, as to converse with me over his shoulder, I won't get so nervous that I accidentally pull the trigger of this pistol."

Kit saw a muscle in Turk's dark jaw clench, and he held his laughter. He didn't know why he found it so amusing, given that most females didn't know one end of a pistol from the other, hence being more of a danger in that respect than any other threat. And the glimpse he'd had of the feral little creature holding the weapon had been anything but reassuring.

Pale wisps of blond hair scattered her brow beneath the brim of a lopsided hat. Though she held the pistol with grim determination, he'd noticed the fine lines of stress on each side of her mouth. Any sudden movement might, indeed, cause her to squeeze the trigger. It would not ensure the accuracy of her aim, however, as the barrel of the pistol seemed to waver halfway between the cabin wall and the ceiling most of the time.

Kit drew back and leaned his shoulder against the wall of the passageway. "I am at your service, madam. Pray, make your wishes known, for I fear we are wasting valuable time."

There were muffled whispers and scuffling feet, and he shot Turk a questioning glance. "What is she doing?"

"Predators of this nature seem to come in pairs, Captain," the ebony giant observed. "We have a full complement of them in the cabin."

"I see." Suddenly wearying of the ridiculous delay in a play that had only one ending that he could see, Kit let his voice take on the hard edge that had been known to make men tremble. "Madam, if you value your life and health, put down that pistol before I take the decision from your hands."

Silence fell. The ship creaked and groaned, and he could hear the thud of cargo bumping against hatches as it was transferred to his ship. He waited impatiently, and was about to repeat his demand in more explicit terms when he heard her refusal.

"No," came the quavering reply. "If I relinquish the pistol, there will be nothing to stop you from doing your worst."

"Damnation, there's nothing to stop me now." He lev-

in
my
sult

"N

"Pe
his. If
if you a
nate as t

He let
promise of
fective than
English gentl

During the p
proaching grou   ...shift of the deck
beneath his feet.   a glance at Turk, and saw
that he had also   ...ected the ship's rising motion. It
should provide a perfect opportunity.

"What will it be?" Kit demanded to distract the girl. "Do you surrender easily, or must we resort to extremes?"

"I . . . I only want mine and my maid's safety guaranteed," came the faintly breathless reply. Her voice quivered, not a good sign as far as Kit was concerned.

As the ship began a slow, stately rise, he moved forward a step, glimpsing the girl's frightened bravado before the ship suddenly dropped again. The brief moment of abrupt weightlessness made the girl stagger, her pistol wavering. At almost the same instant as he, Turk leaped forward. A stifled scream sliced the air, and the booming report of a pistol deafened him as Kit lunged close behind Turk.

the tiny cabin
grunt. Kit had a
slender legs in white
around a fragile wrist.
forward a limp, pale-faced girl
curls. She promptly fainted with
dropping to the floor by his feet. He
tention to the daring assailant, and saw that
her pinned against the bunk with his massive
. The pistol lay on the cabin floor, smoke still curling
from the barrel.

Kit scooped it up with one hand, tossing the uncon-
scious girl to the bunk with his other. He stuck the pistol
into his belt, then turned.

Turk's muscled biceps were streaked with blood, and
Kit muttered a curse.

"Bloody hell, Turk. She shot you."

"So it would seem, Captain. I commend your acuity."

Furious now, Kit reached for the girl, jerking her to
him. Her hat was askew, dipping over one eye and half
hiding her face. His hand tangled in a wealth of loose
blond hair that had tumbled over her shoulder. It felt as
clean and fresh as sunlight on a winter's day; he dragged
her close and tilted back her hat. When her small, patrician nose was only a few inches from his and he could
see terror fill her grass green eyes, he said with deliberate cruelty, "I warned you that you would not like your
fate."

Her pupils expanded to darken her eyes with dramatic
shadows. Fear shone in her gaze, fear and something else
he could not place. He felt her muscles tense, saw the
shadows in her eyes sharpen to purpose. Before he could

react to this unexpected threat, the delicate little creature cowering in his grip brought up a swift, accurate knee.

Unprepared, Kit was caught in his groin by a blow only slightly softened by petticoat and skirts. He grunted in pain and released her to double over. There was a roaring in his ears as if he'd been standing too long on the gundeck. His vision blurred out of focus for a moment as he went to one knee and tried to hold the nausea at bay.

By the time he looked up again, his blond assailant was well in hand. Turk's broad fingers curled around her throat in a menacing grip. Kit rose slowly and took a stumbling step, then another; he finally drew in a deep breath that felt riddled with needles. He straightened to his full height with only a slight wince.

"Take her topside," he said in a voice that sounded strange. He eyed the girl's flushed face for a long moment while Turk rearranged his hold on her. Turk seemed absorbed in the task of using her pink satin dress sash as manacles, and did not glance at him. Kit had the distinct impression that it was more because of a desire to hide his laughter than the pain the shallow burn across his biceps was giving him.

Kit turned away and, with only a slight limp, made his way to the upper deck.

Two

"What did you do to him?" Emily whispered in a quivering voice.

Angela slid her maid an assessing glance. Emily had wakened to utter hysteria, made worse by the pirates' icy indifference. Only a growling threat to knock her out again had ended it. Now they were bound to the mainmast of the *Scrutiny,* hands tied behind them. Rough wood dug into her tender spine, and Angela shifted position in an effort to ease the discomfort. She gave a slight shake of her head that almost dislodged her hat.

"I'm not certain. My cousin Tommy taught it to me when I was fifteen. He said if ever I was accosted, I was to kick him in a certain spot and the man would let me go. Apparently, Tommy was truthful for once."

Angela and Emily watched the proceedings aboard the captured vessel with terrified interest. Captain Turnower stood on the main deck in tense silence while pirates brought up cargo from the hold and plundered the officers' cabins. Captain Saber supervised, occasionally flinging Angela a dark look that made her shiver.

To her surprise, he was nothing like what she had imagined. After hearing all the stories, she'd envisioned a swarthy man with drooping mustache and unkempt beard, armed to the teeth and wearing extravagant, gaudy garments stained with previous meals. Though there were men like that swarming over the decks, the pirate captain was the antithesis of his crew.

Not that he didn't look savage enough, but it was a savagery along the lines of an ornate Spanish sword— beautiful and lethal. Beauty and violence combined in over six feet of lean muscle, dark hair, eyes as blue and piercing as a hot summer sun, and the fluid grace of a wild tiger. It was as breathtaking as it was terrifying.

And just as disconcerting were the simple garments he wore. On any other man they would have been mundane, merely a covering. But on Kit Saber, the fitted black breeches and knee-high boots were an adornment, a showcase for supple muscle and long, lean legs. Angela found herself staring at him. It wasn't that she'd never seen a handsome man before, because that certainly wasn't the case. It was just that she'd never seen one so blatantly—well, *male.* He radiated masculine arrogance; it oozed from every pore, a great many of which were visible beneath a buttonless white shirt open to the waist and leaving bare a large expanse of tanned chest and flexing muscle. She swallowed heavily, confused by the conflicting emotions he produced in her. She should be outraged and terrified, not intrigued. No, it was not the sort of impression that gave her any comfort, and she tore her gaze away from him with a supreme effort of will.

It had been a half hour at least since they'd been brought above deck, and the pirate captain's anger had seemed to grow with each passing moment. She wished she could hear their occasional conversation. Only snatches of it could be heard at times, as the pirates were busy in the hold or on the other ship that was tethered to the *Scrutiny* by grappling hooks. She was very well aware, however, of the hungry glances she and Emily received from grinning pirates as they passed. None had spoken to them, but she had the distinct impression that if their captain gave the slightest signal, they would pounce on the two women like ravening wolves.

Shivering, she looked away from a swarthy pirate clad in the barest of garments. Knee-length trousers were tattered and hung from his hips by only a prayer, it seemed. He wore a scarf around his head and a huge gold hoop dangled from one earlobe. Other than that, there was an overabundance of tanned, bare flesh.

Truly, pirates seemed to have no modesty whatsoever. Nor much compunction in leering at helpless female captives. The pirate she'd noticed had paused and was staring at her with unconcealed interest. Nothing in her life's experience had prepared her for this sort of predicament. She, who had been cosseted and protected her entire life, doted on by loving parents and taught the proper things to say in any social situation, struggled with the knowledge that she was far out of her element this time.

Angela swallowed another surge of fear, well aware of Emily's precarious balance on the edge of hysteria, and held her tongue. What in God's name did one say to a pirate anyway?

" 'Ello, luv," the swarthy, half-clad pirate said with a

laugh, obviously at no loss of words himself. "Ye don't look like ye're havin' much fun."

Angela ignored him with a mixture of utter disdain and blinding fear. He persisted, however, stepping even closer, his bare feet nudging the hem of her bombazine day dress.

"W'at? Too good ta talk ta an ole sea-dog, luv? Mebbe ye'll be glad of a chance fer polite conversation afore th' day is over with."

Angela looked up at last, schooling her trembling voice as close to contempt as she could. "I doubt very seriously that you could ever manage anything remotely near polite, much less intelligent conversation. Go back to your rampant looting and leave us alone."

Anger creased the pirate's brow, and he stepped so close his bare foot trod on the material bunched around her thighs. He crouched down and put out a grimy hand to touch her cheek.

Unable to help herself, Angela flinched away from his hand. "Don't touch me!"

He laughed, revealing a gap where two front teeth had been, and his breath was foul as he leaned even closer. Horrified, Angela realized he meant to kiss her, and she pressed her spine into the unyielding wood of the mast. She could hear Emily whimpering beside her. Closing her eyes to blot out the sight of the pirate, Angela steeled herself for the inevitable.

Then she heard a curious thump and grunt, and felt a whisper of wind as the pirate's hand left her face. After a tense moment of silence, she cautiously opened her eyes.

Instead of the scruffy pirate, she saw a pair of obviously expensive black leather knee-high boots with scuffed toes. She lifted her gaze. Captain Saber stood there instead of the other man, and a swift glance revealed the other pirate sprawled out on the deck. He was groaning and holding his head.

"Get back to work instead of wasting valuable time, Reed," the captain said coldly, and swept Angela a stony stare before turning away.

Instead of feeling gratitude, she felt a spurt of anger that the captain would view her near-assault as a waste of valuable time. Her mouth tightened, and fear melded into irrational fury. How dare he treat her with such callous disregard!

She opened her mouth to fling a nasty comment at Saber when she felt Emily's faint nudge against her leg.

"Miss Angela—what do you think they'll do to us?"

Emily's quivering question brought an instant return of sanity. Angela's anger subsided into caution. She shook her head. "I don't know, Emily. I pray that they allow us to remain aboard the ship unmolested."

It was a faint hope and both knew it. Pirates were not usually known for their generosity toward female captives. And Captain Saber was said to be one of the worst. She couldn't suppress a sudden shiver, and Emily again whimpered softly.

"It will be all right," Angela whispered with little conviction; Emily nodded. They fell silent, watching as the pirates swarmed across the deck.

Seamen from the *Scrutiny* were being interrogated, and unbelievably, some of them seemed willing to join the pirate crew. Angela watched with astonished disgust as they eagerly fell in with the enemy. How could they?

Were there no decent men left? Seething with angry despair, she forced her attention away from them.

Thick smoke from smoldering coils of tarred rope stung her eyes and nose, and she turned her head to try and take a breath of fresh air. From where she and Emily were tied to a mast, she could see the hatch that led below to her cabin. Smoke billowed out in gentle puffs. A steady glow was diffused by the smoke, faint flickers that made her frown and study the opening. Then her eyes widened.

"Fire!"

Her scream brought Captain Saber's head around, and he swore crudely before rapping out orders to douse the blaze. The pirates dropped what they were doing and scurried with buckets of sand and water. They flung the buckets down the opening but, from what Angela could see, made little progress. Her throat tightened. The ship was going to burn. That much was obvious. And more than likely, she and Emily would be left tied to the mainmast while it did, a fit retribution for daring to shoot the pirate officer.

Smoke and angry tears stung her eyes, and she blinked them back. It was quickly apparent that the fire had taken a good hold, and Captain Saber began snapping orders. He then turned to Turnower.

"Take your boats, Captain. You're not so far from shore that you won't be able to get there within a reasonable time, or perhaps be picked up by a passing ship."

Turnower nodded stiffly. "Aye, but we have only two jolly boats that are seaworthy."

Saber stared at him for a moment, then flicked a quick glance at the captured crew. "How shortsighted of Sheridan Shipping not to provide ample room for her crew," he said after a moment. "Well, the decision is up to you, Captain. I leave you to your own."

"Saber!" Turnower called out when the pirate captain spun on his heel and started for the rail. "What do you intend should be done with the women?"

Saber shot him a startled look. "I don't intend that anything be done with them. They're your problem."

"You have them tied to the mainmast. I assumed that to mean that you intended to take them with you."

"You assumed incorrectly." Saber's voice was soft, but held a steely edge to it that made Angela shiver.

Turnower took a step forward. "I cannot take them with me. I did not even want passengers aboard, especially females, and yet the bloody purser took their passage. Take them with you. There is no room in the boats."

Swinging back around, Saber gave the captain a look of contempt. "What a brave Englishman you are, Captain. I see that it would not distress you to leave them lashed to the mainmast."

"Not when it means the lives of my loyal crew."

Emily made a faint sound that reminded Angela of a wounded animal. She blinked against the sting of smoke and horror. She must have been getting lightheaded from the smoke and stress. There could be no other explanation for the exchange that she was witnessing, the callous disregard for her life by the captain of the *Scrutiny*.

But when she closed her eyes and opened them again, she saw that Captain Turnower had turned his back on her and given the order for the boats to be launched.

Men grabbed eagerly at the davits, not one of the *Scrutiny*'s crew so much as glancing in the direction of the two women tied to the mast.

Emily began to whimper, and Angela saw Captain Saber take a step forward again. Her heart pounded, and she hoped he would order Turnower to take them with him.

But he did not. Instead, he motioned for two of his own crew to come forward. Before Angela could give so much as a single protest, the thick ropes tying them to the mast were severed and they were pulled to their feet. To her surprise, her legs would not support her, and she swayed so that the pirate had to grab her. She was glad to see that it was not the one called Reed.

He grinned, his face pushed so close to hers that she recoiled. "Ho, me beauty—grab hold," he said, still grinning. Angela had no time to protest before he lifted her and slung her over his back.

The swift pressure of his shoulder cutting into her middle pushed the air from her lungs, and she gasped for breath as she dangled over the pirate in an undignified heap. A glance upward showed her that Emily had suffered a similar fate. Doubling her hands into fists, Angela beat a protest on the pirate's back as he swaggered past his captain toward the rail.

When he swung her to her feet, she drew in a deep breath, expecting to be flung overboard. Her breath exhaled in a rush when he swept her up again and leaped over the rail. There was a sickening moment of being airborne, and Angela let out a piercing scream as she was swung between the two ships. A yawning expanse of choppy gray waves swirled below, and she quickly squeezed her eyes shut. Then they landed with a jolt. Only when she felt the security of solid wood beneath her feet again did she open her eyes.

Emily appeared beside her as if dropped from heaven, her eyes wide and her hair in charming disarray around her plump shoulders. They clung weakly to one another, watching as pirates still on the *Scrutiny* swung aboard, then pushed the other ship away. Grappling hooks were disengaged, and the chasm between the ships grew larger.

Angela saw that the fire had raged higher aboard the *Scrutiny*, and now licked its way across the main deck. Smoke billowed in dark clouds, and sparks flew into the air. She thought of her trunk, the miniatures of her family, and the music box her father had given her. Unexpected tears stung her eyes, and she felt Emily shudder.

As they watched, the *Scrutiny* began to list. High-pitched sounds almost like human screams emanated from the ship, and halyards snapped and canvas tumbled in flaming sheets to the main deck. Though the decks were aflame, the mainmast still stood intact. Flames licked at it with a growing frenzy, and the ship listed sharply to the leeward side. With a mighty screech of wood, the doomed ship began to take on water more quickly.

Angela could see water pouring through the scuppers. For what seemed an eternity, she watched the death of the *Scrutiny*. Around her, the pirate crew bustled with cheer and chores, hauling lines and shouting orders in what seemed to her to be incomprehensible terms.

"Ready about!"

"Helm's a-lee!"

The bow of the ship nosed about slowly, and canvas flapped loudly overhead as wind tugged at the sails. "Off tacks and sheets!" Lines creaked and whined, and there was a slithering sound as they hummed through sailors' hands and tackles. Yards swung around slowly from the force of the wind, canvas sheets cracking. "Mainsail haul!" came the shout, and sails tautened under the press of wind and tightening lines.

Angela listened in a daze, barely aware of the alien sounds. In such a short space of time, her life and Emily's had changed drastically. She had to think, had to safeguard them from the pirates as best as possible.

"Let go and haul!" rang out across the deck. Angela glanced upward to see the yards shift into line with the others, watching dully as men hauled on bowlines and braces to pull them taut, then began to coil the gear and hang it on the pins dangling neatly at the ship's rails.

As the wind tugged at her loose hair and sent it in tangles around her face, she pulled it away and turned to look for the pirate captain. He was standing on the quarterdeck. His massive quartermaster stood next to him; a white cloth was bright against the dark skin of the quartermaster's upper arm where he'd bandaged it.

A deafening roar startled her and she jumped. Emily let out a scream as the deck shuddered. Before this afternoon, Angela would never have recognized the source, but now she immediately knew the cause. One of the big guns belched a ball and flame over the water.

Angela moved to the rail, puzzled. Then she saw, out

on the waves, the overcrowded jolly boats from the *Scrutiny*. Another gun boomed, and there was a faint whistling sound as the ball arced through the air then splashed into the water near the boats. Even at this distance, she could hear the faint screams and shouts.

Whirling around, she looked up at the quarterdeck and saw Captain Saber watching impassively.

"Stop them!" she screamed, flinging herself toward the five steps that led up to the quarterdeck. "They're going to hit Turnower and his crew!"

Captain Saber gazed at her for a long moment, then shrugged. "That's entirely possible."

"That's . . ." Flabbergasted, she stared at him. "But you'll kill them!" She took another step up, but he put out a hand to stop her.

"They didn't seem too worried about you not so long ago. I thought I'd give them a taste of the same mercy they would have given you."

"But . . ." Another gun roared, and she whirled back around to stare in distress as one of the boats disappeared from view in a froth of foam and water plumes. She put her hands over her ears as if she could hear their screams. When a final shot boomed, she closed her eyes.

It didn't help. She knew the image of those geysers of seawater and cannonballs would stay with her the rest of her life.

She opened her eyes to see the faintly amused gaze of the captain trained on her. Slowly lowering her hands from over her ears, she said distinctly, "You are as villainous as you have been named, Captain Saber. I would rather have drowned with the honest men of the *Scrutiny* than be left to your dishonorable mercy."

"Would you?" His calm voice belied the hot, savage glitter in his eyes. "That can still be arranged if you're feeling sufficiently suicidal."

A flutter of fear caught in her throat. She tried to ignore it. "An honest death is preferable to a dishonorable life," she said with a betraying quiver in her voice.

The captain came toward her, his blue eyes narrowed and his mouth a taut line. When he stood on the step just above her, towering over her, she held her ground despite legs that were trembling. Unable to look into his face, she fastened her gaze on the smooth brown column of his throat where it rose from the pristine folds of his white shirt.

"A noble sentiment from someone safely aboard a ship. I wonder how noble you would be if forced to choose between them," he said in a harsh tone. "Shall we test your resolve, madam?"

Angela's eyes shot to his face. He looked serious. And angry. She briefly regretted her mad impulse to rebuke him, and wondered if she could still retreat with a shred of dignity. She cleared her throat.

"Are you offering me a boat and freedom?"

He gave a harsh laugh. "No. But I will offer you the opportunity to seek an *honorable death,* if you insist. The rail is to your left. Be my guest."

When she hesitated, paralyzed by fright and dread that she had once more spoken too quickly, he reached down and grasped her by one shoulder to spin her around and shove her toward the rail. She half stumbled over a coil of rope and was saved from sprawling onto the deck by Saber's quick hand. He righted her, then gave her another shove toward the side rail.

Angela saw that she had gained the attention of some of the crew. She recognized several former members of the *Scrutiny*'s crew standing at the rail, and wondered bitterly how they could have sunk so low as to join pirates.

Then she was at the rail, Saber's unyielding hand at her back. "Shall I lift you over, or do you think you can manage it on your own?" he asked in a conversational tone. Her hands curled over the wide rail, fingers digging into the wood to hold on.

Wind whipped at her face. Sails snapped crisply, and sea water splashed up to mist the air as the hull sliced through gray-green waves. Her stomach lurched unpleasantly. She stared over the side rail at the churning sea rushing below. Death by drowning was said to be peaceful once one ceased struggling. Perhaps it was. Perhaps it would be better than whatever fate Saber might have in mind for her.

A feeling of despair washed over her. She gripped the rail more tightly. Her hat was awry. Loose hair whipped at her face, lashing in stinging wisps against her skin. She shifted as if to climb atop the rail, then paused. Panic swelled. It was a long way down to the water, and once over, there would be no retreat. White foam clustered on the dark waves, then scattered in lingering wisps of froth as the ship moved forward.

Sagging, she shook her head. Saber's hand was still against her back, palm pressing into her spine as if to keep her at the rail. He released the pressure after a moment and, saying nothing, walked away. She heard his boots scuff over the wooden deck, heard him pause and give orders in a quiet voice, then he clattered down the hatch to go below.

For a long time, Angela stood at the rail contemplating her wretched cowardice and tenacious grip on life.

Three

"Women voyaging aboard the *Sea Tiger*." Turk shook his head. "I never thought to encounter such, Kit."

"We'll get rid of them in the first port we come to." Kit poured a healthy amount of brandy into a snifter and handed it to Turk. He sat down behind his desk and held the decanter up to the fading light that streamed through the gallery windows across the stern. Light glinted in the cut glass container with tiny iridescent sparkles.

Turk rolled the delicate stem of his snifter between his large, blunt fingers, and frowned thoughtfully. "In retrospect," he said after a moment, "there was little else that could be done. That scurrilous dog of a captain would have left them aboard the sinking ship."

As Turk took a sip of brandy, Kit poured some for himself. "Yes, so it seems. Sheridan Shipping is to be commended for hiring such noble officers."

A faint smile curved Turk's broad mouth, and his dark eyes crinkled with amusement. "Why is it you can never resist the opportunity to point out the obvious deficiencies of Sheridan Shipping."

It was merely a rhetorical question, and Kit knew it. Turk loved to hear his own rhetoric, an affection that often caused strife between them. Never serious. Turk had been his friend too long to ever let anything come between them.

Kit sipped at his brandy, the fumes as heady as the taste, and thought of the two young women he'd taken aboard. He didn't even know their names. One was plump and nervous, making him think of a pretty sparrow. The other—beneath her bravado, she had the same regal haughtiness that he'd learned to despise in other women. He knew her type: cool, blond, arrogant. Oh yes, he knew her type well. Hadn't women like her been a major cause of the most traumatic crises in his young life? He'd learned long ago to crush them, or run like hell before they created too much havoc in his life. This one, he suspected, would create a great deal of havoc if he was foolish enough to allow it. She was trouble, and he knew it.

Yet, recalling her frightened bravado, he wondered if there might be more to her than he'd first considered. A rueful smile curled his mouth as he remembered her instinctive reaction to his violent grip on her. Neatly done, if a painful lesson. He'd not thought such an obvious town miss would know anything about rough-and-tumble. He made a mental note not to underestimate her again. And to stay away from her as much as possible.

He looked up at Turk. "Have you seen Rollo?"

"Not in the past few hours. He is probably bunking with Mr. Buttons this evening. You know how he adores sweetmeats, and Mr. Buttons always has an ample supply after we take a ship."

Kit laughed. "True. What a fickle soul Rollo has when it comes to any sort of honeyed treat. I suppose I'll see him tomorrow morning when the treats are devoured and his belly is full."

"Quite a plausible conclusion." Turk swirled the brandy in his small goblet with a thoughtful intensity, then looked up again.

"So, Kit, where do you intend for the young ladies to spend their nights?" Turk watched him over the rim of his brandy snifter. The ship rolled gently on a wave, and the gimballed lanterns swayed with the motion, shedding pools of light in shallow splashes on walls and windows.

Kit gave a resigned sigh. It was apparent Turk would not let the subject of the reluctant shipmates rest until he had an answer. "I have no idea. Are you interested?"

Frowning, Turk said, "Your levity is sadly lacking. No, I am not interested in the manner you obviously imply, merely curious. Your decision could have a detrimental affect on the ladies."

"Or the crew."

Turk's brow lifted. "Perhaps not quite as detrimental for them. The men seem a bit more experienced at depravity."

"But not humanity?" Kit smiled wryly. "Leaving our charming captives on deck would be a grave error, I fear."

Turk grinned. "Exceedingly grave. There would be only bits and pieces left for aquatic life to devour by the time the crew had done." He paused. "I understand that you gave the order they were not to be molested."

"Yes." Kit shifted impatiently, already regretting his momentary insanity in taking them aboard. He should have left them to the cruel mercies of Turnower. At least their deaths would not have been on his conscience. He took a sip of brandy to drown his irritation and said, "I suppose it's not fair to ask Mr. Buttons to give up his cozy little cabin."

"No, it is not." Turk paused. "You seem quite drawn to the fair-haired miss. Have you considered sharing your berth with her?"

Because he had—for a fleeting instant—considered that very thing, it made him even more irritable, and not at all inclined to admit to such damnable weakness. He slammed his brandy to the tabletop and glared.

"Drawn—devil take you, Turk. Why do you say that?"

Shrugging, the huge quartermaster said placidly, "Because I noted the manner with which you regarded her while we were still aboard the unfortunate *Scrutiny*. Not many of the fair sex draw your rapt attention so swiftly."

Kit cursed softly. "Bloody hell. Not many of the fair sex almost cripple me with their knee at first meeting, either."

"True." Turk smiled. "In my opinion, you have had matters in your favor much too long when it comes to women. Do you deny that the pretty English miss attracts you?"

Kit arched a brow. "Do I seem desperate for a woman?"

"Desperate in some respects, perhaps, but not for a woman." Turk sipped his brandy, regarding Kit for a long moment of silence. "The lady is definitely attractive."

Kit frowned into his snifter, then upended it and drained the last of his brandy. It seared a comforting path to his stomach, and he stood. "This time, my friend, you are quite wrong. I shall find the charming, inconvenient misses and inform them that my cabin is at their disposal for the night. Tomorrow, I will find them another bunk."

"There will be plenty of offers from the crew." Turk's chest rumbled with subdued laughter. "I envision both those lovelies draped in hammocks in the forecastle. Perhaps a rather snug berth, but better than the watery berth Turnower intended to leave them. Although that fate would have left your conscience clear, I daresay."

Kit paused at his door. There were times that Turk's words eerily echoed his thoughts. Too often. He shot him a quick glance, but Turk's innocuous expression gave no hint of his sentiments. He shoved open the door and stepped into the passageway without replying.

Night had fallen. Fitful rays of lantern light glinted from smooth, polished rails and brass fittings on the main deck. A brisk wind blew, filling the sails. Decks had been scoured with sand and holystones, cleared of any sign of battle. The crew was cheerful, as they usually were after a good haul, sitting under lanterns tossing dice and gaming away future shares of their profits.

"Cap'n," a laughing voice called as he passed, "I bet I know who you're looking for."

Recognizing Dylan's rich drawl, Kit paused. The youthful pirate stood up in a fluid motion, a half-grin on his face, his boyish features blurred in the subtle glow of a lightly swinging lantern. Gold flecks sparked his eyes.

Kit couldn't help a returning smile. "I'm certain you do. I take it you've seen them loitering nearby."

Youthfully muscular shoulders lifted in a careless shrug. "You might try looking aft. There's a bit of lace peeking out from behind some barrels. I hated to say anything, 'cause they seemed to think they were well hid."

Kit smothered a sigh. Not only females aboard the *Sea Tiger,* but idiotic females. "Just what I need," he muttered.

Dylan stepped away from his comrades. Candle flame glinted in his long dark hair with reddish lights. He moved with lazy grace until he stood close enough not to be heard by the others. "Saber, these women—I hear that you gave the order they were not to be bothered."

"That's true." Kit raised a brow and stared at him. "Do you have a problem with that order?"

Dylan shook his head. A torrent of sable hair brushed against his bare shoulders. He grinned. "Not me, Cap'n. They don't look like the sort who'd know much about the finer points of what I'd want 'em for."

Kit smiled faintly. "Probably not. They seem like the sort who would be more nuisances than pleasurable."

"Are they to be held for ransom, then?"

"I haven't yet decided their fates." Kit paused. "It will be brought up at the next council."

Dylan nodded. "That sounds fair. For us, anyway." He laughed in tones as rich as the Colombian coffee plantation where he'd been born twenty-two years before. The illegitimate son of the English-born owner and one of his servants, Dylan had learned early that there would be little future for him there, and so had set out on the high seas to make his own. Having found little justice in life, he had few expectations. Over the years, this had faded his views of the world, a perception Kit had tried at various times to alter with little success.

"I'll see if there's anything left of them," Kit said now,

ignoring Dylan's implication. "If not, our problems are
over." Not that he really expected them to do the sensible
thing and fling themselves overboard. The blonde had
looked as if she intended to survive with a vengeance.

Kit found them huddled behind barrels strapped to the
aft deck. They looked frightened and, in the pale light
of the glassed-in lantern he lifted above them, wearier
than he had anticipated. He bludgeoned his impatience
into diplomacy.

"Come along, ladies. Your room is ready."

A reedy voice said, "No. Not until you promise to—"

"Sweet Jesus. Do you know where you are? On a
bloody pirate ship. I don't have to promise you anything.
Now come out from behind those barrels."

After a moment of taut silence came the clear reply.
"We'd rather stay here, thank you."

They seemed to draw farther into the shadows, and he
lost what little patience he could claim. "Come out," he
snapped. "Unless you have a desire to sleep on deck
with most of the crew for the night. Not that you'd get
much sleep . . ."

That brought their hesitation to a halt, and the blonde
came out first, straightening her damp, wilted hat with
one hand while she bent to help the other woman crawl
out.

"What do you intend to do with us?" the blonde asked
when she turned back to him. Despite her obvious fear,
her voice was cool. He had to admire that much, anyway.
Apparently, the little chit had good breeding and excellent
training, her brief lapse into brawling notwithstanding.

Out of a perverse desire to see her as uncomfortable
as she'd made him earlier, he set the lantern on the roof

of the coach house and leaned casually against the capstan. Light sprayed over them, illuminating one side of her face and leaving the other in shadow. He studied her with a silent intensity that he knew would be unnerving, letting his gaze rake over her as if measuring her feminine charms. She stared back, and he could see the spark of disquiet in eyes that looked—gray? No, green. Definitely green.

Oddly, despite her disheveled appearance, she would be considered an attractive woman once she was cleaned up a bit. His first impression of a winsome young chit barely out of the schoolroom altered slightly. Young, yes, but not as young as all that. She was slender, and slightly above average height, though it was hard to tell exactly how tall she was with the crumpled mess of her hat still clinging to her head. The stiffened muslin stuck up at an odd angle that made him want to jerk it off, and he reached out to pull the chin ribbon free.

The girl gave a startled little leap, like a frightened kitten, then stiffened. Heat flashed in her eyes, amusing him. So, the little cat still had some fight in her. Maybe the situation would afford him some entertainment, after all.

He yanked the ribbon and tossed her hat aside. The wind caught it and swept it over the rail. Catching her by the chin, he held her face up to the light, ignoring her rebellious glare. A tangled mass of pale hair that had been tortured into curls straggled about her face, partially masking a face with patrician features: straight, pert little nose, full lips that were set in an angry line, and murderous green eyes. He adjusted his grip slightly, still keeping her chin in the wedge of his thumb and fingers as he turned her face in a slow, deliberate motion, study-ing her at leisure and watching her anger mount. It was fascinating to see the flush of color rise and stain her high, delicate cheekbones and milky skin. Only English-women seemed to have that particular coloring, as if they were exquisitely painted porcelain.

Intrigued, he stared at her longer than he'd intended to, dwelling on the vagaries of fate that imbued women with beauty on the outside and such deviant natures in-side. Beautiful women should be outlawed, really, Kit de-cided. They should be penned on a desert isle, where they could do harm to no one but themselves. There were enough problems in the world, in his opinion, without men being distracted by willful, deceitful women.

He wondered just what it was in his face that made this lovely creature stare at him with eyes widening in fear.

"What do you intend to do with us?" she repeated in a voice that now vibrated with anxiety.

Kit released her chin. "I could toss you to my crew. None of us have been this close to a woman in the past few months."

Her gasp diverted his attention to her open mouth. Lips the color and delicacy of a rose petal parted to draw in another deep breath. Intrigued, he watched as her teeth cut into her bottom lip to steady it. One front tooth was slightly crooked, and somehow, that made her appear more vulnerable. Her voice was surprisingly cool, if a bit shaky.

"But . . . you wouldn't do that, would you?"

"I might." Kit didn't bother to repeat his earlier as-surances. Apparently, she hadn't believed them anyway.

When she panicked and tried to bolt past him, he pulled her up short. His fingers bit into her arm. "Don't be foolish. There's no place you can hide on a ship that we can't find you."

She struggled vainly. "Let go, you beastly fiend!"

Kit snorted. "If you allow this to degenerate into name calling, at least be more articulate."

Held tightly, she looked up at him with huge, shadowed eyes. "Please . . ." Her voice trailed into quivering silence that made his anger fade.

He felt a spurt of unaccustomed sympathy. Why he should, he had no idea. The women were a tempting problem aboard a ship full of healthy men accustomed to taking what they wanted. These two may not have realized it, but they were in much more danger here than they'd been aboard the burning *Scrutiny*. At least there, their fates had been certain and swift. Now . . . He didn't finish the thought.

His hand loosened slightly on her arm, and he saw her breath come more easily. She finally looked away from him, fastening her gaze downward, head bent so that he saw only the mass of falling curls atop her crown. Silky, flyaway hair slithered in wayward strands down the sides of her neck and over her cheeks. He resisted the urge to push it from her face, and instead reached out to touch her cheek. She looked up at him again, warily, as if about to take flight.

She was warm and soft, and he could feel the rapid thud of her heartbeat beneath the forearm he was still pressing against her ribcage. Kit frowned. It had been a deuced long time since he had held a warm female in his arms, and his body responded with predictable idiocy. He should let her go. This was no time for a little idle lust, for God's sake.

Watching him, she put out her tongue to wet her lips in a nervous gesture. His eyes riveted on the pink tip as it drew slowly over her lush bottom lip, and he promptly dismissed his resolution to leave her alone. He lowered his head and closed his hands tightly around her upper arms as he bent down. His mouth smothered her startled protest. She tasted sweet, as he'd known she would, trembling under the pressure of his lips. After a moment, he lifted his head and stared down at her through narrowed eyes. She was breathing swiftly, eyes wide, and he felt a surge of anger at his own weakness.

He pushed her away from him. His teeth clenched against a remark that would only make matters worse. Kit reached for the box lantern he'd set on the roof of the coach house. He took a step back, holding the lantern higher, and saw her chin quiver before she steadied it. She put a hand behind her as if to hide her cowering companion in the shadows.

"Well?" she demanded coolly. "Have you done with your rudeness, Captain?"

"Pirates are supposed to be rude. Haven't you heard? Or don't you read the pamphlets detailing our exploits?"

"I do," piped the girl still lurking in the shadows. "And you are one of the worst, sir. Captain, sir."

Kit fought a wave of amusement. "Am I? How pleasing. All my hard work has not been unremarked."

"No, indeed." A mop of brown curls appeared in the fitful light of the lantern. "You are the scourge of the seas. A rapacious rascal with no morals. A defiler of decency and distressed damsels . . ."

"How picturesque. Is that your phrase? No, I thought not. It does sound a bit exalted. Now, as to your disposal this evening . . ."

"Do your worst." Obviously well recovered from her fright, the blond miss flung back the hair from her eyes with a slender hand and stared at him in cool arrogance. "You will not find us compliant, I warn you."

Kit put his left hand over his eyes and rubbed them. They were still stinging from all the smoke earlier. His lungs ached, too, and he'd probably be up all night coughing. He heaved a sigh.

"No, I had not thought to find you amenable in any way. Perhaps you've noticed that pirates don't seem to consider compliancy a necessary virtue. Most ships we take are quite resistant to the notion, so be forewarned—I know how to deal with resistance."

She blinked, her bravado cracking in the face of his coldness. "What do you . . . mean to do with us now, then?"

"A bed. Sleep." He deliberately leered. "I've never 'ad two birds in my bunk at once, luv. I thought I'd—oh, for Chrissake. Don't get all defensive. I'm allowing you to sleep in my cabin for tonight. Alone. Or without me, at any rate."

Turning on his heel, he strode over the deck without looking back. If they chose to follow, fine. If not, they could bloody well take what options would be left to them, which would make going down with a burning ship preferable in comparison.

The shuffle of footsteps behind him were evidence that they'd decided to chance him rather than his crew. A wise choice, in his opinion. Not that his crew weren't good men, but they were not exactly the sort that young ladies of this ilk would find pleasant companions.

He slammed open the door to his cabin with more force than was necessary, then stood in the opening and motioned for the two women to precede him. They scuttled past him with obvious trepidation, and he felt another wave of irritation. Damn them. He didn't really want them aboard the *Sea Tiger* anyway, and he certainly didn't much care for the way they looked at him as if he was picking his teeth with human bones. It only increased his annoyance.

He left the door open and crossed to the cabinet that held pistols and sabers shining lethally in its racks. He locked it, tucked the key into the small placket in the front of his trousers, then turned to eye the two women. They clung to one another as if for safety, and he let go another irritated sigh.

"I'm afraid I'll have to leave the debauchery for another time, ladies. I fear my day has been too long and tiring to be of much use as a despoiler of distressed damsels tonight. Do forgive me."

He'd reached the cabin door before they spoke, and he turned to see the blond take a step toward him. She frowned. "We are to stay alone in your cabin?"

He leaned against the doorjamb and crossed his arms over his chest. "Regrettably, yes. Disappointed?"

She shook her head. "No. Pleasantly surprised. But I would like to ask a favor if I could, please . . ."

"Of course. Being left in peace could not be enough for you, I'm certain. What do you want? Jewels? Gold? Another pistol, perhaps?"

"All that would be quite delightful," she snapped, "but we would much prefer food."

He stared at them. The mundane request seemed anticlimactic after her blazing theatrics above deck.

Indicating her companion, the blond continued, "Emily has a predilection to nausea aboard a ship. I thought if she ate, she would feel better."

"Or have more to empty onto my carpet." Kit straightened from his lazy posture against the doorjamb. "Very well. I'll see what I can find in the galley. The cook has finished for the day, I'm certain, so it will have to be whatever I can manage to find."

The girl stared at him, eyes cool and green and assessing. That, he discovered, irritated him as much as her melodramatic expectations. He shrugged and left, leaving the door open.

When he'd gone, Angela turned to Emily. The girl gazed back at her with wide, shadowed brown eyes.

"He kissed you," Emily whispered, a tinge of awe in her tone.

Angela flushed. "I am aware of that, thank you. And now I would prefer to forget it."

"But . . . was it nice?"

She shot Emily a withering glance. *"Nice?* He's a pirate, Emily. How can you ask a question like that?"

Emily shook her head. "I—I just wondered. I've never been kissed, you see. I had the thought . . ." She paused and flushed painfully. "Well, he is handsome, for all that he's a dreadful pirate."

Angela stared at her. She had no intention of confessing that Captain Saber's kiss had flustered her more than it had revolted her. She should have been horrified, and said something so crushing he would have slunk away like a dog with its tail between his legs. All she had been able to do, however, was tell him he was rude. Her cheeks grew hot at the memory, and she turned her attention back to Emily with an effort.

"Miss Angela, look. He left the door open!"

It swung gently on its hinges, noiseless and inviting, a tempting trap. She nodded. "Yes, I see that, Emily."

"We can escape."

"To where? The crow's nest atop a mast? As he said, there is no place to hide aboard a ship, Emily. He would find us, and be quite angry that we had caused him trouble. No, we'll have to wait here, I'm afraid. At least he doesn't seem inclined to do anything too dreadful tonight. And he does intend to feed us."

Emily gave a dainty shudder. "Why is it that I feel like a sheep being fattened for the slaughter?"

"What an alarming analogy. Perish the thought."

"Perhaps he means to sell us as slaves at the next port," Emily said glumly. "It happens a great deal to female captives, you know."

"No. I didn't know." Angela stared at her with growing irritation. "I declare, Emily, I don't know whether to believe your suspicions at times or ignore them. Do you get all this lurid information from the tabloids and pamphlets that circulate the London streets?"

Emily nodded. "A great deal of it, yes. But the information is based upon truth, Miss Angela. It may be exaggerated at times, but the truth is there." She shuddered. "You know that pirates are cruel and brutal, and if they do not kill their captives, they do horrible things with them."

"Such as sell them."

"Yes. And that is one of the least dreadful fates that can befall gentlewomen." She drew in a shaky breath. "I read that, last year, one of the women Captain Saber took as his prisoner threw herself overboard rather than face her family after what he'd done to her. And there is the matter of his crew. They are said to—"

"Enough," Angela said fiercely. "Perhaps you are right, but I refuse to listen to any more of this. We will deal with what we must when the time comes."

"Yes, Miss Angela." Emily bent her head and stared down at her hands folded in her lap. "At least Captain Saber seems a bit more civilized than the pamphlets reported."

Angela ignored that. Civilized? Hardly. Not with her lips still burning from his kiss. She resisted the impulse to touch them. She was aware, however, even more so than Emily, that he could do much more than he had. A shiver tickled down her spine, and she tried to forget her initial reaction to his kiss. It had startled her. She should have struggled against him, fought him, but instead had been taken aback by the spark of response that had ignited inside her. She shook her head, and thrust the memory from her mind.

Not now, for pity's sake, when she had to think of

a way out of this dreadful situation. She slumped with weariness as she studied the cabin in the mottled light provided by flickering lamps set in holders along the dark-paneled walls. Three sets of windows with thick, leaded glass in tiny diamond panes would flood the room with sunlight during the day. The cabin was quite large.

She was surprised at the tasteful furnishings that could have come from any London drawing room. A thick Turkish carpet of deep red and scattered gold flowers covered gleaming bare planks; several lacquered tables of exquisite craftsmanship held a variety of objects she would not have thought an uncouth pirate captain would wish to own. Delicate porcelain figurines, a Chinese fan in gilt and ivory, and tall, slender vases of the Ming dynasty reposed behind the glass doors of a wall cabinet. Nestled beside it was another set of glass doors holding shelves of leather-bound books. More books were stacked in a haphazard fashion around the cabin.

Angela walked to a table, and lifted a copy of *Castle Rackrent* by Maria Edgeworth in her hands. There was also a leather-bound treatise of the recent discovery of the Rosetta stone in Egypt. She flipped idly through pages that detailed how the stone made possible the deciphering of ancient hieroglyphics. About to close it, a name on the inside leather caught her attention. Apparently, pirates had no compunction about robbing even a duke. The name *David Charles Edward Sheridan, Fourth Duke of Tremayne* had been neatly inscribed there, mute testimony to the previous owner. Really. This Captain Saber was a dreadful man.

Emily made a muffled sound, and Angela turned to see that her face had gone from ivory to a distinct greenish shade. Slowly, Emily sank to the carpeted floor with her hands over her mouth. Angela dropped the treatise back to the table.

"What is it, Emily?"

"I feel ill," came the smothered reply.

Angela sighed. "Again?"

Emily nodded, eyes welling with tears and desperation. Angela searched swiftly for a bowl, and found one in a lacquered cabinet bolted to the floor beneath a swaying lantern. She looked down at it for a moment. This was no crude metal bowl such as the one she'd had aboard the *Scrutiny,* but a Chinese enameled bowl painted with blue horses. Not at all the sort of chamber pot she'd expected to find in a pirate captain's cabin.

Moaning, Emily made a retching noise, and Angela hurried toward her. The continuous pitching of the ship had increased, but she had been too distraught to notice it until now.

She shoved the bowl into Emily's trembling hands just in time, and knelt beside her while the unfortunate girl retched violently. As always, Angela offered what comfort she could, patting Emily's shoulder and holding her hair back from her face as she bent over the bowl. Concerned, she did not hear Captain Saber's return until he spoke.

"What a charming scene. I shall remember it fondly in the days to come."

Angela turned to look up at him with a frown. "Emily

cannot help it. It's the ship's motion that causes her distress. I would think you could be a bit more sympathetic to her affliction."

Saber dropped a wooden tray on a table. "I ooze sympathy. I just do it discreetly. Seasickness has never been a particular problem aboard the *Sea Tiger,* so perhaps you can understand my attitude. Shall I send Turk to you?"

"Turk—oh yes. The Moorish pirate."

"Moorish? Do not suggest that ancestry to Turk. He will debate the accuracy of it with you at some length, and he can become quite tedious."

Emily moaned, and Angela gave her another comforting pat before rising to her feet to face Saber. She fought a faint tremor in her voice as she asked, "Just what is Turk's cure for nausea?"

"Nothing too painful, I assure you." His eyes narrowed. "Did you expect poison? Dissection? No one aboard the *Sea Tiger* has been dissected in several months. We've almost forgotten how, and I'm certain our knives are too dull by now."

Angela looked at him uncertainly. Her perception of him was undergoing a slight readjustment. Though Captain Saber certainly looked as if he could dismember her with a reasonable amount of skill and efficiency, there was none of the look of a rabid dog about him, as Emily's pamphlets so faithfully reported. Still, the earlier scene of his impassivity while consigning Captain Turnower and his crew to the watery depths of the Atlantic remained fixed in her memory as a grim warning that Saber could not be trusted to behave as a gentleman.

She drew in another deep breath. "If you think Mr. Turk—"

"Turk. No Mr."

"If Turk," she continued, "could be of assistance to Emily, I would be most grateful."

Captain Saber's brow lifted. "Gratitude. How alarming. Next thing I know, you'll be eating the meal I brought you without first checking for the dismembered portions of any previous captives."

Angela flushed, though she could not stop a swift glance at the tray. Saber gave a bark of sardonic laughter.

"How absolutely predictable you are. I see that I'm going to have to contact the authors of those pamphlets that circulate London and insist upon some accuracy in reporting the details of my depredations. I assure you, the truth is diabolical enough without embellishment."

Angela didn't doubt that for a moment, but she refused to rise to his baiting comment this time. She remained silent while he studied her with a cool gaze. She took the opportunity to stare back at him, taking in his casual garb with an unsettling admiration. He did seem the very picture of a romantic rogue, with the flowing sleeves of his loose white shirt, and tight black breeches and knee-high boots. A scarlet sash circled his lean waist and held several weapons. She saw the butt of a pistol as well as the carved bone handle of a dagger, while a thin belt held a sword at his left side. He looked well armed and dangerous, an articulate corsair of startling good looks.

His brow lifted at her silent survey. "Do you approve of my haberdasher, madam?"

She couldn't help smiling faintly. "I admit, your tailor does seem to have a flair for the dramatic."

"Ah, and you, of course, are addicted to all forms of drama, I note."

"At times." She cast a quick glance at Emily, still crouched over the washbowl in discomfort, then looked back at Captain Saber. "Do you suppose that Mist—that Turk would be so kind as to bring Emily something to ease her discomfort?"

"It has nothing to do with kindness, and everything to do with an extreme dislike of cleaning a soiled carpet." Saber moved to the door again, then turned back to look at her. "Whatever is your name, by the way?"

She hesitated. The name *Lindell* was well known in some circles. It would not be unlikely to suppose that a man as obviously well read and diverse as Captain Saber would have heard of her wealthy father. Should she risk being held hostage, or was it preferable to an unknown fate?

Saber seemed to read her mind, for his lips twisted with wry humor. "Just your given name will suffice. Very few of us aboard the *Sea Tiger* even recall our true names, nor do we wish to be reminded of them."

"I see. Well—Angela."

His brow lifted, and his mouth curved into a smile so devastating that she caught her breath at his male beauty. His derisive comment quickly banished that appealing image.

"Angela—it means angelic one. How inappropriate. I should think Medusa much more suitable for you."

Four

Kit stood at the rail and stared at the night-dark sea. Faint lights from the ship bobbed erratically, casting glimmers on the choppy surface in gossamer shapes. He wondered once again just why he felt this peculiar attraction to Miss Angela Whomever. It went beyond physical interest, and that baffled him. Though he did, indeed, nurture a healthy physical response to her, there had been a nebulous tremor of something that went far deeper. Maybe it was a sort of admiration for her refusal to collapse into hysteria, as most women would have done, given the same circumstances. Her little maid had certainly seen no reason not to indulge in hysterics, which had, surprisingly, seemed to irritate her mistress rather than tempt her to the same.

It was intriguing. This Angela was the essence of all the women in his life that he despised, with her pretty manners and haughty demeanor. Didn't he know well what happened when it came to women of her kind?

Oh yes, he'd learned early to avoid them, and stick to females of a less complicated nature, females eager to please with little expectation beyond a pretty bauble or two and some careless admiration. Yet there was something about this one that drew him and, at the same time, set to jangling every alarm bell in his defense system.

He had enough to do without being involved with a female hostage, he thought irritably, and turned sharply away from the rail. Boxy shadows clumped over the deck as the night watch answered the bosun's bells. He leaned back against the rail again, regarding the smooth running of the ship as a thing of beauty to be appreciated. Orderliness was a virtue. He subscribed to it faithfully. His early years had been so chaotic, that his need for system and order had become a driving force in his life.

That, and his need for answers.

A brisk wind made the sails flap loudly and tugged at the ratlines as Kit curled his hands over the smooth, polished surface of the side rail. He had to find her. He had to *know.* Too much of his life had been spent searching, and now he was near—so near. He would not rest until he found the answers he sought, and he had no intention of being distracted. This time, he would succeed.

"What is that?"

Angela gazed suspiciously at the concoction in the huge quartermaster's hands. Steam rose from the brew Turk had mixed in a bowl. He ignored her, and poured a liberal amount from the bowl into a cup.

"Drink this," he ordered, holding the cup to Emily's lips.

Emily drew in a deep breath of the aromatic steam, her eyes widening. "It smells like . . . Mrs. Peach's cookies."

"I daresay." Turk nudged the edge of the cup closer.

"It is quite tasty, so you needn't look at me as if I intend to poison you, child."

Emily cast him a quick, frightened glance, then drummed up her courage and took a sip of the brew. For a moment, she waited, as if she expected to fall into writhing convulsions at any second, then she took another cautious sip.

"Good heavens, child," Turk said, his rich voice rife with impatience. "Drink it all. It cannot cure you from the outside."

"Ginger," Angela said suddenly, and Turk looked in her direction. She indicated the mixture. "It smells just like ginger."

"How astute of you. That is precisely what it is." He turned his attention back to Emily, who took the cup and drained the remainder in a single gulp. Turk nodded his approval. "Marvelous."

Angela scooted to the edge of the deep chair behind the captain's desk and folded her hands primly in her lap. "What benefit does the ginger have?"

"It eases motion sickness, which is what your companion suffers from at present."

Intrigued, Angela said, "I suppose sailors must have all sorts of remedies available of that nature, given that you are always at sea."

"Not necessarily." Turk poured another small amount into a cup for Emily and gave it to her, then stood, his full height intimidating in the cabin. "I know of few men at sea who become seasick. Though there are, I suppose, a fair number who might begin their career with that affliction. As we do not generally invite passengers aboard, I have never had to use ginger for this particular ailment."

"No?" Angela glanced at him. His dark face gleamed with a polished luster in the light of the lantern. Some of her distrust of the quartermaster dissolved. Despite the ferocity of his appearance, he spoke like a cultured gentleman. She looked away from his piercing gaze and decided to stay with a safe topic of conversation. "Have you made a study of herbs?"

"Among other things. Eight years ago, I discovered quite by accident that certain foods produced adverse affects. And other foods, if ingested daily, could cure certain maladies."

"And you've investigated this further?"

Turk smiled slightly. "Yes. A member of my family had grown quite ill, and I chanced upon a book, *Macrobiotics, or The Art to Prolong One's Life,* by a man named Hufeland. His studies concluded what I had already learned through studying the Chinese philosophies. It's quite fascinating."

Angela smiled. "And Hufeland's book taught you to use ginger to cure Emily's seasickness."

"Indirectly. Though Chinese practitioners discovered its use as a healing spice over two thousand years ago, it is a versatile little root. Tibetans use it to help convalescents recuperate from illness, and in Japan, a ginger-oil massage is considered quite beneficial in alleviating spinal and joint problems. It is even," he continued as he replaced Emily's empty cup on the tray he'd brought, "useful for the treatment of mild burns. Said to bring almost instantaneous relief."

"Must Emily drink it often?"

"As often as the symptoms occur, I should think." Turk stood with his massive legs braced apart. Angela studied him with open candor as he fussed with the tray and pots.

Clad in a loose white shirt and trousers and a pair of leather sandals, he should have looked unrefined. The opposite was true, however. Perhaps it was his instinctive dignity, or his regal bearing. He was completely bald, and wore a huge gold hoop in his left earlobe. Small bluish lines were tattooed on each of his cheeks. His nose was large and flat, and his mouth was well chiseled and of surprising delicacy for the rest of his features. It would have been easy to envision him clad in the raiment of a king of his native country.

"Captain Saber said that you were not Moorish," she remarked.

Turk smiled. "As customary, he speaks the truth."

Ignoring Emily's appalled gaze at her temerity, Angela pressed, "But if you are not Moorish, what is your nationality?"

"Are you truly interested, madam, or just satisfying a rather morbid curiosity?"

Turk was looking at her now, his dark eyes somber and riveting. She quelled the impulse to mumble that it didn't matter, and steadied her voice.

"I am truly interested. I have never seen a blackamoor this closely."

"Ah. You are mistaken. I am not, as I have noted, a Moor. Therefore, blackamoor is blatantly erroneous terminology."

Angela gazed at him for a moment. A faint smile of

admiration curved her mouth. "Marvelous. Do you speak so fluently in your native country?"

"In my own language, which is much more lyrical and flowing than English."

"What is your language and your country?"

"I was born in the Sudan, into the Monyjang, which is also referred to as the Dinka tribe." A faint smile curved his mouth. "Men in my tribe were also called 'ghostly giants' by some Europeans, referring, of course, to our height and predilection for coating our bodies with ash. Quite an effective sight, I assure you."

"The Sudan is in Africa, is that correct?" Angela asked, and Turk nodded.

"It is, indeed. Just below Egypt. An ancient and beautiful land, inhabited by man and beast since time first began." Turk paused, then added softly, "Though not always equitably, I'm afraid. Man is by far the most dangerous predator in any land, I've discovered."

Emily made a faint sound, and Angela looked at her. The color was coming back to her cheeks, though she still looked a bit wobbly.

"I think I want to lie down," Emily said faintly, and Angela went to her immediately.

"Where can she lie down, sir?"

Turk moved forward, and swept Emily into his huge arms. She made another soft sound that closely resembled the frightened squeak of a rabbit as he carried her across the cabin to a recess. Angela saw it was a bed of sorts, built into the wall and set on gimbaled casters to stay level against the sway of the ship.

"This would be best for her," Turk said smoothly, and placed Emily onto the embroidered cotton quilt. She sank into the mattress with a sigh of contentment, fear temporarily replaced by the delight of a thick feather mattress beneath her.

"O-oh, it's so comfortable," Emily murmured, and rested her dark head into the billowing softness of a pillow.

Angela followed Turk back to the table, watching while he retrieved the tray and the remains of their light repast. Dried fruit and pieces of hard, flat biscuit had been enough to take the edge off her appetite, though Emily had not been able to eat much. The wooden tray rattled with a faint clink of fine china cups as Turk lifted it and looked down at her.

"We shall recommence our discourse at another, more convenient time, miss. Now, it would be best if you were to seek a respite from the day's vigorous activities. If you are truly interested, I shall tell you of the beauties of my native land another time."

"I would be quite interested in hearing of your home," Angela said, suddenly realizing how tired she was. A wave of weariness made her sway. She barely managed a smile when he asked if she would care for some chamomile tea to help her sleep.

"I think that I shall fall asleep the moment my head touches the pillow," she assured him. He nodded his agreement and left, shutting the door softly behind him.

But despite her assurances, Angela lay awake for a long time after turning down the lanterns and undressing. Clad in her sleeveless chemise, she crawled into the bunk beside Emily and nudged her gently.

"Are you still awake, Emily?"

"Unfortunately."

"Shall I help you undress?"

"No. I'm too tired. And I can't imagine that a wrinkled gown could make matters worse than they are now."

Angela smiled at the dismal tone. "It could be worse, you know."

"Oh? How?"

"Use your imagination."

That reply brought several moments of thick silence. Then Emily sighed. "You're right, of course. I allowed my personal misery to overcome common sense. Shall we say a prayer of gratitude that we are still alive?"

Angela hesitated. She felt lately as if she had erred too gravely to be on good terms with Divine Grace, but surely, in these dire circumstances, He would forgive her past indiscretions.

"Yes, let's do, Emily."

After a short prayer of thanks, freely mixed with pleas for continued clemency, they grew silent for a time.

"Emily?" Angela whispered finally. "You've read all the articles about him. Do you suppose that this Captain Saber will truly let us go unharmed?"

"It's hard to say." Emily drew in a long, shuddering breath. "If one believes all the reports about him, we should have already been killed or ravished. Or both. But don't you think it odd, Miss Angela, that he talks like a proper Englishman? I mean, his speech is not at all coarse, though he does look rather wicked." She paused, then added softly, "Handsomely wicked, I should say."

She'd had the same thought, but Angela was not ready to release her doubts. "Lucifer is said to be quite beautiful, you know. Besides, Saber may be handsome in a rough manner, but he is definitely not a proper gentleman."

"No, he could never be that." Emily paused. "Though I do think him rather dashing, in a frightening sort of way."

"Dashing!"

Emily stirred uncomfortably. "Well, you know. Exciting. Bold. That sort of thing."

"Emily, your imagination will get you in trouble one day."

"Perhaps," Emily returned tartly, "but not in as much trouble as your determination has already gotten me."

There was not much to be said to that, and Angela rolled to her side. Honesty compelled her to agree, but she was too ashamed to admit it aloud. She remained miserably silent, and soon heard Emily's soft snores.

Listening to Emily's rhythmic breathing, Angela felt a spurt of gratitude for her maid's presence. What would she have done if she'd had to brave this ordeal alone?

She shut her eyes, squeezing them tightly to block out the sight of the unfamiliar cabin with its elegant furnishings that belonged to a pirate. The furnishings were no doubt stolen from some poor honest merchantman, loot ripped away from the less fortunate and more honorable. How could Captain Saber sleep comfortably in a cabin filled with stolen goods?

But then, how could he sleep comfortably knowing he was responsible for terror and death. . . .

It was not, Angela thought wearily, the sort of situation she'd ever dreamed she would endure. If only she had already been with Philippe, and none of this had happened. Surely he would keep her safe and secure, banish all the terrors that threatened.

Philippe . . .

A sob caught in her throat, and she turned over to bury her face in the cool cotton of the pillow casing. She could not break down. Not now, when the grim situation called for a cool head. She had to remain calm. Thinking of Philippe was all that kept her steady.

Aristocratic Philippe du Plessis, with his dark, cool eyes and beautiful soul. Did he miss her letters? Their correspondence over the years had somehow evolved into love for one another, slipping between the written words and into their hearts. No man had been able to compare with the prose Philippe had written to her, his soaring philosophies that were so near her own.

It still amazed her that her normally intelligent father would view Philippe as a bounder and fortune hunter. She had done her best to reason with Papa, but to no avail. And now she'd fled her home for a chance at happiness.

Squares of bright, silvery moonlight pressed through the mullioned windows across the stern in distorted patterns; Angela watched as they grew pale with the passage of night. It seemed as if she would never fall asleep.

"Two points to starboard! Man overboard! Raise the roger, boys! No quarter! Stick 'em! Slash 'em! Aawk!"

Gasping, Angela sat bolt upright in the bunk, a hand clutching the sheets to her chest. She stared wildly about her, blinking at the sunlight streaming dustily through the gallery windows. Emily wailed loudly as the raucous cries began again, sounding as if they were in the cabin.

"Bloody hell! Bloody hell! Heave to, mates!"

A flash of scarlet flew past with a loud flapping, and

Angela ducked instinctively. Then she snatched up the pillow and flung it in the direction of the screeching voice as it bellowed obscene imprecations she'd never heard before.

Emily screamed, and screamed again as something brushed her cheek. The red, darting arrow swooped away with a flapping sound and Angela blinked, realizing what it must be. She grabbed Emily's arm before the girl descended into complete hysterics.

"Hush, goose. It's only a bird."

Emily buried her face in her palms, words muffled and disbelieving. "Truly? But what kind of bird?"

"I don't know. A parrot, probably."

A flash of scarlet swept past again, and this time she saw it clearly. She glanced at Emily. A red feather fluttered in her mop of curls. She pulled it loose and nudged her.

"See the feather? Only a parrot."

Emily peeped through her spread fingers and gave a sigh of relief when she saw the feather. "Oh. I see."

Angela slid from the bed and balanced precariously on the shifting floor of the cabin. The strap to her chemise sagged from one shoulder, and the hem brushed against her thighs. She reached for the gown she'd draped over a chair.

As she was slipping it over her head, the bird flew past again, this time landing on the back of a chair to peer at her with bright, beady eyes. Angela stared back at it.

"You're a nasty bird," she said calmly as she fastened the row of buttons at the side of her day dress.

The bird shifted from one clawed foot to the other,

tilting his head in the other direction. "Pretty Rollo," he said brightly. "Rollo is a good bird. Have some rum."

Angela couldn't help a laugh. Though she didn't quite dare attempt stroking him, she had to admit he was a pretty bird, with bright green feathers on his head and wings.

"Rollo is a vile creature," she said firmly. "I can only imagine where you heard some of those dreadful things you said."

Emily crept cautiously from the bunk, smoothing her hair back from her forehead as she gazed in fascination at the bird. "He's rather clever, don't you think, Miss Angela?"

"Obnoxious is a more suitable term, I would say."

Rollo took wing, a scarlet flash in the cabin. *"Awwk!* Rollo is a good bird."

Emily laughed. "He disagrees with you."

"No doubt. But he must get his opinion from the captain, remember, and we both know his character."

Emily frowned slightly as she moved haltingly across the floor to the gallery windows. Stuffed cushions in rich brocades of various patterns lined a wide bench beneath the windows. She knelt on the bench and peered out at the sea, which seemed to stretch endlessly.

"Actually, Miss Angela," she murmured as she rested her chin in her palm, "I think Captain Saber has behaved much more nicely than Captain Turnower ever did. At least he did not leave us to go down with a burning ship."

Angela slipped on her shoes and looked up at Emily. "No, but that does not mean we should trust him. He has a reason for keeping us alive. We should wait to discover it before giving him the benefit of the doubt."

"True." Emily turned as the bird landed on the arm of a lamp in a noisy flutter. She stared at it. Rollo stared back, eyes unblinking and intent, head cocked to one side. "How did it get in here, do you think?" she mused.

Angela pushed the hair from her eyes, frowning. "I did not even think of that. . . ."

"I let him in."

Both turned at the male voice, and saw the cabin door opening wider to admit Captain Saber. Seen in daylight, without smoke and dusky shadows diffusing details, Angela realized that this man was an entirely different person from the one she had first met. There was a harder look to him that did not diminish his brand of extreme good looks; indeed, if anything, it only added to them. But the charity she had thought she'd glimpsed simply did not exist. The crescent-shaped scar curving from his left eyebrow to the high, stark cut of his cheekbone gave him a more dangerous look, and thick-lashed blue eyes regarded her coldly.

Angela sternly slowed her rapidly galloping pulse into order and flushed, wondering how long he'd been there, and what he'd seen and heard. She turned, and shooed the bird from the lamp arm. Rollo immediately took wing and, with a rather disgruntled *squawk,* flapped out the open door.

Saber's amused, sardonic gaze flicked over Angela. "I see you've met Rollo. I hope he's not worse for the encounter."

"He needs his mouth washed out with soap. I take it

you are the one who taught him such colorful phrases?" she returned coolly.

"Of course. Most of them I taught him when I was ten. The others he's picked up here and there."

Angela opened her mouth, but thought better of it, and lapsed into grim silence. As if he enjoyed her reaction, Saber lifted a mocking brow. Then he moved across the cabin floor with a graceful ease that spoke of long familiarity with the motion of a ship.

The ship rose gracefully on a wave, then plunged steeply. Angela stepped cautiously to the security of a chair, hoping that she would not stumble clumsily while he was there. She sat down and folded her hands primly in her lap.

Saber did not seem to notice. He bent over his desk and rearranged some odd-looking metal instruments that Angela recognized. A sextant, one of them was called. Her cousin had received a small set of them as a child, but had never allowed her to touch them. "Ship's navigational tools," he'd called them. "Not for *girls.*"

Angela's eyes narrowed as Saber unrolled a large square of parchment with a crisp crackle, holding one end of it with his hand to keep it from rolling back on itself. It looked as if it were a map, and she couldn't control her curiosity.

"Where are we, Captain Saber?"

He glanced up at her. "I presume you mean to ask our location in the Atlantic, and how near to shore we are."

"Of course."

"Not near enough to a port amenable to the *Sea Tiger.*

I fear your stay with us will be a bit longer than anticipated."

Her heart lurched. "Does that mean you do intend to
set us ashore eventually?"

He frowned. "Of course. Surely, you don't think I want
you aboard the *Sea Tiger* any longer than need be."

Rather startled by this disclosure, Angela could not
form an appropriate reply. It was Emily who blurted out
their fears.

"But Captain Saber, do you intend to sell us? Or take
us to some distant port as slaves?"

"Sell you?" He looked from Angela to Emily and
back. A derisive smile curled the hard lines of his mouth.
"I fear that I would get very little profit for either of
you. Giddy girls bring little nowadays in a competitive
market. Unless you have skills that I am unaware of,
perhaps? No? Then I shall just count myself fortunate to
be rid of you before you cost me too much for your
care."

"How noble." Angela rose from her chair, stung by
his contemptuous comments. "If we were more valuable
or talented in certain respects, then I am certain your
charity would undergo rapid revisions."

His smile broadened. "Naturally. However, we don't
have to worry about that. You are neither valuable nor
talented, merely inconvenient."

"That is not at all true!" Emily rose indignantly from
the cushions beneath the portholes to glare at Saber.
"Why, Miss Angela is from a very good family, and her
papa owns banks and businesses that are worth a great
deal of—"

"Emily!"

Horrified, Emily clapped a hand over her mouth, while Angela stared at her with a mixture of irritation and dismay. Then she turned to look at Captain Saber. His expression was cold and intent.

"So," he drawled, and shifted to sit on the edge of his desk, "you are valuable after all, Miss Angela. How interesting. Am I supposed to shout 'Aha!' and send a ransom note to your rich papa now?"

"I hardly think—"

"Don't worry. I still don't give tuppence for what your papa is worth, so all this acting is useless." He uncoiled from his casual posture and moved to her, his action so swift that she had no time to retreat before he'd caught her by one arm. "Listen carefully," he ground out, his face only inches from hers, so close that she could count each individual eyelash and view at close range the scar that curved from his left eyebrow to his cheek. "I detest females who manipulate those around them. I have no intention of keeping you aboard my ship any longer than absolutely necessary. As soon as we come to a safe harbor, I am putting you ashore. I don't give a damn about recompense, only the vast relief I shall feel at knowing that I do not have to suffer you aboard my ship any longer. Is that clear enough?"

It seemed that they had inadvertently stepped on his toes, and she tried to recall exactly what had provoked this reaction. Saber's icy blue eyes were heated with hostility. She managed a nod, more disturbed than she would have liked to admit.

"Good," he said. "Do not treat me to any more of your ridiculous histrionics, or I may actually succumb to my growing desire to see you lashed to the shrouds."

Releasing her with a shove, Captain Saber turned to scoop up the map he'd spread out. He rolled it into a cylinder with swift, furious motions, then stalked from the cabin. The door slammed loudly behind him.

Shaken, Angela stared after him. "What a moody individual," she said after a moment, and then heard Emily's soft sob. She flashed her a look of irritation. "Oh, do be quiet. At least we now know that he does not intend to sell us or hold us for ransom." She frowned. "But he *is* a pirate. What does he consider a safe harbor, I wonder."

"Stupid, idiotic females," Kit snarled, wresting Turk's attention from his breakfast to his captain.

Lifting a brow, Turk asked "Do I detect a singular note of hostility, Captain?"

"Not a single note—a roaring symphony of hostility would more closely describe my emotions at this moment."

Kit flung the leather chart cylinder to the table and straddled a bench. Rigging creaked loudly in the rising wind. Two of the crew slanted wary glances at him as they finished their meal. Kit nodded curtly, then lapsed into seething silence until the men had left the mess room. He looked up at Turk.

Turk eyed him speculatively. "I see that the regal Miss Angela has managed to arouse your ire early this morning."

"I would have done better to have sent Mr. Buttons to fetch the chart. As it is, I've already been accused of trafficking in slave trade, and possibly pandering. Not to mention abduction of an English gentlewoman who is, I've been informed, worth a great deal to her doting, rich papa." Kit raked his clenched fist across the scarred wooden table in an irritated motion. "There are times, Turk, that piracy and its attending profits can be quite attractive."

"Am I to deduce from that cryptic statement that you plan on ransoming Miss Angela to her wealthy parent?" Turk dipped a carved wooden spoon into his bowl of oatmeal, eyeing Kit with a quizzical expression while he ate.

"Not necessarily. If her papa has any sense, he would insist that I keep her. It's just that the options described to me as worthy of a pirate seem infinitely preferable to keeping her aboard."

"Ah, you've still not forgiven her for her . . . low blow, so to speak."

Kit narrowed his eyes at Turk's bland expression. "Why do you say that?"

"You're not normally so irascible this early."

"Normally, I'm not accused of slave trading this early. Nor am I forced to view two witless females in various stages of undress in my comfortable cabin, while I spent the night coughing in a hammock on the quarterdeck."

Frowning, Turk took a sip of strong, aromatic tea. "You are aware of the method to cure that particular affliction, so I cannot feel too much sympathy."

"Hell, that again?" Kit groaned. "I'd rather cough than eat seaweed and rice, thank you."

"A most foolish preference. However, it's your ailing constitution, not mine. Proper nutrition would enhance your health immensely. A macrobiotic diet is the most effective manner of ridding your system of unhealthy poisons."

"I would rather not get into this discussion with you again. It's boring and not at all productive. I refuse to eat food that even a sheep would scorn, thank you."

"Very well. Continue with your present menu and your internal organs will one day rebel completely."

"Then you can say 'I told you so.' Until then, however, I would appreciate it if you would not harp on my diet, my constitution, or my unappreciation of your concern. Let us return to the former topic of conversation, if you please."

Turk nodded. "I bow to your wishes under protest. Dare I ask why you did not send Mr. Buttons to fetch the chart from your cabin for you?"

"Of course. He would have been only too delighted at the opportunity. If I had, he would still be there standing on his tongue, however."

Kit raked a hand through his hair, trying to sort through the conflicting emotions that ranged from irritation to a vague uneasiness he couldn't quite place. Why should he be uneasy? The women in his cabin meant nothing to him—beyond a certain obscure pang of sympathy now and then. Yet the memory of Angela clad in a brief chemise that did nothing to hide her charms was a stinging one.

Recalling the upthrust of her breasts against the thin material, the curve of her hips, and the exposure of her long, slender legs still made him physically uncomfortable. At the time he'd not been able to move, but had stood like a boy paralyzed by the sight of his first woman. He'd been only too grateful that she hadn't noticed his reaction.

Nothing was as it should be. By all rights, the girl should be cowering in a dark corner and be only too willing to cooperate. Kit could recall his own feelings of helplessness as a youth caught in the same sort of situation, and supposed he'd thought she might feel the same.

Helpless. Not her. Helpless as a panther, perhaps. Even Rollo had regarded the illustrious Miss Angela with a wary eye, a most unusual reaction for the intrepid bird.

"Here," Turk said. "Have a slice of dried apple. It will improve your health if not your temper."

Kit glared at him, but took the dried fruit. Chewing it, he muttered, "I knew it was a bad idea to bring those women aboard."

"And still you persisted. How noble." Turk's brow lifted at Kit's surly snarl. "Look at it from another perspective, if you will. The lady obviously does not expect much courtesy from a man reviled as a scourge of the seas. What would you think if you were Miss Angela?"

"I'd think it would be wise to keep my sharp tongue firmly between my teeth instead of prodding the man who held my fate in his hands. Prod the wrong man and situations can grow nasty."

"Yes, we've both experienced that consequence. Miss Angela, I fear, has yet to suffer any graver consequence than missing her afternoon tea."

Kit reflected on that for a moment. Turk's casual comment presented an attractive idea. He smiled slightly. "Perhaps I should educate her."

Turk took another sip of the Japanese tea he favored.

"There are some educations that are beneficial, while others are best averted. Do you think it considerate to educate her in that respect?"

"Not considerate, perhaps." Kit met Turk's gaze. "But necessary if she stays another night aboard this ship."

"I see that you are not to be dissuaded from that end."

"No. I think that Miss Angela Whomever should learn the vagaries of pirate captains when unwisely prodded."

"Do you." Turk applied his knife industriously to the slice of dried apple, dissected it neatly, then speared the individual bites with the tip. After a moment of silence, he looked up. "It would undeniably be a propitious lesson, but I wonder for whom?"

Kit stared at him. "Just what the devil do you mean by that?"

"I anticipate that we shall see soon enough."

"I hate it when you look superior and talk in riddles." Kit rose from the bench and retrieved the leather cylinder from where it had rolled to the edge of the table. Only the fiddles, small racks wisely placed to keep skidding dishes still on the table, kept the cylinder from tumbling to the floor. He held the leather in one hand, sliding his fingers absently over the smooth surface as he wondered what it was about the women that made their fates appeal to Turk. Normally abstaining from any sort of involvement with strangers, and particularly women, the voluble giant had inexplicably gathered these two strays under his wing.

He turned to look at Turk. "I shall be below terrifying the two English misses if you decide to join me. Wear appropriate attire for properly terrorizing them, please. I do not wish to seem the only savage aboard."

Turk waited until Kit had reached the open door of the galley before he murmured loud enough for him to hear, "But you are the fiercest savage aboard."

Five

Angela had almost decided to brave the unknown by going above deck, when she heard the latch lift on the cabin door. She exchanged a quick glance with Emily and rose to her feet, holding tightly to the back of a chair to keep her balance.

It was not a surprise to see the pirate captain enter, and she recognized from his expression that he was still in a nasty mood. The door swung back to bang against the wall, and his steps were firm on the portion of planked floor between rug and threshold. Angela's grip on the curved back of the chair loosened, and the chair tilted sharply away with a clatter, as if it were a wild creature bucking from beneath her grasp. She grabbed at it in vain, and barely kept her balance.

"Sit down before you fall and expect me to pick you up again," Saber shot in her direction as he crossed to his desk. He immediately became absorbed in a large ledger that he pulled from a shelf. Dark head bent, he propped one hand against the gleaming surface of the desk and used the other to riffle the pages. He took up a goose quill pen and scratched notations on one of the pages, apparently forgetting the two captives.

Angela righted the chair and exchanged a quick glance

with Emily, who looked close to hysterics again. Gathering her flagging courage, she blurted, "Emily is better but still weak. Do you intend to feed us this morning?"

He looked up. An unfriendly light glittered in sharp blue eyes. "Eventually. Are you always so governed by your stomach?"

Before she could splutter an angry reply, a pirate appeared at the open door. He was young and muscular, with gold eyes and a long shock of dark hair that fell halfway down his back in a glossy ribbon. Garbed in the disturbing attire—or half-attire—of the other pirates, somehow it seemed to fit him. A sleeveless leather vest hung loosely over his bare chest, and snug-fitting buff breeches ended in knee-high boottops. His amber-gilt glance moved from the women to Saber.

"Begging your pardon, Cap'n, but Mr. Buttons says you wanted to see me."

Saber nodded. "I do. I have a task for you." He straightened and indicated Emily. "Dylan, please escort this young lady to the mess and see that she is fed. I will depend upon your gallantry to see that no harm comes to her."

The pirate brightened, and looked at Emily with a friendly smile. "It will be my pleasure, sir."

Emily didn't protest when he gave her his arm and drew her up to escort her from the cabin, but she shot a doubtful glance at Angela. Her lower lip trembled.

"Captain Saber," Angela said immediately, hoping to prevent more hysteria, "we do not wish to be separated."

"But you do wish for Emily to be fed, do you not? While she is eating, I have something to discuss with you."

There was nothing she could do, and Angela watched dismally as Emily was led from the cabin. Saber looked back down at his ledger, apparently absorbed in it. Minutes passed, and still he had not spoken or even seemed to recall that she was in the same cabin with him. She stirred restlessly, hoping that she could remain on her feet without losing her balance.

At last he looked up at her, and she felt an odd lurching in the pit of her stomach. Instinctively, she met his gaze with a steady stare. He would not see her cower, no matter how frightened she really was.

Saber did not seem to admire her courage, or perhaps he did not notice it. He moved to the front of the desk and leaned back against it, crossing his arms over his half-covered chest. His gaze was hard, with no hint of sympathy or mercy.

Angela's nerves grew taut when he continued to stare at her so coldly. She almost jumped when he finally rasped, "A woman aboard ship is considered unlucky by most crews."

She calmed her jittery nerves. "Really? I thought only barge fishermen were prone to such superstition."

"While I do not encourage superstition, neither do I proscribe it," Saber growled. "I much prefer having a calm voyage, with no complainants brought before the mast. If I hear complaints about our new passengers being too much trouble, or causing problems in any type of manner, I will be forced to take—distasteful action. Do I make myself clear?"

"Yes. You intend to discipline any sailor prone to complaining."

He straightened. "No. I intend to rid myself of the

problem's cause with little delay. As we are at open sea, my only option may be to jettison the source. One piece at a time, if I must. Now am I clear?"

She clutched the chair back more tightly. "Very clear."

"Excellent."

His gaze rested on her face, making her think of a wary wolf. His long, lean frame looked relaxed, almost indolent. Yet beneath that careless facade lay a ruthless purpose that she had only briefly glimpsed on the main deck of the *Scrutiny*. Captain Turnower was fortunate to have been given at least a chance to escape.

She swallowed, and hoped her expression did not betray her. For a long, tense moment, there was only the sound of creaking timbers and vague ship's noises in the cabin, then Saber's boots scuffed over the thick pile of the carpet as he moved toward her.

She tensed, expecting the worst. When he stopped in front of her, she noticed once again how tall he was, so tall he seemed to blot out the light streaming dustily through the high gallery windows across the cabin stern. He made her feel small and helpless, and she hated the feeling of inadequacy and fear that shot through her. To counteract it, she took a step back and lifted her chin, mimicking the gesture she had seen her aunt make numerous times. It had been most effective in the past.

"Keep your distance, Captain. I do not care to be intimidated."

Saber's eyes narrowed ominously. His face tightened to a harsh mask. Without warning, his hand shot out to curl around her wrist in a ruthless grip. He drew her closer.

"I don't think you understand your true situation."

She tried to pull away. "I don't know what you mean."

"The hell you don't. This is not some tea party, or a boring night at Almack's."

"What would a man like you know of Almack's Assembly Rooms?" she snapped, jerking her arm from his grasp. "I seriously doubt that you've ever seen the inside of any decent house, much less an esteemed establishment such as Almack's. Why, Lady Castlereagh would faint at the sight of a rogue such as you."

"Would she?" Saber's mouth curled into a mocking smile. "Somehow, I think Lady Castlereagh is made of sterner stuff than that. In fact, I happen to know the arrogant, oddly garbed Emily is quite formidable in her way."

Angela paused. He sounded much too certain of himself about Lady Castlereagh. Perhaps he did know her. It hardly seemed possible, given his chosen career, though he affected the airs of a gentleman with perfect ease. That, of course, was only magnificent theatrics. But what if he had somehow chanced to meet Lady Castlereagh? As John Lindell was well known in those circles, her last name would then be familiar to him. It could be her salvation or her downfall, and she did not yet know which. She quickly formed another assault.

"At any rate, you needn't assume that I am not well aware of my situation here, Captain. I have managed to fall victim to pirates—any woman's worst nightmare. Do not deceive yourself, sir. I am properly terrified."

Saber seemed faintly startled by her tart rebuttal and stared at her for a long, tense moment. The ship creaked and groaned, rising and falling in a ceaseless motion that might have made Angela queasy if she'd allowed herself to dwell on it. Instead, she focused on Saber's narrowed blue eyes and contemplative scowl. Finally he gave a harsh bark of laughter.

"I came down here to terrorize you into submission. I did not expect such easy capitulation."

"How dismaying for you. Should I put up a defiant front to assuage your disappointment?"

"It would salvage some of my pride," he said wryly, and moved to lean back against the edge of his desk. Still gazing at her, he raked a hand through the dark strands of his hair. "Most females would be swooning in despair by this time. How have I failed?"

"As I pointed out to you—you have not failed. It's just that I am too terrified to swoon. Pray, forgive me."

"Bloody hell," he commented, and pushed away from the desk. "You're a cool one, Miss Angela. I'll give you that much."

"Am I to say thank you? Or was that not a compliment?"

Saber paused to stare at her thoughtfully. After a moment he murmured, "Why don't you do us both a favor, and say what is on your mind?"

She drew in a deep breath. He seemed serious. Was it possible that he might have a touch of decency after all?

"Very well," she replied. "Emily and I cannot decide if you are monster or myth. We have heard so many stories that it is hard to separate fact from fiction. Are you what they say you are, Captain Saber?"

A slight smile tilted his mouth up at one corner. "And what do they say I am, Miss Angela? Murderer? I've killed men, though I can't say I've derived any satisfaction from it. Pirate? Quite true. Though at times, I've stolen things that belong to me, so I'm not quite certain what that does to my redoubtable reputation as a thief and scourge of the seven seas."

He took a step closer, his voice lowering to a husky timbre that sent chills chasing down her spine. One hand lifted to caress her cheek, then slid around to cup her neck in his palm. His fingers gently massaged her nape, and the breath caught in her throat at his ministrations. He smiled.

"What was it your Miss Emily spouted last night? That I am known as—let me see—a *defiler of damsels?* As for that reputation, I gladly plead . . ." His hand shifted, fingers tightening in her hair to draw her head back. Angela's throat closed, and her heart beat so fast and hard she was certain he could hear it. Saber's voice was a husky whisper when he finished, ". . . guilty. I plead guilty, Miss Angela."

She closed her eyes as his face blotted out the rest of the cabin, and when his mouth brushed against her lips, she shivered. Saber laughed softly, and caressed her throat with his free hand. His thumb slid over her bottom lip in a slow, silky glide, curiously rough and soft at the same time. She felt her mouth quiver, then open as his grip shifted to apply gentle pressure. Saber made another sound, this one more of a sigh, and his mouth covered hers. Shockingly, his tongue slid between her lips, heated velvet that tasted like apple. The anomaly startled her, and her eyes flew open.

Saber's exploring tongue made a brief, sizzling foray that drew a whimper of protest from her, and he paused. His eyelids lifted slightly, and he gazed at her through the thick bristle of his lashes. Still, he did not release her, though his mouth barely grazed her lips.

"No. Don't," he said against her mouth. "It's best to just surrender to the magic."

Magic? Her head was whirling, and she was suddenly certain she was as green as Emily in the throes of her *mal de mer.* Almost desperately, she tried to pull away from him before he could wreak more havoc on her rebellious system.

She wanted to push him away, but balked at the contemplation of putting her hand against the taut contours of his bare chest. It would probably ignite a fire, just to touch that smooth flex of sculpted muscle. She leaned away, but still he held her in an iron grip; he shifted one hand to press against the small of her back, holding her body against his. A shudder ran through her. She felt light-headed and weak, and dug her fingers into his upper arms to keep from sliding to the cabin floor in a humiliating heap.

"Please," she heard herself whimper, sounding as if her voice came from a great distance.

Saber laughed softly. Her scalp stung from the pressure of the grip he had on her hair as he tilted back her head. He pulled her into him with an inflexible pressure so that she felt the hard length of his body against hers from breasts to thighs. Her breasts were crushed against him, and even through her bombazine skirts, she could feel his taut, muscular thighs burning against hers. The buckle of his belt nudged against her stomach with an almost painful jab.

"Captain . . . Saber . . . you must . . . stop," she managed to get out in a husky rasp that only made him

hold her more tightly against him. Her senses were swimming in dizzying whirls, and she felt as if she would
truly swoon. Was this what he had meant? This giddy
confusion that enveloped her with the contradiction of
pleasure and torment? It must be, because he seemed to
be enjoying it, and obviously had every intention of pro-
longing her misery.

His hand stroked leisurely along her spine, then slid to
cup her bottom in his palm and lift her against him. She
moaned, and he bent to kiss the sensitive spot in front of
her ear. Another shiver racked her, and Angela felt her
confusion dissolve into turmoil. An ache ignited somewhere in her middle. She shifted, and he put a hand on the
swell of her breast, long fingers gently caressing her.

It was such a shock—no man had ever touched her
there before—that Angela could not move or react. She
stood in paralyzed tension, breath caught in her throat
as he began to lightly tease her breast. The cabin seemed
to tilt, and the floor shifted away as Saber provoked a
heated response with his touch and his mouth. She was
shaking all over, and a deep, throbbing pulse began between her thighs.

Dear God, what was he doing? It felt as if she had a
fever, but chills made her shiver as his lips traced a light
path over the curve of her neck and along her jawline to
her other ear. Her eyes were closed though she couldn't
recall shutting them, and her head was tilted back in helpless surrender. It was insane, and she dimly realized that
she should be offering resistance, but she had never before encountered such a barrage of intense sensations.
The atmosphere of calculated intimidation did nothing to
diminish her reaction, but only heightened it. She had

been in a state of apprehension for too many hours to retain a sufficient degree of resistance, and she was appallingly aware of it.

Disaster loomed. It danced upon the hands of the man who held her much too close and touched her way too intimately, and she was helpless to prevent it. She, who had always been in control of her actions and emotions, was now adrift in a sea of heated responses that could have only one ending. . . . It was enough to make her nauseous, and she struggled against the desire to become violently ill all over Saber's shiny black boots.

But then he released her and took a step back, though he kept one hand on her shoulder as if to steady her. "There," he said briskly, "that wasn't so bad, was it?"

Shakily, she touched her lips with her fingertips and croaked, "Bad?"

Saber smiled faintly. "As opposed to good. You did seem to like it, you know."

Heat burned her cheeks, this time from a righteous indignation at what he had done, as well as what he now suggested.

"You cad!" she spat, and was hardly gratified to hear him laugh.

"Cad? Is that the best you can do, Miss Angela? I am convinced we shall have to improve your education in the proper use of profanity. An afternoon topside with a few of my crew should do it." He rubbed his hands together and said, "Now that you and I seem to have established a certain rapport, perhaps we should discuss the new bunking arrangements."

"Bunking arrangements?" she echoed dazedly. "Whatever do you mean?"

"Why, in view of our newfound—shall we say . . . interests?—I think it much more palatable for us to snuggle cozily in my bunk than to snatch stolen moments in shadowy corners. Do you have a problem with that?"

Angela blinked several times. It took her a moment to grasp the intent behind his words, and then fury deprived her of speech for another moment or two. Almost gasping with outrage, she stuttered out a variety of incomprehensible terms coupled with scathing refusals that seemed to have no effect on Saber whatsoever. He merely lifted a dark brow and regarded her thoughtfully.

"I take it you are not pleased with my suggestion," he remarked when she paused for breath. "How devastating. In that case, I shall find suitable accommodations for you and your little friend. But I warn you, madam, that should you display any tendencies toward verbal pique, I shall deem it as a desire for change in your circumstances. Do you understand?"

Understand? He could hardly have made his intentions clearer. What had just transpired between them was little more than a threat. If she did not cooperate in every way, it was obvious he would have little reluctance in forcing her to his bed.

Angela nodded silently, and Saber gave a nod of satisfaction. "Very good. I see that you do understand. How enlightened of you. Now, shall I escort you to the mess for a bite to eat?"

"I see they are well guarded," Turk remarked to Kit as he regarded the two young ladies seated on a long bench in the mess room. Dylan hovered at the door like a watchdog, giving the ladies his assiduous attention.

"Yes. Dylan seems enamored of his new duties. I may give him the job until we reach port."

"How fortunate for Mr. Dylan. It does seem, though, as if Miss Angela is now quite subdued," Turk said.

"Refreshing, isn't it?" Kit shrugged at Turk's quizzical glance. "Intimidation can be convenient."

"I daresay. A most convenient commodity, indeed." Turk smiled slightly and stepped out into the passageway, ducking to miss the overhead beam. Kit followed, and the two went above deck.

Sunlight washed over them, bright and blinding. Sails snapped crisply in the wind as the ship sliced through the waves. Kit went up to the quarterdeck, and there found Mr. Buttons at the wheel, a rather apologetic expression on the earnest young face beneath his shock of red hair.

"Good morning, Captain Saber."

"I'm glad you think so, Mr. Buttons," Kit replied, and waited for the inevitable. He liked Charley Buttons, but there were moments—as now—when the young officer's addiction to protocol seemed entirely unnecessary. It was due, of course, to his years spent aboard a British man-of-war, a vessel run with strict discipline and astringent adherence to rules. It had left an indelible imprint on the impressionable Mr. Buttons.

Mr. Buttons curled his hands tightly around the spokes of the wheel and looked straight ahead, at a spot just past Kit's right ear. "Sir, I hesitate to bring this up, but as the sailing master, I have been appointed by the men to—"

"What men?"

Mr. Buttons paused, face flushing. "Why, some of the crew, sir. They feel—"

"Why have you been appointed? *Tsk, tsk.* A severe departure from proper procedure, Mr. Buttons. I can hardly believe it of you. Protocol demands that, as quartermaster, Turk be spokesman for the crew. Is there something this crew doesn't feel they can discuss with him directly?"

Again a pause before the crestfallen Mr. Buttons said slowly, "It would seem so, Captain Saber. Shall I continue, or would you rather I have the men concerned bring this up with Turk?"

Caught between irritation and amusement, Kit shrugged. "You've already begun, Mr. Buttons, and Turk would probably prefer hearing this from me. Pray, continue."

"Very well, sir." He took a deep breath. "It seems that there have been concerns voiced over the presence of the two young ladies aboard."

"Concerns? Or complaints?" Kit stared hard at Mr. Buttons, and saw his flush mount from neck to eyebrows, as red as his hair.

"If I were to hazard a guess, sir, I would say complaints. This is the first time you have allowed females to remain aboard ship, and some of the men recall only too well that incident last year off Barbados."

"I'm gratified to hear it. Perhaps some of the men should also recall who owns this ship. We may be regarded as pirates, but it might do to remind them that the *Sea Tiger* does not follow the usual articles applied by other buccaneers. That was made clear before each man signed on, and it still holds true. Shall I go on?"

"No, sir." Mr. Buttons shifted uncomfortably. "I did tell them that, but some of the men were insistent that their grievances be aired. Therefore, to avert any possible trouble, I brought those concerns to you. I regret having wasted your time."

Kit shrugged. "It's not my time that's wasted. Any man on this vessel who is dissatisfied is free to leave at the next port. I adhere to certain rules of my own, and expect them to abide by them. We may be freebooters, but by God, I do not maltreat innocents, which, I perceive, is what the men are complaining about. There will be plenty of whores in the next port. If I find that one of those young women has so much as heard foul language, I'll personally strip the hide off the man responsible. Pass that sentiment on to them, Mr. Buttons."

"Yes sir."

"Is there any other business you wish to discuss?"

"No, sir. That was all."

"Then the crew can save any other concerns for the next council."

"Yes, sir."

"Excellent. I'll take the wheel now so that you may inform them of our decision."

As Mr. Buttons left the quarterdeck, he passed Turk and gave him a brief nod of greeting. Kit waited with his hands on the wheel, the wind tugging at his loose shirt. When Turk moved to take the great wheel that steered the ship, Kit turned to him.

"Those damn women are going to be trouble," he remarked.

"I take it there have been complaints, which explains Mr. Button's flustered countenance." Turk sighed. "It has been my experience that women of any station in life frequently incite disagreeable reactions among men. I find it as inexplicable as I do distressing."

"I find it irritating."

"Indeed." Turk gazed at him with impassive calm. "And which do you find more irritating? The impending difficulty, or your unfortunate attraction?"

"I've been attracted to women before. I've never known it to draw your undiluted speculation, however."

"This is an unconventional fascination. It appears that the young lady is no casual harlot, but a refined female who has little inducement to offer other than a wealthy parent. Ordinarily, she would attract no more attention from you than a gnat. Yet she seems to fascinate you."

"If I hadn't known you so long," Kit remarked, "I would take offense with your misguided meddling. However, as I am well aware of your propensity for interfering in my life with all good intentions, I shall only remind you that whether I am or am not attracted to our lovely captive, it is hardly of any significance to the welfare of this ship and its crew."

"A well-spoken sentiment, Captain Saber."

Kit just looked at him for a moment. Damn it, but Turk could be insufferable when he wanted to be. What the devil kind of point was he trying to make? That Kit found Miss Angela to be attractive? Attractive women were a penny a dozen, and could be found in every port. If he found her tempting, it should make no difference to anyone. Besides, she was just a simple attraction, despite the kiss he'd given her. It had been—as she had seen—a tactic designed as intimidation. That it had worked was the most uplifting thing that had happened since the *Scrutiny* had been spotted. She'd been a quiet little mouse all the way to her breakfast, with only an occasional wide-eyed glance at him.

Damn. It irritated him beyond imagination that he wanted her. He rarely found himself attracted to one particular woman. Most, he accepted as casual encounters, wanting nothing else. He'd learned too long ago not to trust the fair sex, nor to put himself in their hands.

Bloody hell. Why did he have to find himself wanting the cool-eyed little baggage with such ferocity? Of all the inconvenient times, this was one of the worst. And he was damned if he knew why his lust had been aroused. It wasn't as if he was a green youth unable to control that side of his sexual nature, and it wasn't as if she was the most beautiful or desirable woman he'd ever seen. Or lain with, for that matter. Yet, the plain and simple fact was that he wanted her. Lust, that was it, a healthy dose of good, old-fashioned lust. And it would ruin him if he let it.

Turk cleared his throat suggestively. Kit abandoned any attempt at further explanation of his attraction or aversion to Angela, and said instead, "It's been four months since we last scraped the *Sea Tiger*'s hull. I'm afraid we'll have to put in soon to careen her."

Turk deftly adjusted the wheel. "True. I was discussing that fact with Mr. Buttons only yesterday. She's a bit sluggish, and if that last merchantman had not been such a wallowing tub, we might not have been able to overtake her."

"We'll stop in the Azores to do a boot-topping. That

will have to do until we get to Port Royal. There are too many man-o'-wars cruising these waters to make it safe enough for a thorough careening."

"I concur." Turk lifted a brow. "P'raps we shall be able to relinquish our captives in the port of Ponta Delgada beforehand."

Kit shrugged. "It seems the likeliest spot, though I wonder about our reception. The commissioner was suspicious of our true colors the last time we drew a berth there."

"Portugal and England are allies. As a Portuguese possession, they should accept an English flag without objection."

"Our letters of marque are genuine, even if they do not belong to us." Kit grinned. "Commissioner LaRosa did not seem to look too closely once we presented him with all those casks of Spanish wine and French cheeses the last time we were there."

"Indeed, he seemed thoroughly charmed by us afterward. I have the notion that some of the excellent stores we gained from the *Scrutiny* will give him just as much pleasure this time."

"And should ensure the swift, efficient disposal of our annoying guests."

Turk smiled. "Life should be able to return to normal—or what passes for normal aboard the *Sea Tiger*—after that, I presume."

"God. I hope so." Kit moved to stand by one of the twelve-pound cannons lashed to the rail. He raked a closed fist over the cold iron. "I certainly don't need any more problems or delays. If we don't reach Port Royal in time, I may miss her again."

Turk did not ask who *her* was. He merely nodded silent agreement, while Kit stood at the gunwale and stared across the wind-pocked sea.

Six

"What is this?" Angela stared morosely into the wooden bowl in front of her.

"Oatmeal and salt pork." Dylan gave her an encouraging smile. "It tastes pretty good once you get used to it."

Angela shuddered and lifted her spoon. The cereal tasted of tin sweat from its container, musty and unappealing, and the salt pork did nothing to enhance the flavor. Her spoon dropped. The food was nothing like what she was accustomed to from Mrs. Peach's whistle-clean kitchen at home. She looked up.

"I had this for breakfast. I can't eat it again."

Shrugging, the pirate said, "There's nothing better until the evening meal."

"The evening meal?" She brightened. "What do we eat in the evening?"

He grinned. "This being Wednesday, our ration is dried peas, cheese and butter to go along with the oatmeal, hardtack, and salt pork."

Silence fell. After an appalled moment, Angela said faintly, "And that is all?"

"Beer and rum. Water with lime juice squeezed into it to stay off scurvy." Dylan's gold eyes looked sympathetic, and his voice was kinder when he added, "Seeing as how we just got a good haul, the biscuits won't have maggots yet. The *Scrutiny* was only two days out, and the food was still fresh."

Emily made a strangled sound, and Angela glanced at her. Color drained from Emily's round cheeks, and her lips parted.

"Maggots?" Emily echoed, staring down at her empty bowl. "Were there—?"

"No," Dylan said. "I told you. These are fresh biscuits we took from the *Scrutiny*. Besides, Beans knows how to get rid of maggots."

"Beans?"

"The cook." Dylan's gilt eyes danced with mischief. "It's easy. You just put a large dead fish atop the sack of biscuits, and when the maggots crawl out to eat it, you wait until the fish is covered, then toss it over the rail and get another fish. . . ."

This time, Emily clapped one hand over her mouth and stumbled away from the long trestle table toward the door.

"Now you've done it," Angela said, though she was also having trouble taming her heaving stomach. "Emily has a predilection for nausea aboard a ship. Since you caused it, you care for her."

Dylan looked more mischievous than repentant. "I'd be glad to, but I can't leave you unattended. Orders were—"

"You can't leave Emily unattended either, so unless you wish for your vile-tempered captain to wonder why she's out wandering the ship alone, I suggest you tend her," Angela said sharply. "If you're afraid I'll steal something, or eat more than my share, you've nothing to worry about. I see very little I would want."

"Maybe so, but I'll send someone to sit with you," Dylan said, and disappeared out the door.

Angela stared after him. She wished briefly that she had the courage to defy orders, but she didn't. Especially not after Saber's less than subtle warning. That confrontation had dulled her appetite at breakfast, a condition she did not now regret in light of the fare being served aboard ship. Mercy, how did sailors survive? Or was it only pirates who had such unchanging menus? Surely, the men aboard a proper vessel received much better food. She hoped so. She didn't think she could survive on musty water alone for very long. And it didn't seem as if anything better would be offered. Or maybe that was just for captives. She sighed heavily, and decided not to give Captain Saber the satisfaction of starving them to death before he could do whatever it was he intended to do with them.

When Angela tried to bite into one of the biscuits, she found that it certainly lived up to the name *hardtack*. She touched the tip of her tongue to her front teeth to ascertain they were intact, and tossed the biscuit back to the plate. It looked innocent, with nothing alive in it that she could see, but still she shuddered at the thought.

She looked up when a noise at the entrance announced the arrival of the guard Dylan had promised. Hope flared that it would be Mr. Buttons. He had seemed the only respectable man aboard this cursed ship and had expressed genuine distress that two fine ladies were in such a dreadful predicament. However, her brief conversation with Mr. Buttons had been cut short by Dylan, who had warned darkly that it would "go bad for any sod caught where he shouldn't be," and Mr. Buttons had departed with a regretful smile.

But her hope that it would be he who was sent to guard her vanished in an instant. The breath caught in her throat when she saw Captain Saber's unsmiling countenance. His expression was one of irritation, his brows low over shadowed eyes, his mouth set in a sulky line. He moved gracefully to the sideboard, a study in tan leather and flowing muscle that made it even more difficult for her to breathe properly.

Saber leaned indolently against the edge of the sideboard and regarded her with a lifted brow as he crossed his long legs at the ankle. "So," he said, "you're still managing to be an inconvenience."

Angela's cheeks flamed at the undeserved insult, but she bit her tongue to hold back an angry reply. Silent, she watched Saber pick up a biscuit and dip it into a mug he carried. After a moment, he must have deemed it edible. He crunched noisily, while eyeing Angela as if she were a disreputable puppy who had soiled his carpet. Her chin lifted instinctively against his obvious disapproval, and Saber's eyes narrowed.

"You needn't give me that haughty look. It won't help." He took another bite of biscuit.

"Excuse me, but you seem confused. It is not I who am being arrogant," she said.

"No? Then why put your nose up in the air?" Saber took a gulp from his mug. His eyes narrowed at her over the rim.

"Perhaps because I do not like being stared at so rudely, nor do I appreciate being bullied."

"Bullied?" His dark brow winged upward and his mouth curled. "You have no idea just how bullying I can be."

"Oh, I imagine I have some idea. I've been on this ship less than twenty-four hours, yet I've gleaned several important facts. If I were not bound to silence by threats of dismemberment, I would share them with you."

"Then I'm glad I had the foresight to threaten your imminent dismemberment." Saber finished the biscuit in a single bite. He didn't seem to care that it might have maggots. "If you are finished with your breakfast, I will escort you to your new cabin."

"New cabin?"

"Certainly." His eyes stabbed into her, blue and hot as the center of a candle flame. "Mr. Buttons has graciously offered to give up his own comfort for yours. Oh my. You didn't hope to continue sharing mine, did you? How rude of me. Especially since I have every intention of sleeping in my own bed tonight. Of course, if you've changed your mind about that, I can scoot over and make room for you, angel."

Angela's insides gave a funny lurch, but her voice was cool enough. "As much as I appreciate your lurid invitation, I shall decline." She stood up. "I trust our new cabin is far removed from yours."

He grinned. "Far enough away so that I don't have to see you unless I want to, but close enough to reach you in very short order should I feel the need."

Another internal lurch left her voice thin and reedy. "I fervently hope that you never feel that need, sir."

Saber's laugh was wicked, and his eyes gleamed a deep, glittering blue that left her in little doubt that her hopes were of no concern to him. He set his coffee mug on the sideboard and stepped close to her, sliding one hand behind her neck in a gesture that could have been affectionate were it not done so roughly. His fingers cupped around her nape in an iron hold, and though his expression was pleasant enough, Angela took note of the anger vibrating just below the surface of his perfect features.

"Should I feel that need, little one," he said with soft malice, "your hopes will be of no significance to me. I trust you understand that."

"P-p-perfectly," she stammered, hating the reaction he caused with his touch and words. Why could she not shove him away and say something so annihilating that he would be downcast with shame? But not a single rebuff came to mind, and she could only stand in quivering silence while he stared down at her.

After a moment, he released her and stood back. Sweeping a bow that would have been elegant were it not done so mockingly, he said, "After you, my lady."

Angela forced her legs to move, and preceded him into the dim, narrow companionway. A chaotic blend of sounds and smells assaulted her. It was odd, but the *Sea Tiger* seemed to be run much more efficiently than the *Scrutiny*. The decks were scrubbed clean, with every article hanging or stowed in place. Except for distasteful things such as maggots in biscuits and water that reeked of tin sweat, the pirate vessel was the epitome of excellent seamanship.

Saber led her above deck. Noise and stinging sunlight exploded in ringing chaos around her as she stumbled onto the busy deck. Motion was constant. Sails cracked crisply in the hard press of the wind, and lines hummed and sang with taut vibration. Angela blinked and squinted against the burn of sunlight in her eyes, and reached out blindly to grasp at a rail. Saber caught her hand.

"Not that one. Hold on to me instead. Distasteful as you may find it to touch me, I'm going in the right direction."

Angela found her hand tucked cozily in the crook of his hard biceps and forearm, and she was led along like an errant child. Light shimmered and reflected off polished brass fittings, sparkle lending more light to a brilliant day. Wind picked at her hair, tugging it loose from the clumsy braid she'd hastily formed earlier. Beyond the square white sails that seemed to fill the sky, the horizon dipped and rose in an endless motion as the bow of the ship sliced through the ocean. Angela recalled a half-nude mermaid that decorated the bow, impossibly high bare breasts pointing the way. It was the sort of figurehead she would expect a disreputable pirate ship to bear.

Everywhere she glanced, half-clad men worked or watched their progress. It was disconcerting. Angela tried not to look too closely at them, but she couldn't help noticing the predatory grins and leering winks in her direction. She recognized Reed, the pirate who had accosted her that first day while she was still aboard the *Scrutiny.* He was talking with another pirate and gesturing in her direction as they both laughed. It was just as well that the wind whistled loudly in her ears, so that she couldn't hear their remarks. Her cheeks burning, she wondered where Emily was, and if she was enduring the same vulgar scrutiny.

The cry of "Sail ho!" drifted down from above, and

Saber stepped to the rail, taking Angela with him. She saw on the horizon a dark speck that she took to be another ship. Activity aboard the *Sea Tiger* changed abruptly from casual toil to energetic preparation. Men scurried about with cheerful purpose.

Tilting back her head, Angela watched with a puzzled frown when the pirate standard that was usually flown from the mast was lowered and replaced with another. Instead of the roger, or banner bearing the bloody saber, a flag that looked vaguely familiar was sent up the pole with a shimmy. A shock of recognition went through her, and she turned accusing eyes on Saber.

"That's a French flag!"

"Aye," he said cheerfully. "I'm gratified to learn that you can recognize it. Education these days can be so scanty—"

"I thought you were English."

His brow lifted. "I am. What the devil does that have to do with the flag I choose to fly?"

"But . . . but, if you're English, why are you—"

"Ah, of course. What an innocent you are." He put an arm around her shoulder and drew her closer to the rail. "You see, if I were to fly my usual roger, then I could not come within ten leagues of another ship without a great deal of effort. This way, however, that French ship across the water will come close enough to communicate. Of course, once within easy range, I am always more than happy to show my true colors."

"You're despicable," she managed to get out, and he laughed.

"But good at it. Come this way," Saber said then, and she was led along the slightly slippery planks of the deck toward a far door that was painted a glossy blue. He shoved it open with the heel of his hand, and musty shadows enveloped them as they stepped into a narrow companionway that was suffocatingly close and silent. They weren't even in the same area of the ship as his cabin, she noticed, but didn't know whether to be relieved or insulted.

"You'll be safer below anyway," he remarked casually, his voice sounding too loud in the darkness, and Angela turned to look at him.

"You mean from the crew?"

Saber looked amused. "Hardly. They won't touch you unless I give the word. I meant from a stray shot."

Confusion furrowed her brow, and she frowned. "What stray shot?"

"Are you being deliberately obtuse?" Saber shook his head in exasperation, and nudged her down the companionway. "What do you think that ship's reaction to our roger will be?"

Realization struck her, and Angela felt the chill of apprehension. "You mean to attack that vessel."

"Very good. Your comprehension is commendable." Saber paused in front of a door and reached around her to open it, one hand at the small of her back to propel her inside.

Emily perched on the edge of a small bunk and looked up, her face reflecting relief when she recognized Angela. "Thank heavens you're here!" she exclaimed, rising so quickly she almost lost her balance and had to grab at the bunk. "I was worried that . . . that something dreadful had happened."

"Not yet," Angela said, moving toward her. She turned

back to look at Saber where he stood framed in the low doorway. Her throat tightened. His urbane expression was totally incongruous with his profession. How did he appear so aloof and sophisticated when he was a tarred villain of a pirate, for heaven's sake? She didn't understand it, and most of all, she didn't understand the potent effect he had on her. She was to wed another man, yet Captain Kit Saber had the power to set her senses in a whirl with only a glance from beneath his absurdly long lashes.

It was ridiculous, and made her tone sharp when she said in reply to Emily, "But I believe disaster is imminent. We're about to endure another sea battle, it seems."

"Hardly a battle." Saber shrugged. "If they're smart— which they usually are—they will offer no resistance. A shot or two across their bow, and they'll strike their colors in a hurry. Most captains would rather lose cargo than lives."

With that, he stepped back and shut the door behind him. They heard the metallic rasp of a key in the lock. Angela looked at Emily. Fright that must have mirrored her own shone from Emily's round face, and her eyes were wide with panic.

"He's locked us in," Emily whispered. "What'll we do if the ship begins to sink?"

"I don't think they'll accidentally let us drown. It will be deliberate, if anything."

Angela sank wearily onto the hard bunk and looked around her. The cabin was stark and neat. A table tied down with ropes nestled three chairs beneath it. A desk was set into one wall and flanked by shelves that dovetailed into one another. A narrow ledge held in the books on the walnut shelves. A wing-back chair squatted in a corner beneath a lantern and porthole. Drawers with bright brass handles and carvings of whales and porpoises decorated one wall in utilitarian beauty, and as in Saber's cabin, lanterns hung at intervals. Two narrow bunks made up as neat as Mrs. Peach's kitchen pantry were on one wall, one over the other. She spared a moment of gratitude for Mr. Buttons's generous displacement. At least they were in a cabin, and had not been locked in a damp hold somewhere in the bowels of the ship. She sighed, and heard Emily snuffle dolefully.

"Oh, do not cry, Emily. I don't think I can bear it. It is bad enough that we are here. If we panic at every turn, it will be unbearable." She leaned over to give Emily a gentle pat of comfort. "Strange as it may sound, I have all confidence in Captain Saber's ability to take a ship without harm to himself. He seems quite adept at piracy."

"Is that supposed to be comforting?" came a query muffled by Emily's palms and a scarf. Angela smiled.

"Yes. Oh, don't give me that look. It hardly helps to ponder the possibilities. Let us focus on other things. Such as an extreme need for a proper bath and unsoiled clothing. I fear that my gown has undergone a great deal of stress, and yours looks dreadfully wrinkled from having been slept in last night."

Emily looked down at her wrinkled muslin and sighed. Once it had belonged to her mistress, and in fact, had been one of Angela's favorites. The seams had been let out to fit around Emily's more generous curves and the shoulders altered a little for her shorter stature. Before their capture, Emily had looked quite nice in it. Now, the skirts were torn in places, and soot smeared the hem. Angela's blue bombazine gown had fared little better.

"See? More practical concerns can ease our minds if we really—"

A loud crack split the air, cutting off the end of her sentence and making both of them jump. An instant later, another gun was fired, and she felt the reverberation shiver through the ship's timbers. With a quickly beating heart, Angela stepped to the small round porthole over the desk. She dragged the edge of her palm across the damp glass and peered out.

The other ship was closer now, and as she watched, she saw the bright shimmy of its flag rapidly descend a mast. It had apparently decided not to fight, and relief flooded her. She turned to Emily.

"They have surrendered. There will be no battle."

"Thank God," Emily murmured, and Angela realized that she felt the same deep gratitude. Despite her brave words, the thought of a sea battle had terrified her.

In the long hours that followed, Angela noted the transfer of ship's goods from one vessel to the other, huge casks and trunks, and bolts of paper-covered cloth that looked like silk. Piracy could be quite profitable, it seemed.

It took the better part of the day to transfer cargo, and by the time the *Sea Tiger* pulled away from its prey, the western sky was a collage of pinks and saffrons and setting sun. Angela wondered idly if they had been forgotten, then regretted that thought when she heard the clink of a key in the cabin door. She turned with quickened pulses, expecting Captain Saber.

It was Dylan, however, his jeweled gold eyes bright

with laughter at some unshared joke. He was wearing a fine coat of carmine velvet, with frogged fastenings of twisted ebony and decorative cord on the wide cuffs. Beneath it his chest was bare, his trousers a supple leather that clung to well-formed legs. A floppy hat with broad brim and a curling feather perched atop his head, looking incongruous with his fall of long black hair and the huge gold hoop in his ear. He swept them a graceful bow and grinned.

"Look the proper swell, don't I?" he said cheerfully. "I took a fancy to this coat, and the gentleman who owned it was willing to part with it."

"I daresay," Angela said tartly. "At swordpoint, no doubt."

Dylan gave her a reproachful look and turned to Emily. "You like it, don't you, Miss Emily?"

Emily nodded, brown eyes as huge as plates, admiration evident. Angela was startled. Admiration was not an acceptable reaction to a pirate, no matter how magnificent his body or charming his manners. Though Dylan seemed to take great pains to be courteous, there was no doubt in her mind that he would dispose of them without a qualm should he feel it necessary. Or should Captain Saber order it.

Angela cleared her throat meaningfully, and gave Emily a sharp pinch on her arm.

"What we would really like, Mr. Dylan," she said, "is to be allowed a change of garments ourselves. Ours have become stained and, quite frankly, odorous. Do you suppose it possible to find us something suitable in the trunks you pilfered from the *Scrutiny?* Our things are probably below in the hold at this very moment, if we could search for them."

Dylan frowned. "I thought you might want to eat, not go shopping."

"Eat? That bilge you fed us earlier was quite enough, thank you. Did you come to threaten us with another meal?"

"Yes." He smiled slightly. "And to see if you needed anything."

"And as I have just told you, we do. Would it be possible, do you think?"

"Doubtful. But I'll ask around." He hesitated. "If I ask Saber about new clothes for you, I want a promise in return."

Angela exchanged glances with Emily. "What promise?" she finally asked.

"That you stop pissing him off. Every time he talks to you, he ends up in a mood as foul as the bilge on a whaler. Let up, will you?"

"Pardon me, but I do not see how you can hold me even slightly responsible for your captain's foul moods. As he is the sole ruler of the *Sea Tyrant*—"

"Tiger," Dylan cut in.

"Excuse me. A natural enough error. *Tiger,* then—it seems to me that he is solely responsible for his own moods. Can I help it if he enjoys terrorizing innocent victims?'

"You can help how you react," Dylan said frankly. "Not that anything *I* have to say will matter, but if you'd just be a bit more agreeable—"

"Agreeable!" Angela stared at him in angry amazement. "If I were any more agreeable, I'd be in his bed."

"That might help." Dylan gave her back an angry stare. "I hate to be the one to tell you this, but you're on a bloody pirate ship. If you were on a ship with any other captain, you might already be a ride-under for most of the crew, in case that helps you make up your mind."

Tension roiled thickly between them as Angela and Dylan glared at one another. It was Emily who broke the tension.

"Excuse me, but isn't there a less intimate and demanding manner in which to appease Captain Saber?" she asked in a quavering voice.

Dylan visibly relaxed, and his gaze shifted to Emily's face. "Aye. Placate him instead of prod him. Truthfully, he's never had much use for women that I can tell, but he's not deliberately cruel, either. He can be congenial most of the time."

"I've not noticed his congeniality," Angela remarked, "but I will endeavor to placate him at every turn if you will get us clean clothing. And a bath," she added as an afterthought. "We could both use one."

The pirate's eyes widened to the size of Spanish doubloons. "Jeezus. Does this look like a royal pleasure yacht? A bath. Why not ask for steak and kidney pie, something that might be remotely possible?"

"I take it you mean a bath is impossible."

"Nearly. It'd most likely cause a riot if the crew got wind of it. Two naked females in a tub of water? God forbid. I can imagine Saber's reaction if I were dumb enough to even ask."

"I did not request a bath on the main deck for the entertainment of the crew," Angela pointed out. "Only a few minutes of privacy."

Dylan swept off his hat, stroking the curved ostrich feather between his fingers. He looked thoughtful. "Jeez. Do you have to look at me like that? It's not as if *I* care if you bathe. It's the crew. Not a man jack of 'em wouldn't give their best to take a peek. I'm not even certain there's a tub on board anyway. Isn't there something else you'd like more?"

"Freedom, but right now a bath is the most practical and likely necessity that occurs to me." Angela crossed her arms over her chest. "It seems to me to be a simple enough request, especially in light of the request you made for me to throw myself at Saber like a harlot."

Dylan sighed. "I didn't mean it that way, though it would probably put him in a much better mood." He paused, then said, "I think there might be a tub in Saber's cabin. Nothing fancy, though. He usually does like the rest of us."

"Without?" Angela snapped, nettled by Dylan's obvious indifference and refusal to understand.

Instead of being chastened, Dylan grinned. "I admit that my usual baths are taken in a hard rain, but if I soap up quick, I can get most of the dirt off before the rain stops."

"How enlightening. It conjures up a wonderful image." She drew in a deep breath. "However, we prefer being allowed the luxury of bathing in the privacy of our cabin."

"Jeez, you don't mind asking the impossible, do you." Dylan's grin removed any sting from his words. He shook his head, long hair brushing like dark silk over his shoulders. "I won't make any promises, but I'll see. Remember *your* promise. I'm tired of catching hell because Saber ain't getting what he really wants from you."

She should have been affronted by this last, but somehow, with Dylan's sunny smile and engaging face, she found it difficult. An unwilling smile tugged at the corners of her mouth despite her efforts to look disapproving.

"You'd best get used to it," she said. "I do not intend to give him whatever it is you think he wants."

Dylan looked frankly disbelieving, but was polite enough not to argue that point. Instead, he said earnestly, "Theory aside, you need to watch your step with Saber. He's not a man to trifle with on some things."

"Don't I already know that?" she retorted.

"Apparently not. Last I heard, you half crippled him with your knee. A man's not likely to forget that blow to his ego—or his manhood."

With that subtle warning echoing in her head, Angela allowed the pirate to coax them into eating. He had wooden kids in the passageway, he announced, with tasty treats just for the ladies. Would they care to try some honey cakes before the weevils got them?

His wheedling was hard to resist, and soon both Emily and Angela were seated at the small table with trays in front of them. Once the covers were removed, they found to their delight that the food was, indeed, quite edible.

"Umm," Emily said dreamily, with sauce still smeared on her upper lip, "this is quite good."

Dylan smiled as if he were personally responsible for cooking the meal. "You're lucky it was me in charge instead of Turk, or you'd be eating weeds and seeds. I told Beans to outdo himself. I even gave him a book with recipes, so you're his first experiment. What with our recent take, this food would only spoil, I told Beans. And don't he need the practice? Why cook for mates who don't have the experience to appreciate fine food near as much as you two ladies?"

Knowing that it was filched food did not deter Angela's pleasure in the least, which only proved to her that she had already abandoned some of her more refined principles. She devoured the chicken baked in a clever sauce of herbs and vinegar, crusty rolls that were flaky and soft on the inside, and fruit sautéed in butter. The honey cakes were the crowning glory, rich and heavy, sprinkled with chopped almonds and garnished with ripe red cherries.

Dylan watched silently, straddling a chair and swinging his hat idly from the tip of a finger. The feather fluttered with the movement. Once he got up and opened the door wide, "To let in fresh air," he said, and sat back down.

Angela eyed him. "Would you like a portion?" she asked, indicating her half-finished plate. Dylan shook his head and said cheerily that he had eaten already, but thank you very much. His gaze strayed again and again to dark-haired Emily, to her pretty, plump face and generous curves. Angela silently fretted. It would never do for a pirate to form an attachment for Emily. Or would it?

The idea came to her with such sizzling clarity that she was astonished she had not considered it before. Why could they not use Dylan's obvious admiration for Emily to gain their freedom? Women had been doing that sort of thing since time began—all it took was some ingenuity and subtlety. Surely, Emily could manage to coax Dylan into helping them if he believed that she cared for him.

It was certainly a solution, though a risky one. She would have to think on it a bit more before presenting it to Emily. After all, it would require much more than a bit of flirting, she was certain, but she did not know how far Emily would be able to go without blurting out the truth or fleeing. Emily's plain, honest, nature did not lend itself to duplicity, which did not say very much for herself, Angela considered with a silent sigh. But then again, she was desperate.

Philippe would be wondering where she was, and why she had not arrived in New Orleans yet, and oh, heaven forbid if he tried to contact her father! Papa would be beside himself with worry and grief. If he heard that his only daughter had fallen into the hands of pirates. . . . She spared a moment of prayer for Captain Turnower and the ill-fated crew of the *Scrutiny* before reflecting that their deaths had at least spared her father the knowledge of his daughter's fate. It would be some time before anyone knew what had happened to the *Scrutiny,* she was certain. Perhaps she would be able to get a message to Philippe before he began to worry badly enough to contact Papa.

Yes. Though she deplored the method, she saw Dylan's attentions to Emily as possible freedom. Pirates had no compunction whatsoever in impressing their will on helpless victims, so she saw no need to spare a moment's guilt at what she contemplated. All she had to do was convince Emily of that fact. It should be easy enough. They had little to lose if Captain Saber really did intend to hold them hostage or sell them. And there was little she would put past him.

She lifted her head and focused her gaze on Emily. Some judicious warnings of dire fate would be all that was necessary. Once they were free, she could ease her conscience.

And besides—it may be their only chance to escape.

Kit slammed his closed fist against the rail. "Bloody hell," he muttered softly. The bird perched on his shoulder echoed the sentiment with warbling cheer, digging talons deeper into the bunched linen of his shirt. Kit gently detached the talons and swung Rollo to his forearm.

"Yes," Turk said, "I agree with your sentiment. It will be most inconvenient to journey to America. Are you certain of your information?"

Opening his closed fist, Kit held up a crumpled sheet of paper. "If I believe this communiqué from Gabriel, yes. He's never been wrong before, though I seem to be always a day or two too late."

The last was said bitterly, and Turk nodded. After a moment, the tall giant remarked, "A rather coincidental meeting, in my opinion. Rather like the taking of the *St. Denis,* when Gabriel was aboard."

Kit smiled faintly. "Gabriel does have a flair, does he not? He is the most excellent spy I have ever employed. If anyone can find her, he can. And does so consistently."

"Kit," Turk said after a moment of silence, "has it occurred to you that perhaps she does not wish for you to find her? That these near misses are deliberate instead of coincidental?"

Rollo muttered something obscene, and Kit stroked the bright feathers with two fingers, focusing on the bird for a moment. Occurred to him? Oh yes. And more than once. *Constantly* would better describe it. Yet what else could he do? He'd find the bitch, whether she wanted it or not. And he'd find the truth when he did, even if it was not the truth he wanted.

He looked up. "Yes. I have considered that. And it doesn't matter."

Turk looked over the rail at the ship now barely visible on the far horizon. The *St. Denis*'s sails caught dying rays of sunlight and turned pink, a rosy mirage against the dark blue of the water. "I can only hope," he said quietly to Kit, "that the truth does not destroy you."

Seven

A knock at the door barely preceded Dylan's entrance. He wedged his head between door and jamb with impudent and obvious glee; a silky skein of black hair hung down, shimmering in the early morning light.

"Ladies, I have a surprise for you," he announced without preamble. Angela exchanged a quick glance with Emily, who was curled up on one bunk reading *Camilla* by Fanny Burney. That Captain Saber possessed the novel at all had surprised Angela. She much preferred reading his books on theology and history, a rather extensive collection that surprised her even more. Now, Emily's eyes widened, and she closed her novel with a decisive snap.

"What is it?" Angela asked cautiously, recalling Dylan's last "surprise." It had been a dead rat with two heads that one of the crewman had encountered in the bilge area of the ship, an oddity that Dylan had been certain the two women would appreciate. He had been slightly disgruntled at their failure to value his efforts to entertain, and had loftily informed them that they "ain't got no idea of what's a right fair sight." Angela had mulled over his assessment for a few moments before agreeing with Emily that Dylan's idea of entertainment and theirs could not pass within a nautical league of one another.

Grinning, Dylan said, "Remember that bath you wanted?"

"That was three days ago."

"Do you still want it or not?" he demanded. His brows lowered slightly. " 'Cause if you changed your mind after all the trouble I went to—"

"Oh no," Angela put in hastily, "we haven't changed our minds at all. We'd just assumed a real bath to be an impossibility."

"Damn near was," Dylan said frankly. He stepped inside and leaned against the doorjamb, arms crossed over his bare chest. Today he wore a huge diamond earring in his lobe; it sparkled gaily in the sunlight streaming through the high portholes of their cabin. He grinned again. "Saber is having another one of his spells and ain't in a great mood, so I had to do some kind of talking to get permission for you two to use his tub."

"Spells?" Angela shifted uneasily. She hadn't seen even a glimpse of Kit Saber in two days. Since depositing her in the new cabin, he had gone out of his way to avoid her. On the one occasion she'd encountered him, he had been even more brusque than normal. It left her feeling uneasy.

"What kind of spells?" she asked, wondering if Saber had fits of violence. It was not a comforting vision, and she was faintly relieved when Dylan assured them it had to do with a physical malady.

"Coughing," he explained. "Sounds like he's spitting up bits of lung. Smoke usually irritates it more. Or when we have wet weather."

Angela was slightly intrigued to learn that the indomitable Captain Saber had any sort of weakness. Oddly, it made him more human and sympathetic.

"Is it a fatal illness?" Emily leaned forward and asked with wide eyes. Dylan shook his head.

"No. Sounds like it at times, 'specially when he's in one of his worst spells, but Turk says it's only a broom—bron-something condition. Not fatal or contagious. Now—do you ladies still want that bath?"

"Definitely." Angela stood up. "Where shall we set the tub?"

Dylan studied her for a moment before saying, "In Saber's cabin. And don't give me that suspicious look. He ain't there. He's up on the quarterdeck with Mr. Buttons and Turk. This is the best time to do it, and if you refuse, it will be the last chance you get."

With that frank decree hanging over her head, Angela had little choice but to concede. After all, Saber would hardly want to come to his cabin while she and Emily were there, would he? It seemed highly unlikely. And Dylan was promising to stand guard outside the door to keep away any "half-wits who don't mind risking neck and back by disobeying Saber's orders," so it should be quite private.

To their mutual delight, Angela and Emily discovered that Dylan had also managed to acquire a jar of perfumed bath salts, two thick cotton towels, and a silk dressing gown for each of them. It would do no good, of course, to wonder to whom these items had once belonged. It might only mar the pleasure now, so Angela and Emily accepted them with gracious glee.

Dylan's grin grew even wider. "I'm glad you're being

sensible 'bout this. I wasn't sure. The green dressing gown is for you, Miss Angela. It goes with your eyes. And the pink"—he held out a rose-colored gown as if it were a sacred offering—"is for you, Miss Emily. I think it will look bloody swell on you."

Emily accepted the silk dressing gown with a blush, and Dylan held it a shade too long before releasing it to her. Then he swept them a slight bow that was clumsy but enthusiastic before he closed the door and left them to the high-backed brass tub placed in the middle of the cabin. A tall black-lacquered Chinese screen had been placed at a discreet angle around the tub, and a brass bucket of hot water simmered on a brazier.

"You go first," Angela offered, and Emily gave only a token protest. Circumstances had simplified their former relationship in a short time, and Angela thought little of performing the tasks of a ladies' maid for Emily. She helped her unhook her gown, then placed it neatly over the back of a chair. In scant moments, Emily was sinking into the tub with a luxurious sigh of pleasure. Angela laughed.

"You've become a decadent creature, Emily. I don't know if I shall be able to bear you much longer without reproof."

There was a muted splash from behind the screen. "I know. Shocking, isn't it? In less than a week, our lives have been changed forever."

It was a daunting thought, and Angela was quiet for a moment before saying, "I suppose we must learn from our tribulations."

"What do you suppose this particular tribulation is

meant to teach us?" Emily asked to the accompaniment of more splashing. "I already knew about fear."

Angela smiled. "Perhaps we're meant to exercise our minds and think of a way to escape."

"Escape?" Emily sounded uneasy. "I'm not that brave. I don't think I should like the consequences if we fail. Didn't you hear Dylan's comments yesterday about captives who have tried escaping and been caught?"

"He was only trying to frighten us into cowering in our cabins and not asking anything of him that might be the least bit inconvenient," Angela replied. "I'm not at all certain Saber would actually tie cannonballs to our waists and throw us overboard as Dylan claims pirates are accustomed to doing."

"But are you certain that he wouldn't?"

That question gave her pause. No, she wasn't certain of him in any way. Even though on occasion she had the thought that he might truly have been reared as a gentleman, there were too many times Saber had shown traces of ruthlessness to make her believe he had latent tendencies toward mercy. If she was ever foolish enough to believe he might display charitable traits, she had only to bring to mind the memory of Captain Turnower and his ill-fated crew being blasted out of the water by cannon fire.

She suppressed a shiver. That particular memory did fervent battle with other memories, those disturbing visions that came to her mind in the long, dark hours of night when she should be sleeping. At those times, her traitorous mind and body would recall the touch of his hand and the press of his mouth against her lips. It was ridiculous, of course, yet the memories still burned and made her ache at times, a most mortifying response to such a villainous pirate.

"No," she said at last, "I'm not at all certain of his reaction. But I do know that we can govern our own actions and rule our own fates."

"I don't know about that last," Emily said from behind the screen. There was a loud splash and a blur of movement as she rose from the tub and reached out an arm for the towel draped over a chair. "It's difficult to rule your own fate when someone else holds the power of life or death over you."

"But does he? I know that he does to some degree, yet I still think we can overcome any obstacles if we put our full minds and energies to it." Angela paused, then said, "If we are truly careful, I believe that we can outwit Captain Saber."

Emily's head appeared at the edge of the screen, her dark eyes wide and damp strands of hair clinging to her plump shoulders. "Outwit him? How?"

Angela stood up and began to unfasten her gown. "If we are clever enough to make full use of everything we have at our disposal, it can be done. I've thought about it for several days."

Emily looked doubtful. "Do you mean to steal a boat and escape? I'm not a very good sailor, you know."

"I know." Angela pulled her gown over her head and tossed it over a chair, then sat down and began peeling off her stockings. "Sooner or later, we should be near enough to land to form a solid plan. What we need to do until then is ensure that we'll have the means to carry it out."

"I don't understand." Wearing the silk dressing gown

Dylan had provided for her, Emily stepped out from behind the Chinese screen. The thin rose silk clung to her damp body in places, and the hem was much too long for her, dragging over the canvas Dylan had placed under the brass tub to protect the floor. "How can we plan to have the means to escape when we don't even know where we'll be?"

"We may not know, but there are others aboard who do." Angela let that sink in for a moment as she focused on rolling her stockings neatly and placing them atop her gown. She looked up to find Emily staring at her with a puzzled frown.

"The crew? I should hope they know where we're going, but that still doesn't help us. None of them would tell us, I'm sure."

"Not normally, no. But if we have gained the affection and trust of one of them . . ." Angela deliberately let her voice trail into silence while she stepped behind the screen and removed the rest of her garments.

She had poured the rest of the hot water into the tub along with a liberal dose of bath salts and was sinking down into the tub when Emily finally said, "You mean Dylan."

Angela leaned back and draped her arms over the high rim. She raised her voice to be heard over the screen. "Yes. Dylan likes you. I'm certain he would help us if we convinced him our lives were in danger."

Silence.

"Dylan seems *especially* fond of you, Emily."

More silence.

Angela tried again. "Of course, we would have to be so discreet no one would suspect him of helping us."

"You want me to ask him," Emily said flatly, and Angela hesitated.

"Not now," she said after a moment. "Later, when we're close to land."

"It would endanger him as well as us," Emily said in a tight voice. "I don't want to do it."

"You would rather be sold to some Turkish caliph and live in his harem the rest of your life? Or perhaps be sold to a farmer in the colonies and hoe weeds and pick cotton all day every day?" Angela didn't try to hide her irritation. "What is the matter, Emily? Don't you have any sort of survival instinct?"

"Yes," Emily flashed. "If you're so convinced this will work, why don't you try it on Captain Saber?"

"Saber!" Angela dropped her washcloth. "He would see right through me in an instant. Besides, Dylan likes you. Saber hates me."

Emily gave a scornful laugh. "Not a bit of it. I've seen the way he looks at you. And for that matter, I've seen the way you look at him, too."

"Really, Emily, you're imagining things again." Angela scrubbed angrily at one arm. "I do not appreciate your even suggesting such a thing."

"You don't seem to mind suggesting it for me. Don't you have any sort of compassion?"

"Of course." Angela sat up with a jerk, sending a spray of water onto the canvas mat. "I had compassion for Captain Turnower and his crew, and I have compassion for you. Do you expect me to have compassion for a pirate who has probably robbed, raped, and murdered more people in a single year than we can imagine? Emily, *think!*"

A faint sob drifted around the screen, and Angela closed her eyes with frustration. This was not going well. Dear Emily, so filled with guileless trust that she could not even enlist the aid of one of her own captors. Sighing, Angela said aloud, "If it distresses you, don't think about it, Emily. We'll devise another plan."

"Oh good," Emily said with obvious relief. After a moment, she added in a faint voice, "I think I shall go back to our cabin now. I left my hairbrush there, and my hair tangles so badly if I do not brush it dry."

"I'll be along in a few minutes," Angela said, lifting a leg and soaping it with leisurely strokes. "I just want to enjoy my bath."

Emily stepped to the door and called for Dylan. In a moment, his steps could be heard on the steep companionway, and he knocked once before swinging open the door.

"I've a word or two to say to both of you," he called out, and he did not sound very pleased.

"Is there something amiss, Dylan?" Angela asked from behind the screen, but he refused to reply, saying only that he would speak to her later.

"Right now, I'll take Emily back to her cabin while you finish your bath."

"If you intend to give her a piece of your mind about something," Angela observed, "make certain you can spare it."

"Don't be too sassy. You won't like what I have to say any more than she will. Come along, Miss Emily."

The murmur of their voices faded behind the closed door, and Angela sighed. Her enjoyment of the bath was marred by Emily's distress. There was little she could do to alleviate it. If she sympathized too much, then any hope of getting Emily to actually cooperate with her plan would be doomed. No, she simply had to coax Emily into doing it. Their freedom certainly depended upon it, and possibly even their lives. And it wasn't as if she didn't like Dylan. She did. But if he could be tricked into helping them, she would do it in an instant.

Closing her eyes, she allowed herself a few moments of indulgent soaking before she rose from the tub. Dylan would be returning shortly, and she had no desire to risk meeting up with Captain Saber. He was too perceptive, and she had the uncomfortable feeling that he knew what she was thinking most of the time.

Frequently, there was a mocking light in his eyes, as if he knew she lay awake at night and thought of him. She should have been shamed by it, but she was more confused than anything else. How could she have allowed him to kiss her? She should have screamed, or slapped him, or shown some kind of reaction other than a breathless plea for him to stop. That last still left her flushed with humiliation. She'd never considered herself weak or spineless, but apparently, Saber was able to find her frailties quickly enough. She didn't understand it at all. Thoughts of Philippe should have kept her strong, but they hadn't. Oddly, she'd not thought of him for an instant when Saber kissed her. Not until much later, anyway.

Angela sighed and rose from the tub. She reached for a towel. All this dwelling on what couldn't be changed was pointless. She should devote all her energies to escaping. Yet she was more afraid of how Saber made her feel than the possibilities of what he could do to her. She had to escape, and soon, if she was to survive with her soul intact.

Kit stood in the doorway like a stone statue, one hand still on the latch, his eyes riveted to the scene in his cabin. God. He'd forgotten. The Azores were within sight, and his mind had been on business. Intent on retrieving the letters of marque from his locked casket, he'd not given a single thought to the fact that the women might still be in his cabin with their damned bath.

Yet they were. Or one of them was, at any rate. Where the hell was Dylan? He was supposed to stand guard outside the door, but there had been no sign of him. Kit muttered a curse when Angela stepped from behind the Chinese screen clad in a towel that barely hid her torso and left her long, creamy legs bare. She hadn't noticed him as she reached for a silk dressing gown thrown over a chair. The towel slipped dangerously low, revealing the high rise of one breast and enticing shadows. He sagged against the doorframe.

God, he couldn't help it. Angela aroused a fire in him that was as urgent as it was baffling. He hadn't been able to get her out of his mind since he'd first laid eyes on her, and now it would be worse. Much worse. Seeing her in the filmy chemise had been bad enough. He closed his eyes. Visions of tantalizing skin, luscious curves, and bare legs would be pure hell in the nights to follow.

A flash of heat produced predictable physical results. He opened his eyes and wrenched away from the doorframe.

"Must you drip all ever my carpet?" he asked in as mild a tone as he could manage.

Angela turned with a jerk and a gasp, and the towel fell. For an instant, she stood paralyzed, breasts rising and falling with each rapid breath. Kit tried in vain to ignore a prodding sense of urgency. Then she gave another strangled gasp and snatched up the robe to hold it in front of her. It draped in a fall of green silk that hid very little, and she tried to readjust it with clumsy haste. Her quick, fluttering movements made him think of a startled butterfly.

"It really doesn't hide much," he observed calmly. He tilted his head to one side. "You would do better to put it on, I think."

She stood quite still, staring at him with wide eyes as green as the silk robe she held. A bright flush stained her high cheekbones. The flush stained her throat down to the curve of her rounded breasts, a most interesting reaction. He speculated an instant on possibilities before drawling, "At least cover the parts that are too tempting, angel. It's not that I'm not enjoying the show, but have you considered the fact that you might grow chilled?"

That seemed to propel her into action at last. She stepped back behind the Chinese screen and there was a flurry of green silk accompanied by a furious, "How dare you!"

"How dare I what? Come into my own cabin?" Kit folded his arms over his chest and said, "I gave permission for you to take a brief bath in my tub, which is in *my* cabin, in case you've forgotten. I did not give permission for you and your fripperies to actually take over my quarters. Where is your chaperon, green eyes?"

"I suppose you mean my guard," Angela snapped from behind the screen. "He's out tying cannonballs to unfortunate prisoners, I presume. Isn't that what pirates do?"

Kit said evenly, "Yes, at times. At other times, we defile distressed damsels. Or had you forgotten?"

"Not for an instant!" Angela appeared at the edge of the screen, the dressing gown wrapped tightly around her body. There was now a scarcity of visible skin, but he noted with a slight grin that the robe clung in revealing folds to her damp body.

"You seem to find this amusing, Captain Saber," she said stiffly, and he realized she'd misinterpreted his reaction.

Lifting a brow, he said, *"Annoyed* more closely describes my emotions at this moment. Why is it that I stumble across you and your maid in various stages of undress at every opportunity? Don't you know how to keep your clothes on?"

"Yes, but one does not usually do so when bathing. At least, not a *civilized* person."

"Ah, I take it that inference is meant to imply that I am not civilized, Miss High-and-Mighty?"

"Not imply—state unequivocally."

He strode forward, hardly realizing his intention until he had one hand around her arm and had pulled her against him. His hand tightened around her upper arm.

"You're so bloody high-minded. Has it ever occurred to you that given the right circumstances, you might behave in a less than civilized manner yourself?"

"I might be frightened, but I doubt very seriously I would stoop to some of the crimes you have committed."

"Oh do you." He laughed harshly. "Yes, I imagine

you'd like to think so. But I wonder. I wonder just how polite you would be when faced with the possibility of a slow death. Or witnessing the death of someone you knew and loved. Do you think you would courteously request that the perpetrators cease and desist? Or would you look around you for a weapon, and when you had used it and they were dead, would you want to laugh?"

Her face had gone pale, her eyes as murky as green bottle glass. Kit shook his head.

"Yes, I can see by your face that you think it's all a crock of nonsense, but I assure you, sweetheart, that given the right situation, you would do just the same. You're a fighter and a survivor. I noted that about you the first day, when you jabbed your knee into my crotch. Do you think you would not fight? Since you've been on this ship, that's all you've done. Granted, the weapons have been words, but the intent is the same."

"What would you have me do?" she asked in a hoarse whisper. "Yield to unjust demands? Surrender meekly?"

"No. I would never recommend spineless submission to anyone. It will get you killed in the long run."

Her eyes flashed, and she tried to pull away. When he did not release her, she said angrily, "Then why must you torment me? If you approve of resistance, why do you try to suppress it?"

"Ah, because I do not necessarily approve of resistance against me," he said with a laugh. "It depends on the circumstances, angel. While I am not trying to really harm you, only rid myself of you, there are others who would deserve such an enthusiastic revolt."

"I have never before met a man who deserves an uprising more than you," she snapped, and this time he let her go when she tried to get away.

A smile curled his mouth. He couldn't help it. She was such a fierce little creature at times that his irritation usually lost to amusement at her useless bravado.

Her eyes flamed at his obvious amusement. "Damn you!"

He laughed. "I've been damned for more years than you know, angel. But I do approve your usage of profanity. A few more verbose expletives, and you'll be right at home among the crew."

"Among those ravages of humanity?" she scoffed. "I hardly think so. It would take someone with far more excesses of immorality than I have exhibited to feel at home amon—"

He caught a handful of her hair and pulled her head back, effectively cutting off her sneering criticism. Anger made his voice harsh.

"I would like to see how moral you would be when faced with the lives some of those men have led. Some of them were condemned to death for a crime no worse than stealing bread to feed their starving family. Yet they were called criminal, and sent to the gallows. If not for escape, more than one man aboard this ship would be food for the worms by now, because the justice system decrees that it is moral for babies to die screaming for food but immoral for a man to be forced to rob to provide it. Oh, I can see that you don't believe me. Well, it is obviously much easier to live your way, believing that life is all sugarplums and hot bread."

"You don't know what I believe," she said in a voice that shook slightly. "You don't know me at all."

"No, and I don't want to," he said with deliberate cruelty. "I don't want to know more about you than I do, because it would sicken me. I've known enough females just like you to give me a good idea of the workings of your mind. You're selfish and vain, and want only the momentary gratification of whatever whims come to mind."

His grip had tightened in her damp, curling hair; pale strands streamed over his hand and danced loosely. He saw pained tears spring into her eyes, making them glisten darkly.

"That's not true," she whispered. "I want happiness, but not at the cost of others."

"Oh? Is that right? Why do I have the impression that Emily was not eager to go on this journey? She seemed less than enthusiastic about leaving England, yet she is here nevertheless."

Color stained Angela's cheeks, and her lower lip quivered slightly. "I admit that she was reluctant, but it is only until I reach—until I get to my destination. I promised I would send her home then."

"And she was given that choice?"

Angela's lashes lowered over her eyes, and after a moment, she said softly, "No. You are right. I allowed my needs to supersede Emily's. It seemed my only solution at the time."

"Yet Emily is now enjoying a fate similar to yours. How that must upset you."

Her lashes flew up at his mockery, heated anger drying her tears. "I suppose you've never acted unwisely? I suppose your life has been one of perfect and blameless rectitude?"

"At least I'm honest enough to say outright that what I want matters most to me," he shot back. "I don't hide behind self-righteous pratings about morality."

"Don't you?" she mocked. "I seem to recall your condemning Captain Turnower when I've seen you commit acts of piracy that are even worse. I think you do exactly what you want, when you want, with no regard to right or wrong."

"Do you." His grip tightened. "Perhaps you're right. What I want right now is to lay you back on my bed. Maybe I should, and to hell with everything else."

He heard her soft gasp as he pulled her hard against him, and ignored the wordless whimper of protest she gave when he bent his head and kissed her. He drew one hand down over her back, spreading his fingers to hold her tightly against him. He could feel the thrust of her breasts through the thin silk, the nipples hard little points against the bare skin of his chest. God, he shouldn't be doing this, shouldn't be yielding to the heady temptation she presented. The lesson he'd intended to teach her was turning out to be more of a lesson for him. If he had any sense, he would let go, turn her around, and send her back to her own cabin before he went so far he couldn't retreat.

But as Turk had noted more than once, there were moments when a man's reason became clouded. This, apparently, was one of them.

Kit rapidly lost himself in the kiss, in the sweet, luscious taste of her mouth and the feel of her body beneath his palm. It was insane, and he knew it, but he couldn't stop. Not now, not now . . .

"Angel," he muttered in a groan, his mouth against

her scented skin. Kissing her mouth and then her throat, his hand curled more tightly in the wealth of her hair and he coiled it around his fist to hold her still. It should have made little difference who she was or what she was, only that she was there and soft and warm and inviting. It was vaguely surprising to realize that it made a great deal of difference to him, and he wondered why.

Her struggles finally ceased and she leaned compliantly against him, her breath coming in shallow pants, her breasts pressing tantalizingly against him with each intake of air. He explored her soft curves through the robe, shaping her to him, stroking down the small of her back and over her hips, hands molding to her body in caresses that grew bold. She was moving against him, faint whimpers coming from her throat, and with a shock, he felt her hands move in a light caress over his back. Any thought of restraint he might have entertained vanished like smoke in a high wind. He groaned, and without pausing to think, swept her into his arms and carried her to his shadowed bunk.

Laying her down, he leaned over her, bracing himself on one arm. Her hair fanned out over his pillow in a golden stream and the jade dressing gown gapped open, revealing a marvel of cream and pink shadows. He put a hand atop hers when she instinctively moved to cover herself.

"No, don't," he said in a voice so hoarse he didn't recognize it as his own. Her hand quivered under his. She looked up through a thick fan of lashes that shadowed her eyes, mouth trembling. He bent again, closing his eyes as he kissed her and reached for the ties of her dressing gown.

When he gave the silk tie a tug, it came free, and he felt the edges fall apart. With a groan, he bent lower, forearm pressing her back into the mattress of his bunk. His mouth teased her taut nipple through the silk, drawing it against his teeth and wetting the material until she was arching up against him with moans of pleasure.

Losing himself in the damp heat of her body, Kit slid his hand intimately between her legs. He wanted her so badly he ached all over, but he wanted her willing. He wanted her to ache for him, to plead for what he desperately wanted to give her. It was insane and he knew it, knew that he should run before it was too late, but at that moment, nothing could have dragged him away. Caressing her, he slid his hand upward until he touched her intimately, sliding his fingers over her alluring femininity in a leisurely glide. She gave a small cry but he did not remove his hand, even when her thighs closed around it.

Still stroking her, he shifted slightly so that the silk robe slipped away from her breast. The nipple was tightly beaded and damp, and he took it gently between his teeth, teasing it until she began to gasp and tremble beneath him. He tugged at her nipple, one hand moving to her other breast and the other between her thighs. He slid his fingers into her, into the tight, moist heat of her, exploring deeply. When he came to the unbroken barrier of her virginity, he felt a moment's shock. Somehow, he'd not quite expected that. He didn't know why, except that the English gentlewomen he'd known had usually been much more experienced.

He groaned, feeling as if he would explode at any moment. Damn, he had to exhibit some restraint.

Damn restraint, he thought in the next instant when

she arched against him. He had to have her, had to feel her lovely body tight around him. His hand moved inside her again, long glides that made the edges of his reason grow dim and hazy. His blood was pounding, drowning out common sense and the tiny whispers of whatever conscience he had left. Suddenly, he didn't care. Nothing mattered but Angela, the sweet curves of her body and the release she could give him.

Angela cried out, body quivering, and he started to withdraw and reach for the buttons of his breeches. Almost convulsively, she grasped at him, holding him still as her hips arched upward.

"Kit, please," she breathed in a strangled moan, and he wasn't certain if she wanted him to stop or continue. He moved his hand again in a slow glide and felt her quiver. Schooling his raging body into patience, he focused on giving her pleasure, his fingers stroking in and out. Her hands raked the bare skin of his arms and shoulders where the leather vest had fallen away, but he barely felt the sting. Then she was shuddering against him in release, awkward in her inexperience, crying out wordlessly.

For a long moment, Kit hung there, braced on one arm, fighting the impulse to take her. He should. She would yield gladly. But somewhere in the midst of her response to him, he had discovered that he couldn't do that to her. Some small spark of the man he had once been—should have been—would not allow him to take advantage of her innocence.

Lifting his head, he stared down at her small face. Her eyes were closed, and her lips were parted. She made him think of a tiger cub, all hiss and curiosity, and he

fought a wave of unexpected affection mixed with resentment. He sighed, and held her for a long moment
while she tucked her head into the billowing softness of
a pillow as if trying to hide from him.

Finally, into the silence still thick with remnants of
passion, she said softly, "Is that what you did to the
woman who threw herself overboard rather than face her
family?"

Kit went still. He felt as if he'd been doused with icy
water. Damn her. How did she hear that old story? Of
course. Emily would know. She read all the accounts,
true and untrue, of his exploits. He should have expected
this, but somehow he hadn't.

He sat up and swung his legs over the edge of the
bunk. Raking a hand through his hair, he looked at her
for a moment before saying deliberately, "Yes."

Angela's head turned away on the pillow, and she drew
together the edges of her dressing gown. He caught her
hands.

"A little late for that, isn't it? No, don't say anything
else. I think you've said quite enough for now."

He got up and stalked toward his desk, eyeing the
damp spots on his carpet with a scowl. Keys jangled as
he unlocked a drawer and removed the small wood and
iron cask that held the letters of marque giving the *Sea
Tiger* permission to sail certain waters. When he glanced
up, he saw that Angela had gathered up her clothes and
started for the door.

"Where in the hell do you think you're going?" he
demanded, and when she didn't pause, he strode after
her. He caught her by one arm as she was about to exit
and yanked her back into the cabin. Tears streaked her

cheeks and trembled on the length of her lashes, but her mouth was set in a taut line. She shot him a nervous glance and her small chin rose defiantly.

"Let go of me."

"And let you trot up on deck where the wind will whip that thin robe right off you? Fine." He let go of her. "By all means, my lady, gallivant along the decks wearing next to nothing. And when the crew is done with you, I'll toss what's left over the taffrail."

Angela paled. "I could dress first."

"Yes. That would be the intelligent thing to do. Jolly good thing you thought of it, tardy though you may be."

His acid tone seemed to seep into her brain at last, and she pressed her lips tightly together. After a moment, she said, "I cannot dress with you still in here, Captain Saber."

His brow shot up. "How formal we're being now. After what we've just shared, you could relax a bit, you know. It's not as if I haven't already seen all of you there is to see."

With flaming cheeks, Angela glared up at him. "That was not my choice, either. And I refuse to dress for your entertainment . . ."

He put up a hand to stop her. "Spare me the self-righteous mewling. Perhaps the best thing is for me to fetch your chaperon to take you to your cabin."

"How kind of you," Angela said tartly. "I see why you're so popular a captain."

Kit didn't reply. He stuck his head out the door and bellowed, "Dylan!" until he heard the rapid pounding of feet in the companionway. In moments, Dylan appeared at the door, his face carefully settling into a blank expression as he surveyed the scene. Amber eyes moved from the tub and scattered cloths to the bed, and then to Angela's disheveled figure and damp robe. Kit could imagine his thoughts.

"Do you need me?" Dylan asked, and Kit wasn't certain which one of them he was addressing.

Angela was thrust forward. "No," Saber said curtly, "but I want her out of here. *Now.*"

Dylan didn't ask questions, only took Angela by one arm and escorted her from the cabin. Kit slammed the door behind them; he wondered bitterly why he seemed to keep his brains between his legs since meeting Angela. He should have backed out of the cabin the moment he'd seen her. It would have been much simpler.

And when Turk stepped into his cabin several minutes later and glanced around with a brow lifted in mild surprise, Kit wished he'd done the sensible thing and stayed topside until it was clear.

"Mercy," Turk said at last, eyeing the hip bath full of cold, perfumed water and the rumpled bunk, "I seem to have missed something."

"Not much." Kit held out the papers he'd retrieved. "These will do. With England and Portugal such enthusiastic allies against Napoleon, we should be well received."

"I daresay." Turk took the papers and slid them into the inner pocket of his tailored coat. Superfine breeches fit him snugly, and his knee-high Hessian leather boots had been fashioned by Hoby, the most famous bootmaker in London.

Kit regarded Turk with a lifted brow. "Dressed to the nines, I see. Expecting to impress someone?"

"One should invariably endeavor to impress those in a position to do harm or favor."

"Really. I take it you mean to overwhelm Commissioner LaRosa with your tailor?"

"If possible. Should I wear ragged breeches and a leather vest? It would definitely make an impression, but not one I would recommend." Turk studied him for a moment before saying softly, "Your irascible temper is even fouler than normal. I advise you to initiate steps to correct the cause."

"And I suppose you know the cause," Kit said irritably when Turk turned to leave. The quartermaster turned back.

"I am well aware of the motivation for your ill humor. As are you."

"Bloody hell, Turk, leave it be," Kit said savagely. "They'll be gone tomorrow."

"I fervently hope that you do not swerve in that enterprise, Kit. The consequences could be disastrous."

"What makes you think I'll change my mind? The girl gets on my nerves. I'm eager to be rid of the both of them."

"As you say. Nevertheless, I wish to reiterate the importance of them being returned to their homes. It could initiate an incident that would be extremely detrimental to us if we were so foolish as to allow them to linger aboard the *Sea Tiger* much longer."

Amazed, Kit said, "Do I look like I'm enjoying this? I'd rather eat a live toad than take her another league."

A faint smile curved Turk's mouth. "Live toads are not very appetizing. Nor are they healthy. If you insist upon meat in your diet, I suggest white fish or perhaps shellfish."

Kit had learned long before not to take seriously every baiting comment Turk made, but it still rankled. "Thank you for another commentary on my diet when we're discussing a completely different topic."

"Not quite so dissimilar, if you consider all the aspects. You are remarkably intractable about recognizing facts whose existence you do not care to acknowledge. It can be both advantageous and calamitous."

Kit ignored this. "While you are meeting with Commissioner LaRosa, I shall be making the arrangements for our . . . guests to embark on a return journey to England. With a generous payment for our services, of course."

"Excellent. I have the suspicion that Miss Angela would generate industrious investigation if her whereabouts are not divulged in a reasonable length of time."

"If one cares to believe her maid, she is extremely valuable as a hostage. Although I have my doubts that anyone would bother paying for her, the crew thinks otherwise." Kit rose from behind his desk. "Although if I were to be fair, I suppose I would have to admit to a certain astonishment at the young lady's choice of reading material. Despite all appearances to the contrary, it seems she at least possesses a brain."

"If you would actually commence a discourse with her instead of an argument," said Turk, "you would already know that."

Kit shrugged. He was beginning to find the conversation tedious, which was rare when he was with Turk. No other man had ever been able to converse at length with him, matching wit and temper so neatly that it was almost as if he argued with his mirror image. Lately, his mirror image had begun to chafe.

"At any rate," he said, "by this time tomorrow, the ladies will be someone else's problem."

"I certainly hope so." Turk paused in the doorway. "I shall be glad when matters are back to normal."

"Whatever that is."

Turk nodded. "Yes. Whatever that is."

After Turk had gone, Kit moved to stare through the gallery porthole at the water outside. A blur on the horizon grew sharper as he watched. The volcanic rock of Pico Island thrust up from the sea in elephantine folds, barren and desolate. Ponta Delgada on the south side of São Miguel had a decent harbor, and they would be putting into it before dark. It would be a relief to rid himself of the responsibility of Angela Whoever.

He just wished he could erase from his mind the image of her in his bunk, still damp from her bath, and the silk dressing robe barely clinging to her luscious curves, her eyes closed in ecstasy. He tamped down the surge of raw frustration that still gnawed at him. Bloody hell. He'd get rid of her at the first opportunity. He had to, or he'd find himself at her feet like some puling adolescent boy besotted with his first woman.

Kit looked down at his knotted hands, and realized that he'd broken in two a Chinese figurine from the fifth dynasty. He couldn't recall picking it up, but there it was in his hands, snapped as cleanly as a dry twig. Gently, he placed the ruined figurine on a table and reached for the decanter of brandy. He'd best dull the edges, or there would be hell to pay.

Rollo, flapped in through the opened door, perched on the edge of the brass tub and looked at him brightly. "Bloody hell," he chirped cheerily, and Kit held up his brandy.

"A toast, Rollo. To women—if only we could fall into their arms, and not into their hands. Damn all women."

Tilting back his head, he drained his brandy in a single swallow, while Rollo merrily crowed, "Damn all women. Damn all women . . ."

Eight

"Now?" Angela tried to hide the sudden tremor of her hands. "I had no idea that we were even near land."

Dylan turned her around and began to button her dress with a brisk efficiency that would do any lady's maid proud. "Well, we are. How d'ya think I was able to persuade Saber to let you bathe? Be still. I can't fasten these tiny hooks and eyes if you keep turning around to look at me."

She stood stiffly while Dylan fussed with the fastenings of her gown. She had not seen Saber since the episode in his cabin earlier, and prayed earnestly that she would not have to face him again. She couldn't. Not with the memory of what had transpired between them still so raw and vivid in her mind. It made her burn with shame to recall it, and she quickly thrust it from her thoughts.

But like a cork, images bobbed to the surface despite her most vigorous efforts to drown them. Flashes of Kit's face above her on the bunk, his arms around her, his hands moving so wickedly and wantonly, provoking reactions she'd never dreamed existed . . . she wondered what he thought of her now. That she was morally deficient, probably. She couldn't argue with that, either. Why had she yielded so easily?

Maybe it was as he'd said—magic. *Surrender to the magic,* he'd told her, and she had not known then what he meant. Now she did. Oh yes. Now she did. She had never imagined anything would feel like that.

Thrusting it from her mind with a firmness born of desperation, she said as calmly as possible to Dylan, "What is to be done with us?"

"I'm not sure. And don't think you can talk me into interfering. I heard you and Emily talking." His hands straightened a fold of fabric, then he turned her back around. There was no malice or anger in his eyes, only a frank perception that made her slightly ashamed. "You shouldn't talk so loud when you plan a mutiny. There are air vents in Saber's cabin that lead topside, and I imagine if he hadn't been so absorbed in what he was doing, he would have heard you as well. Good thing I made enough racket to drown you out. I don't want to think about what *he* would have said about your plot."

Emily removed her hands from her face and looked up from where she sat on the edge of a bunk. "Well," she said with an unusual show of spirit, "what would you have us do? Just go meekly to our fates?"

"It would be easier. And safer. Look, Saber ain't as bad as you're thinking. I know I told you a bunch of stuff, but that was to keep you from doing anything too stupid. He wouldn't really harm you. Scare you, maybe, but nothing fatal."

"Then what does he plan to do with us today?" Emily asked.

Dylan looked away. Late afternoon light slanted hazily

through the round ports and picked out coppery glints in his dark hair. "It was a council decision," he said at last. "We all voted. Saber intends to arrange your passage back to England once we get to Ponta Delgada."

Angela's heart lurched. Kit intended to send her away after what had happened? Obviously, it had meant more to her than it did to him. Of course. Pirates would be well used to such interludes with women captives.

Lifting her chin, she snorted in a very unladylike manner. "But are we to go as passengers or as prisoners?"

"Does it matter? You've been well treated." He thrust a hairbrush into Angela's hand. "You might as well look presentable, whatever the plans."

Emily made another sobbing sound, and Dylan's expression softened when he turned to her. "Don't fret, love. I can promise you that nothing too bad will happen. You'll be traded for a hefty ransom first, but that's all. No one will really harm you, I swear it."

Moist brown eyes fastened on Dylan. "Ransom? Are you sure?" she whispered, and he grimaced.

"It's the best thing for you. Common enough, you know. After all, it's done all the time and certainly fattens up our purses. Pirates aren't the only ones who do it," he said defensively when Emily gave him a scathing glance. "France and England have been busily engaged in that sort of conduct for years. So has Spain, and every other *civilized* country, so you don't need to look at me as if I'm in league with Attila the Hun."

"How scholarly a comparison," Angela said. "I'm delighted that you've heard of him, though I had in mind a more apt comparison—Blackbeard."

Anger sparked the gold eyes. "Damme, but you don't need to be so mean about it. Saber ain't no Blackbeard."

"Not enough wives?" Angela asked with a malice steeped in hurt. "Or is it the beard he lacks?"

Dylan turned abruptly to Emily. "Believe what you want, both of you, but I hope you've remorse enough to apologize when you're safely on a ship back to England."

Emily colored. "Oh, she didn't mean it, Dylan, truly she didn't!"

"Yes, I did," Angela began, but Emily wasn't listening. She had begun a stammering litany of reassurances that dealt with the sterling character of their "hosts," and degenerated from there into an idealized itinerary of their exemplary treatment while aboard the *Sea Tiger.*

Disgusted, Angela muttered an uncomplimentary phrase that finally drew Dylan's attention from Emily. His dark brow lifted.

"Say what you will, Saber ain't like Blackbeard at all. He's got a conscience, and he's decent. He's never willingly hurt a woman and has gone out of his way to treat both you and Miss Emily well, so I don't know why you won't believe me when I tell you that you won't be harmed."

"Forgive me," Angela shot at him, "but it's difficult to reconcile the Saber you describe with the man depicted in London as a monster. What do you suggest I believe—his well-known reputation or your glowing words?"

"Your own experience would be a good basis, I would think." Dylan's eyes softened slightly. "I understand why you're worried, but there's no need for it. If you'll just give Saber the name of someone who would be willing to ransom you, you'll be on a ship back to England quick as a cat."

Angela turned away from his knowing gaze, coloring hotly as she wondered just how much Dylan knew. Dear God, she couldn't let anyone see how painful this was for her—Kit's rejection after what had happened was an obvious indication of what little value he placed on her. She suspected he must be right, or she would not have yielded so easily to him earlier.

"Oh, I see now," she said with a careless shrug. "You're simply the Trojan horse sent to ferret out our weakness. First you befriend us, then take gross advantage of our belief in you to coerce the names of those to be contacted for ransom. Well, I refuse to cooperate."

"What a stupid notion. And aren't you forgetting *your* little scheme?" Dylan asked with a lifted brow. "It's remarkably close, if you ask me."

"Perhaps. But I have no intention of telling you anything that will allow you to return us to England."

Dylan stared at her as if not quite certain he'd heard correctly. "What?"

"I said, I have no intention of telling you anything." Angela drew in a deep breath. "I wish to go on to America. I have business there and see no sense in going back to England."

Emily moaned, and Angela dared not look at her. To return to England now would be the worst possible outcome of this whole affair. She would be wed immediately to the baron her father had chosen, and her life would be ruined. If she could get to America and Philippe, there may yet be hope for her future.

"You're joking," Dylan said, his voice flat as if he realized that she was not. "You must be."

"I am not." Angela met his gaze steadily. "If we are to be ransomed, it will be in America, not England."

"Miss Angela!" Emily burst out. "You cannot mean this."

Angela turned. "Of course I do. I have no intention of taking a chance ashore here, where we know no one to help us should the occasion arise. And you must realize that, with pirates, it is quite likely that an occasion will arise where we will need aid. So don't be too quick to say anything, Emily."

"But to go all the way to America—it's because of Philippe, isn't it?"

"Yes. But only partly. I've no desire to be left at the mercies of brigands who have no compunction about holding honest Englishwomen hostage. At least in New Orleans there will be someone we can depend upon to see us safely home again. Philippe will pay well."

"With what?" Emily shook her head, dark curls rioting around her face. "He has no money."

"I do. In my own account. I will transfer every shilling to Captain Saber and his estimable crew when I am safely ashore in New Orleans. And it is a sizable amount, as you well know."

Dylan made a sort of whuffing sound and shrugged. "I'll tell Saber what you said. He ain't gonna like it."

"His likes and dislikes are of no consequence to me," Angela said with more confidence than she felt. "If he will not cooperate, I am certain there are those in Ponta Delgada who will feel differently. That is where you said we are disembarking, is it not?"

"Sweet Jesus. You pay attention at the damndest times. Yes, but don't get any grand ideas."

"If Captain Saber does not take me to America, I will tell the authorities exactly who he is," Angela said calmly. "He will be arrested. If I am not mistaken, Ponta Delgada is Portuguese territory. Pirates are not well received in Portugal, last I heard."

Dylan stared at her. "I don't think you want to broach that idea to Saber," he said at last. "He may not take it well."

"Better now than when it's too late." Angela brushed a speck of imaginary lint from her dress sleeve, not quite able to look at Dylan. "It would be dreadful for the captain and crew of the *Sea Tiger* if they were to be hanged as murderous pirates, but I am certain England would be grateful."

After a long moment, Dylan said slowly, "It may be too late. Turk has gone ashore to meet with the commissioner, and Saber is making the arrangements for your safe return."

"Gone ashore?" Angela glanced out the round port and saw nothing but sea. Then she realized that the ship was not moving as usual, but gently rolling. She looked back at Dylan. "But we are not in a harbor."

"No. Saber prefers to remain moored a distance out. They took the skiff in. It's safer that way."

"Safer from what?" Emily asked in a frightened voice, and Dylan gave her a faint smile of reassurance.

"Anyone who might wish us harm. It's easier to fight when there's plenty of sea beneath the ship. We were grounded once, a long time ago, when we made the mistake of mooring close. Tide went out, and there we were, stuck like crabs, scuttling around and firing back until we managed to work our way free. Haven't done it since."

"I'm elated to hear that Saber seems to learn from his mistakes," Angela snapped, and Dylan sighed.

"Look. You really don't want to give him an ultimatum. Listen to me—I'll talk to him. We'll work it out. Don't do something stupid."

"Stupid would be allowing him to ransom us to Portuguese pirates when I can negotiate for our safe delivery to New Orleans."

"New Orleans." Dylan shook his head. "Saber won't look at this as negotiating, you know. He'll consider it blackmail. If you're foolish enough to do it, you'll be sorry."

Angela took a deep breath, ignoring Emily's moan of fear. "Nonetheless, I intend that he shall hear me out."

"You'll be sorry," Dylan predicted gloomily, and she wondered if she was, indeed, being stupid. But there were no other options that she found feasible. And it was the last alternative that didn't involve being sent home like an errant child, or voluntarily ending her days in a convent.

"Oh, Miss Angela," Emily whispered miserably, "I hope you know what you're doing."

So do I, she thought. *So do I.*

Saber thought for a moment he had not heard correctly. Crossing his legs at the ankle, he shifted his booted feet slightly so that Dylan could sit at the table. A trill of violin music from a very bad musician clanged sourly in the great room of the seaside inn. He frowned and focused on Dylan again. Smoke and too much heavy Portuguese wine was having an adverse affect on him, he could tell.

"Say that again, Dylan. There's too much noise in this tavern for me to have heard you correctly."

"I'm afraid not." Dylan pulled a chair from beneath a drunken individual who had made the bad choice of passing out with his head on a nearby table. The hapless man crashed to the floor. Spinning the chair around on one leg, Dylan straddled it and met Saber's narrowed gaze. "You heard me right. She refuses to name anyone who might pay a ransom. She wants to go to New Orleans, where she says she'll pay the ransom herself."

Kit snorted. "Not bloody likely." He tilted his cup without glancing at the floating chaff. Rum would have been better, but the tavern served nothing but wine. "I've already made the arrangements. The swap will take place at midnight tonight. Then we're rid of them. They'll be Nuñez's problem."

"And if they won't give us the name of her rich papa? What then? Nuñez will hardly want them if he can't get anything for them. He'd probably sell them at an auction."

Swirling his almost empty cup, Kit scowled down into the dregs. He didn't want to think about what could happen, dammit. It hadn't been his choice to have them come aboard in the first place, nor his idea to ransom them to some babbling idiots with more money than sense. What the deuce was she doing leaving England anyway? Why hadn't her family stopped her? He gave a harsh grunt and looked up at Dylan's worried face.

"They'd come free with the information rather quickly when faced with that undesirable option, I think. After all, even Emily has enough imagination to guess the consequences."

"Maybe, but Angela seemed pretty determined. And it's Angela who's calling the shots here."

Kit shrugged. "She might be stubborn enough to risk her own life, but I don't think she'd risk Emily's."

"And you don't mind if they're terrorized by Nuñez."

"Damn it, you voted with the rest of the crew to ransom them. I would have been content to just set them free with passage to anywhere they wanted to go."

Dylan's high cheekbones bleached pale and his throat corded. "I know that. I thought it would be the best way to see them off safely. I didn't know Angela would be so stubborn."

Another snort preceded the draining of Kit's wine. When he set the empty cup on the scarred table, he shifted slightly. "You should have. We've been a week at sea with them. Even Rollo has taken to hiding in Mr. Buttons's new cabin rather than face that sea witch after she chased him with a pillow for singing a song she didn't like."

Dylan grinned. "It was the song you taught him about the mermaid who was caught in the fisherman's net."

"Nothing the matter with that song. When I was a few years younger, I used to dream about the same kind of thing happening to me. A woman who is eager to please a man and doesn't talk. Paradise." He sat up, and swung his feet down from the table. "Have you told Turk about this new suggestion?"

Dylan shook his head. "No, he's still meeting with the commissioner, I suppose. No one has seen him."

"Good. Don't tell him. I have no desire to listen to his lectures. We'll proceed as planned, and Miss Angela can discuss her scheme with Nuñez. He may prefer dealing with her than with her papa anyway." Kit rose and stretched lazily. "What's the worst that can happen?"

Dylan stood up. "She said she'd inform the authorities that the *Sea Tiger* is a pirate vessel if we don't agree to take her to New Orleans."

"Did she. And how does she propose to do that if we don't allow her to talk to the authorities?"

"I have no idea, but I'm not at all sure I want to take any chances."

"Neither am I." Kit started for the door. "I hope you left them well guarded."

"Mr. Buttons is keeping an eye on them."

Kit halted and swung around. "Mr. Buttons? Good God, they'll have talked him out of his shirt and be at the helm of the *Sea Tiger* by the time we can get there. Why in the name of God did you leave him as their guard?"

Following behind as Kit shoved open the tavern door, Dylan said, "He was the only one I'd trust with them."

"You'd best hope that he hasn't given them the keys to the powder magazine by this time. Mr. Buttons—that's like leaving a lamb in charge of the wolf pack."

"And you would have preferred that I leave them with Reed, maybe? He would have liked that well enough, I imagine."

"Not even Reed is lust-crazed enough to disobey a

direct order. No woman is worth the top layer of a man's hide, and that's what it would cost him."

Dylan didn't reply to that, and by the time they reached the skiff tied to a pier, some of Kit's anger had faded. He stepped into the skiff and untied the line, tossing it to Dylan.

"Turk can take the dinghy you used. Somehow, I have a feeling that we'd better rescue Mr. Buttons."

But they were only a few yards from shore when they heard a muffled *boom!* and saw a thick cloud of dark smoke billow outward from the ship. Kit swore harshly and let out more sail to catch the wind. Lights danced on board the *Sea Tiger,* shimmering in hazy, broken patterns.

Kit let out another string of curses as he worked the sail. Dylan took the tiller, and the slap of water against the bow made the small craft buck wildly for a moment. Fog had begun to settle lightly on the surface of the sea, misty gray shrouds that drifted between the skiff and the *Sea Tiger.* It did not help Kit's temper any that the explosion aboard the ship seemed to have been minor, for he saw, slicing across the water, one of the commissioner's well-armed coastal revenue cutters.

"Militia," Dylan said tersely.

"I see them." This was all he needed. A quiet halt to unload cargo and unwanted passengers was apparently too much to hope for now. It was apparent that the cutter would reach the ship before he could possibly do so. He wondered if Turk had managed to ingratiate himself with the commissioner. The letters of marque giving the *Sea Tiger* permission to attack enemy vessels applied mainly to American and Italian ships, which should satisfy Portugal's colonial commissioner quite well. Yet there was always the risk that they would be accused of piracy, and ransomed to the enemy government for a tidy sum. It had happened before to others.

When the skiff finally bumped against the side of the ship and the watch shouted down a challenge, Kit stood up and barked back an answer. A line spun down and he caught it deftly in one hand and tied it fast. Dylan began to uncleat the halyards that held the sails, while Kit grabbed hold of the ship's ladder and climbed up to the smoke-hazed deck.

The first person he saw was Mr. Buttons, an expression of fright and guilt on his soot-streaked face.

"Captain Saber, sir," he began, "it was an accident. No damage. I've been trying to explain it to these gentlemen, but—"

"Never mind," Kit interrupted, and swung his gaze to the uniformed militia standing on the main deck. "Is there a problem, gentlemen?"

"That is what we have been trying to decide," one of them replied in a thick accent. He smiled slightly, and rubbed at his thick mustache with one finger. "We heard the blast and, of course, must investigate."

"I see." Kit swept out an arm. "Shall we go below and discuss this over a glass of port, Lieutenant—"

"Garcia. Rafael Santos y Garcia." The officer brightened. "But of course, señor. We are only doing our jobs, you understand."

"I do. The necessary papers are in my cabin below. One of my officers has taken our letters ashore for the commissioner, but should be back at any time. I am certain we will be able to straighten out any problems quite easily, once we get away from all this smoke."

"Sir," Mr. Buttons began, but Kit sliced him such a fierce glance that he immediately subsided into a coughing stammer.

Ignoring him, Kit led the way below. As soon as he opened the door to his cabin, he realized he should have listened to his young officer. Angela and Emily, sooty and with torn garments, were tied to chairs in the middle of the floor. Perched on the arm of a lamp, Rollo swung back and forth in a screeching frenzy.

"Fire! Fire! More rum, boys, more rum," the bird chanted cheerily.

Kit heard the Portuguese officer mutter something under his breath, and Angela looked up with a grim smile.

"Well, so you've decided to come at last," she said. "I wondered how long it would take you."

Striding forward, Kit knelt down beside her, his fingers curling around her wrist in a harsh grasp. She smelled strongly of smoke and—*rum?* He kept a smile on his face and his voice lightly pleasant.

"So, you've managed to irritate the normally placid Mr. Buttons," he said. "I see he has you restrained for your own safety."

"Not exactly," she began, glaring up at him. His grip tightened and she smothered a gasp of pain.

"Now, sweetheart," he said, "you know that Papa will worry if I don't keep you safe." Half turning on the balls of his feet, he looked back at the officers still standing in the open door. "My sister," he explained. "She has run away so often that we're forced to resort to extreme measures. Papa has despaired of her ever being wed, as no man wants a harpy, so I am to take her to a convent until she learns temperance."

"Ah." Lieutenant Garcia smiled slightly. "I have six sisters. They are all high-strung, and we have had to offer a huge dowry for each of them. It is very expensive."

Angela had begun to sputter furiously, and Kit looked back down at her. "Quiet, little one, or I shall gag you," he warned in a solicitous tone that made her eyes narrow.

"Yes, brother dear," she said so sweetly that he looked at her more sharply. "I should hate to make matters worse. Especially as it's been so difficult for you lately, with half the English Navy chasing you—"

His thumb dug viciously into the tendons of her wrist, and he tucked a hand under her chin, his gaze boring into hers. "No, no, I've told you several times—those were French ships."

"Flying English flags?" she chirped. Her soot-streaked mouth curved into a smile when his hand tightened, and she whispered, "We need to talk privately, or I shall be forced to confess all I know to our inquisitive visitor."

"It's hard to talk with a slit throat," he muttered, but heard Garcia cough politely and knew that he would have to silence her. He turned, forcing a smile. "She feels a bit light-headed. Allow me to see her to her cabin, and—"

"My cabin is on fire," Angela said sweetly. "And I feel fine."

"Capítan," Garcia interrupted, "perhaps we should discuss this a bit more. There seems to be a contradiction here."

Kit met Angela's triumphant gaze with a flash of grudging admiration. She had cleverly managed to maneuver him into a difficult position. If he was to avoid detainment at the best, and at the worst—arrest—he would have to bargain with her. As much as it went against his grain to agree, he heard himself murmur, "I understand we are to go to New Orleans."

She smiled. "How considerate of you. I trust we'll have a most amicable voyage."

Turning, Kit said to Lieutenant Garcia, "Please be seated, and my sister and I will endeavor to straighten out any misconceptions you may have."

Nine

"All in all," Turk said thoughtfully, "it was a rather creative effort. In my opinion."

Kit ignored him, which was not easily done. He continued scratching notes in his log, trying to focus on what should be said and what he would like to say about the previous day's events.

"Left Ponta Delgada with cargo intact. Was allowed to take on water and necessary supplies after paying what was required by the commissioner as fees." Pause. He chewed on the end of his pen for a moment, then dipped it back into the inkwell. *"After unfortunate explosion aboard ship, decision was made to sell cargo in Caribbean."* He scratched out the last word and penned in *New Orleans,* then used a blotter on the page.

"What do you propose to do with the young ladies?" Turk asked into the silence, and Kit looked up.

"I find myself torn between sewing them up in burlap bags with heavy rocks and throwing them into the sea, or just tossing them overboard. I lean toward the former myself, as the latter leaves too much to chance." He closed the log book. "And with a woman like Angela, nothing should be left to chance."

"I see."

"Do you?" Kit rose from behind his desk. "I'm glad, because I certainly don't. What the hell did she expect to gain from that little performance?"

"Isn't it evident? She gained what she desired, which is passage to New Orleans. It is entirely coincidental that we just happen to be sailing to that particular destination. Ah, the vagaries of Fate . . ."

"Damn Fate," Kit said shortly. "If I had my way, the little vixen would be sailing back to England in a paper boat at this very moment."

"Indeed." Turk settled his large frame into a Moroccan leather chair and crossed one leg over his knee. "Why is it that my analysis of the situation is so disparate from yours?"

"Because you're too eager to jump to conclusions. Enough, Turk. I'm not in the mood."

"No, I presume you are not. In the mood for a correct evaluation, at any rate."

Kit reached for the decanter of brandy. His temper was short, and he found Turk's attitude aggravating. He poured a large amount in a glass and swallowed it, then poured another liberal portion, aware of Turk's somber gaze on him.

"Alcohol will not help."

"I'll remember that," Kit said nastily. "Alcohol won't help. A handy little slogan to recall in the heat of battle, or when some damned female has again managed to bungle up my life."

"You're blaming Angela for what others have done. I hardly deem that just, Kit."

Turk's quiet reproof was jarring. Kit slammed down his empty glass on the desktop. "No? Then what do you deem fair? Some of the crew opted for ten strokes with the cat, but others think it might kill her too quickly to suit them. Dylan, of course, thinks we should just keep her cozily in a cabin and out of sight until she gets where she wants. That," he growled, "would kill me. So—what do you suggest?"

"Members of the crew are still perturbed that they were denied shore leave. Anger is a natural reaction. They will recover in time. It is you who concerns me, however."

"Me?" Kit gave a harsh laugh and poured more brandy. "How am I a concern? I didn't kill her, though God help me, I was sorely tempted. Once Garcia left, it was all I could do not to curl my hands around her pretty white throat and squeeze until she turned blue. Jesus. I can still envision it." He closed his eyes and smiled.

"Kit."

Opening his eyes, Kit met Turk's dark gaze. Must the man be so knowing? Must he realize exactly what Kit was feeling? His hands curled around the brandy glass and he set it down slowly.

"I know, Turk. She's not Vivian, and she's not Elaine, or even Susan. But she's just like them. She's careless. She's egocentric. She doesn't care about anyone else when her own plans are in jeopardy. And all those wonderful attributes are wrapped tidily in a very appealing package, which only makes it more difficult to understand. Or see through." He picked up his glass again. "And you're wrong. Alcohol does help."

Sighing, Turk shook his head. "No, it only dulls the edges. I don't suppose her declaration of love for this Philippe du Plessis has anything to do with your pique?"

"No. Only a faint stirring of sympathy for Monsieur du Plessis."

"Ah. Then I don't suppose you would care to discuss your plans for her in the interim."

"You suppose correctly." Kit gazed at Turk over the rim of his glass. "Truth be told, I have no idea what I intend to do. All my instincts are screaming that I should drown her, but what little common decency I have left urges me toward caution. She's like a bomb. Or a bottle of rum with a lit rag stuffed into the mouth. My God, she could have blown up the entire ship. Poor Buttons. He was beside himself, wasn't he? I thought he was going to faint at one point."

"Yes, when Garcia left and you dragged Miss Angela from your cabin and to the rail, there were many faint hearts and light heads."

Kit snorted. "The hell there was. Only two—Buttons and Dylan." He sat on the edge of his desk, one leg swinging back and forth. "What is it, do you think, that has generated such compassion from Dylan? For five years I've been trying to find something that would matter to him. Now, these strays come straggling along, and he's a man with a mission."

"Perhaps you should have purchased him a pet." Turk stood up. "Or taken into account that it would be in his best interests to be put in a responsible position for someone weaker than he. It's a rather novel notion for a youth reared to have responsibility for no one but himself."

"I daresay." Kit frowned. "A puppy would have been better. Soiled carpets are minor compared to the damage these two have done in such a short time."

"The cabin is not damaged beyond repair. But I divine

that is not what you are making reference to—am I correct?"

"As always." Kit drained the last of his brandy and set down his glass. "And now, I shall brave Miss Angela in her den—or what's left of it—and do my best not to kill her. It should be a most illuminating interview."

"Slavery? Dear God. Your melodramatics are almost more than I can stand." Saber lifted a mocking brow, and Angela felt her face grow warm.

"Well," she said defensively, "you did intend to ransom us to a man who would show little courtesy toward the paying customer. I thought we were to be sold as slaves. Can you deny it?"

Kit sat forward in his chair with an unfriendly light in his eyes. "It would serve you right. Nuñez is not foolish enough to allow any harm to come to his hostages. They are worth far less if they have been abused."

His mocking assurance did little to lessen her righteous indignation, and Angela's chin lifted slightly as she met his astringent blue eyes. They seemed overly sharp, cold nearly to the point of frigidity. She looked away after a moment, and said, "I apologize for the damage to our cabin."

She felt his amusement when he drawled, "Your apology should be given to Mr. Buttons. It is his cabin." He paused, then said, "Where did you learn to make bombs with bottles of rum, pray tell?"

Angela had no intention of telling him that she'd led a rather carefree childhood in the company of her rowdy cousin Tommy, who had gotten her into all manner of scrapes. She said merely, "I am well aware of the volatile tendencies of alcohol when ignited."

"Apparently. Good thing Mr. Buttons's cabin is located close to the fire buckets or the entire ship might have gone up in flame. Did you stop to think what might have happened?"

"I was confident that Mr. Buttons was watching closely, though I admit I was rather startled at how quickly feather pillows burn. And so much smoke—I probably didn't even need those last few."

Saber stood up. "No more fires, please. We are far from shore now, and it would be a long swim." He started for the door, paused, and turned back to her. "You may thank your good fortune that Lieutenant Garcia did not have the imagination to see the truth behind your ridiculous story. If he had tried to arrest us, yours would have been the first throat I cut."

Angela stared at him. He was so matter-of-fact that she didn't doubt him for a moment. She felt a wave of nausea. There were times she tended to forget that she was dealing with a pirate, a man accustomed to all forms of murder and depravity. Saber's gentlemanly facade lured her into false security at times, and she realized rather shakily that her actions could have led to a very different kind of ending. She swallowed the impulse to babble an apology.

For a long moment, Saber stared at her. A muscle flickered at one corner of his mouth, and his eyes were narrowed. Then he reached out to grasp her chin in his palm, his long fingers cradling her face in a hold that was not quite gentle, not quite harsh.

"There are times," he said softly, "when I forget myself with you. Do not make the mistake of thinking me docile, however."

Bewildered by the contrast of savage expression and inexplicable comment, Angela could only stare at him silently. His grip tightened, fingers digging into her jaw muscles with almost painful intensity. Her breath caught in the back of her throat when his head lowered, and she instinctively closed her eyes.

"Afraid at last, angel?" he purred. "You should be. I'm feeling quite lethal at the moment."

Not quite daring to move or speak, Angela waited wretchedly for his next move or comment. Whatever it was she was certain it would be devastating. Nothing with this man was ever easy, and yet she found herself thinking of him more often than was necessary. Or prudent. Why couldn't she just relegate him to some dim recess of her mind and focus on escape? Why *must* he invade her every waking moment with some form of mental anguish?

And dear God, why must she find herself stirring to just the touch of his hand upon her face? The brush of his fingers against her cheek sparked a hundred different reactions, the least among them being a vague sense of disquiet.

"I'd swear," Kit murmured against her mouth, "that I still smell rum and soot in your hair."

"Probably," she managed to reply with what she hoped sounded like poise. "The closest I've been to water since the fire was when you held me over the rail."

"A memory I still cherish. I've entertained fond thoughts of how large a splash you would have made into the sea."

Angela opened her eyes and tried to match his insouciance. "I have an inescapable feeling that I would have been much better off if you had drowned me."

"Ah, sweetheart, you've no idea how much better off you would have been."

Her stomach dropped, and icy fingers gripped her heart when he tightened his hold for an instant. Then he was pushing her backward until she came up short against the bunk. It caught her behind the knees, unbalancing her. Kit took immediate advantage of the situation, and in an instant, she was sprawled across the bunk beneath his heavy weight.

Catching both her wrists in one hand, he drew her arms up and over her head, pressing them into the mattress, using his weight to hold her. His expression was intent and, to her consternation, as exciting as it was frightening. With his mouth curled into a wicked half-smile and his blue eyes narrowed, he made her think of things she probably shouldn't.

Such as the afternoon of her bath, and how he'd held her then. It always left a queer churning in the pit of her stomach when she thought of that day, and the things he'd done and the way she'd reacted—like now, when he was sliding his hand over her torso and creating quivering sensations that she knew better than to surrender to.

"Kit . . . no," she said in a husky whisper that sounded weak even to her own ears. She wasn't a bit surprised when he ignored her, but continued his explorations, fingers touching and teasing skin that was highly sensitized. His hand tightened on her ribcage then slid upward, opening to cup the full swell of her breast. When his thumb closed on his finger, teasing her nipple, Angela cried out softly.

Kit took immediate advantage of the opportunity to kiss her again, tongue sliding between her lips in a shockingly intimate manner. She wanted to twist away from him, but he held her still, rotating his thumb in a slow, leisurely motion that made her shudder.

Desperately clinging to the shreds of her resistance, Angela gasped out, "Why are you doing this?"

The words gave him pause, and he lifted his head to stare down at her with a dark blue gaze that held no mercy or emotion. She swallowed a half-sob, and his mouth twisted.

"Damned if I know." He sat up, raking a hand through his hair as he released her wrists. For a long moment he looked at her, and she had the thought he was seeing someone else instead of her.

Rubbing at her wrists—she would no doubt have bruises there on the morrow—she watched him carefully, uncertain as to what he would do next. But Kit only rose in a fluid motion and took two steps away from the bunk. Volatile emotions chased across his face. After a moment, he gave her cheek a gentle pat then pivoted on his heel and stalked to the door. It swung open noiselessly, and he stepped out.

When the door had shut behind him, she collapsed into a shivering mass of relief. It did not matter that he had locked her in, or that Emily was being impounded elsewhere. They were alive and on their way to America. That should be all that mattered.

Yet during the next week, Angela found it increasingly difficult to remember her resolve. Boredom set in. Only

Dylan visited her in the tiny cabin where she was kept—imprisoned was a more suitable term, she thought—and the days stretched long and endless. Monotony was her worst enemy now, and she surprised herself at times by thinking longingly of the days when Saber had tormented her with visits and verbal spats.

Dylan refused to argue with her, his face set and remote when she attempted to draw him out. She grew listless and spent long hours lying motionless on the small, hard bunk, sleeping or staring up at the ceiling. Dylan brought her some books. She had no desire to read them or even look through them. Then he brought in Rollo for diversion, but that was hardly successful.

The bird seemed to delight in reciting naughty verses that horrified her almost as much as they intrigued her. When he began quoting diatribes against women, Dylan took him out again and the experiment was ended. She was left alone to while away the long hours, contemplating the pattern of the sun on walls still charred in places.

Turk came one day, his massive frame filling up the tiny room. Even his deep voice seemed too large for the confined space.

"You have not been eating," he said matter-of-factly. "Your health will degenerate swiftly if you do not ingest proper nourishment."

Angela opened her eyes and sighed. "I'm not hungry. I don't like oatmeal, and I hate salt pork."

"Dare I suggest that you venture eating healthy victuals for a change? I realize it's rather audacious of me to propose such a course, but it might be beneficial to you, regardless of our illustrious captain's sentiments."

A faint smile touched her lips. "Weeds and seeds? It does not sound very appetizing."

"Neither does the lactating fluid of a large mammal with two stomachs, but you drink cow's milk, I'm certain. And it is the English custom to consume the unborn embryo of a fowl for breakfast every morning, I understand, along with an odoriferous little aquatic creature that has been soaked in brine."

She sat up and hugged her knees to her chest, amused in spite of herself. "Eggs and kippers, I presume?"

Turk smiled. "Among other unhealthy items. Would you care for some rice?"

"If you insist."

When he returned with a tray, Angela sat up and gazed at the steaming food. Rice and some sort of odd-looking beans that Turk said were sprouts had been piled upon her plate, along with dried, crackling shreds of something that smelled like the sea.

"Dulse," Turk said when she asked what it was. "Dried seaweed. It is a staple in the Maritimes, and tastes better than it smells. Be venturesome. Take a bite."

Angela did and made a face. "It tastes like seawater, only chewier."

"Doesn't it? One grows accustomed to it after awhile, though I admit it is rather a challenge at first. How are the rice and bean sprouts?"

"Tasty," she said after trying them.

Turk smiled. "Excellent. If you eat healthy food, you will grow healthy. I am always amazed at the improvement in those who have tried this particular diet."

She thought about Saber and wondered if he ate the recommended foods.

As if reading her mind, Turk said, "I have exhorted Kit to endeavor to eat more healthily, but he is obdurate in his refusal. It would greatly benefit his bronchial inflammation, if he would only listen to me."

Angela took a sip of hot tea from a delicate china cup. "Is he ill?" she asked.

"He has been afflicted with bronchial congestion for a week, hence his absence. It was the smoke that aggravated his condition, though he has a proclivity for the illness."

"Smoke—from the explosion?"

Turk's dark eyes met hers. "As I said, he is inclined to the disease at even the best of times."

"But smoke from the fire I caused aggravated it." Angela sighed. "I never thought of that. I should be sorry, I suppose."

"Not necessarily. He spent several hours in a smoky tavern that would produce the same result. It has been my observation that Captain Saber has a propensity for self-indulgence, as well as an inclination toward self-abuse. Though it saddens me to watch, I refuse to interfere without invitation."

"A wise decision," Angela said, thinking of her last altercation with Kit.

When she had finished her meal and Turk gathered the tray, she said almost wistfully, "Dylan said the weather was warmer now. Does that mean we are near the American colonies?"

"No, it means we've picked up the westerlies and a good warm tradewind. We will reach the Caribbean Sea soon, where we usually pause to careen the ship and restock our supplies. But I suppose this time we'll wait to stop until our return from New Orleans."

"Car-what?"

"Careen. Scrape the accumulated crustaceans from the keel to enable the ship to progress more efficiently. It is a simple process, but rather time-consuming. And it leaves us in jeopardy while the vessel is lying ashore much like a beached turtle. We had intended to perform a minor version of it in the Azores, but events dictated otherwise."

Angela flushed slightly. She was well aware what "events" he referred to. The repercussions still lingered painfully in her memory.

Turk hesitated at the door, then said in his rich voice, "I recommend that you endeavor not to vex Captain Saber when you meet again. It is imperative that you remain in his good graces until we reach New Orleans."

"Imperative? Why?"

"Let me just convey the opinion that it would be beneficial in the extreme to have him jocular instead of inflamed. He is much more amenable then."

Angela sighed. "I can't seem to help it. Every time I say something, it's wrong."

"Then accept the advice of an observer and remain silent. Not only will it astound him, it will charm him."

"I have no desire to charm him," Angela said tartly, and Turk gave an eloquent shrug of his shoulders.

"As you will. I, however, would much prefer a pleasant conversation than an altercation."

After he'd gone, Angela considered what he'd said. It made sense, of course. It should. Since being taken aboard the *Sea Tiger,* every exchange with Kit Saber had been angry. Or completely out of her control. She thought of how he'd held her against him, and the way it had made her feel.

During the past week, she'd vividly recalled his kisses. Driven by emotions she didn't understand, she'd tried her best to put them from her mind. It was humiliating to recall how he'd held her, how he'd touched her and made her cry out. A thick lump settled in her throat. She'd been unfaithful to Philippe. And oddly enough, it had not felt at all like it at the time. There had been no thought of her betrothed, only of the man who held her in his arms and did those wickedly shameful and delightful things to her.

She buried her face in her palms. She was completely degenerate. It was bad enough that she'd allowed it, but to dwell on it, to wake up from dreams of Kit with the strange restless pulsing still making her ache—it was unbearable. If only they were in New Orleans. If only Philippe were with her. Then none of this would have happened. Somehow, he would have stopped it.

She thought of her parents and their comfortable home in the fashionable part of Mayfair. She thought of sun-lit mornings at the table, listening to her mother's prattle about calling cards and visits and soirees, and realized that she missed them all. Even her father's gruff manner had covered a kind, genuinely loving heart, and she knew that if they had discovered her fate, they would be frantic. She'd been so thoughtless. It had seemed like the only solution at the time, but it must have grieved them deeply. They would not understand her brief note of explanation, nor would they understand her desire to be independent of their decision. Marriage to the baron still seemed abhorrent, but she should have remained in London and been strong. Eventually, her father would have abandoned his wedding plans for her, and as she had already passed the age of majority, he would have been forced to heed her decision.

Hot tears pricked her eyes, and she closed them to hold back the tears. Useless, so useless, and now her life was totally out of her control . . .

It was only when a light tapping sounded on the door that she realized she'd fallen asleep. Rising to her elbows, she sleepily called out, "Yes?"

Dylan swung open the door and stepped inside. He cast a long shadow on the floor, and Angela realized it must be late afternoon. Assuming he was bringing her something to eat, she began her usual refusal, but he cut her off.

"That ain't why I'm here. I brought you something." He held out a silk-wrapped bundle. "Found it with your trunk in the hold and thought it might make you feel better."

Puzzled, Angela sat up and pushed a tangle of hair from her eyes. He placed the silk square in her lap and stood back. She looked down at it for a long moment, her sleep-fogged mind struggling to waken.

"Open it," Dylan said, his voice impatient. "If you don't want it, I'll take it back. Or toss it over the side. Probably the last. If Saber sees it, I don't know what he'd say to me.

Intrigued now, Angela unwrapped the silk—she recognized the scarf her mother had given her for her last birthday—and gave a soft cry.

"My reticule! With the letters from Philippe . . ."

"Quiet, will you? Do you want Saber down here? I don't. He's mean as a tiger with a toothache lately. And he don't need to know about this. He wouldn't understand, and I'm not too sure he'd like it. If he sees them, tell the truth, but if he doesn't ask, don't tell. All right?"

"Oh Dylan—of course. Yes, of course I won't bring up the subject. But you needn't worry about him seeing them. He hasn't been here in a week."

"I know. But that doesn't mean he won't come."

Angela looked up and saw the distress in Dylan's eyes. It was obvious he was struggling with his loyalties, and she felt a spurt of gratitude.

"Thank you. From the bottom of my heart. Tell me—how is Emily?"

"Bored, same as you. She's taken to reading everything I can bring her. If you want the truth, it was her suggestion that I get you these letters. She's been worried about you."

"Tell her that I appreciate it. And tell her—that I miss her. And I'm sorry. For everything. I should have listened to her."

Dylan grinned, a flash of white in a sun-dark face. "I'll tell her. That ought to make her smile. She likes being right."

When he had gone, Angela settled back against the wall with her letters. Her hands shook slightly as she pulled them out and saw Philippe's familiar scrawl. It was as if he were there with her, his dark eyes studying her with somber regard, his handsome face in regal repose.

Closing her eyes, she tried to envision him as she had last seen him, before Papa had come into the parlor and ordered him away.

But only a fragment of blurred image would come to mind. Instead of Philippe, she saw sun-bright blue eyes and a crescent scar, white teeth flashing in Kit Saber's dark face. Slowly, she opened her eyes. How had it happened? How, in such a short time, had Philippe been supplanted by a pirate? It must have been because of that kiss with Saber. That memory had been burned into her mind with a scorching heat.

Damn Kit Saber!

Now, not even her most precious memories were untarnished. All she had left were the letters in her hand, the vows of undying love that she had thought she'd shared, but now knew were no more.

Ten

New Orleans. Angela leaned forward, gazing eagerly out the porthole to catch her first glimpse of the city. To her disappointment, all she saw were thick trees and knobby roots jutting up from murky water lapping at the edges of what looked like a swamp. She turned.

"Where is the city? All I see are trees and a few boats."

Dylan lifted a brow. "You don't think we intend to just sail right up to the docks, do you? That would be suicide."

"Then what—"

"Patience," he soothed her with a faint smile. "First we stop to see some old friends. Then we will take a pirogue up the backwaters to the city."

"A pea what?"

"Pirogue. It's a flat-bottomed boat. Don't worry. The bayou is close to town."

Angela glanced impatiently out the porthole again. "But I thought we were already there. Turk said—"

"That we'd reached New Orleans. And we have. Close enough, anyway. Look, Angela, New Orleans belongs to the French again, and we're English. Even with letters of marque, we could run into problems. Besides, Kit has other fish to fry while we're here, and he don't want it known that we're around yet."

She stared at him. "What other fish?"

Dylan looked away with a shrug. "It ain't my business to be too nosy. And if you want my advice, you'll swallow your own curiosity. It's not healthy."

"For who?"

"You." Dylan turned to look at her. He held her gaze and said softly, "There are some things you don't need to know."

Piqued, she managed a careless shrug. "I don't care at all what he does or why he's here. Only that he takes me to Philippe as soon as possible." After an anxious pause, she added, "He will, won't he? Take me to Philippe?"

"That, you will have to ask Saber. Now listen. Don't look at me like that. I've had enough of female vapors today. Emily has given me fits about being kept away from you, and I can tell you, I don't like being in the middle of it."

"I daresay." Angela turned back to gaze blindly out the port, the landscape blurring in a mist of unshed tears. Would she never reach safety? Must she be continuously on edge, wondering what would happen in the next moment? Dear God, the past weeks had been so horrible, and she was so weary of worrying.

"Angela," Dylan said softly, "it will be all right."

"Will it?" she asked without turning. "I don't think so. Nothing is the same. Everything's changed, and I'm frightened. I don't like to admit it, but there are moments when I feel—doomed."

Dylan laughed, and when she turned angrily, he put up a hand as if to ward off a blow. "No, no, I didn't mean to make fun of you. It's just that you sound so—resigned. And that is one thing I'd never expect from you."

"What do you mean by that?"

"Only that you're a fighter. You'll never just allow things to happen without fighting back."

"That's what your captain said," she replied bitterly. "He seemed to think it a meritable notion except for when it applied to him. Doesn't Saber realize that *he* is what I'm fighting against? *He* is the cause of all my problems, so what am I supposed to do?"

"Angela, as I've said before, you can pleasure him or placate him. Either one would work. All you've done so far is insult him, try to blow up his ship, and get him entangled with LaRosa's revenue cutters so that he had to pay a huge fine. Maybe it's time for a little tact."

"I won't need tact if I'm to be freed," she pointed out. "Unless you have an unpleasant surprise for me?"

Dylan groaned. "All right. Have it your way. I can't help you."

"You mean *won't* help me."

Unperturbed by her hostility, Dylan nodded. "Precisely. I've grown accustomed to my head where it is, which is safely on my neck. And I rather like the fact that it's relatively unscarred."

Whirling around, Angela fought a wave of resentment that rose hotly in her throat. "I should never have expected decency from you," she said without turning to look at him. "Please leave."

After a pause, Dylan said, "Well, at least eat what I brought you. Turk sent it. Said it's healthy, which probably means it tastes like it came from—" He stopped short, then finished, "The pantry. Eat. I'll be back later to get the tray."

When the door had shut behind him, Angela leaned against the cabin wall and yielded to the tears that had been lurking behind her eyes. Would she ever be free? Not only of this hateful ship, but the hateful memories any mention of Kit Saber provoked? Dear God, when she thought of how shamefully she'd behaved—and she thought of it even when she tried hardest not to—she felt waves of remorse at her behavior. She'd been wanton. It would not surprise her in the least to find herself sold as a woman of the streets. Not that she'd put anything past Saber. He seemed to do just what he wanted. Damn him for a tarred villain of a pirate. Damn him for having such brilliant blue eyes and a lopsided grin—of which she saw very little—and damn him for making her think of him when she didn't want to.

Yet, it seemed that even when she closed her eyes to shut out the images of him, they seeped through her closed eyelids and burned into her brain with a tenacity she found amazing.

Doomed. Dylan had not understood at all. It was the only word that perfectly described her situation.

Kit swiped at a thick tuft of grass with the flat edge of his sword and said impatiently, "There's time enough for that later. You know why I'm here. I can't take the time to go on wild chases, even if Miss Angela dictates it. She'll have to wait."

Turk smiled slightly. "As usual, you are in a foul humor. This is becoming all too frequent lately, but I understand the reason."

"Do you?" Kit snarled. "How jolly. Pray, don't share the knowledge with me, because I don't give a damn.

"Ah, but you do. No, do not glare at me so balefully, if you please. I find myself rather vexed as well. It is not a pleasant emotion to entertain. If we do not succeed in our search this time, will you abandon it?"

Turk's sudden change in conversation gave Kit pause. After a moment he said slowly, "You know I cannot do that."

Settling a huge hand on Kit's shoulder, Turk gazed down at him for a moment without speaking. Both knew what the other was thinking, for it had been a topic of conversation too many times to count. Should he continue a search that had so far been frustrating? Or should he accept what had happened so long ago and put it behind him? Neither option was tempting, and he was damned if he knew why. He wished that he knew what drove him to find the answers to all his questions, to find the one woman who could provide him with those answers. Yet he knew he had to, that he could not rest until he did.

Kit shrugged away Turk's hand and took a step closer to the grassy edges of the riverbank. Brown water sloshed rhythmically against the mud and weeds, and a strong breeze rippled the tall grasses. A mile upriver lay New Orleans and maybe the end to years of searching. He had to move swiftly or he might lose her again.

Without turning, he said, "Have Dylan get the two women ready to move at dark. With any luck at all, I can solve all my problems before dawn. Pray that fortune is with me."

"Good fortune or bad?" Turk inquired. "Ofttimes, finding what you seek leads to disappointment."

"No more learned philosophy, please. This isn't the time for it."

"I would think there was no more appropriate time than now, but I shall bow to your wishes."

An unwilling smile tugged at his mouth as Kit turned to look at Turk. "There's a first. Bowing to my wishes? What an innovative idea."

"I did not finish my statement. I should have qualified it with the addendum—*but with reservations*. I am on your side, remember."

"There are moments when I wonder about that."

"You are not that foolish."

Kit nodded. "You're right. But that doesn't mean I like hearing what you have to say at times."

"Honesty. A refreshing quality, and also a rare one." Turk's tattooed face creased into a smile, his dark eyes glimmering with humor. "Do try and remember that one should also be honest with oneself. 'To thine own self be true,' it is said."

"Are you hinting that I am not?"

"I do not hint. I say precisely what I mean. And now, I shall ensconce myself in that distasteful little craft that these swamp people and river rats refer to as a pirogue and journey through the swamps to begin my investigations. We will meet as planned."

"Café des Exilés at midnight."

"A most appropriate spot. Do you think to find Miss Angela's betrothed there as well?"

"It seems likely. Where else would a Royalist émigré go?"

"True."

Turk turned to go, then paused and looked back. "Kit—be careful."

Lifting a brow in surprise, he said, "I always am."

"Ah, so you say."

Kit watched his massive friend walk down the grassy banks to the flat-bottomed boat waiting in the shallows. Delicate streamers of gray moss grazed Turk's head as he passed beneath huge, gnarled oaks, and tall grasses rose almost to his waist. Around the bend in the river lay New Orleans, a teeming city of thousands, while only a few miles away lay swampland and uncharted bayous. The bayous, however, were anything but uninhabited. The swampy backwaters were home to pirates, smugglers, and settlers. Not even the militia dared venture into the area, for the few who had were rarely seen again.

Sliding his drawn sword back into the sheath at his side, Kit moved away from the bank and toward the encampment tucked beneath towering trees. There was a lot to do, and so much depended upon his moving swiftly and secretly. It was as if she knew his every move, and always managed to elude him. This time, he would find her. *This time,* she would not evade him as she always had before. And she would finally answer his questions, by God.

Shivering in the chill night air, Angela whispered to Dylan, "Where are we?"

He made an impatient motion with one hand, signaling her to silence. She pulled the dark cloak and hood he'd insisted she wear more tightly around her and waited. Night birds called, and the incessant chirping of crickets heralded the intruders. A deep-throated bellow sounded occasionally. Dylan had told her it was a 'gator, or alligator. Quite tasty, he'd informed her, laughing at her horrified expression. She'd seen the alligators moving clumsily on land, scrabbling like crabs until reaching the water, where they had slid in sinister silence and grace through murky shallows. The rows of sharp-pointed teeth were ample evidence of danger, and were all she'd needed to see to convince her that she did not want to attempt escape and risk overturning into the water or stumbling over one of the creatures in the dark.

"All right," Dylan said finally, and pulled her with him from the shadows. A road twisted above them on high banks, and he helped her up the side until they stood on level ground. "It's only a short distance into the city from here. Stay with me, don't talk, and answer no questions should we run into trouble. Let me take care of everything."

Still shivering, she nodded. "That's fine with me. But I still don't understand why we had to wait so late. And why wasn't Emily allowed to come along?"

"Too dangerous right now. Don't worry. Once matters are settled, she can join you." He flashed her a glance, amber eyes reflecting bright moonlight and the glow of his lantern. "Remember your promise."

"I remember," she said crossly. "Do you think I would

jeopardize everything by forgetting it? Besides, I gave my word."

"That's not usually a deterrent to most females," Dylan said, so frankly she glared at him.

"Well, it is to me. I can only imagine the sort of females you're accustomed to consorting with, so—"

"Enough." Dylan's grip on her arm tightened. "We don't have time to argue now. Save it for later."

"I doubt there will be a *later.*" Angela felt a tremor of shock at her own words. Of course. If she was reunited with Philippe tonight, she would never see Dylan again. Or Kit Saber. She closed her eyes briefly at the thought, and wondered why it mattered. They were pirates. Villains. Thieves and murderers and worse. Why should she care? And how had she grown so fond of Dylan in only a few short weeks?

Maddeningly, however, it was the thought of never seeing Kit again that pricked her most. She should be grateful, relieved, delirious with happiness at the mere suggestion, but she wasn't. It was inexplicable.

"Come on," Dylan said, and they began to move toward the glow of city lights that she could see just ahead. Now that the moment was almost there, she felt her doubts loom larger. What if Philippe was gone? What if he had given up hope of seeing her again and left New Orleans? All sorts of possibilities presented themselves until she felt sick with worry.

"Stop it," Dylan said after a moment, and she gave him a startled glance.

"What do you mean?"

"I know what you're doing. I can tell by the look on your face. Worry won't help. Things will work out or they won't. If you get too nervous you're liable to do something stupid. If your lover is here—"

"Betrothed, not lover."

"Fine. Betrothed. If he's in New Orleans, Turk and Kit can find him. And if he isn't, you can get on a ship going back to England and wait for him to find you there."

"But he won't," Angela said wretchedly. "He thinks our love is a lost cause."

"I'm familiar with lost causes. If he's any kind of man at all, he won't let a little thing like your parents' disapproval stand in his way."

"You don't understand. Things are simply not done that way. I went far past the boundaries of decency and decorum when I left home as I did." She drew in a shaky breath. "But I saw no other way to be with the man I love."

"Do you?"

"Do I what?"

"Love him." Dylan shrugged at her exclamation. "I just wondered. I never hear you talk about him. The only man you ever talk about is Saber."

"Of all the— Don't be absurd. Of course I love Philippe. Why else would I have traveled halfway around the world to be with him?"

"Angela, don't act too hastily, all right? When you see this Philippe guy again, think about who he is, not who you want him to be.

"What do you think he'll be? Some sort of criminal? A thief, or even worse—a pirate?"

Dylan just looked at her for a long moment while the night birds trilled around them and the *harrump!* of frogs broke the stillness. Then he gave a shrug of his shoulders and said softly, "Let's go. It's getting late, and we don't want to miss Saber."

Streets flanked by narrow banquettes threaded between buildings festooned with lacy iron balconies and drapes of flowers. Tall lampposts provided intermittent light. Carriages and pedestrians filled the wayfare, and Angela recognized elegant French fashion and houses of couture. Surprised by the sophistication of the city, when she had visualized it as a crude outpost at the far reaches of civilization, she stared about her in fascination.

Women with dark complexions like Turk's strolled the streets with large baskets atop their heads, crying out their wares in French. They wore colorful turbans and clothes and seemed unperturbed by the chaos around them, or the late hour.

"In the mornings," Dylan said, "you will see many people here buying their food. The French Market is over there." He pointed to a few low buildings surrounded by canopies and vegetable stalls. "Most leave at dark, but you can still purchase certain goods."

The rich smells of coffee, spices, baked goods, and vegetables mingled with the more pungent odors of fish and chickens. Though most of the canopies had been rolled down, a few were still open to display their wares, and people milled about. Angela caught the cadence of Spanish mixed with French, and another accent she could not place. Dylan smiled when she asked him about it.

"There are many cultures here and some of them have grown together to form their own language. It's not quite French and not quite Spanish. I don't know what they call it, but it's very musical, I think."

As he hurried her past the market, Angela glimpsed parrots in cages, monkeys on tethers, and even a live alligator. She almost forgot their destination and reason for being in New Orleans for a time, until Dylan paused in front of a row of two-story buildings with wrought-iron balconies.

"This is where we wait," he said tersely. "Keep your hood around your face and stay close to me."

She curled her fingers around his arm. "Where are we?"

He hesitated, then said, "Café des Réfugiés. We are to wait here until Saber or Turk comes for us."

"But what manner of place is this?"

Dylan did not reply. Instead he pulled her inside with him. The large common room was filled with smoke and loud laughter, and she found herself edging even closer to Dylan. There was a strain to the laughter that made her uncomfortable for some reason, and she tugged at the edges of her hood to keep it around her face. Men garbed in rough costume sat at tables or stood in groups, and some of them turned to stare. An occasional outburst of profanity rose above the hubbub of voices. Dylan stopped to converse briefly with a tall man with only one ear and a seamed face, then they moved through the crowd.

When they were seated at a table in a far corner, Angela breathed a bit easier. She looked up at Dylan and noted with surprise that he had placed a pistol casually upon the tabletop. Her heart gave an alarming thump.

"Do you expect trouble?"

"One should always be prepared." His mouth twisted

wryly. "This is not the sort of place where trouble fears to visit."

"Why have you brought me here?" she demanded in a low voice. "And where is Philippe?"

Shaking his head impatiently, Dylan said, "I told you, Turk and Kit will find him if he's in New Orleans. Just be patient, dammit."

"Patient? I think I have been more than patient." Leaning forward, she hissed, "Stop treating me like a child! Tell me what is going on."

"You can see what is going on, Angela. We are to meet here—"

"And what kind of place is this?" She glanced around, her voice rising slightly. "Most of these men look like outlaws, not law-abiding citizens."

"They are." Dylan met her gaze coolly. "Pirates, smugglers, and European outlaws favor this establishment, which is why we are here. We might be too noticeable elsewhere."

"You mean *you* might be too noticeable elsewhere!"

"Exactly."

Angela swallowed her nervous laughter. What on earth had she gotten herself into now? Why had she ever thought she would just be escorted to some genteel home where Philippe would be reunited with her? Oh no, Kit Saber would never think of anything like that. He was far too accustomed to the seamier side of life to adjust to anything remotely civilized. She sighed.

"You are impossible, Dylan."

"But we always get results."

"Not always the ones you want, however," she reminded him, and he gave a rueful nod of his head.

"Very true. I admit that I'll be glad when Kit gets here. I'm not at all sure what you'll do next. He seems to be able to control you better than I can."

Her heart gave an odd lurch at the thought of seeing Kit again, and she sternly ignored it. "Mr. Saber is unable to control even his own nature. I hardly think him capable of controlling mine."

Dylan just grinned, and when they were served glasses of some sort of pale liquor, he advised her to give hers to him. "It's too strong for you."

"Is that so?" Angela lifted her glass and took a healthy sip, almost choking on it. It seared her throat like liquid fire. Her eyes began to water, and she saw Dylan's amusement but refused to acknowledge it. She was getting quite weary of having him think her some sort of naive child. She took another sip, this one more cautious, and she felt the liquid burn a path to her stomach.

"Slowly," Dylan cautioned. "You're not used to it and it will go to your head."

"I grew up on fine wines and liqueurs," she said haughtily, lifting her chin to glare at him.

Dylan immediately snapped, "Keep your head down! Do you want to start a riot in here? All I need is for some drunken fool to decide he likes the way you look."

Lowering her head, she muttered, "What is this drink?"

"Rum. You ought to remember it. Don't you like it?"

"Not really. It's rather nasty, but does provide some warmth." She glanced up cautiously. "How much longer?"

"Not long," Dylan promised.

But it was over an hour before Kit stepped into the smoky common room of the café. Angela saw him immediately across the crowded room and her heart lurched. Despite the rum she'd sipped, her hands began to shake as if she were chilled, and she shivered when Kit approached the table.

He wore buff trousers, knee-high black boots, a red sash, and a white shirt with flowing sleeves beneath a dark cloak. The hilt of a saber was visible at his side. He looked every inch the corsair and commanded the attention of more than one man in the room as he crossed to them.

"I see you've managed to keep her relatively peaceful," Kit observed when he paused at the table. "I confess my admiration, Dylan."

"It wasn't as hard as you might think." Dylan stood and scooped up the pistol from the table. Tucking it into the waist of his trousers, he said, "Did you find her?"

A muscle twitched in Kit's lean jaw, and Angela sensed his anger. "Disappointed once again," he drawled. "She left New Orleans at dusk."

"Damn," Dylan said softly. He opened his mouth as if to speak further, then glanced away and asked softly, "Any idea where she went this time?"

"Not yet."

Angela frowned. "Who are you talking about? Who is *she?* Does this person have anything to do with Philippe?"

A faint smile touched Kit's mouth. "Ever selfish Angela. No, *she* has nothing to do with you or your precious Philippe. This is my business."

"I only meant—"

He reached out and lifted her to her feet with one hand under her elbow. "It doesn't matter what you meant. Turk found your—betrothed. Come and see him. I think he'll be most surprised to see you."

"I should think so," she began, but Kit wasn't listening. He pulled her through the room, nodding at acquaintances but not pausing. Once outside, Angela breathed deeply of the fresh air. Her head was swimming and she felt faint. It must have something to do with the rum, though she had been fairly prudent and sipped only a little.

"This way, angel," Kit said, and tucked her hand into the crook of his arm. "You are about to be reunited with your true love, so don't dally. I think I shall enjoy this meeting much more than you."

"I'm certain you're delighted to be rid of me," she said tartly, but Kit only laughed.

It was Dylan who said, "Life won't be the same aboard the *Sea Tiger* without you and Emily."

"Don't be too sure of that," Kit said. "I rather look forward to peace upon the waters again."

Nervous, Angela bit her lower lip to keep from giving Saber a reply that would only start another argument. Lately, it seemed that every exchange she had with Dylan ended that way, and Kit was even more adept at provoking a quarrel.

After walking a few blocks, Kit stopped her at the corner of Royal and St. Anne.

"This is it," he said, and cupped her chin in his palm to lift her head. The hood to her cloak fell back and she stared up at him. There was something in his eyes that she could not read, some elusive emotion that made her shift nervously. Was he regretting the fact that she would be going off with another man? Did he care that he would never see her again after tonight?

The questions trembled on the tip of her tongue, but she could not force herself to ask them. Especially not with Dylan standing silently by, watching and waiting.

"Angela," Saber said, his tone curiously soft, "remember that it has been a long time since you have seen your Philippe. Circumstances change."

"Yes, but love does not. Not true love, which is what we have between us." She took a deep breath. "He is here, then? In this establishment?"

Kit's hand fell away. "Yes. Turk is already inside."

She glanced at the tall building doubtfully. "Is this another place like the last?"

"Similar." He gestured toward the front door. "It is a new house and acts as the gathering place for Royalist émigrés who have escaped execution in France, a logical meeting spot for your deposed friend."

"Yes, Philippe would gravitate here, I am certain," she murmured. She reached up to smooth her hair. "Do I look presentable?" she couldn't help asking, flushing slightly when Kit gave a bark of laughter.

"How predictable you are. Yes, you are beautiful, as you well know. Do not be so vain, angel. It doesn't suit you."

"I am not vain, it is just that I have not seen him in so long, and I wish to appear at my best." She smoothed the skirts of the gown Dylan had brought from her own trunk and took another deep breath. "I am ready."

"Dear God, you sound as if you are preparing to be presented to the king instead of some downtrodden royalist with nothing to commend him but the acquaintance of other poverty-stricken, exiled aristocrats."

Flashing him a dark look, Angela snapped, "I shall be most grateful not to have to listen to any more of your snide comments!"

Kit stepped to the door and pushed it open, holding it wide for her. She swept past him as he murmured, "I hope so, angel."

The atmosphere inside the Café des Exilés was much different from that of the Café des Réfugiés. Though crowded as had been the other, these men spoke in fluent French and flawless English, with none of the crude laughter she'd heard earlier. Lantern light flickered softly, and the conversation was a low hum instead of raucous chaos.

"This way," Kit said, and they followed a dark-clad servant down a hallway to the rear of the house and a steep staircase.

Turk stood outside a door on the second floor and nodded when he saw Kit. "Monsieur du Plessis resides within," he said, and indicated the door. "But I do not believe now would be the most appropriate hour to engage him in polite conversation. He has guests."

Angela stepped forward before she lost her nerve. "I disagree. He will not mind interrupting any conversation to see me, I am certain."

Turk gave her a grave stare, then looked up and past her to Kit.

"Let her go," Kit said with a shrug, and leaned a broad shoulder against the wall. He crossed his arms over his chest. "We will wait here if you like."

"Do as you please. Philippe will take care of me now."

Angela stepped to the door and knocked sharply. She

could hear the muted murmur of voices inside and shifted impatiently when no one called to her to enter. She knocked again, and when there was still no reply, she grasped the knob. It turned easily, and she pushed open the door.

Candlelight flickered in glass globes on the walls and tables, but oddly, provided scant light. It took a moment for her eyes to adjust to the dimness. There was the fragrance of heavy perfume and brandy, and lumps of material were scattered on the carpet. A rustling like dry leaves caught her attention, and she turned toward the sound. A couch stretched against one wall, and several chairs and lounges were grouped about haphazardly.

Then she heard the unmistakable sound of feminine laughter. She stopped when a throaty male voice called out, *"Entrez vous, chérie!"*

"Philippe?" she managed to murmur, her voice trembling. The strangeness of the scene had not escaped her, and she noted the occupied couch across the room. She took a step forward, hands clenched into the folds of her cloak. "Philippe, is it you?"

There was an instant of silence, then a murmured curse in French. *"Sacre bleu!* Angela? It cannot be you."

She froze, slowly perceiving the scene before her with disbelieving eyes. The tangled dark mass on the couch separated into distinct arms and legs and faces, and she recognized Philippe as he disentangled himself from the two women and stood.

"What are you doing here?" he demanded harshly as he strode toward her. *"Mon Dieu,* did you not receive my letter?"

"Letter?" she repeated numbly. "I . . . I don't know

what you mean. I have all your letters. The letters we wrote to one another over the years—Philippe, what is the matter? Are you not glad to see me?"

She could not help the faint note of pleading in her voice, but there was too much to comprehend at the moment. He was moving toward her and taking her by one arm to push her across the room, and she saw dimly that she had left the door open. He shoved her toward it.

"Go back home, Angela. I wrote you immediately upon receiving your letter, telling you not to join me. *C'est impossible.*"

"But—we love one another. Papa will come 'round once we are wed. You know he will. And even if he does not, nothing matters but our love."

Philippe stepped into a pool of light, dark eyes narrowed and cold. His frilled shirt was open to the waist, and the top two buttons of his trousers were undone. Angela looked away, cheeks hot with embarrassment. It was only too obvious what she had interrupted.

"Listen to me," he said coldly. "Your papa will not capitulate. He made it quite clear to me that he would never sanction our union. And I have no intention of wedding a milk-faced girl without any money. Go back home. You have come all this way for nothing. *C'est fini . . .*"

Reeling with shock and disillusionment, Angela could not move for a moment. She stood staring up at him, at his aristocratic face and thin lips, the faint sneer curling them up at the corners.

"But our letters," she whispered, still unable to conceive that she meant nothing to him. "The things you said to me—"

"Lies. I did not even write them, Angela. Père François wrote them for me. The old priest had a romantic soul, *oui?*"

One of the women still on the couch called out something in French and Philippe half turned with a laugh. When he glanced back at her, Angela slapped him across one cheek with her palm. The echo of her blow sounded loud in the room, and she heard an angry exclamation from the couch just before Philippe grasped her by the wrist.

She gasped as sharp pains shot up her arm, and she tried to jerk away. A scream from the direction of the couch was the only warning before Philippe was suddenly flung backward, and it took her a moment to realize what had happened. By then, Saber was standing over the fallen Frenchman, a boot on each side of his torso. Philippe stared up in shock.

"Do not even consider trying to rise, *mon ami,*" Kit said in an amicable tone that did nothing to hide his fury. "I would be forced to pin you to the floor with my sword, and the management frowns on carpet stains. Especially blood, as it is so hard to remove."

Philippe had paled to a pasty gray-white. He gave a short jerk of his head to indicate understanding, then grew very still and watchful. After a moment, Kit stepped back and motioned for Turk to come forward. Philippe's eyes grew wide as the massive shadow moved toward him, and in a very short time, Turk had pulled him to his feet and seated him in a chair.

"Now," Kit said pleasantly, "apologize to the young lady for not only your manners, but your fraud. Then we will take our departure."

"No," Angela whispered hoarsely. "I do not want an apology from him. There is nothing he can say or do that will excuse him."

Shrugging, Kit looked at her. "No, but until you hear it, you cannot forget it." He glanced back at Philippe.

"I apologize to you for my deception and my manners," Philippe muttered ungraciously. "But you have brought it upon yourself with your foolish actions." He gave Saber a defiant glance. "I do not apologize for anything else."

"You should. You're as miserable an excuse for a man as I have ever seen." Kit reached out with one foot and kicked Philippe backward. He crashed to the floor in a splintering of wooden chair and brocade.

Angela realized she must have made some sound, because suddenly Dylan was there, one arm around her, drawing her to the door. "Come along," he said softly in her ear. "Saber will take care of him now."

"He is not worth it," she said numbly. "I do not want to be responsible for anything. Just—just take me away, Dylan. Please. I want to see Emily. I want to leave here . . ."

Turning, she buried her face in Dylan's shoulder, feeling the smooth linen of his shirt cool against her burning cheek. Pain clogged her throat and made her stumble, and Dylan's arm tightened around her.

She barely remembered the return to the ship. It was only a blur of movement punctuated by sharper images. There was darkness and water, and then the blessed relief of seeing Emily again. Turk soothed her with his resonant reassurances and herbal tea, and Emily helped her into a cool lawn gown and tucked her into a wide bunk that she only vaguely recalled. Then she was left in silence, while the familiar rocking of the ship lulled her into a deep sleep.

Eleven

Angela stared over the rail at the distant speck of land on the horizon. Her eyes were shadowed by her lashes and sadness, and pale hair whipped against her cheeks. Kit shifted, leaning an elbow on the rail next to her. Feeling awkward and damnably uncertain of himself, he watched her for a long time before finding a neutral topic of conversation.

Fortunately, it presented itself in the form of a smudge on the horizon that grew steadily larger as the ship sliced through the iridescent blue-green Caribbean sea. When the smudge grew into a land mass rising abruptly from the Atlantic on the north side, the Caribbean on the south, he gestured toward it.

"See that deep-water harbor? That's St. Thomas. I know you've heard of Blackbeard. He favored the town of Charlotte Amalie on this harbor as his haunt. When we get closer, you'll see a tall stone tower. It's known as Blackbeard's Castle. He used it as a lookout post for Spanish galleons."

Turning to stare up at him, Angela shaded her eyes from the sun with her palm. A faint smile touched her lips. It was the closest he'd seen her come to any emotion other than apathy in the past week since leaving New Orleans.

Curiosity now sparked in her eyes as she looked up at him. "I suppose Dylan told you about my Blackbeard remark."

"He did mention your comparison between us, yes."

She sighed. "Well, I always thought Blackbeard was more myth than truth—rather like you. How do you know all about him?"

Shrugging, Kit resisted the urge to touch her. It took him much too long to curb the startling surge of tenderness that welled inside at her sad expression. Damndest thing, but ever since seeing her crushed by her betrothed's callous rejection, he'd felt a compassion for her that he hadn't suspected. Maybe it was more empathy than sympathy, but he could certainly understand how hurt she was. Hadn't he had the same sort of experience himself?

Clearing his throat, he said, "Legend is sometimes based on fact. Blackbeard was real, all right. Maybe not larger than life, as some think, but just as villainous. Of course, legend mixes freely with fact, but there's enough of both to satisfy even the most curious."

"Emily would swoon with ecstasy at hearing this."

Kit smiled. "Then you'll have to tell her. If Dylan hasn't already."

Angela frowned slightly. "Emily and Dylan spend a great deal of time together, I've noticed."

"And you disapprove?"

She looked startled. "Actually, I don't approve or disapprove. I don't know what to think."

"I thought you liked Dylan."

"Oh, I do. I do. He's been wonderful to me and to

Emily. I can't think how I would have survived if not for him."

Kit struggled against a surge of jealousy that astonished him as much as it annoyed him. Jealous? Of her affection for Dylan? He'd thought himself beyond such an emotion. Obviously, he gave himself too much credit for having any sense. He managed a careless shrug.

"Dylan should have been given a pet a long time ago. He's adopted you two for now."

Leaning back against the rail, Angela smiled. "Meaning that we are only temporary amusements, I take it."

Kit scowled. "I didn't say that."

"But it's what you meant."

"Don't put words in my mouth."

She laughed, and he realized that it had been a long time since he'd heard her do so. He couldn't help a grin.

When Angela said, "You're very handsome when you aren't wearing that terrible scowl, you know," he felt his throat tighten. He kept his voice light with an effort.

"I always assumed you considered me in league with the devil."

"Oh, certainly. I haven't really changed *that* opinion. But I would have to be blind not to notice how handsome you are."

"I see. A man could never grow too vain with you around, I perceive."

"My nanny used to tell me that beauty is as beauty does. One's acts can make them more beautiful or turn beauty into ugliness. I believe that must be true." She turned to stare back over the water that shimmered blue-green in the sunlight, her gaze focused on the shore line growing steadily larger.

"Angela."

She turned back to look at him, and he reached out to pull her close. She looked startled, her eyes widening to huge green pools and her lips parting. He smoothed her wind-blown hair with one hand and gently stroked her cheek with the other, as he would a frightened kitten.

"You'll get over all this," he heard himself say, and knew that he was stepping out on a ledge that may have no retreat. He wanted to stop, to keep the distance between them, but found it impossible not to offer some sort of comfort, however clumsy. When she shook her head in obvious distress, he said softly, "Yes, you will. A woman as beautiful as you will have many men at her feet."

Her lashes lowered to hide her eyes, and her bottom lip trembled. "Even if that were true, only one man would be enough."

He ignored the implications, teasing, "You can't be that blind. Are there no mirrors in the world you live in?"

"Of course. But different people see different things when they look into a mirror." She looked back up at him. "You say you see beauty when you look at me. When I look into my mirror, I see a credulous fool."

"Maybe you're looking into the wrong mirror. Listen, angel," he said, grasping her hands when she started to turn away from him, "your only mistake was believing in someone who wasn't worthy of you. People do it all the time. Do you think you're the first to trust someone who didn't deserve it? You're not. And you won't be the last. God knows, I've been a fool often enough."

"And you have no intention of being one again," she said, startling him. He shrugged.

"True. But I don't put the blame on myself for trusting people I shouldn't have. I place the blame where it belongs—on their shoulders."

"That's a very nice solution, but unfortunately it doesn't work for everyone," she said bitterly. "I think of the years I wasted, the qualities I thought Philippe had when he didn't, and then I recall Papa trying to tell me the truth. I wouldn't listen to him. And I didn't listen to Emily when she tried to tell me, either. And bless her, she has not once said 'I told you so,' when she certainly could. And should."

"Angela, you're not being fair to yourself. Didn't Dylan tell you that? If you won't believe me—believe him."

"It has nothing to do with believing one person over another." She hesitated, then said, "But maybe that's wrong. I *did* believe in one person, one person I thought was very special. And he wasn't."

Kit fought the urge to shake her. Why did she have to look so damn miserable? She shouldn't waste an instant of regret for du Plessis. But Kit knew better than to tell her that. Few women would welcome the suggestion that the man they had loved was anything but worthy of it, even when he wasn't. Unless, of course, it was their idea. He had seen enough to know that, and knew that listening was the wisest course.

Taking a deep breath, he said merely, "We'll slip into a cove under cover of dusk. Of course, we can't sail right up to town for obvious reasons, but if you like, once we're ashore, I'll take you into Charlotte Amalie. The governor doesn't particularly like pirates in town, but the merchants certainly don't mind doing business with us, I've noticed. Their full warehouses attest to that."

Her eyes widened. "They trade with pirates? Willingly?"

"Most willingly. And would also be the first to see us hung or thrown into the deepest cell of Fort Christian once they'd made a tidy profit, I might add."

"Do I detect a note of bitterness in your voice?"

"Probably. I find it rather amusing in one way, but hypocrisy has always annoyed me. I usually avoid St. Thomas. But the ship has to be careened—I don't know if you know what that means, but—"

"Yes. I do. Turk told me. The barnacles must be scraped from the ship's hull so it will move more swiftly through the water. That way you can attack innocent ships much more efficiently."

He grinned. "Right. At any rate, with the ship beached, we'll be here for a while. The crew works hard during the day, but at night we seek other amusements."

"I shudder to think what those might be."

"Oh, more harmless than you might imagine. In fact, I'll take you to a place that might interest you."

She looked uncertain, and the shadows in her eyes deepened until he was determined to banish them.

"What kind of place is it?" she asked.

"Horrible. Laughter. Entertainment. Dancing. I'm certain you'll hate it."

Some of the shadows in her eyes faded, and the suggestion of a smile worked the corners of her mouth. "I probably will. You must realize that I detest all forms of amusement."

"Do you? Then what I have planned should be sheer torture." He caught both her hands and held them. "Stop wallowing in self-pity, and forget everything for a while. There will be time enough later to face what must be faced."

"Self-pity!"

"Yes. That's what you're doing. No, don't try to pull away again. Think about it. I'm right, and you know it. You may have plenty of reason to feel sorry for yourself, but that won't get you a damn thing."

She looked away, but did not try to step back from him. He watched her, noting the play of emotions that shimmered like tiny stars beneath the creamy surface of her skin. Circles smudged the skin beneath her eyes, looking like faint bruises in the sharp, clear sunlight, and he fought another wave of anger toward du Plessis. He felt no regret at having beaten the Frenchman before leaving New Orleans, though he knew that if Angela learned of it, she would never understand why he had done so.

"My return to England," she said slowly, "will not be exactly what I had envisioned."

"Nothing ever is."

Sighing, Angela looked back up at him. "True. Tell me. Why are you being so nice? For weeks, I saw nothing of you. If I did see you, you made a point of being nasty to me. Why the sudden change of heart?"

"Damned if I know. Maybe it has something to do with disillusionment. I've had enough of that to know how to deal with it."

Now, for the first time...

You can find Janelle Taylor, Shannon Drake, Rosanne Bittner, Sylvie Sommerfield, Penelope Neri, Phoebe Conn, Bobbi Smith, and the rest of today's most popular, bestselling authors

...All in one brand-new club!

Introducing KENSINGTON CHOICE, the new Zebra/Pinnacle service that delivers the best new historical romances direct to your home, at a significant discount off the publisher's prices.

As your introduction, we invite you to accept 4 FREE BOOKS worth up to $23.96

details inside...

We've got your authors!

If you seek out the latest historical romances by today's bestselling authors, our new reader's service, KENSINGTON CHOICE, is the club for you.

KENSINGTON CHOICE is the only club where you can find authors like Janelle Taylor, Shannon Drake, Rosanne Bittner, Sylvie Sommerfield, Penelope Neri and Phoebe Conn all in one place...

...and the only service that will deliver their romances direct to your home as soon as they are published—even before they reach the bookstores.

KENSINGTON CHOICE is also the only service that will give you a substantial guaranteed discount off the publisher's prices on every one of those romances.

That's right: Every month, the Editors at Zebra and Pinnacle select four of the newest novels by our bestselling authors and rush them straight to you, usually *before they reach the bookstores*. The publisher's prices for these romances range from $4.99 to $5.99—but they are always yours for the guaranteed low price of just *$3.95!*

That means you'll always save over $1.00...often as much as *$2.00*...off the publisher's prices on every new novel you get from KENSINGTON CHOICE!

All books are sent on a 10-day free examination basis, and there is no minimum number of books to buy. (A postage and handling charge of $1.50 is added to each shipment.)

As your introduction to the convenience and value of this new service, we invite you to accept

4 BOOKS FREE

The 4 books, worth up to $23.96, are our welcoming gift. You pay only $1 to help cover postage and handling.

To start your subscription to KENSINGTON CHOICE and receive your introductory package of 4 FREE romances, detach and mail the postpaid card at right *today*.

We have 4 FREE BOOKS for you
as your introduction to
KENSINGTON CHOICE
To get your FREE BOOKS, worth
up to $23.96, mail the card below.

FREE BOOK CERTIFICATE

As my introduction to your new KENSINGTON CHOICE reader's service, please send me 4 FREE historical romances (worth up to $23.96), billing me just $1 to help cover postage and handling. As a KENSINGTON CHOICE subscriber, I will then receive 4 brand-new romances to preview each month for 10 days FREE. I can return any books I decide not to keep and owe nothing. The publisher's prices for the KENSINGTON CHOICE romances range from $4.99 to $5.99, but as a subscriber I will be entitled to get them for just $3.95 per book or $15.80 for all four titles. There is no minimum number of books to buy, and I can cancel my subscription at any time. A $1.50 postage and handling charge is added to each shipment.

Name _____

Address _____ Apt. _____

City _____ State _____ Zip _____

Telephone (___) _____

Signature _____

(If under 18, parent or guardian must sign)

Subscription subject to acceptance. Terms and prices subject to change.

KC1294

We have
4
FREE
Historical
Romances
for you!

(worth up
to $23.96!)

Details inside!

"And your method is—"

"Distractions. It doesn't take long to focus on something else in your life, and soon, whatever happened to upset you fades away to a vague memory."

"Really." She pulled her hands from his and leaned back against the rail, her arms spread out on the smooth wood. "Like you've done, I suppose you'll tell me. Somehow, I think you're better at giving advice than taking it."

For a moment, Kit didn't say anything. She was more perceptive than he'd thought she would be. Dylan must have told her about Vivian, though it seemed unlikely. Or was his obsession with finding her that obvious? He shook his head slowly, smiling.

"Probably so. I'm getting to be like Turk. He loves to give advice, but is quite offended if one attempts to tell him anything. He's of the opinion that he knows all."

"I've found him to be quite wise in his way."

"Yes. At times. And annoying as hell, too."

Angela laughed. "Well, I wasn't going to say that, but he can be rather— *forceful* with his opinions."

"A tidy way of putting it." Kit shifted slightly to get the sun out of his eyes. Despite his better judgment, he was liking her more and more by the moment. Turk had been right, damn his hide. And Dylan—he didn't even want to think about what that young man had found the nerve to say to him just the day before. It had bordered on outright insult as well as insolence.

"You're just too stubborn and stupid to see what's obvious to anyone else who has any sense," Dylan had snarled at him. Then, apparently unsure as to whether he'd been blunt enough, he'd added, *"You might as well*

get it over with and admit that you feel a lot more for Angela than you want to . . ."

Only great restraint had kept Kit from knocking Dylan to the deck. If anyone had overheard, he would have felt compelled to do so anyway. Fortunately for both of them, they had been alone on the poop deck. Kit had been content with a cold, "You're overstepping the boundaries of friendship as well as good sense." Dylan must have agreed, for he had turned and walked off and they had not spoken since.

And now here he was, feeling slightly foolish and very awkward, trying to charm Angela into a better mood. There was probably some divine justice in this particular whim of fate—as well as a certain macabre humor.

"So," Angela was saying, drawing his attention back to her, "what sort of infamous entertainment could you possibly provide that would not horrify me too much?"

"You'll see. Wait until we're anchored. Tonight will be a celebration for the crew, since they've been at sea so long without one. Tomorrow is soon enough to start work."

"I suppose the entire crew will be ashore?"

"Except the watch shift." Kit paused, not really wanting to remind her how precarious a situation they would be in while the ship was anchored. Once the *Sea Tiger* was beached, they were almost completely helpless until she was afloat again. If a roving man-o'-war happened by, they would be especially vulnerable to capture. To stave off that possibility, he intended to anchor in a secluded cove with plenty of trees and mount his guns atop earthworks. Not only government ships, but other pirates might take advantage of any ship found in that condition, and he knew as well as they did that to depend upon luck was to invite disaster. He'd almost been trapped that way once before, and he had no intention of it happening again.

"So here you are," a resonant voice said behind him, and Kit turned to see Turk approaching. Dark, almond-shaped eyes moved from Kit to Angela, then back. "I should have divined that the pair of you would find a peaceful locality in which to converse without interruption."

"Of course," Kit pointed out, "we're being interrupted now."

"Ah, and so you are." Turk's smile flashed. "How dismaying for you. Do I dare inquire as to the nature of the conversation? You both seem rather calm, and I can detect no blood spilled upon the decks."

"I hope you haven't come to rectify that situation. Lately your conversation has drawn enough blood."

"Testy again, Kit? Can it be that my opinion is of interest to you at last?"

Turk was well aware that their recent conversations had all concerned Angela and ended in impasses that neither could resolve. He had stated this very fact to Kit only that morning, and their disagreement on what should be done with the girl still rankled. He gave an impatient shrug.

"Your opinion is always of interest to me, Turk. You know that. I rarely agree with it, but at least you manage to be entertaining most of the time."

"I'm devastated. Not all the time?"

"One can't be perfect."

Turk shrugged his massive shoulders. "So it is said. We will reach land soon. The crew is already impatient, and I have informed them of the shifts when they will be allowed to go ashore. Is that agreeable?"

"As always. Save room in one of the skiffs. Miss Angela will be joining us this evening."

The blue tattoos on Turk's cheeks seemed to grow darker as he stared down at Kit with a shocked expression. *"Joining* us? Have you taken leave of your senses? Joining us where?"

"At Bloody Bob's Tavern. I promised her entertainment."

"Dear God. You *have* taken leave of your senses. Or gotten too much sun. Whyever would you take her there?"

"Because it's a diversion and she seems in need of one. Do you really think I would allow anything to happen to her?" Kit asked irritably.

"But Bloody Bob's—it is not exactly the sort of establishment to which a young lady of breeding is accustomed, Kit. I beg that you reconsider."

"She'll enjoy it, dammit. You surprise me, Turk. After all, it was your idea that she visit the Café Des Réfugiés in New Orleans. This is no worse."

"Nor any better." Turk took a deep breath, started to say something else, then looked at Angela and lapsed into silence. Kit paused and slanted a glance toward her. She was gazing at them with a faintly perplexed frown, and he knew she'd sensed the tension. Well, it couldn't be helped.

"I will see that there are places made for both of you," Turk said. "And for myself. I have a driving desire to be there this evening."

"As participant or guard?"

"Both capacities are feasible, I should think."

Angela, staring from one to the other of them, was confused by the barbed comments. She had never known Kit and Turk to bear animosity toward one another, and recognized that both of them were circling one another like wary dogs. The most prudent course seemed to be silence, and she settled her spine against the polished rail behind her.

Kit turned abruptly and told her to go below. "You've had enough air for the afternoon. I'll send Dylan for you when it's time to go ashore."

Shrugging, she flashed Turk a faint smile and made her way over the rolling deck to the hatch leading below deck. Several of the crew watched her progress, and she heard soft laughter from the man named Reed. He frequently watched her when she was above deck, his eyes narrowing with malice. Apparently—and Emily had sworn it was true—he had been unwise enough to drink too much rum one night and speak out boldly. To Reed's dismay, Kit had overheard him. The incident had cost Reed several stripes across his back.

Angela ignored Reed as she passed, but did not feel easy until she had stepped into the musty shadows of the companionway. Not that she was afraid of him. No, she'd learned that despite what he said to her in private, Captain Kit Saber had no intention of allowing anything to happen to his female captives. Yet Angela did not delude herself that it had anything to do with deep emotions for her. It was simply his nature, as Dylan had once told her. Whatever else he was, she had come to the conclusion that Kit was also a gentleman in the strictest sense.

Really, so much had happened in the past month and a half that she was growing quite accustomed to the changes

in her life. To alter a hard-held opinion was the least remarkable change. More remarkable, was the way she now
felt about Kit Saber. It had been a complete revelation to
her the day before when he had stuck his head in the door
of her cabin and inquired about her health.

It had occurred to her then, as she'd stared at his
handsome face, that she had been much too preoccu-
pied with him for some time. Even before Philippe's
bitter betrayal, she'd thought of the pirate captain more
than she should. And since then—well, it did not help
in the least that Dylan had correctly summed it up for
her just that morning.

"Don't be mule-headed. Anyone with half a brain can
see that you've gone over the rail about him," Dylan had
said.

At the time, she'd been quite irritated with Dylan for
his presumption. Since then, however, she'd considered
it carefully and come to the conclusion that he was right.
All the signs had been there. She'd just refused to acknowledge them.

It left her more confused than ever.

How could she have thought herself in love with
Philippe, yet fall in love with Saber, too? Or had she
ever been in love with Philippe? If not, would she be
able to recognize love when it happened? Did she really
love Saber, or was he just an attractive man who had
been too much in her company of late?

Angela stepped into her cabin and shut the door, leaning back against it with closed eyes. Stuffy and still
smelling faintly of charred wood, it provided a cozy retreat in which to contemplate her growing confusion. It

made her head ache just to think about it all. She wished Emily would come to talk to her. That might help.

Left alone, images of Kit Saber were much too prevalent in her mind. She could not keep at bay the memories of his hands on her, or his mouth, or the heated press of his body against hers. She thought of his earlier words about distractions, and wished fervently that she could be distracted enough not to think about him in that way. He thought that she was distressed over Philippe's betrayal.

But the truth of the matter was that after the shock of Philippe's cruel rejection had worn off, she'd found herself relieved more than grieved. It was as if a weight had been lifted from her shoulders, and the guilt she had felt over betraying Philippe, in mind if not body, had vanished, like a puff of smoke.

There was, she decided ruefully, a certain freedom in being rejected out of hand. What bothered her was the uncertainty of what she would have done if Philippe had welcomed her with open arms. Would she have stayed with him? Despite how she'd begun to feel about Kit Saber? And dear God, how could she ever explain her feelings about a pirate captain to her parents? Papa would never understand. Mama would swoon and have to be brought around with smelling salts, and her friends—well, she would definitely be ostracized. Polite society did not normally accept pirates into their ranks. Pirates were even more frowned upon than penniless French royalists.

A knock sounded on her door just behind her ear, startling her. She turned to open the door, smiling when she saw Emily's face. "Emily! I'm so glad you've come."

"I can't stay but a moment. I'm helping Dylan pick oakum."

"You're helping what?"

Emily laughed, and Angela had the thought that the nervous girl who had left England was completely different from this confident woman who stood before her now.

"Pick oakum," Emily repeated as she hugged her. Her brown curls smelled of wind and sea air, and there was fresh color in her cheeks that made her dark eyes sparkle. "Turk set him to it for some infraction of the rules—I think it had to do with being late for his watch because he was with me—but anyway, I said I'd help. It's not bad, really. One must take old rope and shred it to stuff into the ship's seams as caulking. It swells when it's wet."

"Oh. And you *like* picking oakum?"

"Not particularly. But I do like being with Dylan, and as long as we don't flaunt our friendship, no one seems to mind. Of course, I think that is largely due to Captain Saber's orders. He won't allow any of the crew to even swear in front of us. Don't tell me you haven't noticed?"

"No," she said slowly. "I suppose because Dylan has been known to swear in front of us."

"That's different. He is in charge of our protection."

Frowning, Angela moved across the cabin to her bunk and perched on the edge. She plucked idly at the comforter folded neatly on the end. "Emily, have you considered what you're going to do about Dylan when we get back to England?"

A shadow crossed the girl's face. "No. I can't make myself think about that now. The time will come all too quickly, and I guess I'll deal with it then. And you—what will you do about Captain Saber?"

Startled, Angela's head jerked up and she stared at her. "What are you talking about?"

"You know what I'm talking about. I cannot see Mr. Lindell allowing you to bring home a pirate for dinner. My parents are dead, and I have just my aunt. I've no one to answer to, but your circumstances are quite different."

It was something to think about. Even after Emily had left her and gone above deck, Angela could not get the question out of her mind. Once back in England, she would probably never see Kit Saber again. The thought was crushing. And worse, there was very little she could do about it.

Sighing, Angela moved to the trunk Dylan had placed in her cabin and pushed open the lid. If she was to be taken to a tavern, she should dress appropriately. But what on earth did a *young lady of breeding* as Turk had referred to her, wear to a Caribbean tavern?

Twelve

"This is Bloody Bob's?"

Kit glanced down at Angela and smiled. "Yes. Looks rather comfortable, doesn't it?"

It was an understatement, and he knew it. Tucked beneath an overhang of palm trees and thick vegetation, the hut resembled a crofter's cottage in Yorkshire more than it did a tavern. Instead of thatching, palm fronds formed the roof, and rough poles supported a porch that ran the length of the front of the building. Torches sputtered, giving off smoky light. Open windows provided glimpses into the dimly lit tavern, and music and laughter drifted out into the soft night air. Sand and crushed seashells lined the path.

"It's very—quaint," Angela murmured, and Turk snorted.

"Another term for decrepit, I presume."

She looked up at Turk with a smile. "Oh no. I think it very charming. And it looks like fun. I've never been to an establishment such as this."

"No," Turk said dryly, "I daresay you haven't."

"Enough chatter," Kit cut in. "It's much more entertaining inside than out here in the road."

Putting his hand beneath her elbow, he steered Angela

toward the door, leaving Turk to follow behind. It was dim and cool inside, despite the press of bodies crowded into the common room. Lanterns hung from the ceiling, shedding pools of erratic light. A long bar stretched across one end of the room, and behind it stood a dark-haired man with a thick mustache, a red kerchief wound around his head and a huge gold hoop earring dangling from his left ear.

Looking up and spying Kit, he grinned broadly. "It's about time you showed up again, Saber. I was beginning to think the government cutters had got ya."

"Not yet." Kit made his way toward the bar, one arm around Angela's shoulders. He saw several interested gazes in her direction, but no one dared approach.

"You must be Bob," Angela said when they reached the bar, and the man laughed.

"Not hardly. Bob owns the place. I just run it for him. And I do a damn good job of it, too."

Kit grinned. "Angela, this is Monroe. Don't listen to a word he says. He's not only the worst tavern keeper in the Caribbean, but the best liar."

"I'm grieved that you should think so low of me, Saber," Monroe said with a sad shake of his head that made the earring sway. He winked at Angela. "Saber just gets too damn impatient."

"Only after requesting a bottle for the fourth time. Until then, I'm an easygoing fellow."

Monroe reached beneath the counter and lifted out a bottle of rum, slamming it to the surface. "There. Without even asking. I should be well paid for such service, but I ain't."

"A bottle of light wine for the lady, please," Kit said,

and Monroe's jaw dropped slightly. "Don't say it. I know you have some in the back, so bring it out."

"That's Bob's private stock," Monroe began to protest, but Kit shook his head.

"Not for the right price, and you know it."

Throwing up his hands, Monroe left the counter and disappeared into the back. When he returned, he held a bottle of wine in one hand. "This what you want?"

Kit tossed a gold coin to the counter and took the bottle from Monroe. "I knew you'd find what I wanted for the lady."

Monroe's dark eyes slid over Angela with appreciation, and he smiled broadly. "Only the best for such a fine lady, eh, Saber? I admire your taste in both women and wine."

From anyone else, Kit would not have tolerated such obvious admiration, but he'd known Monroe far too long to be insulted by his comments. He escorted Angela to an empty table that Turk had managed to commandeer for them and seated her in a chair with her back to the wall so that she could view the entire room.

She looked totally out of place, with her blond hair neatly braided atop her head and her dress much more demure than any worn by the few other women in the tavern. It was obvious she was fascinated with the friendly chaos of the tavern. Her eyes were wide, lips slightly parted as she stared around her, and he tried to envision the scene through her eyes instead of through his own, which had long ago been jaded by similar sights. It was an assorted group, from wealthy indigo planters to rough pirates, with only a few women among them. Those, he knew from experience, were not the kind of females to which Angela was accustomed. He wondered what she thought of them and if she was sorry that Emily had not joined them.

As if reading his mind, Angela leaned forward and said softly, "Emily was right—she would have been terrified to come here."

"And you're not?"

Her delicate brow lifted. "Should I be?"

"Probably." Kit ignored Turk's muffled comment and pulled the cork from the wine bottle. "I would not recommend the glassware here as particularly clean, but there should be no harm in drinking from the bottle."

Angela looked faintly scandalized, but intrigued. "You mean, do as I have seen the crew do when they drink rum?"

"Think you can handle it?"

In reply, she tilted the bottle to her lips and took a sip. The red wine dribbled onto her chin, and she lowered the bottle and wiped it away with her fingers, laughing.

"I didn't do very well at that."

"It takes practice."

"Yes," Turk said, "if one desires to be an expert at that sort of thing."

Kit gave him a long stare. "Are you going to sit there and radiate disapproval all night? I have little desire to be in your company if you are."

"How vexing for you, as I intend to linger near for the remainder of the evening."

Though he knew well enough what was behind Turk's disapproval, Kit could not shake off his irritation. It didn't help any to know that he didn't trust himself to remain aboard the *Sea Tiger* with Angela and stay away

Virginia Brown

from her, yet he did not want to leave her behind. The only alternative had been to bring her along with him.

Shrugging, Kit accepted Turk's impassive announcement without further comment. If his conscience wasn't already overloaded, he mused, he supposed he would feel guilty about bringing Angela to a raucous tavern. But as he had noted, it was already brimming over with other more important matters. This would hardly ripple the surface.

"Shall I get you a napkin?" he asked pleasantly when Angela dripped more wine down her chin, and she smiled at him.

"Your handkerchief will do nicely, thank you. I believe I'm getting better at this."

Before he could say that he did not carry a handkerchief, Turk had produced a spotless square of linen from the breast pocket of the leather vest he wore. He held it out with solemn attention and watched silently as Angela cleaned droplets of ruby wine from her chin and lips.

"You may keep it," Turk said when she started to hand it back. "I should have no need of it tonight, and it seems that you will."

Kit lifted the bottle of rum and pulled out the cork, then took a long swallow. It burned down his throat like liquid fire, wet and potent. Damn Turk. Weren't matters difficult enough without any dissension between them? He took another swallow, aware of Turk's dark gaze resting on him. The sting of his disapproval was like the lash of a whip, irritating him more by the moment.

Laughter rose from a far corner, and Kit turned to see

a dark-haired woman stumbling drunkenly in the steps of a dance. Men cheered her on, laughing uproariously at the spectacle she was making of herself as she flitted from one to the other in search of a partner. His eyes narrowed when the woman turned, and he swore silently when she started toward him.

"Kit!" she cried, pushing at a tangled mat of curls hanging in her eyes. "You're back."

He half rose from his chair, intending to head her off before she could reach the table. His effort was unsuccessful, however, as she managed to reach them before he could avoid her. With a drunken crow of delight, she flung herself at him, arms going around his waist as her lips sought his mouth. He barely managed to turn his head in time, so that she only grazed his jaw in a wet, sloppy kiss.

Well aware of Angela's wide-eyed stare, Kit tried to push the woman away. "You're drunk, Kate," he muttered, holding her at arm's length.

She laughed. "Aren't I always? What of it? I've seen you suck out the bottom of a rum bottle a time or two yourself." Her puffy brown eyes crinkled, thin lips stretching into a grin. Though she would never have been considered pretty, any claim she might have once had to being attractive had long ago evaporated. A hard life had toughened her features, and her complexion was muddy and faintly scarred. She reeked of cheap perfume. A lank mop of brown curls hid her face, and she pushed at her hair with one hand, reaching out for him with the other.

Kit groaned silently. This could get him in trouble if he wasn't careful. He could feel Angela's intent gaze resting on them, and wondered what she was thinking. He didn't even want to imagine what Turk was probably thinking.

"Dammit, Kate," he growled when she rubbed up against him despite the arm he put between them. "Stop it."

"Why?" she purred. "You never minded before, did you? C'mon, Kit, let's—"

Desperate, he dug his fingers into her arm and swung her around. "Kate, this is a friend of mind, Angela. Angela, this is Kate. She works here at times."

"And drinks here often," Turk murmured, not flinching when Kit flung him a dark stare.

Kate gave Angela a raking glance, then laughed as she leaned back against Kit's chest. "Nice to make yer acquaintance, Angela. Kit is a special friend of mine. I've known him for years—our names are alike, so we—"

"Speak whenever we see one another," Kit finished for her. He had no intention of allowing Kate to imply something that had never happened. While it was true he was guilty of dallying with women, Kate had never been one of them. In truth, he felt rather sorry for her most of the time, an emotion she misinterpreted as interest. Until now, it had seemed pointless to correct that impression. But with Angela pale-faced and staring at the woman, it was suddenly imperative she not be misled.

Kate, however, had different ideas. Pushing away from Kit and avoiding his restraining hand, she pulled a stool to the table and perched on it, dingy skirts flowing around her bare legs. "Mind if I join you?" she chirped, and not waiting for an answer, reached out for the rum bottle. She tilted it back with an expert motion, not spilling a drop as she drank deeply. Then she set it back on the table, eyeing Angela for a moment before leaning close, her words slurred.

"So," she said, "are you his latest ride-under? Not that I mind. He's man enough to handle both of us, don't you think?"

Angela cast Turk an uncertain glance, and Kit recognized his friend's growing anger. Kit tucked a hand under Kate's arm and lifted her from the stool, turning her around and propelling her toward the bar.

"Let me buy you your own bottle," he said when Kate began to protest, half stumbling against him. "And you can damn well drink it elsewhere."

By the time Kit was able to get Monroe's attention and purchase Kate a bottle of rum, she was draped over him and busying her hands on any part of his body that interested her. He resisted the temptation to slap her, and focused on getting rid of her. When he saw one of his crew lounging nearby, he steered Kate toward him.

"Dane, I think I've got you some company for the night," he said, shoving Kate toward the surprised crewman. "She comes equipped with a full bottle of rum as well as a very willing nature. Are you interested?"

Dane surveyed Kate for a moment, obviously weighing the attraction of the rum, then nodded. "Sure. It's been a while since I've been with a woman, and all cats are gray in the dark."

"Excellent." Kit pushed Kate toward him, and she laughed and slung an arm around Dane's neck, draping over the big blond crewman as easily as she had done Kit.

But when Kit made his way back to the table in the corner, it was empty. A wine-stained white linen handkerchief lay wadded on the table, along with his bottle of rum. Turk and Angela were gone.

Swearing, he grabbed his rum and headed for the door. By the time he reached the path leading to the beach, he saw Turk pushing the skiff out into the harbor. White sails dipped and swayed, and in the moonlight, he could see the pale glow of Angela's hair in the prow of the tiny craft.

Turk had been right after all. It had been a very bad idea to take Angela to Bloody Bob's Tavern.

Shivering, Angela held her arms around her chest as if she were cold, though it was a very warm night. The sea breeze lifted back her hair and cooled her face as she stared over the water to the torch-lit building on the beach. She clung to the sides of the skiff when it hit the edge of a wave and bucked wildly, still gazing at the beach as they drew farther out into the harbor.

"If it is any consolation to you," Turk said as he maneuvered the craft into the wind, "Kit would never lower his standards enough to actually have intimate dealings with a woman of Kate's appearance and moral stature, not to mention her lack of intelligence."

She didn't look at him. "I am certain it is no concern of mine who he wishes to be with."

"Ah."

"What do you mean by that?" she snapped.

"Exactly what I said."

"Do you think I'm jealous? Do you think that is why I wanted to leave?" she demanded. "It's not. I decided that I did not want to be there anymore. That is all."

"I see. A wise decision, if a bit tardy."

Angela turned to glare at him. "I do not care if Kit Saber has a hundred women clinging to him. If he prefers a hideous creature like that *Kate* to—to—"

"To you?" Turk supplied helpfully when she jerked to a halt. "That *is* what you were going to say, isn't it? Ah, Miss Angela, I can only offer you the assurance that women like Kate are pathetic enough in their own right. Few men wish to burden themselves with such creatures except for the shortest length of time and the most obvious of purposes. Perhaps you did not notice, but Kit was doing his best to rid us of her undesirable presence."

"You're right. I did not notice that. What I noticed was the way he put his arm around her and walked her to the bar." Angela swallowed the knot in her throat with an effort, damning the tears that stung her eyes. Why should it bother her if Kit was with the woman? Indeed, Angela had only been fooling herself that she cared about him. It was a natural reaction to being jilted, and she had deceived herself into thinking her emotions were real and sincere.

For several moments Turk did not reply. His strong back bent to the task of working the sail and bracing the tiller. A brisk wind punched the sails, pushing the skiff around the wooded inlets toward the hidden cove where the *Sea Tiger* waited to be careened.

Miserable, Angela watched silently. Moonlight glittered in the water in silvery ribbons, and reflected from Turk's smooth, dark skin. There was sympathy in his face and eyes, and that only made it harder. She closed her eyes for a moment, and when she opened them, the ship loomed before her in a huge, bulky shadow that blotted out the night.

Turk called a halloo to the watch, then made fast the lines and lifted Angela to the dangling rope ladder that swung against the side of the ship. She felt that she was becoming quite adept at scaling rope ladders as she made her way up to the rail and reached for the hand held out to her.

"Back so soon?" Dylan asked, and her head jerked up to meet his amber gaze.

"It would seem so." She stepped onto the deck and adjusted her skirts, hoping he would not press for answers to the questions she saw in his face.

No such luck.

"Where's Kit?"

"Captain Saber has remained ashore at the tavern," she replied coolly, and swept past him with a finality that even he could not ignore.

By the time she reached her cabin, hoping somehow that Emily would be there, Dylan had caught up with her. She heard his footsteps, light and agile, in the companionway behind her before she could open the cabin door. He caught her by one arm.

"Turk said you were upset because Kit ran into an old acquaintance."

"You have been misinformed." She grasped the latch and shoved, and the door swung open. "If you will re-

lease me, I can go to bed. I'm tired and have a headache."

"No, you're jealous because Kit was dumb enough to
let some ugly tavern wench come between you two. Stop
it. She's not worth a misunderstanding."

Angela leaned wearily against the door. "Dylan, that's
not it at all. Don't you think I know how I feel? I don't
care if Kit Saber has a dozen tavern wenches stowed all
over the Caribbean. Perhaps you have forgotten, but I am
still grieving for my betrothed, and—"

Dylan swore crudely, startling her into silence. He
grasped her by both arms and gave her a slight shake.
"Now look, I don't care if you're in love with Kit or not,
but I do care if you're happy. You didn't give a damn for
your precious betrothed. He was just an illusion, and you
knew that even before we got to New Orleans. Do you
think everyone is as blind as Saber? He chooses to be
blind, but I'm not him. Try being truthful with me, dammit. I thought you were my friend."

Tears stung her eyes. "I am your friend. It just seems
that I'm not a very good friend. Look what I did to
Emily."

"Emily? She seems happy enough now, though I admit
it's taken a while for her to adjust." His voice softened.
"Angela, don't be so hard on yourself. You've made mistakes, but they were honest ones. Don't ruin everything
because of another one."

"Ruin everything?" She shook her head. "I don't
know what you're talking about."

"Yes, you do. Kit's the closest thing to a big brother
that I've ever had. He cared about me and took me in

when no one else was willing to, and he's tried to teach me a few things along the way."

"Such as piracy? What kind of thing is that to teach a friend?"

Sighing, Dylan shook his head. "You don't know half of what you think you do. There's a lot more than appearances at stake here, but that's another story. Right now, what I'm trying to tell you is that Kit truly cares about you. I can see it in his eyes whether he wants to admit it or not, and I don't want to see him hurt."

"Hurt? I couldn't hurt him. On the contrary, it is I who am much more likely to be hurt." She wrenched away, pulling back to stare at Dylan in the dim light of a lantern. It hissed above her head, sputtering and throwing a feeble glow. "Don't you care about my feelings?"

"Why do you think I'm wasting my time standing here?" Dylan raked a hand through his dark hair, exasperation marking his face. "I could be snuggling up to Emily instead of trying to convince you of a truth you don't want to hear."

"Then go snuggle up to her and leave me alone. I'm going to sleep."

Dylan thrust a bottle at her. "If you really want to sleep, drink your wine. There's not much gone, and you can always blame your headache on too much to drink instead of the truth."

She snatched the bottle from his hand, glaring at him. "I think I will, thank you. You've given me a wonderful idea."

Ignoring his frustration, Angela stepped back and firmly shut the door on Dylan, then leaned against it. In a moment, she heard his steps echoing down the corridor. Still distressed, she looked down at the bottle in her hand. Why not? Wine might ease the worst of her mood, though it would still be there to contend with on the morrow. But tonight—tonight she needed a respite from the black despair that seemed to grip her whenever she dwelled on Kit Saber for too long.

Only a few swallows of wine were enough to convince her that it would not offer any lasting solution, however, and she set the bottle into a bucket in disgust. She crossed to the bunk and threw herself across it. Her moods swung from anger to anxiety to despair, then back to anger as she lay there staring at the low ceiling of her cabin. The only light was a small lamp on the wall and the bright press of moonlight through the port window. It gave the tiny cubicle a hazy unreality that made her think she must be going mad.

How else could she explain her confusion? She should despise Kit, yet she didn't. Deep inside, there was a part of her that could not deny her feelings no matter how much she tried to ignore them.

Time passed as she lay there in numb misery, listening to the ship's noises that were somehow muted as they lay at anchor in the secluded bay. Instead of the familiar heavy flapping of sails filled with wind, there was the steady creaking of the ship against the mooring lines. The lilting cries of seagulls drifted on the night wind. Voices still sounded—the night watch, no doubt—and in the distance, she could hear the twang of a fiddle and singing. Mercifully, they were too far away for her to make out the words. There had been times when she had pulled a pillow over her head to stifle the lyrics to certain songs the crew was fond of singing, her face flaming as she wondered if it was all fantasy or there was any feasibility to the antics mentioned in the song.

Finally, with the gentle rocking of the ship lulling her, she drifted into sleep.

Thirteen

Kit swung below deck, landing on his feet in the dimly lit corridor leading to Angela's cabin. He paused, his eyes adjusting slowly to the change in light, the familiar smells of the ship washing over him. Warm wood and fragrant reminders of a previous cargo of cinnamon and ginger they had taken from one of Sheridan Shipping's merchantmen out of India made him smile. He loved this ship in a way he had never loved any home; not even a sprawling estate of gray stone and turrets could give him this kind of feeling.

Of course, he had not considered England home since he was a boy barely out of leading strings. The land of his birth held more painful memories than joyous ones, and on the few occasions that he returned, he was always reminded of why he had left. Oddly enough, though, he felt a fierce loyalty to England and never passed up an opportunity to aid her in the struggle against Napoleon.

Napoleon. Though at the moment there was a treaty that had been signed at Amiens between England and France, Kit did not expect it to last. Napoleon was too greedy, too power-hungry and autocratic to allow England and her wealth to slip from his grasp without a struggle. With his armies divided, some in Santo Domingo to put down the revolt begun by Toussant L'Ou-verture, the little Corsican was only biding his time, Kit was certain. War would come again. And when it did, he intended to pit his money and energies against the French.

Until then, he had his own private pursuit that haunted him day and night, leaving him restless and frustrated most of the time. Vivian. He always missed her somehow, and he knew Turk was right. She must know he pursued her, and thus always cleverly managed to evade him. Why? Why would she not face him? He would not rest until he got an answer, even if it took him the rest of his life.

Yet lately, he had found himself distracted from his purpose by a most unlikely obstacle—Angela. It amazed him that he could spend even a fraction of his time dwelling upon the vagaries of a female, especially one that seemed to epitomize all the deceitful women he had ever known. The suspicion that she was, as Turk insisted, very different from Vivian, Elaine, and especially Susan gave him long moments of pause. He would have liked to believe it. Life, however, had taught him that rarely was anything as it seemed, particularly regarding people.

Despite Turk's belief that without blind faith a man and a woman could not have a significant relationship, he had seen nothing to recommend such a course. His relationships with women had degenerated into quick physical ones, and he told himself that he did not miss the warm intimacy that came with trust. The crushing blow of being betrayed was not worth even a decade of happy gullibility.

Which conclusion left him baffled as to why he was

so angry that Angela had left Bloody Bob's Tavern as she had. He should just shrug and forget it. There were enough other women to occupy his time if not his mind. Why did he find it so difficult to dismiss Angela?

He still had no answer to that question when he quietly pushed open the unlocked door to her cabin and stepped inside. He found her asleep on her bunk, moonlight spilling over her face and glittering from the silvery tracks of dried tears. That brought him up short, defusing some of his anger. She'd been crying. Over him? Or was it over Philippe?

If he had any decency, he thought, he would leave quietly and she would never know he'd been there. But as Turk had noted dourly, his sense of decency had vanished as of late. It probably had to do with his sense of frustration being so prevalent. And most of that frustration was because of Angela.

Slowly, he sat on the edge of the bunk, lowering his weight atop the folded quilt on the end. Angela did not stir, except to sigh softly in her sleep. Her hair had come undone from its braid and framed her face in soft tangles. One hand was propped against her cheek, fingers curling lightly toward her palm. He resisted the inexplicable urge to slide his hand through hers, opting instead to touch her hair. It was fine and silky and, when he leaned close, smelled as fragrant as the air after a summer rain.

What was it about her that engendered this tender response? He'd been angry when he arrived at the ship, after having to commandeer a skiff to get there, as furious with her as with himself. He shouldn't have given a damn if she'd gone, yet he did and that was even more maddening.

And now he was here, and instead of rudely awakening her and demanding to know why the hell she'd fled Bloody Bob's like a scalded dog, he was contemplating kissing her. Her lips were half-parted, her lashes making long shadows on her cheeks, her breasts rising and falling in a regular rhythm. Unable to resist, he bent and touched his mouth lightly to the curved slope of her cheek.

Angela stirred, and her lashes fluttered but did not lift. He kissed her again, this time on the mouth, insinuating his tongue between her lips until she opened for him. He explored gently, lightly, kissing her until she began to move restlessly beneath his weight. He could still taste the wine she'd had earlier, a fruity bouquet clinging to her mouth and tongue.

Moving lower, he kissed her chin, the curve of her throat, the creamy expanse of skin just above the lace fichu covering her breasts. When he deftly unfastened the pin that held the lace and tossed it carelessly to the floor, he glanced up to see her watching him, eyes glistening in the pale moonlight. He paused, the back of his hand resting in the warm valley between her breasts.

"What are you doing?" she whispered. Her tongue flicked out to wet her lips, and she stared at him with fathomless eyes.

There didn't seem to be an answer to her simple question; not one he wanted to voice anyway. He took a deep breath and shook his head, then bent to kiss her again. She did not turn away, but there was no response, and he drew back to look down at her.

"I'm sorry you were upset," he said after a moment, half-surprised to find that he meant it. "That should never have happened."

"Is she—is she a very good friend of yours?"

"If you're asking whether I've ever been intimate with her, the answer is no. We've shared a few bottles of rum together in the past, and that's all. Kate's not exactly the kind of woman who interests me."

"She doesn't seem to think so."

He drew in a long breath. "Don't hold me responsible for what she thinks. I doubt she's ever had a sensible thought in her head anyway. She is not exactly an intellectual."

"I'm not sure it's her mind that interests you."

"Dammit," he snarled, losing patience, "will you forget about Kate? She's not worth a second of your time. I think you're just using her as an excuse."

She stared up at him in angry disbelief. "An excuse for what? Not liking you? I don't need an excuse for that."

"Liar," he said softly. "You're using excuses like bricks to build a wall between us. I recognize your tactics, but they won't work anymore."

Sitting up with a jerk, she tugged at the bodice of her gown where it barely covered the swell of her breasts, snapping, "What did you do with my modesty bit?"

He held up the scrap of triangular lace. "You don't need it tonight." She grabbed at it, and he held it easily out of reach. "We don't need to degenerate into wrestling like children over a toy. If we try, surely we can communicate like two adults who want the same thing."

"I hardly think that applies here. What is it you think I want?"

Kit tossed aside the scrap of lace and leaned forward, his weight pushing her back against the bunk, one hand propped on each side of her body. They stared at one another, lungs competing for the same air to breathe, tension crackling around them like summer lightning.

"I know what you want," he muttered, "because I've seen it often enough in your eyes. Do you think I've forgotten that afternoon I surprised you at your bath? I haven't. And I can remember how you held me and how I made you feel, the way you cried out . . ." His voice roughened when she caught her breath in a little gasp and tried to squirm away. "Oh, no you don't. Damn, I haven't been able to get that afternoon out of my mind. It's all I think about, when I should be thinking about other things."

She made an inarticulate noise low in her throat and rose to her elbows, green eyes wide in the press of moonlight that seemed to fill the cabin with a silvery glow. "Tell me Kit—why do you think about me?"

In answer, Kit lifted one hand and caught hold of her hair at the nape of her neck, tilting her head back as he bent to kiss her. This was no gentle kiss, but a harsh possession, a branding. This time she did not try to push him away, but moaned again, lifting her arms to curl them around his neck.

"You know why I want you," he muttered harshly against the skin just beneath her ear. "You've known it from the first day, you little sea witch. Why must a woman insist upon hearing what she already knows?"

"Reassurance—"

He stopped her with his mouth, a scalding kiss that made them both breathe heavily when he pulled back. This was insanity. He should know better, but there was no stopping now, not when it seemed as if he had waited forever for this moment.

It took much too long to unfasten her gown and divest her of the garment. Beneath that, she wore petticoats and a chemise, as well as stockings. He tamped down a wave of savage impatience.

"Take this off," he muttered, plucking at the lacy straps of her chemise. "Unless you don't mind if I rip it."

Angela was shivering, whether with chill or reaction he wasn't certain, and he reached out to help her trembling fingers. "That's right, love," he murmured when she faltered, "like this." He kissed the smooth flesh bared by the removal of one strap, then moved a bit lower, his lips lingering on the swelling round of her breast. She gave a soft sigh that penetrated to his marrow, and he saw that his own hands were slightly shaking as well when he helped her with the other strap.

Slowly lowering the bodice of her chemise, he fought an overwhelming wave of desire. She was beautiful. His memory wasn't faulty after all.

Unfortunately—or was that fortunately?—she was everything he'd remembered, pink and cream and seductive shadows that made him ache with all the fervor of a man long denied. God, he had to go slow and not ruin the moment. She wanted him; that was evident. And he wanted her to yield to him eagerly.

"Kiss me," he whispered, and groaned with pleasure when she lifted her face to his and teased his mouth with the tip of her tongue.

"Like that?" she murmured archly, and he grabbed her around the waist to hold her, his hands sliding over soft skin in a long glide.

Bared from the waist up, golden hair tumbling loosely over her shoulders, Angela was the epitome of innocent beauty. He shifted his hands to her shoulders, thumbs riding the crest of her collarbone as he held her lightly. "Like that," he agreed in a voice that sounded much too hoarse to be his.

The sweet fragrance of her perfume filled his senses when he nuzzled the side of her neck, holding tight to what was left of his restraint, trying not to go too fast for her. Her head fell back and she clung to him, palms resting on his shoulders, fingers bunching the linen of a shirt that had grown suddenly restrictive. He wanted to feel nothing between them, no barrier between his body and hers.

Releasing her, he shrugged out of his shirt. There was the grating sound of ripping fabric, then cool air washed over him as he stood beside the bunk and began to un-button his trousers. Angela discreetly turned her face away, not moving until he lay down beside her. Then she turned, lashes lowered shyly as she timidly touched his bare chest with her fingertips.

Biting back a groan and the impulse to take her in swift, fierce possession, Kit forced himself to lie still while she explored the ridges of his body with a timorous touch that was discreetly arousing. Wherever she touched, he burned, and his hands closed into fists at his side when her fingers skimmed over his stomach. His flesh contracted involuntarily, and when she moved lower, he grabbed her hand in his.

"Not yet," he said in a soft groan.

"I . . . I have never done this before," she blurted out, and he bit back a smile.

"I know. If I go too fast or hurt you, tell me and I'll stop." His body burned, and he reached to take her into his arms, rolling atop her in a lithe motion that startled her. "Shhh," he murmured against her ear when she gave an involuntary protest, "I only mean to lie here with you right now."

Sliding his knee between her thighs, he began to stroke her cheek with light motions, then let his fingers drift to her lips to outline them with feathery touches of his fingertips. She sighed softly, eyes closing when his hand drifted from her mouth to the curve of her throat, then lower.

His attention focused on the swell of her breast, his mouth going dry at the tempting beauty. Perfect. Round and creamy and pink and miraculous . . . he had to shift his attention quickly before he moved too fast for her, he decided reluctantly.

He sat back, letting his fingers drift over her soft body. She shivered and he caught her gaze on him, wide and green and slightly dazzled. He had to swallow hard before he could say, "You're beautiful, angel. Much more beautiful than I deserve."

A spark lit her eyes, and her mouth trembled in a smile. "I could probably agree with that, but then I would sound quite vain, I think."

He laughed softly. "Right ho, angel. I'm not certain what I do deserve, but this cannot be among my just deserts."

Whatever she might have replied was smothered by a gasp when he bent to trace a circle around her nipple with his tongue. Angela arched upward, fingers sliding over his back and down his arms. Kit licked a path from one breast to the other, then moved downward, his lungs trying to match the quickening tempo of the blood pounding through his veins. His knee shifted, spreading her thighs wider apart as he wedged his body between her legs, and he heard her soft moan of surprise.

Ignoring her cry, he focused on the rich tapestry of her body, hands exploring her with delighted sensuality. From the flat mound of her belly to the apex of her thighs, then her knees, he kissed and touched with hands and tongue and appreciation. Angela was quivering, her breath coming in soft little pants, her body writhing beneath his when he finally paused. His blood was raging, and he wondered how much longer he could wait.

"Angela," he muttered, his voice cracking. "Christ. You're enough to drive a man insane. . . ."

His sentence trailed into a groan as he slid his hands up the curve of her thighs, and Angela inhaled a steadying breath. Dear God, was this what it was like? This aching yearning that only seemed to grow more intense? His weight and the force of his legs against her bare thighs, solid and heated and somehow vaguely intimidating, served only to increase her excitement. Kit was staring down at her, his hands moving between her thighs to focus there on the place that seemed to throb with the pulse of desire.

Despite a longing to close her eyes, to somehow separate herself from what he was doing and the fiery tumult he was creating with his touch, she found herself gazing up at him. His breath was coming fast and hard, the curved muscles of his chest rising and falling in a rapid rhythm. Her throat ached with the need to tell him how beautiful he was, a fallen angel with the ability to steal souls. . . .

"Kit," she said instead, her voice breaking on the single syllable. She opened her mouth to try again, but could not remember what she had wanted to say. Words were unimportant at that moment. All that mattered were the sweet sensations he was sparking inside her. She pressed upward, her hands slipping over the flex of his arms, her fingers digging into hard muscle.

"Here," he muttered, and took her hand in his to slide it over the ridges of his flat belly and lower. Her face flamed, but curiosity was greater than embarrassment when he put her hand on him. For a long moment she did nothing, but lay with her fingers curled around him, holding him while he buried his face in her hair. Then, timidly at first, she began to explore, her hand moving lightly over him in gentle explorations.

"Enough," he said at last, his hand closing over hers to hold her still. His voice was rough and guttural. "Enough for now."

Angela didn't move, but waited, and when he relaxed his grip on her hand, she removed it regretfully. It had been very interesting to see how she could provoke such an instantaneous and startling reaction in his body. It was even more interesting to note that he seemed much more affected by it than she did. She tilted back her head and studied the muscular contours of his body in appreciation.

"Are you certain you want me to stop?"

"Don't give me difficult choices." Kit pushed himself onto one elbow, his eyes glittering hot and blue. "I may not choose correctly."

"Is there a right and wrong way to do this?" She ran one finger down the middle of his chest, admiring the ridges and smooth flex of muscle.

"Sometimes," Kit answered her, "but we won't worry about that now. Now, we should concentrate on getting to know one another better."

"I should think that what we've been doing has pretty well acquainted us," she murmured, and he laughed softly.

"Oh, angel, we've only just begun."

Rising suddenly to his knees, he knelt between her legs and slid his hands beneath her hips. His palms molded her buttocks, lifting her from the soft quilt spread over the bunk.

When he moved forward, Angela felt him press against the heated warmth that was left open to him. He was hot and hard, stroking over her with a leisurely, luxurious motion that took away her breath and made her clutch at the quilt with both hands. He slid easily over the moisture there, sending splinters of pleasure radiating through her. Again and again he moved against her, his hardness caressing her until she thought she would explode from the sheer pleasure of it.

Then he shifted, giving a quick, firm thrust that made her suck in her breath at the pressure. Her body opened for him, accepting his invasion with a blend of pain and pleasure.

"God," he muttered hoarsely, looking up at her as if for reassurance.

Angela put her arms around him wordlessly, and he gave a soft groan and pressed deeper. She felt her body stretch until she was certain it would be painful in the next moment . . . or the next. But there was only a breathless kind of anticipation, a yearning for an ease to the aching pulse that throbbed endlessly.

"Kit," she whispered against the curve of his shoulder, "please . . . please. . . ."

He seemed to understand what she wanted when she wasn't certain herself, and moved deeper, giving a final thrust that made her cry out. Shuddering, she held to him more tightly, moaning softly in his ear.

Kit kissed her cheek, then her throat and mouth, then lay his forehead against hers and went still. He held her for a long moment, not moving, letting her body become accustomed to his.

Hot tears stung her eyes, but they were tears of release. She had never felt so completely whole as she did now, as if she had finally discovered the reason behind everything. This moment gave her life meaning, she thought hazily, to find this one man and give all to him. Her life, her love, her body. And it had taken her so long to realize it, when she should have recognized her destiny from the very first moment she had seen him. So much had come between them, but no more. Now, together they would face whatever life had to offer, despite all the odds, despite everything. Her arms tightened around him.

Finally he began to move again, stinging strokes that first felt uncomfortable, then exhilarating. Under her curved fingers, she felt the heat of his skin and the tightly curving muscle of his shoulder blades as she slid her hands down his back in a helpless motion. With her face nestled into the taut curve of his shoulder, he thrust again and again, taking her to realms she'd never dreamed existed.

This, then, was what it was all about—this giving and taking between a man and a woman. And she lost herself in him, with his harsh breathing in her ear and her body filled with him, hot and heavy inside her, love in its most primitive form. Now, she thought with a faint sob, she understood it all.

And when he gave a long, shuddering groan and stiffened inside her, thrusting more deeply than she'd thought possible, she felt the shattering waves of her own response and yielded to them with an abandon she'd never dreamed she could have. Nothing mattered now, nothing but this man, this devil of the high seas whom she now knew she loved beyond all else.

There would be no more tilting at windmills or foolishly trying to capture the wind. Now, she had found love . . .

Fourteen

Fine white sand glistened under the hot sun, and foamy breakers crashed endlessly upon the beach. Sitting beneath the shade of a canvas tent erected as shelter, Angela gazed at the scene with appreciation. Paradise. Never had she imagined such beauty could exist far from the green shores of England. This was a wilder beauty, nothing like the cultivated fields and neat stone fences of her experience.

Broad-leafed plants and exotic creatures existed in a harmony of vivid greens and blues, so bright at times it hurt the eyes. Colorful splashes of butterflies beat pastel-hued wings in tiny, delicate flutters. Brilliantly plumaged birds twittered in the treetops, and tiny reptiles that Dylan told her were lizards and iguanas scurried up trees and on the ground.

"Stay near the beach," Dylan warned. "If you get lost, it could take days to find you."

Judging from the thick undergrowth, Angela took his advice to heart. It was too hot and humid to take long walks anyway, she decided, so most of her daylight hours were spent with a book under the shade of her tent or watching the crew work while Emily napped in the shade.

A block and tackle had been erected, using a huge tree with roots as thick as a man's torso, to haul the *Sea Tiger* from the water and up onto the beach. It lay on one side, looking, Angela thought, rather like a sea turtle that had been flipped onto its shell. The top mast had been taken down, and the cargo and most of the guns were removed. Several long guns now perched atop limestone boulders at the mouth of the cove, a deadly warning against any predators or trespassers.

Clouds puffed across a hot blue sky, and sunlight beat down with a vengeance, glittering off both the waters of the bay and the white cliffs that rose on each side of the sandy beach like jagged teeth.

Fanning herself lazily with a palm leaf fan, Angela sat beneath the shade and watched as the crew worked to clean the keel of the ship. It was a long and laborious process, especially with the sun beating down mercilessly. Crewmen scraped at the wooden hull to remove weeds and barnacles, checking closely for marine borers. Turk had told her that though the *Sea Tiger* was made of a fragrant, worm-resistant cedar, there was always the chance that the tiny, destructive mollusks could chew through the planking and weaken the structure. As a form of protection, the ship was double-planked with a layer of felt and tar, and cleaned as often as possible.

It had been too long since the last careening, and as a result, the ship had been much too slow and clumsy. It could cost them more than time, Turk had said solemnly, and she'd shivered at the unspoken warning. It was always a shock to recall that any government man-o'-war would be only too delighted to intercept and destroy the *Sea Tiger*. The reminder was doubly disturbing now that she had given herself so completely to Kit.

He was a pirate, for heaven's sake, a man who preyed on the weak and innocent. Why had she fallen in love with him? And why did he seem to be avoiding her these past two days?

Hugging her knees to her chest and trying to ignore the innumerable grains of sand in her shoes and beneath her thin skirt, Angela gazed out over the sun-chipped waters of the cove and tried to come to terms with her newfound emotions. It was more difficult than it should have been.

So many complex reactions assaulted her that she had trouble sorting them out. Falling in love with a pirate was tantamount to social and emotional suicide. Pirates were notoriously short-lived, and their careers entailed certain disagreeable habits—such as robbery and murder. She closed her eyes, groaning softly. Though she had to admit that she had not seen anyone die at the hands of the *Sea Tiger*'s captain and crew, neither was she convinced that it was not entirely possible.

Sighing, Angela leaned forward and lifted a palm full of sand, letting it trickle between her fingers. It was a mystery to her why she felt as she did. If she had any sense at all, she would find a way to flee as far and fast as possible.

But love rarely made sense, she had heard, and now she was inclined to believe in that maxim.

"Do you mind if I join you?" a resonant voice asked, and she looked up to see Turk approaching.

"Of course I don't mind. I welcome the company. Everyone is so busy scraping barnacles and seaweed that I find myself feeling a bit lonely." Unable to stop herself, she glanced toward the ship, where Kit was working, then forced her attention back to Turk.

He folded his huge body into a sitting position beside her, his liquid dark eyes resting on her as he returned her smile. At that moment, Rollo, caged for his own safety and placed beneath the shade of her tent, chose to warble a particularly nasty sea ditty. Angela flushed and threw a cloth over his wicker cage.

"He's a dreadful bird," she muttered. "I cannot imagine why Kit keeps such a foul-tongued creature."

"For entertainment, I suspect," Turk replied. "Rollo has been with him since Kit was a boy. There's a peculiar bond between them that I refuse to speculate upon."

Angela laughed. "Probably a most wise decision. Rollo says the most awful things, and I'm quite certain I know who has taught him most of it."

"True." Turk spread his huge hands on his bent knees, still smiling. "Miss Emily, I take it, is still napping in the shade of her tent."

"Yes. This heat is too much for her."

"And not for you, Miss Angela?"

"Well, not as much as Emily." She plucked at the damp fold of her skirt. "I'm afraid I am not as addicted to modesty as Emily, and have discarded certain articles of clothing without remorse."

Turk laughed softly. "I presume you mean your petticoats. A display of remarkable good sense, I must say. If I were you, however, I should also divest myself of those shoes. No one shall mind."

Struck by the notion, Angela needed no coaxing. She

slipped off her shoes and stockings, stuffing them into a corner of the tent before stretching out her legs and letting the cool breeze wash over her bare feet.

"Ah," she sighed, "that is so much better."

Turk smiled. "I should think so. One must admire your adventurous spirit. So many ladies would recoil in horror at the very suggestion of such impropriety. I applaud your lack of false modesty."

"Thank you. Modesty can be a bit uncomfortable, I've found." She smiled again, digging her bare toes into a hill of warm sand. The shade from the tent made it a little cooler, but the sand retained the heat. It felt peculiar, coarse and grainy as it oozed between her toes and crusted the bottom of her feet.

"You know," Turk remarked, "I could see you enjoying yourself on a South Sea island, tanned as dark as the native girls, wearing grass skirts and dancing around the fire on a moonlit night."

She looked up. "Have you been there? To the South Seas?"

"Oh, yes, on several occasions. It is a most enjoyable area in which to visit. In fact, I do believe it is my favorite of all the places wc have been since I first met Kit."

Curious, she asked, "When did you meet Kit?"

"It has been a good fifteen years, I would say." He looked thoughtful, then nodded slowly. "Yes, I would say it was fifteen years ago. He was still studying at Oxford then."

"Oxford!" Angela stared at Turk. "Do you mean the university?"

"Yes." Turk looked amused. "He is not quite the illiterate bounder that he has been reputed to be. A bounder at times, perhaps, but a well-educated one. In fact, he compressed eight years of studies into little more than four before he decided to, shall we say, pursue other interests. Does it surprise you so very much?"

Angela floundered for a response, then decided upon complete honesty. "Yes. I admit that it more than surprises me—it shocks me. How on earth would Kit have the resources to go to Oxford?"

Frowning slightly, Turk adjusted a metal buckle on his sandal strap, then shrugged. "Let me just say that he had a wealthy benefactor who believed in his ability to do so."

"But . . . but to go to *Oxford*—it seems so unlikely. I mean, the university is so prestigious and expensive, and Kit seems as if . . ." She paused, suddenly recalling the many books he had, books on theology, history, philosophy, and mathematics. That would explain his catholic tastes in literature, though it still seemed incredible that he had actually attended Oxford.

She shifted position on the canvas mat spread beneath the tent, trying not to sound too curious when she asked casually, "Did you attend Oxford with Kit?"

Turk's mouth twisted wryly. "Probably not in the manner you're considering, though I was there in a certain capacity. Kit was generous enough to take me under his wing when he discovered my propensity for learning, and saw to it that I was given every opportunity to avail myself of an education. If not for Kit . . ." His voice roughened slightly. "If not for Kit's concern, I might never have come as far as I have."

Angela said carefully, "But Turk, how far is this? I

mean, living on a ship, robbing and plundering as a way of life? Is this really your life's dream?"

"Miss Angela," he said after a moment, "I am well aware of appearances. I might suggest that you not always judge a person on how matters appear. And that includes Kit."

Kit. The most alien and difficult of all males to understand. She frowned slightly, and resisted the urge to look toward the ship.

"Why does he distance himself from me as he does? I thought once we . . ." She halted, her face flaming as she realized she'd been about to blurt out the fact that they had been intimate.

But Turk, if he noticed, ignored her blunder and said merely, "Kit finds it difficult to trust in anyone, and because of his past betrayals, he has more reason than most to suspect the fairer sex of duplicity."

"Betrayals? I suppose most people have been disappointed in others a few times." She hugged her knees to her chest, thinking of Philippe and his cruel rejection. "I have been betrayed also, and have not allowed it to embitter me."

"Ah, but Miss Angela, there are circumstances of which you are unaware."

"So enlighten me. Perhaps then I can understand why he does and says certain things."

After a brief hesitation, Turk said slowly, "Let me just say that there was a young woman of excellent birth and breeding whom he was very much in love with at one time. Miss Susan chose to break off the betrothal in a very public and humiliating manner. Added to the soul-searing betrayals he had already suffered at the hands of his mother and stepmother, Kit left England behind and took to the high seas. It has been a purging of sorts for him, and very beneficial in ways you might never quite comprehend."

"I daresay." Angela realized there were reams of things she did not know about Kit Saber. She had not seriously thought about his previous life, and why he had become a pirate. Now she wondered if she really wanted to know the reasons. The thought of him being in love with a woman named Susan left her feeling uncertain and more jealous than she had been over the sleazy tavern girl. Even at the time, she had known that Kate was not the sort of woman he would want, though her precarious emotions had catapulted her into impetuous reaction.

"Turk," she said after a long silence broken only by the distant sounds of the crew working on the beached ship, "does he still love this Susan?"

"No. But he still recalls her betrayal."

"You say his mother and stepmother betrayed him. How?"

"Ah, that is something he will have to tell you, Miss Angela, though I will impart this information: You look enough like Elaine to be her sister, and that, I believe, may be part of the reason Kit has occasionally reacted in certain ways."

"Elaine—his mother?"

"No. His stepmother. Or perhaps I should say, his former stepmother. She died several years ago. Of an excess of spleen, in my opinion."

"She sounds very disagreeable."

"More than disagreeable. Elaine was one of the few

people I've met who can safely be called wicked. I cannot imagine what Kit's father saw in her."

"Is his father still alive?"

"Very much so." Turk uncoiled his long body, rising to his feet to tower over her. "I greatly fear that should I linger much longer, I will begin to divulge information best heard from the party most concerned."

Angela's mouth twisted into a wry smile. "I take that to mean that you are fleeing my company before you say too much about Kit."

"As usual, your acuity is commendable." Turk gave her a half-bow that would have been elegant in any drawing room, despite the incongruity of his loose garments and sandals. "I shall consolidate my efforts with those of my fellow crewmen, so that we may decrease the time required to service the ship. If you should need us, we are only a shout away."

Angela glanced toward the beach's edge, where surf washed up in foamy curls to lap at the stern of the ship. Men stood knee deep in tide, scraping furiously at the hull, while others coated the scraped areas with wax, tallow, and tar.

She recognized Kit, his chest bare and gleaming in the hot sun as he worked alongside his men. He would have been easy to recognize anywhere, and from any distance. With his lean grace and predatory stance, he stood out in a crowd. She'd seen that much in the tavern, where heads had turned and people had parted to allow him through. He radiated ferocity at times, but more than that, there was the regal air of authority about him that drew others' respect. Bit by bit, she'd learned that though normally pirate captains were elected by the majority of a vote and kept only as long as they were popular, on the *Sea Tiger* Kit was undisputed master. He controlled the ship, and he controlled everyone on it. Including her.

"Where do we go from here, Turk?" she murmured, wondering what lay in store for her. Would Kit keep her with him? Did she want to go home now, when her life was so entangled with his?

"London, I believe."

She jerked her gaze from the beached ship to Turk, shading her eyes with one hand. "London?"

"That is where you make your home, is it not?"

"Yes, but I thought—I mean, since we have come to . . . to an understanding, I thought Kit would want me to remain with him for a time." Her cheeks grew hot at Turk's steady gaze, and she knew what he must be thinking.

His voice was gentle, however, when he said, "You must not depend upon conjecture, Miss Angela. It is always best to rely on knowledge."

"By that," she said crossly, "I assume you mean that I should discuss it with Kit before I speculate on what will happen next."

"Yes. That is precisely what I mean." Turk knelt on the hot sand so that his face was almost level with hers. "Do not expect too much of him at the present. As I have told you, he is a man accustomed to betrayal in all its most virulent forms. It is my opinion that he will not easily trust in others."

"But I have not betrayed him."

"No, and that is a conclusion that he will certainly reach on his own one day." Turk paused, then said slowly,

"Give him time, and if you love him, I think you will be most pleasantly rewarded in the future."

For a long time after Turk had joined the crew working feverishly on the ship, Angela sat pondering what he had said. It had come as a shock to her to learn that Kit was educated. It was not so shocking to learn of the past betrayals in his life, though she was curious as to what his mother had done. She frowned. If his stepmother had only recently died—was his mother dead as well? Perhaps that explained his bitterness. If only Turk had told her more.

It was Emily, however, who relayed more information, in her innocent, off-hand manner. Angela sat cross-legged beneath the overhang of Emily's small tent, watching afternoon shadows and making small talk.

"Oh, Captain Saber's mother abandoned him when he was quite small," Emily remarked, fanning her warm face with a large palm leaf. She lay back upon a heap of pillows in a tent that had the sides tied up to allow cooling breezes to pass through. Heat, it seemed, was another affliction that left Emily pale and listless.

"Abandoned him?" Angela gazed at her friend in annoyance. "Why would she do that? And why is it that you know all these things about Kit, and I don't?"

Emily looked faintly surprised. "I have no idea. About either. I just know that Dylan told me Kit has searched for years for his mother after she abandoned him as a child. That's all I know—really." She paused, breathing deeply. "I don't know how people live in the heat. I feel drained. Must we stay here much longer?"

"Only another day or two." Angela tamped down her frustration. Emily looked really ill. And she had to admit that the pressing heat made her lethargic as well. Only the nights were cool, with brisk sea breezes ruffling palm fronds and tugging at tent flaps.

Leaning over, she murmured to Emily, "We shall soon be on our way again. Then you will feel much better."

Emily's dark, curly lashes lifted as she fixed Angela with a somber gaze. "I hope so. Even if it takes me closer to parting from Dylan, I would like to see England again soon."

Angela did not reply. She couldn't. The thought of parting from Kit left her floundering in a sea of conflicting emotions. What would she do when the time came?

Fires dotted the beach at intervals, orange and crimson tongues lapping at the dusky sky and sending up showers of sparks. Standing on a ledge of rock that jutted into the bay, Kit shifted restlessly as he watched some of his crew turn spits loaded with fresh game. Wild pigs and fowl inhabited the thick brush and trees, and some of the crew had gone hunting for their evening meal. There was an air of festivity, despite his prohibition against free rum. That order had brought grudging assent and more than a few complaints, but he had remained firm. He had no intention of being caught off-guard with most of his crew too drunk to fight should the need arise. Too much drink had caught more than one pirate unprepared, and he had no desire to join their ranks.

"Our task should be completed by the morrow," Turk said, joining him on the rocky promontory. A spray of sea foam shot up onto the rocks and washed over their feet. "I confess that I am most relieved to have this done. When in town, I heard alarming rumors of an escalated attempt by the governors to scourge pirates from this area."

"Yes. I heard the rumors myself." Kit eyed the darkening sky where it met the horizon. Nothing moved in the distance but a few gulls, their pale feathers looking pink in the light of the setting sun as they swooped gracefully over the water.

Damn, but he had this growing feeling of disquiet that he could not dispel. There was no discernible reason for it, but he could not shake it. And he would not ignore it. Instinct had saved his life too many times.

"Station extra guards up on the rocks tonight. And warn the men not to stray." Kit glanced at Turk, and saw agreement in his eyes. He knew as well as Kit what could happen if they were careless.

"You realize," Turk said after a moment, "that the crew is most unhappy about your latest mandate. They feel we have been too long at sea without proper recreation not to take advantage of it now."

"Too bad. They had last night. A few more hours of drinking and whoring would mean little if stopped short with a hangman's rope."

"My sentiments exactly." Turk paused. "However, the majority of the crew have become rather surly and tend to listen to the complaints of a compatriot."

"Reed?"

Turk smiled slightly. "You are perceptive as always. Reed is a malcontent. I recall recommending his dismissal some time ago."

"So you did. And I refused. If he disobeys a direct order, I will take care of him."

"As you did the last time?" Turk eyed him silently for a moment, and Kit tensed at the implied rebuke.

"He deserved it. Any other captain would have hanged him from a yardarm. I settled for a few stripes on his back."

"I am well aware of that. As are most of the others. However, Mr. Reed is supremely indifferent to the fact that he summoned judgment upon himself. He views you as an autocratic tyrant."

"That is redundant." Kit shifted position on the flat rock. "Perhaps your verbal assessment should be limited to the usage of *tyrant.*"

"Dear Lord. I am being tutored on proper English by you, of all people. Is it to distract me from our topic?"

Irritated, Kit snarled, "Enough, Turk. I would prefer keeping this discussion on a platonic level."

"Are we degenerating to enmity, then?"

"It seems that's all we do lately." He raked a hand through his hair, and grimaced at the sticky residue left by sea winds and sweat. "At least this argument is not about Angela for a change."

"Ah, and it so often is."

Turk glanced toward shore, and Kit followed his gaze. The sides of the tent erected for Angela billowed softly with the wind. It was differentiated from the other tents by a swath of green silk fluttering from the center pole—a warning, Dylan had said, to the crew members not to trespass. He could barely make out Angela where she sat with a book beneath the overhang. It had been all he could do during the day to stay away from her. He had been much too aware of her sitting there, her dress drawn up to her knees, her bare legs stuck out in front of her like a schoolgirl's. The endearing portrait had been more distracting than he would have ever liked to admit.

He looked back at Turk. "Leave it alone. What happens between me and her is none of your business, Turk."

"I could not agree more."

Kit's brow lifted. "Then why do you continue to interfere?"

"You are quite mistaken, Captain, if you think that my interest in the girl is mere interference. I like her. I admire her spirit, her courage, her heart. I would not like to see such fresh vivacity quelled by your mishandling."

"Mishandling! Is that what you call it?"

"For lack of a better term—yes."

Kit's eyes narrowed. "What would you view as *proper* handling, then?"

After a short, bristling pause, Turk asked, "Do you really wish to know, or is that merely a rhetorical query?"

"No rhetoric. Tell me. I'll be fascinated to learn what you consider proper in the handling of a young English gentlewoman who has fallen into the hands of a desperate man."

"Ah, so you recognize that fact . . ."

"I presume you mean my usage of the term *desperate.* Yes. But I never thought there was any question of it."

"Not for some time." Turk shifted slightly, and sea foam laced his bare toes on the wet rock. Fading light picked out the bluish lines of the tattoos on his face, making them appear darker than usual. "Very well," he said, "it is my opinion that you have desired Miss Angela

since the first moment you saw her aboard the *Scrutiny.*
Only your bloody-minded sense of chivalry kept you
from taking her that first night. I saw it then, and tried
to warn you. Now, her emotions are fully involved and
you are still denying yours."

"Let me get this straight—are you angry at me because I didn't take her that first night, or because I took
her at all?"

"Angry is not the correct term. I should think *disappointed* more closely describes my sentiment."

"Bloody hell, Turk." Kit took a step back, caught between anger and amazement. "Am I supposed to fall in
love with every chit I sleep with?"

"Not at all. Neither are you required to sleep with
naive young women who have the misfortune to fall in
love with you. I thought better of you, Kit. You took
advantage of her frailty, when you have no intention of
allowing yourself to return her feelings."

"You don't know what the hell I intend."

"Sadly, no. But neither, I think, do you." Turk looked
at him for a long moment, while the wind plucked at the
loose tails of his full white shirt, making them snap. "It
is time for you to pause and reflect on your motives.
This could be even more important to you one day than
your futile search for answers which you may not want
to hear."

Kit said through his teeth, "I've heard enough."

"Perhaps you have." Turk took a deep breath. "And it
seems that I have spoken out of turn. I was motivated,
however, by concern for Miss Angela and nothing else."

Smarting from Turk's censure, Kit growled, "When did
I become such a despot that I would harm a woman?

Have I ever been known to harm even those who deserved it most?"

"Kit, there are ways to harm others that have nothing to do with physical violence. The outer bruises are ofttimes the easiest and quickest to heal. It's the inner bruises that cause the most painful suffering and may never heal. You should know that last well enough."

Pivoting on his heel, Turk left the promontory and crossed the beach. His large frame made long shadows on the sand, and the fading light blurred both after a moment. Kit watched silently, making no effort to stop him. It didn't help to suspect he was right. Though he had not physically harmed Angela, he knew that she read more into his actions than he was prepared to give.

But he couldn't stay away from her, couldn't even when he wanted to most, even when he knew that it was all going to end one day soon. He couldn't give her what she thought she wanted because he didn't have it to give, and he was being unfair every moment he was with her. He knew that, and knew, too, that when the time came to say their farewells, she would be hurt. If he was any kind of man at all, he thought bitterly, he would stay as far away from her as he could get. Turk was right. It was the inner pain that hurt the most. Didn't he know that well enough?

The kindest thing would be to stay away from her, to ignore the hurt, puzzled shadows in her eyes when he kept his distance and let what had happened between them fade into memory. Yes, that would be the kindest thing for both of them.

Kicking at a loose rock, Kit bent and picked it up to fling it far out into the water. The impact sent up a small geyser of spray that was quickly swallowed by the waves rushing to shore.

He stared at the spot where the rock had disappeared. Not a ripple remained. There was only the vast, anonymous blend of seawater, blue melding into green until it was one color. That was what he wanted—for his feelings about Angela to meld into all the rest, leaving not a trace behind. It was the best thing for both of them.

Glancing toward the tent where she sat, he wondered if he had the willpower to manage it. Just the memories of his night with her still made his brain sizzle, and if he allowed himself to focus for more than a moment on the images jostling for attention, he found his mind lingering on husky whispers and silky skin rather than the business at hand, whatever it might be. It was enough to drive a man to drink.

Maybe Turk was wrong. Maybe the best thing would be to let Fate make the final decision. Too many times he'd tried to hold on to someone who wasn't meant to be his—this time, he would let destiny run its course unimpeded. This time, he would enjoy the moment and not look toward tomorrow. It was the safest path to take.

Fifteen

Angela looked up as a shadow separated from the dark night beyond the fire. Her heart lurched crazily, as it always did when Kit came near. Lithe, familiar, dangerous, he approached her tent with a loose stride. There was an animal grace to him that always caught her off-guard somehow, made her think of things no proper lady should dwell upon.

Yet she did. She couldn't help it. She couldn't help gazing at his fine-limbed body and lean muscles and re-calling how he had held her, the things he had whispered in the night and the way he'd made her respond. She briefly closed her eyes and shivered, hoping he hadn't noticed how she stared at him. It was still so new, the intimacy, the amazing pleasures she had felt with him—did he realize how she felt?

She managed a smile, hoping it didn't betray her as he knelt on one knee in the sand beside her canvas mat. Light from the lantern hanging on her tent pole picked out details in his face.

He tilted his head, leaving one side of his face in shadow. She gazed at the clean line of his features, and the scar that curved from his eyebrow to his cheek, a wicked memento of his very first battle, he'd told her once. He had added the shocking information that he'd been eleven at the time, and the cutlass he'd wielded had been almost as long as he was tall.

"Did you already eat?" he asked now, his knee digging into the sand hill and disturbing a tiny insect that scuttled over his boot trying to escape. He reached down to flick it away, then glanced up at her from beneath his lashes, his gaze dark and unsettling in the flickering light.

"Yes." She pulled her knees up to her chest and wrapped her arms around them as she tried to meet his eyes. "Dylan brought me roast pig that wasn't too charred, and some kind of wild potato that was quite tasty."

"Good." A breeze lifted strands of his dark hair from his brow, and he turned his face slightly as he looked out to sea. Her throat tightened. He appeared remote, unapproachable, and she wondered if the intimacy they had shared had somehow changed his feelings for her. She had heard it whispered that if a woman was foolish enough to yield what should be given only after marriage, the man would consider her soiled goods. Was that how Kit now viewed her?

The question trembled on the tip of her tongue, but she said merely, "Yes, the meal was surprisingly good. Except for the sand. I don't believe I care much for grit in my vegetables."

Kit looked back at her, amusement curving his mouth. "I expect not. Sand is very adequate roughage, however."

"That's almost exactly what Dylan said."

"No doubt." Amusement still marked Kit's face when she asked cautiously, "Is it true that we will be leaving this island tomorrow?"

Glancing toward the beach where the *Sea Tiger* still

lay scuttled on the sand, Kit shrugged. "I hope so. The keel has been scraped and tarred, and the mast set in. We can move her back into the water with the morning tide, then reload the remaining cargo."

"Turk said you sold most of the cargo in town, except for items you feel will sell better elsewhere."

He looked back at her, nodding. "Yes. As I told you, the merchants here may despise us, but they like the profits they make from our goods. Our profit has already been divided among the crew."

She didn't reply to that. It still rankled that the world seemed motivated by greed. The past weeks had taught her some very valuable lessons about life and reality, but they'd shattered any illusions she'd had that honesty always prevailed.

And they'd failed to teach her how to carry on a casual conversation with the man who mattered most to her, she added silently. Pushing at hair blowing into her eyes, she asked, "What is our destination when we leave here?"

Kit shrugged. "Wherever the wind blows best."

It was an evasive reply, and she understood that he had no intention of telling her anything. That much was normal. He rarely divulged information. She always had to learn things from Turk or Dylan. She had hoped for some sort of sign from him that he wanted her with him, but his closed expression left her floundering. What did one say to a man when he behaved as if he'd forgotten their intimacy?

Angela was still trying to decide what to do next when Kit reached out to take her chin in his palm. The shock of his touch left her reeling, while a hundred different reactions raced through her quivering brain and took root in her body. A shudder surged through her like a tidal wave, and Kit must have felt it because his touch altered slightly, becoming more of a caress.

"You're so beautiful," he murmured, and the husky tenor of his voice penetrated to her very center.

She caught his hand, turned it, and pressed a light kiss on his rough palm. Calluses scuffed the surface of his skin, an imprint from years of hauling hemp lines and climbing masts. Angela kissed each one, and heard the sharp intake of his breath.

He started to say something, then stopped when a burst of raucous laughter rose from a group of men only a few yards away. Tents sprouted around them like mushrooms in a rain-wet cow pasture, much too close for anything resembling privacy. She saw the flash of frustration in his eyes, and his mouth thinned into a taut line.

When he pulled her to her feet, Angela hesitated. "Kit, where are we going?"

For an answer, he slid an arm around her waist and pulled her with him, moving past the fire into the night shadows. Members of the crew grouped around driftwood fires, some playing fiddles and singing, others talking. Kit walked her past them without speaking, but she detected interested gazes in their direction.

Clumps of tall grass sprouted up from the ground at intervals, resembling graceful dancers in the moonlit breeze. She moved slowly beside him, her feet sinking deeply in the sand. Then she stepped on a sharp object and stumbled.

"A conch shell," Kit said, bending to lift it and hold it out to her. She took it, marveling at the knobby texture of the outer shell and the satiny smoothness of the curling interior. Even in the fading light she could see the delicate colors, shading from a pale pink to a deep purple. Smiling at her delight, Kit said, "Hold it to your ear and you will hear the roar of the ocean."

Skeptically she did so, and was amazed at the muffled sound of the sea emanating from the shell's interior. "It's just echoes," she accused, and he shook his head.

"No. Actually, it's the sound of your own pulse you hear, but that's not nearly as romantic."

His smile made her breath catch in her throat and sent the pulses he had just mentioned pounding in a rapid rhythm. Trade winds lifted her hair from her neck and sent it in light caresses across her flushed face, and as if he knew what she was feeling Kit took her free hand in his. She allowed the contact, and they walked hand in hand over the clinging, wet sand.

When she stumbled again, Kit swung her up and into his arms, ignoring her squeak of protest. She turned her face into his shoulder, knowing what the crew must be thinking as they watched them. Intimacy was still so new to her that she inwardly quailed.

"Where are we going?" she asked again, the words muffled by his linen shirt.

"Somewhere we can talk." His arms tightened slightly. "Do you have any objections to some privacy?"

Objections? When she'd sat in the shade with her heart on her sleeve and watched him work all day? No, she certainly had no objections, but she doubted the wisdom of telling him how deeply she felt when he had not revealed his own feelings. She shook her head in reply, unable to voice her doubts.

A brisk wind blew off the water of the bay when Kit

paused to lower her to her feet. The sand was wet, with tiny puddles here and there reflecting the moonlight. Stepping gingerly, she avoided the water and a chunk of driftwood as she followed him.

"Watch the jellyfish," Kit cautioned. He stopped and pointed to a shimmering glob of what looked like a translucent silk balloon. "If you step on it, you'll regret it."

"Why?" she asked even as she was skirting the creature. "It looks harmless enough."

"Does it?" Kit picked up a piece of driftwood and knelt, then nudged one of the long, slender tentacles trailing in the sand. Immediately, the thready appendages coiled around the driftwood. Kit looked up at her. "If that was my hand or foot," he said, "I'd have festering sores by now. It stings like the devil. I've seen men almost lose a leg after being stung."

Disengaging the wood with a brisk shake, he stood up. "This is a small one. A larger one would be around my arm."

"Why is it on the beach?"

"Probably stranded by the tide. When the sun comes out tomorrow, it will dry up and die. Jellyfish have to stay wet."

"Oh." She caught at his arm. "Can't you put it back in the water?"

He flashed her a strange glance. "Why?"

"Because it will die if left here. Oh Kit, please. I hate to see it lie here waiting to die."

An amused smile curved his mouth. "So, the tenderhearted girl child can't stand to see even a fish die? What do you think you eat whenever you get the chance?"

"That's not the same thing. This doesn't even look like a fish, and besides—I don't have to watch my meal die."

"I fail to see the logic in that, but never mind. If you think I intend to touch it, you've lost what little sense I supposed you had."

"You'll think of a way to save it."

Kit stared at her in the moonlight, and Angela had the notion he was wondering if she'd lost her mind. Then he shrugged.

"All right. If it will make you happy."

She watched while he removed his shirt, using it and the piece of driftwood to cautiously scoop the quivering jellyfish from the wet sand. One of the tentacles slithered toward him and he jerked back, swearing. The look he shot Angela made her quail, but she murmured encouragement that only made Kit swear again.

"Damn bloody jellyfish—if it stings me, it'll be your fault," he muttered, reaching gingerly for the edge of his shirt to close the top and entrap the creature. It made a shallow trench as he dragged it out into the water, where the tide washed up to his ankles. He lifted the edges of his shirt and gave them a shake, dislodging the sea creature. It made a slight splash as it tumbled into the waves, then bobbed on the surface.

Wading back to her, Kit muttered disgustedly, "It'll just be washed back up on the beach, and now I've got wet boots."

She smiled. "But you saved it for me. Thank you."

He gave her another strange look, wringing seawater from his shirt with both hands. "Which only goes to show that I've lost what little sense I could claim. Why is it that you always have me doing things I don't normally do?"

"Such as?"

"Such as rescuing a stranded jellyfish, for one." He gave her an exasperated look. "And rescuing stranded females for another. I should have left you aboard the *Scrutiny*. My life would be much simpler."

"Do you really wish that?"

"What—that I'd left you aboard a burning ship?" He wrung the last of the water from his shirt and shook it out. "I'd be better off, but no—I don't wish that."

"I was beginning to wonder. You've remarked more than once that I'm a nuisance."

"And so you are." He caught her arm when she took a step back. "But a pretty nuisance. I've grown accustomed to you by now."

She didn't try to avoid his touch, but said, "And here I've been thinking you were trying to avoid me these past two days."

"Ah." He released her arm. "Perhaps it escaped your notice that I've been rather busy scraping barnacles and other determined crustaceans from the hull of my ship."

"Not at all." Escaped her notice? When she'd sat beneath the overhang of a tent and eyed him with a hunger that half amazed her, half shamed her? She could never admit that. "I do recall seeing you in that vicinity," she said instead. "I wasn't aware, however, that you were engaged in honest toil."

Kit snorted. "You're not alone. You must have been talking to Turk."

"Yes, he was able to find time to visit with me, however briefly."

"Nag, nag, nag. Is that all women do?"

"Hardly," she snapped. "If you brought me out here just to pick a fight, I would as soon go back to my tent."

He caught her arm when she turned away, dragging her back to him. "This isn't a fight. This is what passes for casual conversation between us. Or haven't you noticed? We rarely chat idly."

It was true. She could count on the digits of a one-handed pirate the number of times they had enjoyed casual conversation. But it still stung to hear him blithely acknowledge this lack of civility between them, especially when she wanted so desperately to learn all she could about him.

"So," said Angela with what was—she hoped—a nonchalant shrug, "why don't we try that some time?"

"What? Informal discussions? How novel. It sounds delightful, but I'm not at all certain either one of us can manage it. We're rather like flint and tinder, I've recently been told."

"Dylan's words, no doubt."

"Ah, you're quite perceptive. Come with me. No, I'm not going to drown you, angel. There's a boat behind these bushes, and I had visions of a romantic moonlight sail."

Pleased—and more than a little surprised—Angela allowed him to lift her into the small dinghy. It rocked alarmingly, and she gripped the sides with both hands. Kit pushed it away from shore and clambered in, splashing water and sand on her.

"Somehow," she remarked as she brushed wet sand from her skirts, "I never envisioned grit in my romantic dreams."

"Ah, a decided lack of reality. But one should allow for certain intrusions into fantasy in order to enjoy it at all."

Leaning back, Angela watched the play of moonlight and shadow on Kit's face as he picked up the oars and began to row. The slap of water against the small craft was soothing, and the fact that she was with Kit made her almost giddy with delight. This was how she had hoped it could be with them, this playful teasing and enjoyment.

In the distance, she heard the cries of night birds in the trees and could still smell the faint fragrance of roasting meat from their evening meal. It was mixed with the salt tang of the ocean and a heady scent that she could not place.

Shrugging when she asked him what it was, Kit said, "Spanish jasmine, I think. Some kind of flower. The island overflows with them. If we had time, I'd take you to the north side, which is a lot greener than this side."

"We passed a lot of small islands, I noticed. Wouldn't you feel safer careening the ship on one of those?"

"Definitely. But we needed to rid ourselves of a lot of cargo, so we took the chance of coming here." Kit bent to the oars, and moonlight reflected from the smooth flex of his muscles.

Angela watched, admiring the muscled curves of his bare arms and chest. She supposed that the taxing work he did kept him in shape and had the detached thought that he would look elegant in a well-tailored coat and doeskins. Yes, Kit Saber would turn any woman's head, whether in London or the stews of the Caribbean. The elegant line of his jaw and high cheekbones gave him an aristocratic mien that would be at home in a royal drawing room or the most sophisticated club in London. It was a thought, and she wondered how he would react if she suggested that he give up a life of piracy for the more sedate, accepted lifestyle of a London gentleman.

After all, he'd attended Oxford; he couldn't be a complete barbarian, for he must have acceded to society's rules at one time. Would he do so again? Especially if she asked him?

Worrying her bottom lip with her teeth, Angela regarded Kit in silence, paying little attention to their destination. It wasn't until the boat bumped against shore again that she looked around her.

A thickly wooded cove silvered in moonlight surrounded them, and she could hear the muted splash of water in the distance.

"Where are we?" she asked, sitting up in the boat.

"Careful. Don't tip us over. I've no desire to bail water from the bottom of this thing." Kit stood up in the prow, and the tiny craft rocked wildly. "Don't worry," he said over his shoulder when she gasped and grabbed at the sides, "I won't dump us."

Leaping agilely from the prow, Kit caught up the line and beached it before returning to help her out. He lifted her easily, placing her on dry sand before he returned to the craft.

Curiosity pricked, she eyed the bundle in his hands when he rejoined her, but refrained from asking about it. It wasn't until they were several yards up the beach that he unrolled the canvas he carried, and she saw with delight that he'd brought candles, a thin mat, blankets, some cloths, and a package that smelled temptingly like roast meat.

"A picnic—Kit, what a wonderful idea. But at night?"

"That's the best time. All the ants are asleep." He flashed her a grin as he tossed down the mat and motioned for her to sit. As she did, he stuck the candles into the sand and dug in his pocket for a flint and tinder. In moments, he had the candles lit, small ellipses of light that stabbed the darkness and added a rosy glow to the beach.

"The ants may be asleep, but you forgot about the other insects," she observed when a flurry of pink-winged moths descended upon the candles, and he shot her a wry smile.

"So it seems. Let's hope they'll be more interested in the flame than flesh."

Hugging her knees to her chest, Angela sat quietly while Kit set out food and a bottle of wine. When he looked up at her once, his eyes a dark blue in the shadows, she felt her throat tighten almost painfully against a surge of love. She wanted to tell him of her feelings, and how very touched she was by this gesture, but didn't quite dare.

What did she really know of love, anyway? Did she trust herself to recognize it? Perhaps it was all an illusion, as had been her feelings for Philippe. She'd wasted the words on a man who had not wanted nor deserved them. She'd been too foolish, too blind and innately selfish to understand what they really meant in terms of a loving relationship.

Now, she no longer had silly virginal ideas about the realities between a man and a woman, yet didn't know how to express herself. Mere words sounded so inadequate for how she felt, for the wealth of emotion bottled up inside her heart.

Kit came to sit beside her, crossing his long legs and reaching for the wine bottle. He pulled the cork, glanced around, then swore softly. When she gave him a startled glance, he smiled crookedly.

"I forgot glasses. Well, do you still remember how to drink from a bottle?"

"I think I can manage well enough." She took the bottle and tilted it, swallowing a small amount. As she held it out to him she said, "Much better than last time."

"Agreed. Jolly good thing, too. I forgot napkins."

Laughing, Angela asked, "Aren't you going to drink any wine?"

"I've already had some, thank you." He stuck the bottle in the sand, adjusting it so it wouldn't tip over. "Our friend from Bloody Bob's was generous enough to deliver a sufficient supply for the return voyage. I sampled a bit earlier."

She stiffened at mention of the tavern. "What friend?"

His brow lifted, and he grinned wickedly. "Monroe. Who were you expecting?"

She looked down, chagrined that he could read her so easily. "No one. I just wondered."

"I'll bet. Don't worry—I doubt if Kate would dare come to our camp."

"She looks like the type who would dare anything," Angela couldn't help muttering, and looked up angrily when Kit laughed.

"Jealous, sweetheart? Don't be. Last time I saw her, she was quite taken with my chief gunner, Dane. He's a good-looking blond chap with a big hairy chest. Just her type. I'm quite certain he's keeping her busy."

"I really cannot imagine why you think I should care,"

she said with a disgruntled sniff. "I was only curious as to who would have brought wine to our camp."

"So now you know. Here. Try this." He held out a strip of meat that was slightly charred. "Don't worry—it tastes much better than it looks."

Angela tried it, and found it delicious. "What is it?" she mumbled.

"Pigeon, I think. Some kind of wood fowl that one of the crew shot earlier. A bit gamy if not cooked properly, but I think Dylan found the secret of using wood that smokes. It gives it a most interesting flavor."

Stripping off a liberal portion, Kit chewed silently for several moments, while Angela tried to eat daintily. It was a near impossible task, as there were no utensils and no plates. A cloth full of fruit provided their second and third courses, and when she was happily stuffed, she leaned back on the canvas mat with a sigh of satisfaction.

"Most excellent," she murmured. "I cannot think of a better meal."

Kit eyed her with a lifted brow. "I can almost hear the collective groans of dismays from all the chefs in London at that encompassing statement."

"Perhaps the quality of the meal has something to do with the quality of the company," she retorted.

"In which case, I accept your compliment with all due humility." He stuffed his last bite into his mouth and wiped his hands on his trousers, ignoring the cloth she held out to him. Rising in a fluid motion, he held out his hand. "Those are towels. We can wash our hands in the sea. Mother Nature has provided us with an entire ocean full of water for our convenience."

But when they reached the water's edge, Angela discovered that Kit had more than washing on his mind. Grabbing her around the waist, he held her up against him, his mouth next to her ear.

"Ever been for a midnight swim, milady?"

She drew back slightly to look up at him. "I don't swim."

"No? That can be rectified."

"Kit—no," she protested, struggling when he began to unfasten her gown. He stopped, but there was a militant gleam in his eyes that should have warned her what he intended.

"All right. Have it your way." His hands moved to his waist and he flicked open the buttons on his trousers with a deft motion while she spluttered.

"Don't you dare!"

"No?" Moonlight gave his face a hellish cast as he grinned at her with unabashed amusement. "How can I teach you to swim if I don't go in the water with you?"

Angela turned away, her face flaming as he stripped away his trousers. She fled to the water, and to her surprise, found it warm and silky as she waded out up to her knees. Plopping down, she was covered up to her neck, her gown floating about her in billowing drifts.

"Oh no you don't," Kit said, coming up behind her. "Coward. Come on. It's just you and me. No one else is here. Besides, the bugs won't bite if we're in the water."

The water looked black, the only light coming from the moon above and the candles behind them, and Angela shivered. "It's too frightening," she murmured at last. Kit knelt beside her in the sand and water and took her hand.

"I won't let anything hurt you. Trust me."

She hesitated, then nodded, allowing him to draw her

out deeper. He was surefooted, keeping one hand on her waist to guide her and the other supporting her arm. Though she half expected him to touch her elsewhere, he didn't. The water lapped around her, loosening her hair from its braid so that it floated like pale seaweed around her shoulders and in front of her, making her think of the tentacles of a jellyfish as it coiled and moved with the waves.

There was a sensuous delight in the warmth of the water and Kit's hands supporting her, and finally some of the tension left her and she began to enjoy it. There was a sense of weightlessness, of being free of restraint as he lifted her off her feet, and after she had conquered the first surge of panic, she relaxed. Kit smiled, his teeth white in the murky light.

"You like it, don't you."

It was more a statement than a question, and she nodded. "Yes. But you tricked me."

"Would you have come in if I hadn't? No, don't answer. You and I both know you wouldn't have." He shifted slightly to move in front of her, and put both hands on her waist.

Lightly holding her, he said softly, "You would make a beautiful mermaid, angel."

"Like the one in the story Dylan tells?"

He laughed. "God, I hope so. But you may have heard a different version from the one I'm familiar with."

"No doubt," she said tartly, and he laughed again. The water was up to her chin now, and she grasped his arms. "Don't take me any farther out. This is deep enough."

"Where's your sense of adventure?"

"Excuse me, but being captured by pirates was adventure enough. Swimming with their captain exceeds even my imagination."

"I never knew you were so limited in imagination. No, don't pull away. I won't take you any deeper if you don't want to go." His voice lowered slightly, and his hands moved up to her rib cage. "Haven't you ever been in over your head, angel?"

She caught her breath. She knew he wasn't talking about the water. There was an underlying current to his words that made her heart lurch, an unspoken question that she didn't know how to answer.

Resting her hands on his shoulders, which were well above the water, she whispered, "Kit, what do you want from me?"

For a moment he didn't answer. Then he leaned forward, one hand moving to hold her head while his other slipped beneath the hem of her dress to slide over bare skin. She drew in a quick breath at the sensation of his warm hand against her thigh.

"What do I want, angel? This. And . . . this . . ."

His mouth found hers, hot and searching, almost rough with urgency. Curling her arms behind his neck, Angela held on, buoyed by the water, her body sliding sinuously against his in the warm, silky waves. There was an exotic pleasure in the way she rubbed against him, in the pressure of his mouth and the feel of the water around them, binding them, somehow, into a single being. It was sensuous, voluptuous bliss, paradise lost and found and encircling.

"Here," he said against her mouth, his voice a low rasp that barely penetrated her sumptuous haze, "we don't need this anymore, do we?" Somehow, her gown was open and sliding over her shoulders, then floating away on the current. Her unrestrained breasts made contact with his chest, the nipples hardening at the abrasive brushing of his body against hers. The slightest movement sent a shock of sensation shuddering through her.

Kit must have felt her involuntary reaction, for his mouth left her lips and explored the damp region beneath her hair, his hand lifting the heavy mass of taffy-colored curls to facilitate his heated exploration. Murmuring a reassurance when she clung to him in quivering response, he returned to her mouth for a moment, then abandoned that luscious spot for the inviting curve of her throat.

Angela's head tilted back, supported by the weight of his arm behind her neck. Liquids washed around them, salt tang and seaweed, a steady pulsing rhythm of sea that seemed to beckon through the heated haze that Kit was creating with his hands and mouth. She was barely aware of moonlight or wind, her senses so finely tuned to Kit that the rest of the world faded away. Vaguely, she saw the glitter of moonlight on water and felt the cool press of wind against her bare skin, but she was much more aware of the delicious slide of his hand over her body.

"Put your arms back around my neck," he whispered, his breath stirring the wet hair over her ear, and she shivered as she complied.

"This . . . this is crazy," she said, gasping a little when his thumb and finger closed over her nipple. "Are you sure . . . we should . . . be doing . . . this . . ."

Kit laughed softly at her reaction. His mouth nuzzled the curve of her cheek and throat before he lifted his head, and she saw the glitter of his eyes as he studied her for a long moment.

"Don't you like it, angel? Um. You taste like the sea."

"Kit . . ." She stopped, helpless to respond, not knowing what to say.

He seemed to understand. "Never mind. Don't talk. Just be still and let me fill you with love. . . ."

His words reached that empty space inside her, filling her with a surge of hope and joy, but when she drew back a little to tell him so, he was lifting her up, one strong hand beneath her thigh to place her leg around his waist. That brought her into abrupt contact with his body, and she felt the urgent prodding of him against her stomach. The evidence of his desire made the world around her tilt crazily for a moment.

With a sigh, she moved against him. It felt so right, so wonderful to have him with her like this. The intimacy they had already shared washed away any uneasiness she might have felt. This was familiar, and affirmed her hope that he truly cared for her.

As he slid between her thighs, rubbing against her cleft in a slow, unhurried motion that made her catch her breath, Angela leaned back against the arm at her waist and lifted her other leg. Kit groaned, sliding his hands down to her buttocks to support her weight. Then, gripping her, he slid inside in a smooth motion that made her cry out softly.

Never had she dreamed anything could feel like this, the strange sensation of being weightless combined with the invasive thrust of his body inside hers. Resting her hands on his shoulders as she leaned back, Angela could feel the waves of her hair washing over her breasts and against his chest. Kit moved inside her, heavy and full and powerful, his hands holding her hips for his strong plunges.

Twice, he brought her to the brink of explosion, until her quivering fingers dug into his shoulders in a frantic plea. Her breath came in short little gasps for air, and she whimpered brokenly for the release she knew he could give her.

His forearm braced her back while his other hand reached for her head, his fingers splaying against her to hold her still for his kiss, a hot, fierce possession of her mouth that left her aching. Arching, she rotated her hips against him in an undulating move that made him groan against her lips.

"Sea witch," he muttered hoarsely. "God. You're right. This is . . . crazy. I must be . . . to . . . come to . . . you like this. . . ."

Lifting her body forward, she tangled her hands in his wet hair and kissed him just as fiercely as he'd kissed her, tightening her thighs around him. She could feel tremors in his chest, the deep vibrations of pleasure that made her senses soar. She clung to him, breathing faster, her tongue outlining his lips in tiny flicks like fire. He pressed his face into her wet shoulder, his mouth opening against her skin in a heated wash of his tongue.

Flexing into the solid thrusts of his body into hers, Angela felt the first wild tremors of release. "Kit . . . oh Kit . . ."

At her cries, he rocked against her with the rhythm of the waves, plunging again and again. Her back arched, breasts pressing into his chest as she exploded into ecstasy. As if her release signaled his, Kit shuddered and went still, his breath hot against her damp skin.

For several long moments they remained that way, clinging to one another in the water as waves washed over them. Then Kit moved slowly toward shore, still supporting her weight as he moved through the water. Once in the shallows, he sank to his knees, Angela cradled in his lap. She buried her face in the curve of his throat and shoulder, suddenly shy.

The roar of the waves crashing against the shore sounded much louder than it had earlier, and she closed her eyes, shivering at the chill of the wind against her wet skin. Overhead, gulls gave lilting cries that sounded mournful in the dark.

"I thought," she murmured against his shoulder, "that you were going to teach me to swim."

His soft laughter mixed with the sound of the wind and surf. "One never swims after eating, my sweet. It causes cramps. Didn't you know that?"

"You're a devil," she said, and discovered to her surprise that she half meant it.

Nodding, Kit nuzzled her neck and said, "So I've been told a time or two."

After several moments, Kit rose to his feet and carried her ashore. As if she were a child, he took one of the cloths and dried her body and hair, brushing away the sand before wrapping her in a blanket. He found her dress washed ashore, and spread it over a bush to dry after shaking away the sand and grit. Then he spread another blanket upon the canvas mat and moved beside her, pulling her close to him as candlelight flickered in the night and the ocean moved ceaselessly.

Before her eyes drifted shut, Angela had the hazy thought that she had never been quite so happy. Then she fell asleep in his embrace. She didn't know how long she had slept before something woke her, an alien sound or movement that jarred her."

"Listen," Kit said suddenly, as he sat up straight, pushing her slightly away. "Did you hear that?"

Still dazed, she shook her head, clawing at the wet hair in her eyes as she looked up at him. The candles had guttered and gone out, and there was a strange stillness in the air, devoid of living sounds. Not even a bird warbled. Only the waves could be heard crashing against the sandy shore. She shook her head again. "Hear what?"

Before he could answer, she heard it—a deep, loud *boom* that seemed to fill the air with sound and make the ground shake. In the distance, against the dark sky, a bright flash lit the horizon, then another.

"Bloody hell," said Kit softly, "sweet, bloody hell. . . ."

"What?" Angela almost screamed, still sleepy and dazed. "What is it?"

Kit was grabbing at his clothes, snapping at her to get dressed, and she obeyed numbly, terror-stricken when she heard him say, "Militia."

Sixteen

His mind racing, Kit put all his weight behind the oars, sending the small craft bucking through the swelling tide. Damn. Though the *Sea Tiger* was still hidden from sight behind a wall of thick trees, spiky vegetation, and limestone boulders, he knew from the brittle clang of cutlasses and pistol fire what was happening. Battle was an all too-familiar sound. Above the din of cannon, sword, and pistol, he could hear cries of pain and rage. The acrid smell of sulphur rose above the bend of trees and sand, and his sense of urgency grew.

He had to safeguard Angela before it was too late, and he scanned the dark line of trees for a possible spot to put ashore without being seen. The heavy boom of a cannon thundered, and he flinched.

He could only hope that Turk, Dylan, and Mr. Buttons had rallied swiftly and not been caught totally by surprise. If they had been . . .

Unable to finish that thought, he flashed Angela a quick glance. She sat white-faced and stiff in the stern, her hands gripping the sides so tightly that her knuckles gleamed as pale as ivory dice in the pearly light of dawn. There was nothing he could say to comfort her that wouldn't sound forced, so he didn't attempt it. Using one oar to steer, he swung the dinghy around and nosed into shore behind a jumble of rocks and stunted shrubs.

"You stay here," he said when it looked as if she intended to get up. "Remain in the boat until someone comes for you."

"Wonderful. And if no one comes?"

Her tart rejoinder was at least ample evidence that she wasn't near hysteria.

"If no one comes for you, do your best to steer for town. Ask for a man by the name of Maurice Lavateer. Tell him who you are, and he'll help you." He stepped over the side and into the knee-deep water, facing her. Curling waves of pale hair framed her frightened face, and he put a hand beneath her chin and said softly, "You'll be fine, angel. I fully intend to come back for you."

"Kit . . ." Her voice quavered and ended in a choking sob, and he reached up to pull her close. The boat rocked, and after a moment, he released her and stepped back.

"Stay here, no matter what you hear. Do you understand me? I can't fight and worry about you at the same time."

"But Kit—"

"No." He reached into the bottom of the small boat and took out his sword, damning his carelessness in leaving behind his pistols. He should have taken them with him last night, but he'd been so full of high-minded romance and wine, that he'd thought of only the barest necessities. Turk was right. Whatever portion of his body he'd been using to think with lately, it certainly wasn't his brain.

Not looking at her again, Kit anchored the boat, then

splashed onto shore and into the dense line of brush and trees. Darkness immediately surrounded him, foliage blocking out what little light there was to the early morning. He followed the ever-growing noise of battle, at times hacking a path through the brush with his sword.

He emerged from the woods onto a small spit of sand a few yards down from the battle. The scene on the beach was just as he'd expected, and he paused to assess the damages. The government sloop, *Justice,* was broadside at the mouth to the bay, guns blasting toward the beach. Somehow, the *Sea Tiger* had been maneuvered into the water, but sat as helpless as a lame duck in the bay. Kit could see crew members working feverishly to position her guns. The big cannons mounted on each side of the bay were all that kept his ship from being blasted out of the water, and he recognized Turk's broad frame shouting orders beside a thirty-two pounder. The huge cannon belched a deadly load of chain shot toward the enemy's rigging, shaking the ground with the force of the explosion. Canister and grape shot spewed back from the *Justice,* and Kit saw several of his crew go down.

Sprinting toward Turk, Kit dodged splinters as a shattered tree spat deadly missiles of trunk and limb in the air. Leaves and grit showered down on his head, peppering him with debris as he bent low and ran.

Turk looked up, his ebony face wreathed in smoke and wrath when Kit reached the limestone and dirt rampart. "Delighted you could join us, Captain."

"What are the damages so far?"

"As you can see, we had enough warning to put the ship to water, though it seems likely to be sunk at any moment." Turk gave a signal, and an iron ball blasted from the cannon with another mighty roar.

Momentarily deaf from the percussion, Kit waited for his hearing to return, scanning the beach with a critical eye. Though the tents were destroyed, along with most of their provisions, he saw that there were not as many casualties as he'd first thought. Only a few bodies lay scattered on the sand. Apparently, there had been enough time to form some sort of defense.

Turk confirmed this a few moments later, when both of them moved away from the huge cannon to converse briefly. "Actually, if not for Monroe's warning, we would have been caught completely unaware."

"Monroe? From Bloody Bob's Tavern?"

Nodding, Turk said, "It seems that on his return voyage to town, he happened upon some individuals with extremely valuable information. He scurried back to warn us, giving us enough time to get the *Sea Tiger* into the water, though alas, without some of her guns. Beyond his warning, our crew was completely taken by surprise."

"Where were the guards I stationed?" Kit snapped. "They should have been able to sound an alarm."

"I agree." Turk's gaze was steady. "This may not be the most propitious moment to mention it, but a member of our crew found it expedient to supply the others with rum from our cache meant for the return voyage."

Kit's jaw clenched with fury. "After I gave the order none were to have more than the daily allotment?"

There was no need for a reply. Kit saw the answer in Turk's face. "Who was it?" he demanded, and wasn't surprised to hear Turk say, "Reed was in charge of the rum barrels."

"If he lives through the battle," Kit said, turning toward the beach, "he'll hang."

Before Turk could reply, another explosion shook the ground, sending showers of sand raining down on them. Shaking grit from his hair and eyes, Kit moved back to the breastwork to survey the battle. An enemy boat filled with militia launched from the *Justice* attempted to work its way toward the beach.

"They intend to capture our guns," Kit said, and gave an order for one of the twenty-four pounders to be trained on the small craft. Despite a volley of canister and grape shot, the boat made the beach. More boats were sent out from the *Justice* and hand-to-hand fighting raged across the sand.

Leaving a band of men to keep the cannons secure, Turk and Kit joined those on the beach, fighting their way toward the guns mounted on the other side of the bay. Thick smoke swirled around them, choking and blinding Kit at times. Still he moved, his sword slashing, meeting resistance and slashing again. It was all too familiar, the sounds and smells of battle, a nightmare come to life.

Glimpsing the lethal downswing of a glittering blade, he ducked and twisted, swinging his cutlass up in a murderous stroke at the same time. There was an instant of resistance, then an easy slice of blade as he freed it. He had a moment's glimpse of a contorted face before his forward momentum carried him along several yards. Stumbling over an object on the beach, he barely managed to keep his balance, but still went to one knee. Then he recoiled.

It wasn't just debris he'd stumbled over, but one of his

crew lying in a tangle of canvas tent and splintered wood. Hauling himself upright, he glanced at the man. Dane. It was the big blond man who had distracted the tavern whore for him—and lying close beside him, half-nude and with her frowsy brown hair covering her face, lay Kate. She was dead, her body a twisted, bloody mess, but Dane was still breathing. There was only a shredded stump where his right arm had been, and his intestines oozed onto the sand in a pink, glistening coil.

Sweat beaded his forehead as Kit took a step back, swearing softly. Dane's eyelids fluttered. He looked up at him, his eyes unfocused. "Cap'n," he muttered in a wheezy breath, "help me. . . ."

There was nothing he could do, and Kit knew it. Still, he took a moment to kneel beside his fallen crewman. Smoke swirled around them in heavy shrouds, smelling of sulphur and death and making his lungs ache.

A sword was clutched in Dane's left hand, and his fingers curled around it tightly. "Never . . . saw 'em comin'," he wheezed. "Too . . . much . . . rum, I guess."

Kit put a hand on Dane's shoulder, holding him quiet with no effort. "Rest, Dane. I'll send a man back to help you."

The blond crewman's mouth twisted. "No . . . need. Wish I hadn't . . . drank so . . . much. But Reed said . . ."

"Never mind." Kit looked up and saw Mr. Buttons nearby, his face as red as his hair. He beckoned to him. "Charley, get a man here to pull Dane to safety and tend his wounds."

Mr. Buttons lifted a brow, glancing at the fatally

wounded crewman, but nodded without hesitation. He had to know as well as Kit that Dane would not survive.

"Certainly, Captain. You're needed on the south rampart. We think the *Justice* is hit below her water line, and the men want to know what we should do next."

Kit turned, surveying the government sloop. It listed badly on the port side, and he could hear the shouts and confusion aboard her top deck. He smiled grimly.

"Good. If I know Turk, he'll be pouring on the chain shot and cannonballs. If we can't send her to Glory now, we don't have a prayer of escape."

Surging to his feet, Kit left the dying Dane with Mr. Buttons and raced toward the rampart several yards away. There was still a chance they might get away. . . .

Angela trembled so badly she could hardly stand. She knelt in the bushes at the water's edge, anxiously gazing up at the small bluff. Just beyond lay the beach. It had taken her a great deal of effort to fight her way through the trees and find the camp, but now that she was here, she wondered if she should have remained with the boat.

It was just that she'd been so terrified, listening to the heavy thunder of cannon and pistol fire and hearing the clang of swords, and screams and shouts . . . dear God, she had covered her ears with both hands and still been able to hear it. Not knowing what was happening, who was winning and whether Kit and Emily were still alive, had finally prompted her to action. She could no longer just sit and wait to be found. She had to see for herself.

Parting the brush with both hands, she peered at the stretch of beach that curved toward what had once been their camp. Now it was a shambles, canvas tents shredded and poles splintered, provisions scattered haphazardly over the sand or still burning. Thick gray clouds of smoke hung over the beach in billowing shrouds, the wind occasionally blowing it high enough so that she could see the tops of the trees. Her fingers curled tightly around a slender limb as she saw bodies dotting the ground. Nothing had ever prepared her for this, certainly not her sheltered life in London, and not even the brief skirmishes on the open sea when the pirates had taken a ship.

Then, though there had been the reverberating thunder of heavy guns, few ships had dared return fire, and not once had the *Sea Tiger*'s crew engaged in hand-to-hand combat. Now, she realized just how fortunate she had been not to witness a battle.

Fear clogged her throat, not just for herself but for Kit, Turk, Emily, and Dylan. She thought of crew members who had teased her, or fetched things from the hold for her, always polite, and sometimes asking shy questions that revealed their longing for home and the gentler sex. Her stay aboard the ship had not been all bad.

Rising from her knees, she brushed sand from her hands, palms scraping against her still-damp skirt in an absent motion as she judged her next move. Fighting raged closer to the water now, where boats from the man-o'-war had beached. Men swarmed over them in waves, cutlasses clanging. It looked as if the enemy was attempting to return to their ship, and her hope flared. Perhaps this would end soon.

Her bare feet sank into sand littered with shells and debris as she made her way cautiously through the line of bushes toward the rampart that held one of the *Sea*

Tiger's cannons. The smell of gunpowder and smoke was sharp and acrid, burning her nose and stinging her eyes. It hung so thickly in the air that she began to cough.

Putting one hand over her mouth to stifle the sound—rather pointless, she thought, as there was so much noise no one could possibly hear her—she fought her way through the bushes toward the rocky foot of the rampart. Limbs snagged her skirt, and she fell once and scraped her knee against a rock half-hidden in the sandy dirt. With the sun rising higher in the sky and giving the beach a hellish cast, the heat began to press down. Beads of sweat trickled down her face and neck, and her damp hair clung to her face. Insects buzzed around her in persistent swarms.

She slapped at a huge insect on her arm and missed. Dreadful creatures. Why had God even made them, when they were so annoying? Sand fleas nipped at her bare feet and legs, making her stop to scratch and mutter more imprecations against the thoughtlessness of Creation.

A strange, whistling sound came from somewhere alarmingly close, and she looked up, stifling a cry when a cannonball landed only a few yards away with a thundering roar. Dirt shot into the air, and she fell to her knees and put her arms over her head as sand rained down in heavy thuds around her. A rock struck her arm, making it bleed, and a scratch on her cheek seemed to attract more insects. She huddled beneath a bush, terrified. For several moments she could hear nothing except a distinct, pulsing crackle in her ears. Panicked, she clapped her hands to test her hearing and still heard nothing.

God, she was deaf . . . what would she do? Sitting back on her heels, she drew a deep breath. Then there was a pop and a faint sizzle, and a muted roar. Relief flooded her as sound surged back in waves. Beyond the bushes, men shouted, and she leaned forward to peer through tangled branches. There was the noise of fighting as pirates pushed their attackers back to the sea. The crippled man-o'-war listed badly, and looked as if it had somehow run aground.

Stumbling to her feet again, she began to run. A sense of urgency filled her, driving her toward the rampart. She wanted to see a familiar face again. Oddly, she felt no desire to flee to the governor's men. Only a few months ago, she would have thought there would be no question of choosing between pirates and government officials. But now she feared the pirates would leave her behind. Had she been forgotten in all the confusion?

Rocks tore at her palms and bare feet when she began to climb the rampart, intent upon reaching the big gun manned by some of the crew. With the hot sun beating down and the blast of shells around her, Angela focused only upon her goal. It loomed overhead. The ground shook each time the cannon was fired, the heavy *boom* assaulting her ears. As she drew closer, her ears began to buzz again.

Perhaps that was why she didn't hear her name called. It was only when a hand grabbed her arm and jerked that she realized anyone was near. Panic-stricken, she twisted, lashing out at the same time. She was screaming, yet she heard nothing. There was a blur of motion and color, but nothing defined into recognizable form until she was finally pinned to the side of the boulder. Sharp rocks pressed painfully into her back, and she writhed in panting fear and fury as someone held her down.

Shifting aside the thick waves of hair that obscured her vision, her assailant peered down at her with a worried frown. She could see Charley Buttons mouth words at her, and knew that he was expressing concern. Slowly, the fear that pumped through her body began to ebb, and she sagged wearily.

After a moment, he seemed to understand that she could not hear him, and some of his tension eased. Angela managed a quivering smile, and he returned it. Stepping back, Mr. Buttons raked a hand through his red hair. It was coated with ash and soot, and black marks streaked the side of his flushed face. He looked distraught.

Pointing at her, he mouthed, "Are you hurt?"

She shook her head and saw his relief. He helped her to her feet, and indicated that she should come with him. More grateful than he probably knew, Angela clung to his arm as he led her up the steep rock, assisting her when she stumbled.

By the time they reached the top, most of her hearing had returned. The big gun sat silent, and crew members scurried to gather necessary ammunition and provisions.

Mr. Buttons paused, one hand still on her arm, and said, "I was sent to find you. We need to hurry. Are you up to it?"

She nodded. "I can manage. Is Emily all right? Where's Kit?"

"Miss Emily was taken to safety as soon as we received the warning. Captain Saber is quite safe, but concerned about you." He glanced around, anxiety marking his face as he took a deep breath. "Now we must get you to safety as well. Though it seems as if the *Justice* is floundering badly, they are determined to take as many prisoners as they can. I would rather face a hangman's noose than Captain Saber if I allowed anything to happen to you."

Shivering, she allowed Mr. Buttons to lead her down the steep embankment. Smoke still hung in heavy shrouds over the beach, but the noise of battle had dimmed. Her throat closed as she saw people lying in tangled heaps of clothing and blood on the sandy shores. Moans drifted up from some of them, and she stared in horror when she saw the unmistakable form of a woman sprawled lifelessly in the sand next to another body. She jerked to a halt, her heart pounding.

"Mr. Buttons—" Her throat closed on the words. Emily was the only other woman in camp. Freeing herself from Mr. Buttons' grasp, she went to kneel beside the woman. Brown hair curled in dirty tangles over the face, and Angela put out a shaking hand to brush it away. No, no, not Emily, with her bright eyes and sweet nature . . . dear God, don't let it be. . . .

Blood smeared her fingertips as Angela pushed away the hair to reveal female features that were almost unrecognizable. Then relief flooded her. Not Emily. Though there was a gaping hole where the nose and mouth had been, she saw enough to know it was not Emily.

Feeling sick, she looked away as Mr. Buttons put a hand on her shoulder. "At least death was swift for her," he said softly. "It is not always so kind to others."

Angela's stunned gaze fell upon the man lying next to the woman, and saw his eyes on her. He was alive, even though the open, brutal wounds on his body should have killed him instantly. One arm had been torn away, and there was a huge slash across his middle. Charred flesh still smoldered. Nausea rose in her throat, and she put a hand over her mouth.

The man's lips twisted in a grimace. "Ain't . . . pretty, is it? At least Kate . . . died . . . quick."

For a moment, Angela didn't comprehend. Then it hit her, and her gaze shifted back to the woman. Kate. The girl from the tavern. God. She wouldn't have known her. It didn't help to recall that she'd disliked her. She was dead now, and the waste of life seemed so pointless.

"Dane," Mr. Buttons was saying, "we have to move quickly. I need to get Miss Angela to safety."

Nodding, Dane's eyes registered his fate. He knew he was dying, and only awaited the end. "Go . . . on," he wheezed, blood bubbling from his lips and into his beard. "Ain't . . . nothing . . . you can do for . . . me now."

"No," Angela said, pulling away as Mr. Buttons pulled her to her feet. "We have to help." She felt a compulsion to stay, to somehow ease the suffering the pirate must be enduring. But Charley Buttons did not listen to her protests, and resorted to literally dragging her down the beach.

"Listen to me," he said sharply, exasperation in his features when she still resisted. "There is nothing to be done for that man. And if you persist in delaying, you may very well end up like Kate. Do you understand what I am saying?"

Shocked, and angry at the needless waste of life, Angela snapped, "Perhaps I am not as inured to death as you seem to be, Mr. Buttons!"

He put a hand briefly over his eyes, then looked at her. "One never grows accustomed to death, Miss Angela. But one must still strive to survive. If you will not be sensible, I must be."

Survival. She remembered Kit once telling her that when faced with death, people would do whatever it took to stay alive. Maybe he was right. It certainly didn't ease her conscience to think of how blithely she had once announced that death was preferable to dishonor. Faced with the harsh, ugly reality of dying, she realized that he was right. She didn't want to die like Kate had, nor as the blond pirate was dying, slowly and painfully. She wanted to live, and the fear that had been temporarily replaced with horror made her tremble.

As if sensing her appreciation of their danger, Mr. Buttons said more kindly, "Just trust me to help you. I'll do my best."

Angela looked back and saw that Dane was already dead.

She allowed Buttons to pull her across the beach, ignoring the dead and dying, thinking only of reaching safety. She had thought he intended to take her to a shelter in the trees, but instead, he led her to the very edge of the beach. A boat bobbed in the curling surf, and she saw Emily seated on a thwart in the stern, her round face terrified. At her feet, a wooden cage held a squawking Rollo. His wings beat against the slats, red feathers flying.

"Emily. Oh God—you're alive. Are you all right?"

Stumbling, Angela splashed into the shallows. Water wet the hem of her skirts and reached her knees. She gripped the sides of the boat when Emily held out a hand.

"Oh! Oh, I was so frightened for you, Miss Angela. . . ."

The little boat rocked wildly when Emily stood up,

and a pirate standing guard barked at her to sit back down or they'd all be in the water. Mr. Buttons came up behind Angela.

"Get in quickly. There's no time to waste."

"But where—"

A muffled roar smothered her words and Angela screamed. She heard Mr. Buttons curse, heard the other pirate shouting and Emily crying. Above the din, Rollo screeched obscenities.

Angela turned, watching in horror as a half-dozen uniformed men swarmed toward them brandishing cutlasses and pistols. More shots rang out, and the acrid bite of sulphur filled the air. Everything was a blur; as if seen through leagues of water, Angela saw Mr. Buttons and two other pirates engage the militia in a flurry of steel. She stood in the water, paralyzed with fright and terror as the skirmish surged toward her.

Over the chaos, she heard Emily's screams rise to a new level. Turning, she saw a man clamber over the side of the boat and reach for Emily. Sunlight glittered from the length of steel in his hand. Without pausing to think, Angela put both hands on the rail of the small boat and put all her weight into it. The craft tilted, catching the man off-balance.

When he scrambled to regain his balance, she pushed again, this time succeeding in tilting the boat. Emily screamed as it capsized and she plunged into the water. She stood up, sputtering and coughing, but Angela had no time to help. Debris from the boat floated around her, and she could see Rollo's cage bobbing in the waves. She made a grab for it and missed, then realized she had a bigger problem. Their attacker stood up in the water right beside her, coughing and cursing.

Then he saw Angela and lifted his dripping sword with a snarl. "Bloody bitch—d'ye think ye can drown me?"

Angela tried to step back, but the water surging around her knees tangled her skirt between her legs and she went down hard. Jarred by the fall, she tried to scoot back in the chest-high water, fumbling for something to use in defense. The man laughed and lifted his sword higher.

Her hand brushed against an object in the sand, and in desperation, Angela grabbed it from the water. The carved hilt of a sword fit her palm, and she swung it up and out just as the man stepped forward to bring down his sword. A numbing thud sent shock waves down her arm as the sword caught her assailant in the middle. He folded over the blade in a curiously slow motion, his eyes widening with shock.

Releasing the hilt of the sword, Angela fought a wave of revulsion when he fell atop her, one arm flopping limply over her shoulder. She screamed, then screamed again, kicking at him so wildly that water drenched her. His weight pushed her deeper into the sand, so that in a very few moments, waves were washing over her face and filling her nose.

Then Mr. Buttons was there, pushing the dead man off, calmly saying that she'd done well and they must hurry. He lifted her from the water, and Angela saw with shivering horror that there were bloodstains on her dress. The body bobbed in the water, bumping against her legs.

"I must . . . wash," she murmured, but Mr. Buttons was lifting her and putting her into the righted boat, telling her that there was no time. She huddled next to Emily, who held Rollo's cage tightly in her lap.

"Get them to the ship," Mr. Buttons told the pirate at the oars. "I'll join you as soon as possible."

Vaguely aware of Emily's coughing sobs and the very wet Rollo's sputtering imprecations, Angela huddled in the front of the boat in numb misery. She had killed a man. She had taken another life. She looked down at the brownish stains on her dress. Marks of murder. And it had been so easy. There had been no question of morality, only the driving need to survive. She was, as Kit had once told her, capable of doing anything to live.

It was not a pleasant realization.

Seventeen

Pandemonium reigned aboard the *Sea Tiger* when Kit boarded with Turk right behind him. Charley Buttons waited at the rail, his face tight with concern.

"We've sustained two hits, none serious," Mr. Buttons announced. "Three of our guns remain on shore, the thirty-four and twenty-four pounder still situated atop the bluffs. As our chief gunner is dead, I've taken the liberty of appointing another to take his place, sir."

"And the women?" Kit snapped. "Did you find Angela?"

"Both are safe." Mr. Buttons hesitated, then added quickly, "I had a bit of trouble finding her at first, and she suffered a bit of an . . . an upset, but she's aboard."

"An upset. What the devil—wasn't she where I said she'd be?" Kit paused, judging from Mr. Buttons's face that that was not the case. Well, he didn't have time to deal with it now. "Good work," he said instead. "Females are a deuced inconvenience aboard ship, and a bloody disaster in a battle. You did well."

When he turned, he saw Angela staring at him from behind a bulwark. Her hair and clothes were drenched, and her eyes were a wide, vivid green that bore traces of shock. At her side, Emily sobbed loudly, clutching Rollo's cage with white-knuckled fingers.

"Get below," he said curtly. "Now is not the time for female hysterics."

"I'll escort them," Mr. Buttons offered hastily, and rushed forward to take Angela by one arm and Emily by the other.

"Well done, Mr. Buttons," Turk said gravely. Immediately, the quartermaster rapped out orders, and men scurried to obey.

Kit turned his attention to urgent matters. With the *Justice* grounded on a sand bar, they had a chance to escape. Despite their grim situation, however, the crew aboard the grounded ship were still firing lethal volleys at the *Sea Tiger*. A ball landed much too close, spattering water and wood splinters over the deck.

"Turk," Kit said, gesturing at the man-o'-war, "I think those gentlemen have too much time on their hands. What do you think our chance is of giving them something else to do other than fire those guns?"

"What did you have in mind?"

Kit smiled. "Fighting fire with—fire."

At first Turk looked faintly perplexed, then he smiled. He turned to look at the huge ship. "I understand completely."

"I thought you would."

It took a very short time to load a small dinghy with two barrels of gunpowder. Lengths of tight rope stretched between the two barrels, with one end set afire. If he had judged right, Kit mused, the barrels should ignite and explode just as the dinghy floated past the *Justice*. If he erred, it should at least provide a short diversion in which the *Sea Tiger* might be able to work past the man-o'-war.

"Are all our men aboard?" he asked, watching tensely as the small boat was set afloat in the current. Waves lifted it briefly, taking it closer to the man-o'-war.

Dylan stepped close to the rail beside Kit. "All that aren't too badly wounded or dead are aboard. Those left ashore won't survive long enough to be hanged."

It was the best a pirate could ask for, Kit thought, to die in battle. Not many pirates died of old age. The nature of the profession provided a high mortality rate, as evidenced by the day's battle.

"Look," Dylan said, and Kit turned his attention to the man-o'-war. Someone aboard had spied the small dinghy wafting toward them on the current, and sounded an alarm. Men scurried to divert it before it reached them. He saw several crewmen dive overboard and swim toward the craft.

But luck was with the pirates that day, because a huge breaker lifted the small dinghy high and swept it just out of the men's reach, sending it careening into the side of the man-o'-war. Shouts were heard, and someone leaned over the rail with a long grappling hook to push it away.

It was too late. There was a blinding flash and deafening roar as the man-o'-war exploded. A series of explosions erupted in shattering chains, and the sky was filled with thick black smoke and hot ash. Wreckage shot high into the air, then splashed into the water. Bits of wood and debris struck the decks of the *Sea Tiger*.

"Bloody hell," Dylan said softly, "we hit their powder magazine."

A beatific smile spread over Turk's face. "How propitious."

"It is if that's the only man-o'-war in the area," Kit observed. "That explosion can be seen for miles. If it doesn't draw attention, we might get away."

Dylan snapped into action. In short order, sails shimmied up the mainmast and caught a good wind. Driven by the punch of the wind, the ship glided out into the open sea.

It wasn't until the island of St. Thomas was only a faint dark line against the horizon that Kit drew an easy breath. No pursuers. By the grace of God and a miracle, they had avoided certain capture and death. It had been a narrow escape. Much too narrow. He didn't want to think about what would have happened to Angela and Emily if they had been taken. The pirates' fates were a foregone conclusion; not so with the women.

Standing on the quarterdeck, with a stiff wind blowing them farther and farther from the island, Kit came to a decision. He had to get Angela to safety. He could no longer risk her well-being for admittedly selfish reasons. Damn. He should have sent her home to London from New Orleans, but he hadn't. No, he had been—as Turk surmised—unable to give her up. It certainly didn't help to realize it now, and he could only hope that she would understand his reasons.

If he could ever understand them himself. . . .

Heartsick, Angela clung to the rail with both hands. She couldn't look at Kit, and fought the pressing desire to put both hands over her ears. Relentlessly, he continued, his voice calm and pragmatic, as if he was discussing the weather instead of her life.

"Once back in London," he said, "I will ensure that you are taken to your parents as soon as possible. Turk has concocted a tale that will explain your circumstances satisfactorily to those interested. Your association with a pirate, of course, will not be discussed. It will be as if you had never met Kit Saber."

She turned to look at him finally, avoiding his eyes. There was nothing in his expression to indicate that he felt anything more than a desire to be rid of her as diplomatically as possible. She had the fleeting thought that he looked more relieved than concerned. Not once had he mentioned regret, or love, or what had happened between them. It would have been gratifying to match his insouciance, but her tone was less indifferent than she would have liked.

"Very well, Captain. Emily must also be advised of the proper explanation, of course. Once I would have doubted her ability to acquit herself without giving it all away, but she has changed a great deal in these past weeks."

"As we all have."

Meeting his eyes at last, she was jolted by the intensity in his gaze. For a moment she said nothing, then managed in a soft, thick whisper, "Yes, some of us have changed a great deal."

Her throat closing, she found more speech too difficult. Instead, she focused on soft pink shreds of cloud on the far horizon that veiled the sun as it sank below the water. The ship's noises were familiar and comfortable—the snap of wind in the sails and humming lines, men talking in low baritones or toying with a fiddle or flute. Kit stood with his back to the spectacular sunset, his face in shadow, diffused light a bronze halo around his dark head.

Why had she not suspected what he would say? Something should have warned her, some small word or deed that would give her a hint that her days aboard the ship were soon to end.

Perhaps it should have been the horrible episode with Reed. It still haunted her, the finality with which Kit had pronounced sentence on him for disobeying an order. It didn't seem fair to her, as the crew had willingly drunk the rum Reed had passed out, but no one wanted to listen. Her protests had earned her hard looks, and Kit had ordered her taken below to her cabin. Dylan had tried to explain it to her after he'd escorted her below.

"Lovey, listen to me," he'd pleaded, "even on a pirate ship there are rules. Reed broke a cardinal rule. He endangered all of us by giving out the rum—"

"But the crew drank it," she argued hotly. "Are they not just as guilty?"

"Technically, yes. But the argument was presented that since Saber was not present and the rum was being given out, the responsibility was Reed's. He was in charge of the barrels, and he disobeyed a direct order. His punishment is warning enough to the rest of the crew. Think about it—if not for Monroe's warning, we might all be swinging from a gibbet right now."

"But it was so horrible," she'd whispered, still shocked by the vision of Reed choking out his life at the end of a noose hanging from the yardarm.

"You weren't meant to see it." Dylan's sigh conveyed

his dismay. "I was supposed to lock you in your cabin. I forgot."

Shuddering, the image of Kit's hard face as he had placed the noose around Reed's neck convulsed Angela's stomach into a tight knot. There had been no mercy, no compassion in the features of a man she'd thought capable of both. The contradiction frightened her.

"Angela," Dylan said gently, "he only did what he had to do. That's his job. That is why he can command men who'd just as soon cut your throat as not," he'd said matter-of-factly. "Do you think a weak man could control this band?"

It was not a comforting thought. And now, when Kit's face held no tinge of mercy or love, only determination, she knew she should have been prepared for his rejection.

When the tension between them grew unbearable, she turned away from the rail to leave. Kit's voice stopped her.

"No need to run away, Angela. You must realize that I'm only concerned for your welfare."

She had almost forgotten how easily he could control her with a few words or a gesture. It was much too irritating to be manipulated so easily. She whirled around, anger shooting through her like a poisoned dart. "Concerned? Or burdened? I've not inconvenienced you until now, I notice."

"Our vulnerability has not been so bluntly evident until now." His calm tone contradicted his savage expression, but it wasn't until she turned again to leave that he grabbed her arm. "There are times one cannot run, Angela. I'm trying to avoid the next crisis."

She twisted her arm from his grasp. "With pirates,

there are always more crises. What makes you think you can avoid the next one?"

"Perhaps I can't, but I can ensure that you won't be in any danger from a cruising Spanish man-o'-war or a French frigate. Do you think I liked hearing that you killed a man?"

The blood drained from her face, and a cold chill raked her with icy fingers. Shocked into silence, she could only stare up at Kit. There was no condemnation in his eyes, only a bitter acceptance. The death had not been mentioned, and she had not thought he knew. The searing memory of that moment still haunted her. How dare he bring that up now, of all times?

Whirling about, she made the escape pride had not allowed her to make a few moments before. Nausea curdled her stomach, and her hands were trembling so that she could barely grasp the latch to her cabin door. It was more the rolling motion of the ship than her efforts that swung open the door at last, and she lurched inside with a choking cry.

Without realizing she'd crossed the cabin, she was facedown on the bunk, hands curling into the soft cotton quilt in a convulsive motion. Hot tears smeared her cheeks and the quilt, and she closed her eyes. Did Kit only pretend to be concerned for her welfare? If he truly cared about her, he would not take her home. Did he think he could stay with her once in London? It was highly unlikely he'd get past the London Bridge gate without being arrested. Even with a clever disguise, the *Sea Tiger* would most likely be recognized if he sailed anywhere close. Oh yes, he wasn't fooling her with his lame excuses.

Thank God she'd made it to her cabin before surrendering to tears. It would have been humiliating to be reduced to sniveling like a schoolgirl in front of him.

"You really should learn to shut doors behind you," a voice drawled from her doorway, and she turned on the bed to see Kit standing in the open portal. Hastily, she wiped away her tears.

"Get out," she snapped at him, sitting up. "I don't wish to talk to you right now."

Ignoring that, he stepped inside and closed the door. "Too bad. I'm in the mood to talk to you. Do you suppose you could explain the meaning of this little drama you're enacting? I would be positively fascinated to learn why you're behaving as if I've just announced my decision to sell you on the block in Barbados."

Schooling her rebelliously quivering lower lip into stiffness, she managed to say coolly, "I really don't know what you're talking about. You have stated your intention to return me to London—which is what I have been asking you to do for the past month—and I have acknowledged it."

Kit's mouth twisted into a sardonic smile. "Have you. Pardon me, but we have differing views. It was more an assault than an acknowledgment. Am I to deduce from your reaction that you don't want to go home?"

She turned away without answering. Of course she wanted to go home. But not like this. Not because he didn't want her to stay with him. Dear God, why must this be so difficult? Why didn't he just go away and leave her alone?

"Angela." The mattress dipped as he sat down, but she refused to look at him. Before long his hands settled on the slope of her shoulders. Gently, he pulled her backward to hold her against his chest, and she could feel the steady rhythm of his breathing. "You're the stubbornest woman I've ever met," he muttered as his fingers slid beneath her heavy hair to caress her.

Predictably, his touch sent shivers through her, and she held tightly to her anger, using it as a shield. He would not smooth over his actions with honeyed words and promises he didn't mean. She'd had enough of that from Philippe.

Kit began to massage her shoulders with light, circular motions, his clever fingers occasionally exploring the sensitive whorls of her ear. Shivering, she pulled away and turned to look at him.

He observed her in silence for a moment, then said in a light, faintly amused voice, "Though rumors may contradict me, I do not usually make a habit of abducting innocent young English women, however beautiful they may be. If you will recall, I rescued you. There is a sizable difference, in my opinion."

"I also recall the reason I *had* to be rescued," she said tartly, and he grinned.

"Ah yes. The unfortunate fire aboard the *Scrutiny.* Whatever would you have done had I not been there?"

"Continued my voyage to New Orleans, most likely," she shot at him. "Had you not attacked us, there would have been no fire."

"And had you continued on to New Orleans, you would have found your precious betrothed awaiting you at the wharf, no doubt."

His sarcasm penetrated to her marrow, and she sucked in a sharp breath. She was well aware that had she managed to find Philippe at all, the outcome would have been the same.

Warily, she asked, "Are you insinuating that you have alleviated my . . . my shock at finding Philippe with . . . in—"

Floundering to a halt, she glared at Kit when he finished for her, *"Inflagrante?"*

"In a compromising situation," she corrected angrily.

Kit waved a dismissive hand. "Just another way of saying the same thing. He wouldn't have been waiting for you, and you would have taken the next ship home. That is what I am doing for you now, if you will only be sensible and tell me why you're so irritated about it."

"Because you're only doing it now when I've become an inconvenience for you," she blurted. "Do you think I'm deaf? I heard you quite clearly."

His brows lowered. "Surely, you aren't referring to my choice of words when I reached the ship after fighting my way across the beach. Even a complete idiot would understand that I was in no mood to be diplomatic."

"Excuse me, but as a *deuced inconvenience,* I find it difficult to distinguish between diplomacy and truth."

Kit put a hand over his eyes. "Dear God. I had hoped for a modicum of restraint here, but I can see it was in vain." He looked at her over the edge of his palm, then shook his head. "Angela, if I have hurt your feelings, I apologize."

She sat quite still. It was the first time he had ever uttered anything near an apology. For a moment, she didn't know what to say. Then she asked softly, "Are you certain you wish to admit to committing an error?"

Faint lines bracketed his mouth in a smile. "Perhaps

this one time. It would help, however, if I knew exactly what I was apologizing for . . . was it the inconvenience remark?"

"Partially." She heaved a sigh. Communication, it was said, was the key to avoiding misunderstandings. If she took a chance and told him how she felt, perhaps his explanation would at least provide an answer.

Lacing her fingers together, she took a deep breath and said, "I feel that you are merely trying to rid yourself of a burden that has grown much too inconvenient by returning me to London. Is that the case, Kit?"

She couldn't look up at him, afraid of what she might see. His laughter was soft and beguiling. "No," he said gently, "that is not the case. I am returning you to London for the very reason I stated—it is too dangerous for you to remain aboard the *Sea Tiger.*"

Looking up, she asked, "And that is all?"

"That is all." He paused, then added, "Besides, it's becoming bloody annoying to issue threats to members of my crew who stare at you a bit too closely."

"Have you?"

"Actually, it is Dylan who has been the most energetic on your behalf. I can think of three individuals who do not stand very high in his estimation at this moment because they evinced too much interest in your . . . form . . . when you boarded ship in your wet dress."

That unpleasant memory—the bloodstained dress had been tossed overboard as soon as she could manage it—made her shiver. Angela looked back down at her entwined fingers, and Kit reached out to touch her lightly on her bent head.

"What else is bothering you, angel?"

His soft concern was her undoing. The tears began to flow, hot and searing, choking her. He said nothing, but drew her into his embrace and held her, rocking silently until she finally stopped. Then he offered her a corner of the quilt on which to wipe her eyes and nose, wryly observing that she should really carry a handkerchief for such emergencies.

When he tucked a finger beneath her chin to tilt her face up to his, she did not try to avoid him. There was a subtle change in his expression, one she had not seen before. She shifted slightly, snuffling in a most ungenteel fashion.

"You're not a woman who should make a habit of weeping," he said lightly. "Your nose is as red as a cherry."

"Thank you!"

Laughing, he drew her close again, this time pulling her into his lap. She lay her head against the strong bend of his arm and shoulder, sighing.

"I know what's bothering you, angel. Mr. Buttons told me how brave you were when you were attacked." She shuddered, and his embrace tightened. "Listen to me— you did what you had to do. Do you think you're the only one who has ever been forced to that end? I can tell you that you're not."

"Nothing excuses what I did." Her voice broke slightly, and she steadied it before saying, "I killed a man."

"Some are forced to it at a very young age."

A tinge of bitterness had crept into his voice, and she recalled how he'd once mentioned the fact that he'd been in his first battle at the tender age of eleven. That was when he had received the scar that curved from his brow to his cheek. Odd how she never even noticed it now, when it had first made her shiver with dread at his wicked appearance.

"As you were forced to it?" she asked before her courage failed her. When he didn't reply, she pulled slightly away and looked at him. "Tell me, Kit. I need to know that I'm not the only one who has ever felt this way."

Instead of answering, he removed her from his lap and rose to his feet. He stood for a moment, looking down at her in the thickening gloom. Light through the tiny portholes had dimmed, and the cabin was filled with shadows.

"Where's the lantern?" he asked, and she pointed toward it.

When it was lit, he came back to sit down beside her on the bunk. Lifting her hands, he studied them for a moment, gently caressing her palm, then her fingers.

"Such small hands," he murmured, "to wield a sword." He looked up at her. "When I was first taken by pirates, I was only six. By the time I actually fought in my first battle, I was a veteran of three score or more. Being the youngest aboard ship, I was a powder monkey. My job was to deliver fresh gunpowder to the gundeck. At times, the decks were so slippery with blood and pieces of my mates, that I could scarcely make my way across them. I was so scared at first. The noise, and the screams and moans of the dying. . . ." His gaze grew distant, and she had the eerie impression that he was seeing that small boy instead of her. Then he seemed to recover, raking a hand through his hair and smiling slightly. "I was a quick learner, they told me. Quicker than any boy they'd ever had sail the Spanish Main with them before. Of course, that was probably because I lived longer than any boy who had sailed with them before, too."

After a moment, she managed to ask, "How . . . how did you come to be with pirates?"

He gave her a faintly cynical smile. "That is an excellent question. I still ask it myself."

When it seemed as if he didn't intend to elaborate, she said, "I suppose it happened to you in almost the same manner as it happened to me."

"God, no."

The harshness of his voice took her aback, and she sat in shocked silence. As if he understood how he'd shocked her, he tried a smile that was more of a grimace.

"It's really not a pleasant tale, angel. You're better off not knowing it, believe me."

She reached out to touch him, her hands curling around his in a comforting grip. "If ever you want to talk about it, I will be glad to listen."

Lifting their entwined hands to his mouth, he kissed the tips of her fingers, smiling slightly. "I intended to comfort you. Why is it that you're trying to comfort me?"

"I think," she said softly, "we are comforting each other."

"Ah. So that's it. I should have known you'd turn this around on me."

Despite the lightness of his tone, she heard a thread of his usual cynicism. This time, instead of distressing her, she recognized and accepted the reason for it. It was the only method he had of dealing with his pain. She had the release of tears, but Kit could never allow others to get even a glimpse of his anguish.

"Of course," she said with a shaky little laugh. "I couldn't let you win, could I?"

"No, angel. Not you." He leaned forward and kissed the tip of her nose. "You never surrender easily."

Closing her eyes when he pulled her against him, Angela felt her heart constrict as he bent his head to kiss her. The first, brief contact of their lips sent a shiver through her, and he could feel her trembling.

"Cold, sweeting?" he murmured against her mouth, his breath warm and enticing. She managed to shake her head, and heard his soft laughter. "I thought not . . . no, don't pull away. I think I've found another method of sharing comfort. . . ."

Kissing her mouth, her eyelids, then her cheeks, his mouth moved lower, tasting and teasing until she was clinging to him with all her senses swimming. As she pressed close to him from chest to waist, Angela's pulses began to throb with wild expectation. It wasn't just what he was doing—though his hands were certainly coaxing sweet responses from her body—it was the fact that he had shared more with her than ever before. There was an intimacy between them now that had nothing to do with sex.

For the first time, Kit Saber had given her a glimpse into his deepest soul, and she felt as if they were one indivisible being. This was what she had thought she'd shared with Philippe, this knowledge of another's heart. But now, she knew differently. Now, she knew the heart of a man worthy of her love.

For Angela, it made all the difference in the world.

That night, while new moonlight streamed through the portholes and lantern light swayed with the rocking of the ship, she gave her heart and soul to a pirate captain. There were no reservations in her mind, no lingering doubts. The soft whispers and hushed murmurs they made filled the cabin and her heart.

Eighteen

Just after midnight Kit suffered a sudden and acute attack of bronchitis. He woke her, coughing and hacking, sounding as if he were dying. Angela ran for Turk, pounding on his cabin door. He opened it at once, looking as if he had not slept.

"It's . . . Kit," she gasped out. "Coughing so dreadfully. . . ."

"I shall come at once." Turk stepped back into his cabin and grabbed a small leather bag, then followed her.

Kit had staggered from Angela's cabin into the companionway, and was bent over, still coughing. Turk lifted him as if he were a small child, carried him to his own cabin, and placed him gently in his bunk.

Frantic with concern, Angela hovered about like—in Turk's words—a hen with its only egg. Turk ordered her from the cabin, relenting only when she pleaded to stay.

"Very well, but you must cooperate fully with my regimen of medication," he said, and she agreed. Soon, the cabin smelled strongly of pine, eucalyptus, and sandalwood. Huge vats of steaming water created moisture on the walls, dispersing aromatic clouds of herbs. Kit huddled over bowls of the water with a towel over his head, his body jerking in racking coughs.

During one of his worst attacks, Turk moved behind him and applied pressure to points on Kit's throat, neck, and upper back. It seemed to help lessen the fits of coughing.

"What caused this?" Angela whispered as she dipped another towel into the steaming water.

"All that smoke from the battle, I imagine." Turk did not pause in his ministrations, and Kit seemed beyond response. "It inflames his bronchial tubes. This is not one of his more serious attacks. I would say he should be doing excellently by morning."

Angela gazed doubtfully at Kit. His complexion alternated between red from the steam, and a gray pallor that was distinctly unhealthy. Turk had ordered a drink made of willow bark to be given him, and Kit had drank it without a murmur, a grave indication that he was truly ill.

To her amazement, by morning, as Turk had predicted, Kit was much better. Still weak, however, he remained in his cabin most of the day. Angela sat beside him reading, and when he woke from a frequent nap, she brought him cool water or more medication.

"You don't need to sit with me," he said crossly in late afternoon. "I'm not a child."

She smiled. "No, but you are certainly as cranky as an infant. Here. Drink this willow bark tea Turk sent down for you."

"I don't want it."

"But he said—"

Sitting up with a snarl, Kit said coldly, "I don't give a damn what he said. Take it away."

She jerked to her feet, her chin lifting angrily. "Very

well. If you insist upon behaving like a naughty child, then you deserve to be ill. And you can shout for someone else to bring you more water because I shan't be here."

With that, she left his cabin, slamming the door behind her as hard as she could. Being crafted from heavy oak, it didn't make as loud a noise as she'd hoped, but she was certain it conveyed her irritation with him.

"He's cross as an entire nest of wasps," she told Dylan a few minutes later, leaning on the gunwale to watch the sunset.

Dylan turned, a faint smile on his face. "What else is new? At least you still have your head."

"So to speak." She smiled wryly. "I think I shall visit Emily. She is much more pleasant company. Has she recovered from our ordeal?"

"Much quicker than I thought. She's in the galley telling Beans how to steam vegetables. Maybe you ought to rescue both of them. Beans ain't the most patient of cooks, and Miss Emily is not the most rational of females. They might both end up throwing around pots and pans before it's over."

Laughing, Angela went to find Emily. The kitchen was small and greasy. Clutter lined walls and shelves; strings of garlic and herbs hung from hooks in the ceiling and on the walls, and tin jars of spices added a pungent scent to the air.

Beans and Emily were toe to toe, both glaring at one another when Angela arrived. "Get her outta here," Beans snarled, gesturing at Emily with a dripping wooden spoon. "I ain't steamin' no damn vegetables."

A huge cauldron simmered on the stove, and several

smaller pots rattled cheerfully as steam boiled into the air in aromatic clouds. A vat of beef soaking in brine sat in one corner.

"It's better for you," Emily insisted. She gestured at the soaking meat. "Who wants to eat that?"

"Come along, Emily." Angela took her arm and escorted her, protesting, to the galley door. She paused and looked back at Beans in his filthy apron. A triumphant smile curled his mouth. Angela couldn't resist saying, "We shall send Turk to advise you on food preparation instead."

A dismayed howl followed them down the companionway as she and Emily made their escape. "There," Angela said, "That was all you needed to say to him. I imagine there will be some steamed vegetables at our next meal."

"I hope so. I was beginning to enjoy staying on the island. The food was fresh and delicious." She paused, then asked, "How is Captain Saber?"

"Better, but as surly as a wet cat. Turk has some remarkable cures at his disposal. Too bad he hasn't found one for an ill temper."

Emily laughed. "I have a feeling you wouldn't want Saber to change a bit."

"Perhaps not. But it would be nice if I knew what he was thinking at times." Angela hesitated, then said, "Emily, do you suppose he's being truthful about his reasons for wanting me to go back to England?"

Emily's brown eyes glanced away from her, then back. "I don't know," she said frankly. "It seems logical. After all, it hasn't exactly been the safest voyage in history. I do think, however, that he'd rather you stay with him."

Leaning against the smooth, polished rail of the fore-deck, Angela said, "Well, I hardly think he'll send me away now." She flushed when Emily gave her a quizzical look. "We've grown quite close, you know."

"Yes." Emily looked away. "So I understand."

Silence fell between them, broken only by the familiar ship noises of wind in the sails and creaking lines. Angela looked up at the swelling canvas where it strained against lines and masts. The wind was a steady force, pushing them ever onward. When it died, the *Sea Tiger* lay motionless in the water, at the mercy of the next good wind. It could buffet them in a storm, or die off completely. There were moments she compared Kit to the wind, and despaired of ever capturing his love. But surely he would never send her away now, not after the night they had spent together. No, he must have changed his mind.

"It's much better this way." Kit dug his fingers into the smooth wood of the gunwale, not looking down at Angela. He didn't want to see the shadows in her eyes, or the slight quivering of her lower lip that she was trying so hard to steady.

"Yes," she said in a low voice. "I agree."

"You'll be home soon, and this will all be behind you."

For a moment, nothing else was said. Pipe smoke drifted on the wind, pungent and fragrant, mixing with the familiar scents of wet rope and wood. Perched atop a spar, Rollo croaked a ditty that usually angered Angela, but she didn't seem to be paying attention this time.

Instead, she said without looking at him, "I suppose I won't see you again."

He hesitated. A three-masted sloop rode at anchor on the starboard side of the *Sea Tiger,* waiting to take Angela and Emily aboard. Negotiations had already been made, and in a short time, the *Swallow* would dock at the Pool between London Bridge and the Tower. Angela would be safely home.

Promises were so easily made and so deuced difficult to keep. Why break her heart when he didn't know what might happen? A brisk wind stirred pale tendrils of the hair that peeked from beneath her muslin bonnet, and he resisted the urge to tuck it back under the scooped brim.

"You do know," he said, "that since the fracas on St. Thomas, every man-o'-war in the Atlantic is looking for us. I can't promise that I'll see you soon."

"Of course."

Damn. Why couldn't he say what he knew she was waiting to hear? Three little words that came so easily to some and so bloody hard to him. He'd said them to only one person, and the memory of that time in his life still scalded him. No. It wasn't the right time. Later, when he saw her again, he would be free to tell her how he felt. By then, he would have resolved the unanswered questions in his life one way or the other.

"They're waiting, Angela," he said gruffly, and took her by the arm. The brief contact jolted him, even through the embroidered sleeves of the spencer she wore over her day dress. Dylan had added new garments to their limited wardrobe, filched only the week before from the trunks of a French aristocrat bound for the Indies. Needless to say, he had not informed Angela or Emily whence the new

clothes had come. Kit had to admit that the style suited
Angela perfectly, with the low, square-cut neckline
trimmed in lace ruching and barely hiding the swell of her
breasts. After seeing her clad in light, simple gowns for
so long, it was as if he were seeing her for the first time.
This Angela he could well visualize in an elegant drawing
room.

"The ship is waiting, Angela," he said again, and gestured toward the rail where Dylan and Turk waited. Emily
stood with a tear-stained face next to Dylan, but thank-
fully, she was not hysterical.

Dylan gave a quick twist of his head that sent the long
dark rope of his hair over one shoulder in a graceful
motion. Sunlight picked out blue glints in his hair and
made his cat-gold eyes glitter like Spanish coins. He took
Emily's hand in his and bent to give her a gentle kiss.
They whispered softly to each other, oblivious of the
glances they received.

Smothering a twinge of envy at their indifference to
those around them, Kit fought the impulse to take Angela
in his arms.

He gestured to the opening in the rail instead. "I'll
help you over the side and into the jolly boat."

Shaking her head, Angela avoided his eyes. "No, Turk
has already offered to see me safely aboard the *Swallow.*
As my trunks have been loaded, they need only their
passengers to make sail. The captain is beginning to look
quite impatient, I fear."

Kit glanced up and saw Captain Hastings signal to
him from the *Swallow.* It was obvious he wanted to be
on his way. Any more delay, and he was quite likely to

change his mind. That would never do. Kit knew his duty, however unpleasant it might be.

"Take her, Turk," he said stiffly, and pushed her ever so gently into the waiting giant's hands. "I'll be below if you should need me."

Angela did not protest, but glanced at him with green eyes silvery with tears. There was a taut set to her chin, as if she dared not relax her guard. "Farewell, Kit," she finally whispered, and he gave a terse nod, unable to force words past the tightness in his throat.

Pivoting on his heels before he lost the thread of reason that had compelled him to send her away, Kit crossed the deck. He never turned to glance back, afraid that, like Lot's wife, he would be turned to a pillar of salt by the vision of Angela disappearing from his life. Ridiculous, really. He hardly knew her. How could one know a woman's mind well in only a few weeks?

Ah, but he could recall the sweet slope of her shoulder and the tantalizing swell of her breast well enough, as well as other portions of her that were even more alluring. It didn't help to recall the sound of her laughter, low and musical, like the light tinkle of silver bells. Nor was it easy to reflect upon her rather touching courage in the face of adversity, and her stiff-necked pride when any other woman would have dissolved into maudlin wails. *Damn.* How could he send away a woman who insisted upon saving the life of a stranded jellyfish, and a few hours later killed a man to save her friend's life? It was beyond his comprehension, but he'd done it.

Someone should paint a picture of this scene, he thought tiredly as he entered his cabin and sank into his deep-cushioned chair. It could be entitled *Fool at Work*. Or any other appropriate title that utilized the word *fool*.

Rubbing a hand over his eyes, he sat in his cabin long after he heard the unmistakable sounds of the *Sea Tiger* getting under way. Afternoon shadows lengthened and grew dim, and Rollo muttered a sleepy chorus and tucked his head under a wing. Kit couldn't even remember the bird joining him, and wondered if he was growing balmy. He must be, or he would have already shrugged off the depression he felt at sending Angela on to England. There was too much to do to wallow in self-pity.

Rising from his chair, Kit made his way topside.

Gravesend was the first town on the Thames as the *Swallow* sailed upriver. The Pool, where the center of the maritime world thrived, lay between the Tower and London Bridge. Rubbish floated on the surface of the river as the vessel slithered around the quays and lines of warehouses. Angela had forgotten the smell of rotting wood, dead sea life, and refuse, but it came back to her in a rush when she went to stand at the gunwale.

"Ugh," Emily muttered through a handkerchief at her nose. "It doesn't smell at all like the cove on St. Thomas."

Angela didn't reply. She didn't want to think about St. Thomas. Or the *Sea Tiger*. Or Kit. Numb from sleepless nights and an aching heart, she could only stare miserably as the ship nudged against the dock. London's familiar sights held no interest for her at this moment. All she wanted was to find a soft bed that didn't rock and lie in it.

"Miss Angela," Emily interrupted her misery excitedly, "look who is waiting for us!"

Fighting a sudden surge of hope, Angela turned to see her parents standing on the stone quay peering anxiously up at the rail of the ship. Her heart clutched. Her mother looked the same, her short, curly hair lightly dusted with strands of silver and her abundant figure impeccably gowned. But Papa—there were deeper lines carved into his face, and his dark hair was almost all silver. His eyes scanned the rail of the ship in a searching gaze, and she lifted a hand in greeting. Her mother, she saw, began to cry immediately, while her father patted her with his usual distracted motions, lifting his arm to return Angela's wave.

Angela's smile and pleasure were genuine when she met them on the dock. She was enveloped in a tight embrace by her mother, who wept copiously onto her neck and said over and over that she had thought she'd never see her daughter again, while her father hovered just behind like a bee over a flower, offering a word here and there.

"My poor girl, my poor girl," Alicia Lindell kept saying, while John Lindell *harrumphed!* and said "Now Alicia" several times. The "poor girl" altered to a litany of "it's over now."

"Oh, I'm so very glad to see you again," Angela said at last, and discovered that she truly meant it. If she could not be with Kit, she at least had her loving family around her. Gently disengaging herself from her mother's clasp, she turned to include Emily in their circle. "We are both glad to be back," she said pointedly, and Emily beamed when Mr. Lindell put an arm around her shoulders and gave her a squeeze and a gruff "Welcome home, Emily."

A light rain began to fall, and Mrs. Lindell scurried toward the waiting carriage, calling to them to join her while their trunks were fetched. In a very short time, the elegant landau rolled away from the docks.

Angela gazed out the window, paying only the scantiest attention to her mother's chatter about friends and acquaintances who would be thrilled to have her home again. Rain spattered against the windowpanes in trickling rivulets, diffusing the familiar landmarks. They passed the Mansion House, where the lord mayor of London resided, traveled down Cannon Street past St. Paul's Cathedral, then crossed the intersection where Blackfriar's Road changed to Farringdon. With St. James and Piccadilly soon behind them, they entered the fashionable district of Mayfair, where John Lindell had built a most comfortable residence ten years before.

As the carriage turned up their street, John Lindell said into the growing silence, "My circumstances have grown even better since you left us, Angela."

Dragging her attention to her father, she murmured, "How nice for you, Papa."

"Yes, yes, quite so. Only a month ago, I was approached by an important man—well, perhaps not the man himself, but one of his barristers—who made me a most lucrative business offer. Of all the men in London he could have chosen, he chose me."

Angela managed an interested smile. "I'm certain he made the wisest choice."

"I like to think so." Mr. Lindell sat back with a satisfied smile. "Rubbing elbows with Charles Sheridan is not something one does every day, you know."

Frowning, Angela tried to recall where she had heard that name. "Charles Sheridan? Why does that name sound familiar?"

"Because," Lindell leaned forward to say with an even wider smile, "he is the Duke of Tremayne. Imagine—we have been invited to a soirée at his home. We shall be in company with nobility, if you please."

Alicia Lindell fanned herself briskly and said in a faintly breathless tone, "I cannot imagine what I shall say! Or wear. Oh my—it is so fortunate that you have returned from your perilous voyage in time to join us, Angela." Her wide blue eyes narrowed slightly as she regarded her daughter. "That time shall, of course, be explained with a most prosaic article in the papers. Your father has already attended to it, so we shall not mention it again."

Angela gazed at her mother. Alicia's fan moved rapidly back and forth. So, her capture by pirates was to be explained with a—*prosaic*—article. Kit Saber's name would never be coupled with hers in any fashion, because that would be too detrimental to her father's career. And her mother's social life. She swallowed a tart reply, and turned her attention to the rain-wet street outside the carriage window. It was as it had always been. Not that she minded, really, for she had expected little else from her parents. She was being unfair. They loved her and wanted to protect her. But she was expected to adhere to society's rules with no volition of her own. At least she knew what was required of her. And she knew they wanted only to shield her from cruel gossip and snubs. It would never have occurred to either of them that she might want anything else.

But she couldn't help wondering if her mother had any interest in knowing what had really happened these past two months. Would she care that her only daughter had fallen in love with a pirate? Or that she missed him horribly and wondered if he ever thought about her? Somehow, she didn't think it would occur to her mother to ask those questions.

Morning sunlight streamed through the windows of the breakfast room with a cheery glow when Angela entered the next morning. Her father looked up from his daily paper and smiled at her.

"You are radiant as always, dear," he said as she took a chair at the table. "I cannot tell you how much you've been missed."

Angela returned his smile. A good night's rest had restored her pleasure at being with her family again. "Thank you, Papa." She unfolded a snowy linen napkin over her lap while a servant offered her food from silver chafing dishes. John Lindell had gone back to reading his newspaper, but looked up again when she asked if there was anything of note in the news.

"The usual. Napoleon and his machinations are wreaking havoc over half of Europe. I cannot imagine why Parliament has signed a treaty with him when they must know he will break it as soon as is expedient. *Humph.* He has spies everywhere. Everyone knows they are spies and still entertain them blatantly. It's foolish and ridiculous."

Amused, Angela said, "If spies are being entertained, there must be a good reason for it, Papa."

"Hah! Some men will allow a beautiful woman to get away with anything, even political treachery. Foolishness, I say, pure foolishness."

"A beautiful spy, Papa? I'm fascinated. Whatever are you talking about?"

"This Frenchwoman, La Diabolique. Diabolical is an astute term for her, I admit. Rumor has it that she's devastatingly beautiful. Raven hair, blue eyes, and skin like Devonshire cream—it's pathetic. She must be forty if she's a day, yet men fall at her feet like sparrows in a hailstorm." He leaned forward, shaking his paper angrily. "It was even said that Pitt entertained her, and if that should happen, government secrets would never be safe!"

"But you know how rumors are. Few of them are true and are often so well embroidered with fantasy that they bear little resemblance to the truth. Perhaps this La Diabolique only requested an audience with the Prime Minister. Out of that could have come this fantastic tale of an alliance."

"True enough, I suppose," Lindell said grudgingly. "Still, I say she should be put on the next ship across the Channel. The infernal woman is everywhere, I'm told. At soirées, royal balls—the prince made an absolute cake of himself by tailing after her all one evening and engaging her in earnest conversation. But what can one expect from a prince who married Mrs. Fitzherbert? Dear God. What a mess this country is in." He leaned forward slightly. "That is why I am so impressed with the duke. He has vision."

"The duke?"

"Tremayne. I told you—Charles Sheridan. He is very adroit not only in business, but in politics. The man casts a long shadow, and I am most impressed with some of his ideas."

Not at all interested in the machinations of the government at the moment, Angela asked if her mother would be joining them for breakfast.

"Alas, no. She has one of her headaches and took a powder to soothe it." After a short pause, he added, "I think it was the excitement at seeing you again. We were so worried, you know." Another pause. Then, "When the captain of the *Scrutiny* told us that you had been taken by pirates. . . ." He let his voice trail into a pregnant silence, and Angela tensed.

"The captain of—do you mean Captain Turnower?"

"But of course. How else do you think we knew about it? When everyone else was either taken prisoner or murdered by those beastly pirates—it was a miracle Turnower escaped—he was all that was left to tell of your fate. Oh, we agonized so many nights, wondering if you were still alive and unharmed."

Her fork clattered to the edge of her plate with a brittle clink. "Captain Turnower is a coward and a liar."

John Lindell stared at her. "Whatever do you mean?"

"He would have left us tied to the mast of a burning ship rather than give up room in the lifeboats to two women he did not want aboard his ship in the first place. If the pirates had not taken us, we would have gone down with the *Scrutiny*."

"That's a rather hard accusation, Angela."

"But true." She took a deep breath. "I was there, Papa. I know what happened."

Lindell's hands crunched the pages of his paper with a loud rustle, and his face took on a hard expression. "If this is true, then I shall see that Turnower is properly punished."

"*If* this is true?" She stared at him. "Do you doubt my word?"

"No, no, not at all. But I had heard . . ." He stopped and looked down at his plate.

"You heard what, Papa?"

He looked back up at her, sighing. "I heard that you were taken by the pirates, not rescued. There is a vast difference, and I assumed—Angela, I never told your mother about it. She knows only that you were picked up by a passing ship when the *Scrutiny* went down, and it has taken you some time to get back to England."

Gesturing to the newspaper he still had wadded in his fists, she asked carefully, "And the article released about our rescue? Does it go into lurid detail, or is that only for those adept at reading between the lines?"

His mouth thinned into a hard line as he murmured, "It states that you have been abroad for a holiday before your marriage to the baron."

"Marriage!" Shocked, she stared at him for several long moments. The faint clatter of dishes in the steward's pantry behind closed doors indicated that the servants were craning their necks to listen. Angela smothered the burning desire to shout her defiance and said calmly, "And who am I to marry?"

"Baron Von Gosden-Lear, of course. I am well aware

that you did not marry your Royalist. His letter arrived here two weeks after you had gone."

"And you read it."

"Of course. Angela, I was frantic. I would have read the king's correspondence if I had thought it would give me information about your welfare."

Slightly shamed, she nodded. "Very well. I understand. But I do not understand your insistence upon my wedding the baron. Has it not occurred to you that I am well past the age where you may force me into such an action?"

"Naturally. But in light of the scandal that your disappearance could have caused, what else was I to do? I had to concoct a plausible explanation that would not damage your reputation and render you unfit for marriage to any proper suitor. Surely, you understand."

"I know, Papa. But I am back now and all is well." Pushing at a coddled egg with the tines of her fork, Angela knew he was trying to maneuver her into doing as he wished. But not for nothing had she managed to survive aboard a pirate ship, and she looked up at him after a moment and said softly, "I refuse to wed the baron. It is useless to pursue that course. Should you persevere, I will think little of telling the truth about the past few months of my life."

John Lindell just stared at her without speaking, until the silence dragged on unbearably. Finally he gave a helpless shrug and said, "Do as you will, Angela. I cannot fight both you and your mother. I have too much else on my mind at the moment."

It was not the most auspicious way to begin her first day back in England. Angela had the dismaying thought that she would have much preferred remaining aboard the *Sea Tiger* with pirates. At least the battle lines there had been clearly drawn.

Nineteen

Alicia Lindell grasped her daughter's arm tightly. "Just look," she whispered. "So many earls and dukes . . . why, even a baron is of little consequence here."

Rather chagrined by her mother's reaction to the elegant drawing room filled with guests, Angela whispered, "Of even less consequence is an untitled banker."

Her mother shot her a frown. "Don't be impertinent. Are you not the least impressed by the assemblage here?"

Truthfully, she had to admit to a certain awe. Where else but in London could one find such a vast and glittering array of jewels and nobility in one gigantic room? Ornate gold pillars and wall coverings embroidered with birds in flight and leafy palm fronds provided an elegant background for the sumptuously garbed guests that danced beneath five—no, six—massive crystal chandeliers that held several hundred candles apiece. It was all very impressive and ostentatious. Appropriate, Angela thought with a trace of cynicism, for a duke said to dabble in politics and profit.

In the two months since she had been back in London, she had heard more than enough about Tremayne. Urbane, sophisticated, witty, his present held as many mysteries as his past. Rumors flocked about many of the peerage, but Tremayne seemed to have gathered more than his share of gossip. His first wife had died under mysterious circumstances, it was said, and his second wife had succumbed to a fever several years before. Neither wife, rumor held it, had been very pleasant.

Then there was the matter of his only son and heir. It was whispered that there had been a violent quarrel and the duke had killed his own son. The cause of the quarrel was said to be a woman, which lent spice to the rumors. No one had seen or heard from the heir in years. All portraits of him had been removed from the walls, and if mention of him was made, the duke refused to respond. It was as if he had never existed. Few could even recall his name, and those who did forbore repeating it. It was as if he had disappeared off the face of the earth.

"Very mysterious," John Lindell had agreed testily when she confronted him, "but hardly sinister. If the boy died, it must have affected the duke greatly. Is it any wonder that he avoids mentioning him?"

Angela's efforts to determine the exact nature of the business between her father and Tremayne had been futile. Lindell was as close-mouthed as a clam, as Dylan would say.

"Look dear," Alicia whispered excitedly, "here comes the duke with your father . . . oh, my, he's going to introduce us!"

Turning, Angela saw a tall, handsome gentleman with silver-flecked dark hair at her father's side. She had the thought that he looked exactly as a duke should—austere, reserved, and aristocratic. He carried himself with the air of a man who knew his own worth and did not have to flaunt it. Angela had never met him or anyone like him.

Dukes had not frequented her social set. Yet there was something about him that was vaguely familiar.

The duke's steady gaze was unnerving, and made her much too self-conscious. She hid a tremor of nervous reaction with a graceful curtsy when her father made the introductions. Childhood hours of deportment classes came to her rescue, so that she was saved from embarrassing herself.

"Your Grace," her father was saying, "may I introduce my wife and daughter. . . ." John Lindell sounded as if he were about to burst with self-importance as he made the introductions, and Angela kept her gaze trained downward while the duke spoke to her mother.

"I believe we have corresponding ties, Mrs. Lindell. My mother was by way of being your mother's fourth cousin, is that not so?"

Hand fluttering at her throat, Alicia stammered, "Why, I . . . I never knew that, Your Grace."

"A small tie, to be true, but a tie nonetheless."

Then Charles Sheridan bent forward over Angela's hand, his voice low and well modulated. "It is a very great pleasure to meet you, Miss Lindell. I see that the rumors about your beauty have not been exaggerated."

"You are very kind, Your Grace," she murmured, and met his eyes with a small sense of shock. They were a deep blue, thick-lashed and penetrating, seeming to see through her to the very marrow of her bones.

"No, not at all," he replied with a faint trace of amusement. "Many things may be said of me, but never has the appellation of *kind* been applied to my character. Truthful to the point of tactless, perhaps, but not kind."

Floundering for a polite reply, Angela was saved from the necessity by her mother's intervention.

"Your Grace, we are so pleased that you honored us with an invitation this evening. It is a lovely affair."

Bowing slightly in Alicia's direction, the duke released Angela's gloved hand at last. "I am pleased that you are enjoying it. So often, these things can be such a bore." Raking Angela with another searching glance, he turned to her father again. "Would it distress you, John, if I were to ask your daughter to honor me with the first dance?"

Shocked, Angela heard through a buzzing in her ears her father's delighted acceptance, then the duke took her hand again in a light grip.

"Miss Lindell, it would give me great pleasure if you would accompany me on the dance floor. It is customary to begin with a minuet."

"I . . . I would be honored, Your Grace," she managed to say. Dear Lord. She had not danced in months. What if she stumbled, or forgot the steps?

But the painstaking drills of the dance master her mother had insisted she have as a child came in good stead, and when the musicians began the stately strains, Angela found herself in the middle of the vast dance floor with the Duke of Tremayne. Other couples danced beside them in the slow, elegant steps of the old French dance. She could feel sidelong glances and open stares and knew most of the guests were wondering who she was. John Lindell may have been well known in business circles, but this was an entirely different matter.

When the dance was over and the duke had returned her to her mother's side, he left with a formal bow and murmur of appreciation. Angela could feel her mother trembling with excitement.

"He has effectively ensured your acceptance," Alicia whispered in Angela's ear. "I cannot believe our good fortune. Look at the way everyone is staring at you and whispering."

"This is ridiculous," Angela murmured. "I feel like a porcelain doll in some grotesque masquerade. Do you suppose we could sip punch for a few moments, then steal away without being noticed?"

Giving her an astonished glance, Alicia asked, "Why-ever would we want to do that? Your arrival into the *ton* has just been secured."

"Because this promises to be a deadly dull evening. I know hardly anyone here, and those I do know are insipid bores."

Alicia fluttered her ivory and lace fan rapidly, hiding her frown. "You just danced with the duke, for heaven's sake." Her voice lowered dramatically. "He is a widower, you know. This could be the beginning of a new world for you, Angela, an introduction into the realms of the elite. Can you not see beyond the moment?"

"Mother, really. . . ."

The ivory and lace fan snapped shut with a vigorous click. "I have always envisioned a wonderful life for you," Alicia said with an accusing frown. "Why must you thwart me at every turn? After all, you could be spending this evening with Arthur, instead of at a soirée where the aristocracy is whispering about you."

Arthur being the boring Baron Von Gosden-Lear—who had, just the week before, politely retracted his offer of marriage—Angela decided not to force the issue. It had been an extreme disappointment to her mother that the baron chose not to wed a young woman with a "cloud" over her reputation. The months spent away from London had not been so easily explained to the man intending to wed her, and though Angela had been most satisfied with his decision, Alicia had not.

"Very well, Mama," she said. "I shall endeavor to find some amusement in the evening."

"You could try," her mother said sharply, "to find a suitable husband."

"There isn't one in London I'd choose," Angela murmured, and sighed when her mother's fan flipped open then snapped shut again. It was apparent they would not agree on the subject, and she wished she had kept her misgivings to herself.

A particularly ebullient gentleman in tight knee-breeches and a yellow satin waistcoat chose that moment to approach them, one hand folded over his corpulent middle as he bowed.

"Mrs. Lindell, isn't it?" he said, beaming at them. "And the lovely Miss Lindell. I don't suppose you remember me. . . ."

"Of course I do," Alicia replied with a delighted smile. "One could never forget such a charming gentleman as yourself, Lord Brompton. We first met at Lady Jersey's soirée, did we not?"

"Ah, an excellent memory, Mrs. Lindell. We did, indeed. At that time, I believe your daughter was still abroad." His gaze returned to Angela. "Did you have an amiable journey, Miss Lindell?"

Briefly considering then discarding the notion of telling the truth, Angela contented herself with a faint smile and a nod. Lord Brompton, however, was not to be satisfied with that.

"Come, come, Miss Lindell, surely you can expound upon your journey. Do not be shy." He beamed at her, his fleshy face creasing into a spider web of lines.

"It was . . . quite long," she said, mentally scolding herself for not being more inventive. "And . . . refreshing. But I am glad to be home in England once more." *Another lie.* "Tell us, Lord Brompton, of your recent visit to—Greece, wasn't it?"

She prayed that she had remembered correctly, but her mother chattered so about people she'd met and the things they'd said, that she could hardly be expected to recall them all. Fortunately, his lordship had, indeed, recently visited Greece, and began to regale them with the details. Angela listened politely until he paused to take a breath, then she excused herself and escaped.

Laughing silently at her sudden freedom, she made her way to an alcove near a set of French doors that opened out onto a veranda. She stepped behind the delicate fronds of a huge, potted palm and leaned against the wall. From her vantage point, she could see the crowd yet not be easily seen herself. It was perfect. She wondered why she had not thought of it at once. This sort of affair was her mother's domain, certainly not hers.

Alicia Lindell thrived on social settings. Angela tried to avoid them as much as possible. Even before her fateful voyage, she had not been one to enjoy lavish parties. She had preferred long walks in Hyde Park, or visits with friends, or even just reading in the garden. Now, since coming back to London, these affairs were truly torturous for her.

Frowning slightly, Angela tugged at the fitted fingers of her elbow-length white gloves as she wondered why a man as prominent and influential as the Duke of Tremayne would single her out for notice in front of half of London. She did not flatter herself that it was her beauty, nor did she think he was attempting to ingratiate himself with her father for business purposes. It was a mystery to her why he would bother with the daughter of a banker, no matter how wealthy and powerful that banker might be. Dukes had their own connections and authority; John Lindell would be merely a small cog in the massive wheel of enterprise.

There was another reason. She was certain of it.

Batting absently at the hanging froth of scarlet trumpet vine in his eyes, Kit Saber listened without surprise to the spy he had employed some time ago. Gabriel—no last name had ever been divulged—was nearing the end of his recitation.

One knee bent and nudging against his chest as he sat on the sand, Dylan listened as quietly, if not as attentively. His attention seemed to wander these days, drifting into mind-space where no one else visited. It was quiet on this curve of beach, with the lilting cries of sea birds a musical accompaniment to the rush of surf and distant clatter of the Greek fishing village.

Turk stood with massive arms folded across his chest, the blue tattoos on his face shining brightly in the noon-day sun. Behind the quartet, scattered up the slopes of a mountain thrust from the Aegean Sea, stuccoed buildings reflected white heat. But in the busy marketplace of Limenas on the isle of Thassos, the sea breeze blowing in from the harbor was cool and brisk.

"So," Kit said at last when Gabriel had finished, "she has gone full-circle. Appropriate enough, I suppose, if one considers all that has happened." He stared up at the pine-thick mountains ranging behind the harbor town, where slices of bare rock gilt-edged with sunlight peeked through.

Coughing politely, Gabriel murmured, "And I also have news of the young lady who so recently frequented your company, *mon ami.*"

Stiffening, Kit gave him an icy look. "Do you. Did I ask for news of her?"

"No, no," Gabriel said, "but I thought you might like to know that she is safely in London. Apparently, her ordeal did not affect her. She has become quite the—how do you say it?—*rage* in society. Due mainly, I think, to the Duke of Tremayne's intense interest in her."

Kit went still. *Bloody hell.* Of all the men in London, why him? Fate, it seemed, was laughing up its treacherous sleeve. *God. . . .* Impatient suddenly, despite the peace and beauty around him, Kit rose to his feet. "I think," he said with a deliberation that surprised him more than those listening, "it is time I returned to England."

Gabriel nodded. "It would seem the most auspicious of times to do so. I believe you may at last find the success you have been seeking for so long."

Kit turned to look at him, meeting the dark, liquid gaze that seemed to hold so many secrets. "Why would you think that?"

Giving a Gallic shrug, Gabriel smiled slightly. "Because the one you seek is willing for you to do so, *mon ami."*

So that was it. He had long suspected that this game of cat and mouse had been at her whim, not his persistence. Turk had suggested it more than once, but he had not been willing to listen. It was not in his nature to allow others to direct his course, but he was slowly learning that there were times one must yield to the inevitable.

After Gabriel had accepted his payment of gold coins and departed, Kit turned to Turk. The wind tugged the long white tails of Turk's loose shirt, and they billowed outward.

Nodding slowly, Turk said, "You are correct. It is time to confront what must be confronted. You are aware, of course, that there is more than one devil to vanquish in London."

Kit drew in a sharp breath that made his lungs ache with the pressure of salt air and sea spice. "Of course I'm aware of it. Do you think I haven't counted each and every one?"

"On the contrary—I am certain of it. I cannot help but wonder, however, which issue you will deem most important."

"Neither can I."

Silence fell, broken finally by Dylan's muttered remark that he was returning to the ship. "I'm tired of bread soaked in olive oil and honeyed walnuts. Don't they have anything else on this bloody island?"

Amusement creased Turk's face. "Silly boy. Pine honey and olive oil are the two most important exports on Thassos. It is comparable to the production of wine in France."

Dylan shot him a sour glance. "I'd rather sample the wine, thank you."

"Not to worry," Kit interrupted. "We've lingered here long enough. We leave on the next high tide." He stared out over the bay where huge blocks of marble quarried during the time of the Romans still lay half-submerged in the lashing waves. He had wasted too much time. Now that he had made his decision, he was ready.

Twenty

"*Another* invitation?" Angela resisted rolling her eyes. She turned to face her mother, who held the square of vellum in one hand, tapping it against her cheek thoughtfully. "I don't wish to be constantly with the duke," Angela added, knowing even as she said it that it would not dissuade her mother in the least.

"Have you no sense at all, girl?" Alicia snapped irritably. The vellum square was tossed back on the silver tray lying upon the carved mahogany table in their entrance hall. She followed Angela into the parlor to continue the discussion. "He is honoring you with his favor. Every eligible woman in London would love to take your place by his side at this ball."

Flinging herself into a brocade wing chair, Angela said wearily. "Then let them."

Exasperated, Alicia pleaded, "Why do you not care for his company?"

Angela sat up. "Oh, but I enjoy his company. How could I not? He's handsome, intelligent, witty, urbane, sophisticated—have I left out any of his more glowing attributes? Oh. I forgot—wealthy beyond all imagination."

"Then why," moaned Alicia, "don't you want to accept his invitations?"

"Because I have the inescapable feeling that his interest is only superficial. After all, the man is more than twice my age." Angela fielded the blank stare her mother gave her with an increasing swell of frustration. It was not something she found easy to explain, even to herself, but when she was with the duke, she felt as if his attentions were cursory and perfunctory. Oh, he was the perfect gentleman. At every soirée or social event to which he invited her, his manners were impeccable. He gave her enough attention to draw whispers, but not enough to launch rumors. Her parents were included often enough to squelch any unsavory speculation, yet there were rides in Hyde Park and the occasional morning visit that gave rise to her mother's hopes for the duke as a future son-in-law.

Added to the rumors she'd heard about him, the duke had become an increasingly mysterious force in her life. No other gentleman approached her any longer, sensing that to step on the toes of the Duke of Tremayne would be an exceedingly unwise course.

"Angela," her mother wheedled, "if his interest is only superficial, then you should endeavor to endear him to you. Just think—you could be a duchess."

She shot her mother a sardonic glance. "Really. And I could make a cake of myself by throwing my affections at his feet. I cannot believe you would actually want me to do that."

"Not make a fool of yourself, no. But it wouldn't hurt for you to be nice to him."

"Exactly what," Angela asked carefully, "do you consider being *nice?* I have not offended him by uttering unladylike words, nor have I dumped a cup of tea in his lap, or even expressed disinterest in his attentions. What is it you're asking me to do?"

Throwing up her hands, Alicia said, "You are the most stubborn girl."

"Mother," Angela said, leaning forward in her chair to fix her with a steady gaze, "I am no longer a girl. I am a grown woman, and I know my own mind. Please do not treat me as a child any longer." She stood up, managing a smile at her mother's open-mouthed expression. "Allow me to make decisions about my life without interference, please."

Alicia sat in silence for a moment, then sighed heavily. "You've changed a great deal. Exactly what happened to you while you were gone, Angela?"

How did she say she'd met a pirate, fallen in love, and become a woman? She didn't. It would not only shock her mother, it would hurt her. And it would be pointless anyway. Alicia Lindell would never understand why her daughter still awoke most mornings with a tear-wet pillow.

So she said merely, "I grew up. Adversity has that affect on some people."

"I daresay. Even flighty Emily has changed. She's prone to long periods of dismal silence now, when once one could rarely get her to cease her endless, silly prattle." Her voice faltered suddenly. "Angela dear—I only want your happiness. Truly, I do. I shall be gone one day, and I want to go to my grave knowing that you shall never want for anything. Please do this for me."

After a moment of potent silence, Angela said, "Very

well. If it will please you, I shall accept the duke's invitation."

Only her mother's intense pleasure alleviated the dismay she felt at capitulating. Angela half listened as Alicia babbled happily about gowns and gloves and jewels for the ball. The prince was to be there, so it was extremely important that Angela be well turned out, of course, and oh, did she think that she might be presented to Prince George?

Angela answered her mother's queries in a murmur, wishing she had more fortitude. It promised to be another tiresome evening listening to stilted conversation and sly innuendoes that she knew were meant for her. After all, she was hardly a member of the exclusive set, and there were those who considered it their duty to make her fully aware of that fact. Never in front of the duke, of course. No, they were much too clever for that. It would have earned them one of Charles Sheridan's famous set-downs, and after that they would be viewed as *de trop* in proper company.

Thank God it was still a fortnight away. She had plenty of time to brace herself for the inevitable dull evening.

Carriages lined the curved drive leading up to the graystone mansion. Footmen waited patiently while the drivers jockeyed for position in the slow-moving line, while ahead lights glittered as if all the stars had fallen from the sky to adorn the house.

"You're lovely, Angela," her mother observed from the coach seat opposite her. "Amaranthus is a perfect color on you. I knew it would be. And Mother's ruby necklace and earrings are just the right touch. They bring out the pink in that purple."

"Shouldn't I be wearing a crown with this?" Angela could not resist asking and saw her father smile.

"Don't be saucy." Alicia gave her a reproving look, but was in too good a mood to be irritated. "Be careful not to wrinkle your train. You aren't sitting on it, are you?"

"No, Mama. I cannot imagine why I ever let you talk me into having a train, however. It's a dreadful bother."

John Lindell surveyed his daughter with a critical eye. "Is her neckline supposed to be that low?" he asked finally, and Angela smothered a laugh.

"Don't be absurd, John," Alicia said with a tap of her fan on his arm. "Of course necklines are low. You have never complained about mine."

"Perhaps because Angela is more—endowed," he muttered, then lapsed into silence when Angela laughed aloud.

Glancing at her husband, Alicia ignored his comment, and the remainder of the ride was spent in silence.

"Impressive," Angela murmured when they arrived at the front door and she was helped from the coach by her father's footman. She surveyed the crowd with growing dismay. "This will be a dreadful crush."

"Isn't it wonderful?" Alicia warbled, and Angela exchanged a rueful glance with her father.

Only Alicia truly enjoyed these affairs. John Lindell went to please his wife and advance his business interests and contacts. Angela, of course, attended most reluctantly.

After ascending the curved flight of stairs to the ballroom, the Lindells were announced by a solemn-faced servant at the entrance. People turned, but to Angela, the sea of faces was an anonymous blur. Several guests spoke as they made their way through the crowd, and she found herself nodding and smiling automatically.

This was a much larger room than the one used for smaller soirées and gatherings. Angela had no doubt that her father's entire three-story house would fit into this cavernous space. No less than twenty crystal chandeliers hung at twenty-foot intervals from the high, vaulted ceiling. Groups of musicians were situated in alcoves or tucked into small balconies spaced around the room. Despite the vastness of the ballroom, the air was already hot and stuffy, cloying with perfumes and scents and the pungent smell of tobacco.

There were so many guests that it was almost impossible to keep the train of her gown from being stepped upon, and Angela despaired of getting through an entire evening without having it ripped away. She had no patience for this; even with the train looped gracefully over one arm, it was a nuisance.

As soon as possible, Angela began to make her way to the safety of an alcove despite her mother's efforts to keep her in the midst of the crowd.

"The duke will appear soon," Alicia hissed, grabbing at her arm. "At least stand here until then."

"If he wants me, he can find me," Angela said firmly. "If I linger in this crowd much longer, he will find me stretched on the floor in a dead faint. Do you want that?"

She did not wait for her mother's reply, but pushed her way through the crowd until she reached a secluded area. It was not as remote as she would have liked, being much too near the musicians, but was better than the stuffy press of people milling about in noisy gaiety. Whyever did her mother find these things so entertaining? All it took was a half hour of listening to the brittle laughter produced by too much alcohol or the effort to impress to convince Angela that she was in the wrong place.

For a moment, while she stood near a potted fern that trailed lush green fronds onto the floor, she was reminded of the island of St. Thomas. Ferns had grown wild there, cascading over the forest floor in luxuriantly lacy abandon. Under them, one could find tiny scarlet flowers, or a thick, springy moss that was as soft as swansdown. The air had been rife with the clean scent of salt tang, wind, and the heady fragrance of tropical blooms.

She briefly closed her eyes, then opened them with a sigh. It was behind her now, and she was caught in a world that she had once thought she wanted. How different life was from what one planned.

Settling her spine against the right angle of the alcove wall, Angela watched the crowd from her vantage spot. The musicians on her right began to tune their instruments, though she could hear music spiraling down from one of the balconies. The discordant sounds were irritating, and her head began to throb. Really, this was too much even for a dutiful daughter.

She began to long for fresh air and quiet. Sets of French doors on the far end led to a balcony, where—she was certain—she could find at least some fresh air. Determinedly, she set out for the doors, but made slow progress. What her mother would say when she tried to find her, Angela had no idea. Reaching the balcony was paramount in her mind.

She had traversed almost the entire length of the ballroom when a swell of excitement rippled through the guests. Voices that had been overly loud only an instant before abruptly halted. Curious to see what had caused this sudden cessation in chaos, Angela paused and turned toward the source of the crowd's interest.

Charles Sheridan stood with his erect, military-like bearing in the center of a group, and he appeared to be introducing one of his guests. Puzzled as to who could garner such intense interest, Angela recalled that the prince was supposed to attend. That would explain the crowd's reaction. Well, she had no desire to meet the prince. From all she had heard, he was a rather pompous, silly man, for all that he was royal.

But as she turned to continue toward the doors leading to the balcony, she heard the duke call her name; she groaned. He would insist upon introducing her to the prince, and there was little she could do. She'd been snared as neatly as a herring in a net.

Determined to make the best of it, Angela turned with a smile, doing her best to keep her train looped over her arm and off the floor. Focusing on the duke, she hoped that she could remember how to address a prince as Tremayne said formally, "Miss Lindell, I wish to introduce you to Lord Westcott. Christian, this is Miss Lindell, daughter of my business associate, and a very amiable companion."

Not the prince, she had time to think gratefully, but when she turned her gaze toward the man stepping forward, her heart lurched and her stomach dropped to her toes.

Furious blue eyes caught and held hers, and she resisted a wave of panic and confusion as their gazes locked.

Kit Saber. . . .

Twenty-one

"Your son?" Angela echoed feebly, and turned green eyes filled with confusion toward the duke. Kit fought a wave of fury. So, she hadn't known. It was just like his father to spring this sort of thing on her. Didn't he know that well enough? History had a way of repeating itself, it seemed.

But he'd be damned if he'd let either of them know he was the least bit affected.

Sweeping an elegant bow, he took the hand Angela finally held out to him. Her fingers trembled as he made an elaborate gesture of kissing her hand, holding it a shade too long. He could feel his father's amused gaze resting on him as he straightened and said, "I'm delighted that my father has found such pleasant and lovely company in his declining years."

As he released her hand, Angela looked from one to the other of them with a stunned expression in her eyes. He could well imagine what she might be feeling at this moment. Once the shock wore off, she may well feel the same savage anger he was feeling. But he doubted it. Angela, it was certain, had never dealt with Charles Sheridan's treachery before. He was only too accustomed to it, however, and wondered bitterly why he had ever thought things might change. Nothing had.

Except, perhaps, Angela. If anything, she was even lovelier than before. Her filmy gown suited her, though he thought the heavy ruby necklace a shade too much. Simplicity was more her style. Such as nothing but a thin cotton gown, damp from the ocean and clinging to her body in diaphanous folds that could make a man ache for days. Damn. That was hardly something he needed to remember at this time.

"Christian," his father was saying, "why don't you lead Miss Lindell in the first dance? I believe the musicians are ready to play a minuet."

He would have refused, finding gracious words so that none would suspect his raging fury, but some quirk in his nature that must enjoy self-torture prompted him to offer an arm in mute invitation. Angela took it after a slight hesitation, and he escorted her to the middle of the floor where a space had been cleared for dancing.

With all eyes on them, they joined the other couples while the musicians began to play. The mincing steps of the dance occupied Kit's attention sufficiently so that he was able to mask his feelings, yet with each dip and swirl and glance at Angela's pale, set face, he fought an increasing urge to sweep her out the door. But that would only create more speculation, which was already running through the crowd like a rabid weasel. Scraps of whispered comments floated about his head like a flurry of dry leaves in a wind eddy. Most of them he could ignore. Angela was a different proposition altogether.

Did she have to look like a beautiful, pale ghost? Not even the brilliant hue of her dress and jewels could disguise the pallor of her cheeks or the fine lines on each side of her mouth. Damn Charles Sheridan and his mania for unpleasant surprises.

Engrossed in his inner turmoil, it took Kit a moment to realize that the minuet had ended and a Scotch reel had begun. He jerked to a halt, ignoring the couple who bumped into him as he looked down at Angela.

"We need to talk," he heard himself say, and she nodded.

Murmurs followed them as he escorted her from the dance floor to the French doors leading onto the balcony, but at that moment, he didn't give a damn what people thought. Especially his father. What he did care about was some sort of explanation from Angela. What the devil was she doing keeping company with his father, for God's sake?

Staring up at him in the light of moon and lantern, Angela did not answer that question for several moments. Kit had the brief feeling that he should have posed it differently, but it had slipped out exactly as he'd been thinking it.

"What the devil," she repeated slowly, leaning back against the wide stone balustrade, "am I doing seeing your father?" Her steady gaze remained fastened on his face for another long interval before she said, "I did not even know he *was* your father. For all I knew, you had no father. Perhaps you don't remember, but you were never very free with information about your life. And while we're at it, perhaps you'd like to tell me why you never divulged the knowledge that you are not only the son and heir of the Duke of Tremayne, but you are also the Earl of Westcott. Did you not think that was important enough to tell me?"

Amazed at her subtle conversion from shock to anger, Kit floundered for a moment before recovering. Damn her, how dare she look at him with accusation in her eyes? He wasn't the one who seemed to have forgotten what had transpired between them.

Forcing himself to remain cool, Kit said evenly, "How alike women are. I should have guessed that you would attempt to place the blame upon me for your transgressions."

"Transgressions!" Her eyes blazed with green fury as she glared up at him. "Perhaps my major transgression was in ever believing in you. It seems that you are nothing but a sham. I was a fool to think you honorable. You were wise to choose piracy as a profession, sir, for it suits you well. Now, if you will excuse me, my mother will be worried about me."

When she started to storm past him, Kit grabbed her arm and whirled her around, forcing her back against the stone ledge with his body, unable to stop himself. The condemnation in her eyes was more than he could withstand. Determined to banish it, to erase that assessing denouncement in her gaze, he grasped her chin with one hand, gripping it so firmly she winced.

"Damn you," he rasped. "Are you condemning the trade of piracy, or are you angry because I did not inform you of my potential worth as an earl? Or has the lure of the big fish distracted you from a mere earl? I admit, a duke wields much more power and wealth, but doesn't my inherent charm count for anything?" He tightened his grip when she tried to wrench away, unable to stop himself from saying, "Doesn't what was between us count for anything?"

"Just what was between us?" she managed to gasp out. "Pardon me, but if there was anything between us, you never told me."

"Did I have to tell you? Bloody hell, Angela, I thought it was plain enough."

She glared up at him. "What was plain enough? That you wanted to bed me? Oh yes. You made that very clear. But I need more than that, Kit. I need what you don't have to give, it seems. There's more to life and love than a casual tumble between the sheets."

Fury knifed through him. Casual? Is that what she thought? When he had practically turned himself inside out to stay away from her? And nearly had his entire ship taken to keep her safe? Was she really that blind?

Releasing her with a contemptuous shove, Kit stared down at her for a long moment. Angela met his gaze with a level stare of her own, almost daring him to prove her wrong.

"I thought so," she finally said with a mocking curl of her lips. "You have courage enough to speak your own mind, but not enough to listen."

Without realizing he had even moved, Kit had her in his arms, hands gripping her so tightly that she gasped. "Is it courage you seek, sweetheart?" His hands shifted to her shoulders, fingers sliding up the nape of her neck, thumbs wedging beneath her chin to tilt back her head so that she had to meet his eyes. "Is it courage," he repeated softly, "or a lapdog that you want? I'm not a lapdog. You can't snap your fingers and command me to heel, or speak, or feel whatever it is you want me to feel at that moment. I'm a man, with a man's needs. Or have you forgotten how easy it is to be a woman?"

"Damn you!"

Her hand flashed up and back, as if to strike him, and he caught it easily, twisting her arm behind her back to hold it there. That action had the effect of pressing her tightly against him, and he could feel the rapid, furious rise and fall of her breasts. He glanced down at the enticing shadow between her breasts, and the creamy mounds that strained against her low-cut gown. It had the usual effect on him.

"Angela. . . ." The word was a harsh groan, quickly lost in the heavy mass of her hair when he pressed his lips against her temple. She struggled against him, but he could only think of the times he had held her, the nights aboard ship, and the night they had made love in the ocean. How had she forgotten them so quickly? Did she really think that all he wanted from her was this . . . and this?

His hand skimmed down her back over bare skin and curves, coming to rest on the gentle slope of her hip to pull her even closer against him. Maybe she was partially right. He did want her. God, he'd thought of her during more long nights than he cared to recall, remembering the silky feel of her skin beneath his hands, the sweet curves of her body. He knew she could feel his desire—Christ, she could probably hear the heavy pounding of the blood through his body. There was something infinitely arousing about an angry woman. This angry woman, anyway.

Kit bent his head and kissed her, holding her chin in the cradle of his palm so that she would not twist away, his mouth burning across her parted lips until he felt her begin to yield. The heady taste of wine was tantalizing, the tentative touch of her tongue against his even more so. Senses reeling, he backed her slowly along the balustrade to the leafy bower of a potted tree with long, trailing branches. He paused beneath it, slivers of light like tiny stars across her face as she gazed up at him. Her lips were slightly parted and her cheeks flushed, her breathing as rapid as his. Kit felt a spurt of satisfaction.

"Now," he asked huskily, "do you deny that you feel the same desire for me?"

For a moment, she just stared up at him. Then Angela lurched several steps from him, her voice a halting series of sobbing breaths. "How . . . dare . . . you! You do not . . . know me . . . at all. Do you really think . . . that bedding you is . . . all I want?" A tear escaped from one corner of her eye, trickling over her cheek and making a silvery path through her face powder. Kit lifted a hand to touch her, but she took a hasty step back, putting both palms outward to fend off his touch. "No. I've heard enough. This night is . . . is too much. Leave me alone. Nothing is what I thought it would be . . . nothing."

Turning, she tossed the trailing train of her gown over one arm and lifted her skirts above her ankles as she ran the length of the balcony to a flight of stone steps leading to the garden below. She disappeared from sight while he stood like a statue, staring after her. She was right. Nothing was as he'd thought it would be. Nothing.

Time did not erase all wounds, nor did it alter the past. It only distanced it until one was able to view it from a distorted angle. But one thing was certain—Charles

Sheridan had not changed. He was still the manipulative bastard he'd always been.

Pivoting on his heel, Kit stalked to the French doors leading into the ballroom. The time had come to have a long overdue father-son discussion. There were some things that needed to be said.

Charles Sheridan's elegant brow lifted in a languid slant. "My dear boy, I have no idea what you are talking about."

Slamming his hands to the surface of his father's polished mahogany desk, Kit snarled, "The devil you don't! You know very well what I'm talking about. We have been through this before—remember?"

"Christian, have you dragged me away from my guests just to rail at me about ancient history? Can it not wait until a more appropriate moment?"

"No." Kit straightened. "It will not wait. Did you think I wouldn't realize what you're doing? You interfered in my betrothal to Susan, and somehow—God only knows how—you found out about Angela. You're doing the same thing. I recall your tactics quite well, so don't play the innocent with me. Divide and slaughter. Offer enough inducements, and the silly chit will grab at the brass ring in the pudding quickly enough. It worked with Susan, but by God, don't you dare try it again. I won't have it."

"Won't you." Sheridan sat down in his huge leather chair and leaned back, fixing Kit with a supercilious smile that did almost irreparable damage to his temper. "I don't really see that you have much choice, Christian. Miss Lindell was left here in London on her own, and I took rather a fancy to her. She's a sweet little thing, don't you think?"

With great effort, Kit resisted the urge to throttle the duke. Logic demanded that he not murder his father with several hundred guests only a few rooms away.

"Why are you doing this?" he contented himself with asking in a much calmer voice than he'd thought possible. "Do you hate me that much?"

In the process of lighting a cigar, the duke went very, very still. He stared at his son over the flaring match until it burned his fingers and he dropped it with a muttered oath. Then he carefully placed the unlit cigar in a glass dish and leaned forward, meeting Kit's eyes.

"Quite the contrary. I have never hated you. I spent ten years of my life scouring the entire world for you. And for my pains, I recovered a hostile brigand who loathed me upon first sight. Hate you? Oh no. I may correctly be accused of many things, Christian, but that is not one of them."

"Then why?" Kit shook his head slowly. "Why are you doing this?"

For a long moment filled with silence and the steady, sonorous ticking of the ornate clock upon the mantel, Charles Sheridan gazed at Kit. Then he gave an elegant shrug of his shoulders. "You are mistaken if you think I am deliberately trying to sabotage you in any way. If anything, I have gone out of my way to alleviate any difficulties in your life. You simply choose to misinterpret my intentions."

"Alleviate—" Kit bit back a choking snarl, amazed at his father's allegation. "Am I supposed to throw myself at your feet now and thank you for *alleviating* my difficulties? Do you think I don't know why you beguiled Susan away from me?"

"Exactly. You have no idea why I chose to show you the young lady for the greedy little baggage that she was." The duke lifted his unlit cigar with an irritable motion. "Wasn't her defection proof enough to you that her emotions were not involved?"

"And is that what you're trying to do with Angela?" Kit leaned forward, placing his palms on the desk and bending until he was within inches of his father's face. "Let me offer you a warning—do not attempt to manipulate me again. Especially not with Angela. I'm a grown man now, not a heartsick youth."

"Dear me, does this mean you won't run away from home again? The last time was such a noble statement, fleeing like a scalded cat instead of staying to face what any man with backbone would confront." He struck another match, deliberately holding the flame to the end of his cigar with disregard for Kit's proximity.

Kit drew back, his voice tight. "I was barely twenty. I thought I was in love. To have it revealed in public that the woman to whom I was betrothed was now my father's mistress was a bit more than I could stomach. I didn't leave England because of cowardice; it was revulsion that drove me to the sea."

"And an affinity for piracy." Putting out the match, Sheridan tossed it into the glass tray. "Your childhood prepared you well for thievery, while I did my best to instill proper values in you. If you think I forgot you once you left the country, you are very much mistaken. I was aware of every ship in the Sheridan line that fell into your hands, and of every port where you docked. I knew how much cargo you took, how much profit you made—all of it. You show an aptitude for trade that would delight a burgher. Why do you think some of my well-armed ships did not return fire upon you? Did it ever occur to you to wonder why ships in the Sheridan line would return fire on any flag but yours? Or did you even notice." Tapping a long ash from the end of his cigar, the duke laughed softly. "Details, Christian, details. They are the very marrow of any thriving business. Ignore them, and you may find yourself on a corner begging for bread."

"I noticed," Kit said tightly. "But it suited my purpose to inconvenience you at every opportunity. I thought it a rather fitting reprisal against your arrogance."

Sheridan nodded thoughtfully. "Then that explains several puzzling events. Very well—so you were astute enough to play both ends against the middle. Eventually, one must tally up the sums to see who has won."

"The problem here is that I was not seeking vengeance or victory. You were just useful. My pursuit involved something quite different from what you may imagine."

"Ah yes, the eternal quest for Vivian. You have heard, by the way, that she is back in London?"

"Damn you." Kit stared at the duke. "Have you always known where she is?"

"Approximately. She is a relatively easy woman to pursue, once one discovers the trick of it. I admit that it was not always so easy. She can certainly be a conniving piece of work when she wants to be."

Reeling, Kit felt as if he had been caught unaware by a ground swell. It was as if the carpeted floor had just been yanked from beneath his feet. "Where is she?" he asked hoarsely.

Charles Sheridan rose to his feet and crushed the cigar into the glass dish on his desk. "Patience, son. Work out one problem at a time. Do not fear—she will not be leaving London soon. When you see her, you must be well prepared." His mouth twisted into a cynical smile that looked vaguely familiar to Kit. "I would not have you taken by surprise as I was. Vivian is a very unique individual, and a very dangerous one."

Striding past Kit, the duke reached the door, then turned around with one hand on the latch. "This has been a most enlightening discussion for me, Christian. I hope it has been as revealing for you. Now, I must return to my guests before the gossip about your reappearance gets quite out of hand. Someone must be there to be certain the rumors are steered in the right direction. Oh— and welcome back. Your arrival was most timely this morning."

Echoes of the closing door reverberated softly in the huge study, and Kit stared blindly after his father. He had been expected. It had been no sudden shock or revelation to arrive at the house this morning, except for his own surprise at finding the bustle of preparations for the evening's ball. He should have known. Filbert's bland countenance and lack of shock should have more than prepared him. Why had he thought he could discompose Charles Sheridan in any way? The duke's network of spies would make a king envious. More than likely, news of Kit's arrival in London had reached the duke long before the *Sea Tiger*—disguised, of course, with a dragon bowsprit and new name—had even docked at the Pool.

Turk, as usual, had been quite correct in stating that the Duke of Tremayne employed many methods of gathering knowledge. It was glaringly apparent.

So what did he do now? He had bungled his first meeting with Angela, but the shock of not only seeing her there, but having her introduced as his father's *amiable companion,* had thrown him off-course. Instinct advised him to tread softly around her. God, he had probably ruined everything now. What had happened to his earlier plans to woo her slowly? Gone in a moment of anger . . . now he had to start over. He'd thought—hoped—to court Angela as any proper suitor would do, to allow their relationship to grow slowly and steadily, without the restraints between them that had been formed upon their first meeting.

After all, he reflected wryly, it was hardly conducive to romance to have the object of one's affections as a prisoner. That state in itself entailed certain disagreeable formalities. Turk had been right. As usual. So what did he do about it now? When she was publicly his father's companion? It would hardly be to his credit to press his suit when everyone in London assumed that the duke and Miss Lindell were "keeping company."

Kit drew in a deep breath. The best he could hope for at this time was to keep his head and not make any more mistakes. After all, no betrothal had been announced. Instinct told him that his father's emotions were not involved, and he was certain that Angela was more bemused than in love. All he could do was bide his time and wait.

* * *

Having repaired the damage done to the rice powder liberally applied to her face, Angela joined her mother after a lengthy search through the crowd. Alicia turned anxiously, relief on her face at her daughter's appearance.

"There you are. Angela—it's the most exciting thing! You will never imagine in a hundred years just who has made an appearance here tonight."

"Lord Westcott. The duke's son."

"Oh. You must have heard." Alicia turned to survey the crowd. "Have you seen him yet? I caught only a glimpse before he disappeared. Everyone is talking—he's an earl in his own right, they say. Where do you suppose he has been for so long? Lady Farnsworth—her husband is Sir Percival Farnsworth, a baronet—said that Westcott must have been tending the duke's foreign interests all this time. Do you think that possible?"

"Anything is possible," Angela murmured. "Mama—I am feeling quite ill. My head aches, and I . . . I feel nauseous. Do you suppose you could fetch the carriage and we could leave?"

Alicia looked dismayed. "Dear me—shall I see if there is a spot where you can lie on a couch until you are better? This is such an important affair, Angela, with the duke's son arriving and the prince due to make an appearance—I should hate for you to miss it all. Have you spoken with the duke?"

"Yes. Mama—I would much rather go home. Perhaps Papa can fetch me a hired cab."

Desperation tinged her voice, and some of it must have seeped through to her mother, for Alicia gave a disappointed nod. "Very well, dear. If you are ill, you are ill.

And I must say, you are dreadfully pale. I shall send a footman for the carriage to take you home at once."

Gratefully, Angela sagged against the wall while her mother beckoned for a liveried footman. The press of people and constant hum of conversation and clink of glasses vied with the musicians in a turbulent blend. The shock of seeing Kit had unnerved her. Just meeting him again would have been disturbing enough; discovering not only that he was in London, but also that he was the Duke of Tremayne's son had been mind-numbing. Why had he never told her? Did he think her that grasping and greedy?

Apparently, she answered her own question, recalling with a sting his earlier words. He thought her intimately involved with his father. If it was not so infuriating, she would have laughed at him.

She put her fingers to her temples and rubbed slowly. Her head ached. Her legs ached from hours of standing, and her eyes stung with the effort to hold back tears. She was miserable. This was the worst night of her life, and she'd thought she had already had that. No, somehow, the emotional impact of being confronted by six feet of hostile male whom she had once assumed cared for her had taken even more of a toll. There had been no love in his eyes, only a raging fury and animosity that had stunned and wounded her.

Kit's actions tonight had only proven what she had tried not to think since her departure from the *Sea Tiger*—he had never loved her. She had been only a convenience, and though Emily had tried time and again to convince her that some men just found it hard to say farewell, she now knew in her heart that had not been the case with Kit.

Pushing away from the wall, Angela tried to tear her mind away from Kit. She had to escape, before she saw him again. It would never do to flee the duke's ball in tears.

"Angela," her mother said at her elbow, "the footman has gone to fetch the carriage. It will take a few moments, however, so why don't you just wait here with me? He will send inside for you when it has been brought 'round."

Agreeing with a silent nod, Angela had begun to lean back against the wall when she heard her mother call a greeting to Lord Brompton. She sighed inwardly and prepared herself to put on a pleasant face.

"Lord Brompton," Alicia was saying, "how delightful to see you again."

"Yes, indeed," Brompton said with a broad smile. "One does tend to knock about in such a press, what? I have lost sight of my companions in this crush, but am making amends by meeting such lovely friends again." His eyes strayed to Angela, and she managed a smile.

"Lord Brompton," she murmured in acknowledgment of his greeting.

"Have you heard the news, Miss Lindell?" his lordship inquired, leaning forward as if to impart vital information. "The duke's prodigal son has returned home. Just today, I understand. Conjecture is running rampant as to the explanation for his long absence from England. Some say business; I say—perhaps not."

Fascinated, Alicia Lindell asked eagerly, "Why do you say that, my lord?"

Wagging his head wisely, Brompton lifted his brows. "Gossip has it that there was a serious disagreement between the duke and his son years ago. I am inclined to agree. Being a bit older than some in this crowd, I can recall things more clearly. The earl was betrothed to a most charming young woman at the time. Susan Witherington, daughter of Baron Heathrow. At any rate, the duke took a fancy to her, the way I heard it, and the young lady, of course, decided that being a duchess was much better than being a countess. Perhaps if she had not made her decision known at a very public ball, the young earl would not have taken it so to heart. But Miss Witherington was not the most generous of young ladies. That is why few felt sorry for her when the duke shifted his attentions elsewhere once the earl left England."

Angela wished she could transport herself to another spot without hearing any more. Poor Kit. No wonder he had not mentioned his betrothed. Or his father. Perhaps he had come home to mend the rift between them. And now—now he thought that the duke was her admirer . . .

Straightening as if shot from a crossbow, Angela earned a rather startled glance from Lord Brompton. "Excuse me," she said. "I . . . I just saw someone I know."

She turned blindly, not knowing which way to go through the crowd, when she saw Kit approaching her. His tall frame was easily seen among the nattily dressed gentlemen and multihued ladies. She had been right, she thought distractedly. Kit looked exceedingly handsome in a cutaway coat of deep claret. Beneath the vee of his white satin waistcoat, his linen shirt protruded in a cascade of frills topped by an intricately tied cravat. Buff doeskin trousers fit snugly to his muscled calves. He looked every inch the dandy, something she had been too shocked to notice earlier. Even his hair was romantically ruffled onto his forehead in the Greek style so favored by the fashionable young man.

"Look," Alicia whispered excitedly to Brompton, "there is Lord Westcott now!"

Angela's heart lurched when she saw that Kit intended to pass her by without speaking. It was Lord Brompton at her side, however, who snared not only Kit's attention, but that of everyone within earshot.

"I say!" he exclaimed loudly. "That cannot be Westcott . . ."

Kit stopped and turned toward him, raking the corpulent baron with a narrow stare. "Can I not? Pray, tell me why not."

"Why, be—because . . . I made your acquaintance only a few months ago. Do you not recall it?" Brompton shifted uneasily, apparently aware that he was creating a scene that might not be to his advantage. It would never do to alienate the duke or his son. "We . . . we played cards. In Greece."

A sardonic smile curled Kit's mouth. "Ah yes. I do recall you now. You were drunk as a friar under a grape arbor in Limenas. We played whist and I won ten pounds from you. You are a very bad gambler, my lord."

Indignant, Brompton blurted, "Only because I was afraid to say anything about the way you deal cards, sir. Did you think me fool enough to challenge a pirate such as Kit Saber about his method of—" He stumbled to an abrupt halt, his face flushing then going pale.

The little pocket of silence around them rippled into

soft murmurs, but the sardonic smile on Kit's mouth never wavered. He merely lifted a brow.

"Method of what? I did not have to cheat, Brompton. But you were very wise not to suggest it. You're quite right about my possible reaction. We pirates are notorious for being insulted by vague accusations of cheating. At times, the reaction can be quite—dangerous."

The baron's color receded again and he made an odd, wheezing sort of sound. "My lord, I never meant—"

"Do not trouble yourself, Brompton. I have taken no offense." Kit looked around at the gawking faces pressed close, and for a brief instant, his eyes met Angela's. Then his gaze swept over her as if he had never seen her before, and with a nod of his head, he turned and made his way through the crowd.

Angela realized she'd been holding her breath when her lungs began to ache, and she released it slowly, not surprised to see others around her doing the same. Whispers began immediately.

"A pirate," someone said softly. "Can it be true?"

"Kit Saber?" another inquired. "The *notorious* Kit Saber?"

Lord Brompton, apparently deciding that he had risked his welcome quite enough for one evening, managed to melt into the crowd with a dexterity that Angela found more amazing than amusing. She looked around her at the variety of reactions, and knew that whatever else, this evening had certainly exceeded the anticipation of all the guests. Not only had the duke's son reappeared after a mysteriously long absence, but he was none other than the notorious pirate captain Kit Saber. Yes, this ball would be one long remembered in the annals of London gossipmongers.

Angela didn't know whether to laugh or cry. Despite her apprehension that the ball would prove to be boring beyond all bearing, it had been the most memorable in her life.

Twenty-two

"This has been," Alicia Lindell said, "the most exciting month that I can recall. Do you not think so, John?"

Not glancing from behind the *Morning Post,* Lindell muttered an indistinct reply that his wife took to be assent. Alicia took another sip of tea, sighing contentedly. "Of course, one can almost feel pity for the duke. He has been beset on all sides with vicious rumors about his heir. Imagine. A notorious pirate captain. I can only envision some of the depredations the young earl must have initiated while roving the seas."

Angela did her best not to look up from her book. It was raining again, or she would have gone to the garden to read. Her mother's endless prattle about the topic of conversation that had all of London buzzing with new tidbits every day was beginning to wear upon her nerves. And she had yet to inquire of her father if he knew about her stay on the *Sea Tiger.* He had not mentioned it, and neither had she. Did he realize that it was Kit Saber's ship that had taken her from the burning *Scrutiny?*

Sliding deeper into her cushioned chair near the fire, Angela tried to concentrate on her novel. Her mother's conversation had turned from pirates to romantic speculation, a familiar drone in the background. She murmured occasional responses for the sake of courtesy, wishing that her mother would run out of information. It wasn't until a name caught her attention that Angela looked up.

"Excuse me, Mama? Who did you say?"

"Christian Sheridan. Westcott, of course."

"No, I meant the other one."

"Ah." Alicia took another sip of tea, delighted to have captured undivided attention at last. *"La Diabolique,* some call her. I have never seen her, but Letitia Crandle claims that she is one of the most beautiful women ever to grace London. It is rumored that she is a notorious spy, but that is probably untrue. The government would never allow her to roam about freely if that was so. Let's see . . . she has another name . . . Contessa Villiers, I believe. Of course, that is probably one of those Royalist affectations. It would be my guess that the number of deposed Royalists has doubled from the actual number, for every Frenchman who comes across the Channel claims ties to the royal family." Sniffing disdainfully, she took another sip of tea before continuing, "All the same, it must be most distressing to the duke to have his son following about after such a woman."

Angela closed her book. "And is he?" she asked carefully.

Her mother gave her a blank stare. "Is who what?"

"Is Westcott following about after Contessa Villiers?"

"Why—I should think so. I have it from a most reliable source. Why do you ask, dear?"

"No reason." Angela traced the embossing on the leather cover of her novel with one finger, staring into the fire. "Curiosity, I suppose."

When she turned her gaze from the flames dancing in the grate, she saw John Lindell gazing at her with a troubled frown. Her mother had moved on to another topic concerning the broken betrothal of a viscount's daughter Angela had never heard of. Rain pattered against the windows with a hissing sound, and flames crackled and popped. On the mantel, a clock ticked loudly.

Opening her book again, Angela stared down at the printed pages without seeing them. In a moment, she heard her father's paper rustle as he lifted it. Christian Sheridan and the contessa were not mentioned again that afternoon.

It was almost bedtime that evening when Angela turned restlessly to Emily. A cool September breeze drifted in her open window and lifted a strand of her loose hair.

"Emily, where do you go every night?"

Hesitating, Emily flushed and looked down. The linens she held were wadded in her hands. "How do you know I go out?"

"Because I looked for you one night and couldn't find you. Mrs. Peach told me that you go out almost every night after you are done with your work."

"And if I do?" Emily asked with a defiant tilt of her chin. "I do my work first."

Angela smiled slightly. "Dear Emily—I am not questioning your right to do as you please on your own time. It would make no difference to me if you did no more than dust the parlor every morning and then went out for the remainder of the day. Heavens, after what we went through together . . ." She halted, then said more quietly, "I just want to know if you're meeting Dylan."

After another brief hesitation, Emily nodded. "Yes.

Often as I can, anyway. He . . . he has his own things to do, you know."

It was difficult to ask the next question, but Angela could not help herself. "Have you . . . seen Kit?"

"Only once. He was with Turk, and they were having a very *loud* discussion. When they saw me, they stopped. Turk gave me a potion for a rash I got from washing powder." She looked down at her hands, and said softly, "And Captain Saber asked after you."

"Did he." Ignoring the sudden clutch of her heart, she had the bitter thought that Kit had been in London a month and not bothered to call upon her. Not a card or a note—nothing. On several of her walks along the winding banks of the Serpentine, she had seen him in an open carriage with various gentlemen, but he had not seen her.

Yet the duke had kept up a faithful correspondence with her—notes, flowers, small gifts delivered to her home— nothing overtly romantic, simply gestures of friendship. An invitation to a night at the opera had arrived from him just the day before. She had not yet responded, despite her mother's urging to do so. It would be unbearable to attend a function and see Kit with another woman on his arm.

Oh yes, she'd heard those rumors, too. Despite the taint of piracy attached to his name—some were now calling it by the more polite but identical title of privateering—Christian Sheridan enjoyed an enormous popularity. Women flocked to his side at every social event, and his name had been linked with many other ladies besides the contessa. It was amazing that in such a short time, he should have become the darling of the *ton*. Of course, there was the matter of his title and wealth to consider. He would have commanded attention for that alone, even if he'd been cross-eyed, knock-kneed, and toothless.

Rubbing wearily at her eyes, Angela asked Emily if she had spoken to Kit about her.

"Not really. Except to say that you were quite well. I saw no need," she said defensively when Angela looked up sharply, "to let him know you were at home pining about him. He would only get ideas."

"Or discover the truth." Angela smiled wryly. "Thank you, Emily. I appreciate your concern. Would you . . . would you do me a favor?"

Wanly, Emily nodded. "If possible."

"Tell Dylan I would like to see him. If he feels uncomfortable coming here, I will meet him wherever he likes. I still consider him my friend, whether or not he knows it."

"Oh. Yes, of course. He worries about you. I know he will want to see you." She hesitated. "Would you like to see Turk as well?"

"Very much."

"Then why don't you go with me one evening?"

"Go with you? What a simple solution. Do you think Dylan would mind?"

"He'd be very happy."

"Then I'll go. Are they staying aboard the ship?"

Emily smiled. "They hate staying on land. Especially Dylan. He says he feels safer aboard the ship."

"Then tomorrow night, I'll go with you."

A brisk wind blew the smell of rotting wood and refuse over the quay. There was none of the salt tang of the ocean in this brackish water; it moved sluggishly, wafting against stone and wood, diluted by river water and hundreds of ocean-going ships.

Wood shuddered beneath his feet as Kit strode up the brow and onto the deck of the *Sea Tiger*. A familiar feeling of belonging enveloped him when he once more stood amid the neatly hung spars and furled sails. Lines creaked gently with the rocking motion of the ship, and water slapped against the sides. A faint murmur could be heard from the direction of a burning lantern, and he directed his steps toward it.

Passing the watch, who nodded a greeting, Kit pushed open the door and stepped down into a companionway. Giving a sharp rap on the door left ajar to Dylan's cabin, he swung it open. Then he came to an abrupt halt.

"What the devil are you doing here?"

Wide-eyed, Angela turned to face him, her cheeks leaching color like a sun-faded flower. Though her lips trembled, she said nothing, and it was Dylan who answered that she had come to visit him.

"You didn't say I couldn't have any visitor I wanted," he added with a trace of belligerence.

Kit supposed that his surprised demand had sounded more than a bit accusatory. He cleared his throat. "No. I didn't. I just didn't expect to see her here."

"Well, she is. Shall we leave?"

"No. No, that's all right. I can change my plans." He turned to go, then paused. It had shaken him more than he had expected it to, seeing her like this, and he wondered why. Gesturing toward Angela, he said, "She can stay as long as she likes."

"Angela," Dylan said. "Her name is Angela. Remember?"

Something in his face must have betrayed his surge of savage anger, because Dylan stepped protectively in front of her. Kit shook his head. "Don't bother. I would not lay a hand on her." He paused, then said, damning the odd thickness in his throat, "Angela, I trust you will enjoy your visit."

When the door had slammed solidly behind him, Kit drew in a breath that felt riddled with needles. His chest constricted, and though it had nothing to do with illness, he was suddenly reminded of the time he'd suffered a bronchitis attack and Angela had helped Turk tend him. Wet, dripping cloths, cool drinks, and infinite patience had eased the worst of it for him, and he could still recall her soothing voice and the soft, loving words she'd used.

God, he was a fool. If he wasn't, he wouldn't be fighting this pressing need to hold her again. He should just let her go. It would be the kindest thing for both of them. After all, even if he did tell her how he felt, it would do neither of them any good. Who would want their daughter to wed a man with the taint of piracy attached to his name? Not even his father's wealth and reputation had really smoothed over that rumor, though few would dare repeat it to his face. Kit smiled wryly.

Leaning back against the door, he struggled against the growing desire to go back inside. It had been a cozy scene, as Angela's face glowed with pleasure and Emily giggled, while Dylan laughed at both of them. Memories of other nights when he had joined them still haunted him at times. Only the lucid vision of Angela at his father's side kept him from turning back. One could never revisit the past. It was foolish to want that which would never be. Didn't he know that well enough?

The reason he had come here tonight was part of that hard-earned lesson. Now he would have to confront his long-awaited appointment elsewhere. If she showed at all. . . .

Rattled by Kit's unexpected appearance, Angela paced the floor of the cabin despite Dylan's efforts to ease her. Finally he said resignedly, "You might as well admit that you still love him. If you didn't, he wouldn't have the power to affect you like this."

Turning, Angela glared at him. "Did you know he was coming here tonight?"

"I told you, no," he said patiently. "This is the first time he's been here in over a week. He don't have to make an appointment, you know. It's his ship. He can do what he likes."

"Don't remind me." She lapsed into gloomy silence, thinking of all the things Kit liked to do and did. It didn't bear study for too long, and she swerved her attention back to Dylan's glum expression. "I'm sorry. I suppose this wasn't such a grand notion after all. It seemed so thrilling, sneaking out of the house in disguise and coming down here to meet you. Perhaps, next time, you should come visit me at the house."

"Oh no." Dylan shook his head. "I know how that would be. I'd be shown to the tradesman's door—which would suit me well enough—but if your father saw you talking to the likes of me, he'd bundle you off to a convent or some such. Then Saber would really be mad at me. No, I won't risk it."

Her brow lifted. "Saber mad at you over me? I hardly think so. He hates me now."

"No, he just hasn't stopped to think things through yet. He will. When he does, he'll see that he's being ridiculous."

Dylan stood and came over to put an arm around her shoulders. "Don't give up on him, Angela. There's a lot going on that you don't know about."

"Well, would someone please tell me just what I need to know? It seems dreadfully unfair for everyone else to know things when I don't."

"It may be unfair, but I like my head where it is—attached to my neck." Dylan lifted his shoulders in a shrug. "I can't, lovey. You must know I would if I could."

Because she did know, Angela accepted his decision graciously. After a few more moments of idle chatter, Emily rose and helped Angela with her cloak, then reached for her own.

"We need to return. I dare not keep Miss Angela out too late."

"I'll see you back," Dylan said, "since Turk is not here yet. I can't imagine where he went. He's always here."

Leaving Dylan and Emily in the cabin for a few moments of privacy, Angela made her way topside. Lantern light sprayed over her in shifting patches. A wind had sprung up, noisily snapping loose lines and tugging at furled sails. The ship rolled gently from side to side, and Angela grasped the rail to keep her footing. Odd, how quickly she had forgotten how to keep her balance aboard a ship. It had been a hard-earned lesson much too easily neglected.

The rough scrabble of carriage wheels on cobbled stone made a scrunching sound, and she looked up, peering into the misty gloom of the quay. Fitful light from carriage lanterns stabbed the darkness in quivering globes, and for an instant, she thought it was a carriage come to take her and Emily home. Then she realized as she reached the wooden brow leading from ship to quay, that the closed carriage was already occupied.

One hand still lifted to hail the driver, she froze when she recognized Kit Saber's deep voice in the shadows beyond the light. There was the rusty squeak of a door opening, and silhouetted against the running lights, she saw a woman perched on the carriage seats. A low, feminine laugh purled lightly, and Angela's heart lurched. Kit had reached the side of the vehicle and was speaking to her, leaning against the side in a leisurely posture that didn't fool Angela at all. She recognized the tension in his tautly held shoulders and heard it in the tone of his voice though she could not quite hear his words.

Holding her breath, uncertain if she should risk exposure by fleeing back up the gangplank to the deck, she clung tightly to the railing and stood in the shadows with trembling legs. A capricious gust of wind carried scraps of their conversation to her ears.

". . . you said no one would be here," a pouting feminine voice complained in a vaguely familiar accent.

Kit's reply was partially obscured by the muted clang of ship's bells, fragments of it drifting to Angela. ". . . did not know. Impossible to . . . perhaps we could meet elsewhere. . . ."

Cutting across his explanation was the cold, *"Non!* I will make another appointment. . . ."

Kit must have protested, for Angela could see the woman's dark head shake firmly. Additional words were obscured by more bells, then as Kit shifted position, lantern light illuminated his mysterious visitor. Angela's heart skipped a beat. The woman was exotically beautiful: raven hair, milk-white skin, and aristocratic features of a perfection few could match. Then a shadow eclipsed her again and thickening mist curled in drifts.

The sound of a slamming door jerked Angela from her trance, and she turned to flee back up the tilted wooden walkway as carriage wheels rumbled in the fog. In her haste, she caught a foot in the hem of her cloak and stumbled. Falling to one knee with a painful jar, she swallowed a gasp of pain as she tried to regain her balance. One hand flailed for the support of a rail and missed, and she grew even more hopelessly tangled in the treachery of her voluminous cloak.

"Here," came the voice she least wanted to hear at that moment, "give me your hand before you tumble into the water."

Scalding heat flushed her cheeks as Kit grasped her by the arm and hauled her to her feet, his grip not especially gentle. "Did you come out to spy on me?" he demanded when she was standing in front of him.

Angela jerked her arm from his grasp. "You overrate your attraction, my lord. I have no desire to spy on you for any reason."

"Is that so." His cynical reply was accompanied by a lift of his brow that was infuriating. "For a young woman who has no interest in my activities, you seem to be in my vicinity a great deal at times. Do you always take long walks along the Serpentine during the afternoon?"

So. He had noticed her when she had thought him oblivious to her presence. If there was any gratification in that, she failed to see it. Apparently, he had not felt sufficiently interested to acknowledge her existence. She looked up at his shadowed face.

"Pardon me, but I was unaware that you now owned the park. Pray, forgive me for trespassing."

"Must you always overreact, Angela?" he inquired tautly. "I find it curious that you are so sensitive about certain subjects. Could it be a guilty conscience, perhaps?"

"My lord, whatever I might have a guilty conscience about, it would certainly not involve you. Do not flatter yourself."

When Kit moved into the light of a lantern, she felt a flutter of apprehension at his expression. Barely concealed savagery narrowed his eyes and thinned his lips, and fine white lines cut deep grooves on each side of his mouth. The last time she had seen a similar expression on his face had been just after the battle on St. Thomas. Residue of stress from the fierce bloodshed had been understandable then; it was less so now.

Swallowing the impulse to proffer an apology for some unknown sin, Angela stood in silence while the ship rocked gently and the fog curled around them in light flutters like cats' paws. The tension stretched, and she sensed Kit's tightly controlled effort to keep his temper in check.

Finally he said, his voice a rough rasp, "Perhaps this is the time to talk, after all."

Without waiting for her agreement, he cupped her elbow in his palm and turned her around, steering her toward his cabin. It didn't seem like the appropriate time to offer a protest or an argument, not with his mood so unpredictable. Apparently, his brief meeting with the mysterious woman had left him with a raw temper.

A painful rush of emotion engulfed her when she once more stood in Kit's cabin, with its familiar furnishings. Time flashed backward, and she saw herself arriving aboard the *Sea Tiger* for the first time, terrified and apprehensive, certain she and Emily were about to meet dire and dreadful fates. Kit had surprised her then, as he was surprising her now.

Releasing her arm, he closed the door and stalked to a cabinet to pull out a crystal decanter. She recognized brandy, and when he poured a small amount in a snifter and handed it to her, she took it gratefully. Liquid courage was better than none, and it might stop her legs from trembling so violently.

It was Rollo, however, that eased the worst of her tension.

"Bloody hell," the bird croaked from a shadowed corner, sounding cross. "Batten the hatches!"

"Are we," Angela couldn't resist asking with a spurt of amusement, "expecting a storm?"

"Possibly." Kit eyed her over the rim of his snifter. "I have heard it said that dumb creatures are best at predicting natural disasters."

"Are they." Feeling more confident with the brandy warming her stomach lining and throat, Angela crossed to a chair and seated herself in as graceful a motion as she could manage. "Odd, but I would never have classified Rollo as a dumb creature. Annoying, perhaps, but not inarticulate."

"The term *dumb* should be translated as meaning unaware, I suppose." Kit took another sip of brandy. "Whatever Rollo is, he is certainly vocal."

Conversation about the bird was safe. But there was a vast territory beyond casual discussion that loomed like a lethal coral reef waiting to wreck the conversational ship, and Angela was well aware of that. She was not at all certain she wanted to leave these safe waters.

Kit, however, seemed to have no inhibitions about steering their discussion into dangerous regions. Twirling the stem of his brandy snifter between thumb and forefinger, he murmured, "I would be vitally interested to learn more about the depth of the relationship between you and my father."

There. It was out. The gambit she had been dreading. If she denied any relationship, he would not believe her. If she told him exactly how she interpreted the duke's attentions, it was very likely he would not believe that either. So what did she say? That she had no idea why Tremayne was showering her with gifts and attention? That perhaps he was just being cordial to the daughter of a business acquaintance? It all sounded pathetically contrived. Appalled by her ignorance, she sat in helpless contemplation.

Silence deepened, until finally Kit glanced up from the perusal of his brandy snifter and gazed at her for several long moments. "I see," he said, his tone conveying the opposite message. He set the half-empty snifter on the desk with a deliberate motion, then perched on the edge, his hands curling over the top as he caught and held her gaze. "I cannot say I'm surprised by your refusal to explain. Perhaps I should just tell you how I view this . . . situation."

Hotly, she began, "You have no idea—" but he cut her off with a warning lift of one hand.

"Don't. Denial is only one step away from admission. I should know. I've dealt with this same situation before."

She knew what he meant, but she had no intention of allowing him to compare her to the Susan who had so heartlessly betrayed him. Surging to her feet, Angela snapped, "I know all about it, but I am not the same woman. No, you listen to me for a change. Nothing is the same, except your warped perception of the—situation. From all I have heard, your father was only trying to demonstrate the . . . the lack of loyalty of your betrothed. I think he did that successfully, however poorly he went about it. Has it escaped your notice that he did not marry her?"

"Foolish child," Kit chided gently when she paused for an angry breath, "he did not wed Susan because he was still married to my stepmother. I never thought he offered honorable marriage to her, only a position. It was, perhaps, the only time in my life I felt the tiniest bit of sympathy for Elaine. Not that she would ever have appreciated that. Barracudas have little time in their busy, destructive lives to appreciate anything they have not personally engineered."

"Elaine," Angela repeated blankly. "Who is Elaine?"

"Was. Haven't you been listening? My stepmother. In lieu of my mother, who has also contrived to make my life hell. It seems that I am destined to be beset by women convinced that their duty is to plague me with whatever torment seems most expedient at the moment."

Memory returned, of that afternoon on the beach when Turk had revealed tidbits of Kit's life. Elaine had been his stepmother. Even Turk had considered her evil. But that only partially explained Kit's willingness to lump her with the rest of the deceitful women in his life, and Angela resented it.

Fixing him with a contemptuous gaze, she said distinctly, "Isn't it time you stopped whining about the past? Must you behave as a thwarted child? I should think you would be more willing to accept loyalty where you find it, instead of being so suspicious of anyone who attempts to love you."

She hadn't quite meant to make that oblique confession, but it was out and there was nothing she could do about it. Besides, Kit was staring at her with an expression she was afraid to interpret. It hovered somewhere between amazement at her audacity, and fury at her assessment.

"I find myself," he said in a much calmer tone than she expected, "floundering for words. One of us has completely missed the boat, but I'm damned if I can figure out which one."

"Then maybe," she said, striving to keep her metaphors in the same realm as his, "we should book passage on another ship."

To her surprise, Kit laughed softly. "You always have been a fighter, Angela. I knew that the first moment I met you aboard the *Scrutiny*. As I recall, it was a rather . . . painful . . . introduction to your stubbornness."

Not wishing to dwell upon the fact that she had jabbed

her knee into the most vulnerable portion of his anatomy, Angela said hurriedly, "Would you have me just lie down and meekly submit to any fate?"

"Ah no, sweetheart. Never that."

It was the first hint at a lessening of his temper, and she took a deep breath. "Then Kit, please—give us both the chance to learn from the past instead of repeat it."

There was a subtle change in the deep blue shadows of his eyes, so subtle she almost missed it. If not for the chance roll of the ship that sent a splash of lamplight across his face, Angela might not have noticed. But she caught a glimpse of his pain, and the brief flare of hope that sputtered before he squelched it. She wanted to weep with frustration when he looked away from her, long lashes veiling his eyes in a sulky drift that was as revealing as it was crushing.

Unable to stop herself, she rose and went to him, putting a hand on his arm. Muscles bunched beneath her fingers, and he gave her a swift, impatient glance before removing her hand.

"It's no use, Angela. Go home. Forget about the past. I certainly should have."

"But . . . but I can't." She sucked in a deep breath when he looked away from her again, his face set in a cold mask. God, how could she reach him when he put a wall between them? She tried again. "Kit, please. I don't want to give up if there's a chance for us."

"Dammit," he snarled, turning to her and grasping her arms, "haven't you been listening to me? You were right. Nothing has changed. I haven't changed. You haven't changed. My father hasn't changed. London hasn't changed. The same set of people inhabiting the same

circles, doing the same things year after year—God. I'd
go crazy if I stayed in London. And you would never
leave. This is your world, Angela, not mine. Not anymore. If it ever was. I came here seeking answers, and
maybe they weren't the ones I wanted, but I have most
of them. Others . . ." He looked up and past her, his
grip easing slightly. "Others," he continued softly, "I
will never get, just as Turk warned me. Damn him."

There was such pain in his bleak tone that Angela
leaned forward and lay her head against his chest. She
heard the sharp intake of his breath, then his arms went
around her and he was pulling back her head to kiss her,
his mouth harsh on hers. She didn't care. Nothing mattered but that he hold her again, that he kiss her and
touch her as he once had.

Sliding her hand behind his neck, she held him, her
fingers tangling in the damp, dark hair that curled in fine
waves on his nape. He smelled of wind and sea; it was
a familiar, haunting fragrance, making her think of soft
tropical nights and sandy beaches and the sensual rhythm
of the waves breaking around them.

"Kit," she whispered against his mouth, "hold me."

He went still, then lifted his head, his shadowed eyes
studying her face for a long moment. Outside, the distant, muted clang of a bell rang in the night. The ship
rolled gently from side to side, and the lantern flashed
a pool of light over them. Rollo gave a sleepy squawk
and flutter of feathers as he tucked his head beneath a
wing.

Drawing in a deep breath, Kit lifted her in his arms
and crossed to his bunk. He lay her down gently. The
bunk dipped beneath his weight, and he bent to kiss her,

this time soft and easy, his mouth moving on her parted lips with sweet tenderness. Angela slid one hand over the familiar contours of his face, the sharp angles and planes, her fingers caressing the crescent-shaped scar from his eyebrow to cheek. Her fingers moved lightly over the chiseled outline of his mouth, his thumb sliding over his lower lip in a silky glide. He caught her hand in his and bit her thumb gently.

"Oh, Kit," she whispered, and he gave her a faint smile. She slid her free hand into the open collar of his loose shirt, and flicked open the buttons one by one. The cool linen of his shirt was still damp from the night air, but the bare skin beneath heated the backs of her fingers.

When her hand reached the last button at his waist, Kit drew in another deep breath and straightened. He gave her a crooked, sardonic smile that made her breath catch and her throat ache.

"Does this," he asked lightly, "come under the heading of love, or desire? Perhaps I should know the proper definition, just in case I'm taken to task for it later."

Angela sat up quickly, as if a bucket of cold seawater had been poured over her head. Kit lifted a brow and caught her chin in his palm.

"Well," he purred, "which is it, love?"

She knocked his hand away and lurched to her feet, her face flaming with embarrassment and anger. It was just like him to throw her own words back in her face, and only what she deserved, she supposed, for trying to seduce him with his own methods. Why had she ever thought anything she could say or do would make a difference to Kit Saber? Or Christian Sheridan, or whoever he chose to be—they were all the same man, locked up in a prison of his own making.

She drew in a deep, calming breath and managed a careless shrug. "Does it matter? You've spoiled the moment now, anyway. I don't see how you've acquired such a tantalizing reputation as a lover. Perhaps other rumors have some basis in fact, but not that particular one."

"I'm devastated."

His cynical comment jerked her head up. "No doubt. Well, since you seem determined to repeat the past, I can see that I'm wasting my time."

Kit's eyes narrowed. "I have learned," he said in the cold tones that had once sent chills down her spine. "And I do not intend to repeat my mistake, whatever you may think." He stood up and came to her, grasping her chin in his rough palm in an oddly tender gesture. "Once, perhaps, I thought I could escape my past. But I can't, angel. None of us can. It can't be escaped or changed. Only the most reckless would dare to ignore that."

Releasing her chin, he stepped back, and she tried to hold in the bitter tears burning her eyes. "Very well," she managed to say. "Off with the old, on with the new. I suppose now you will race off to chase the very lovely contessa. That should do the trick. No contessas in your past, Kit? Is this some novel and unusual sport, perhaps?"

She had thought to sound worldly and cynical, matching his jaded views. But to her shock, Kit gave a harsh bark of laughter that sounded anything but amused or impressed with her panache.

"So you have heard about Contessa Villiers, have you? I should have guessed. Gossip is the number one sport of the idle in London." His mouth twisted into a sardonic curl. "Do not be fooled, little one. The contessa is not new. She and I go a long way back. Longer than any other woman in my life."

Unable to stop herself, Angela blurted out, "Then it's true? You are seeing her?"

"Every time she will allow it. The contessa, you see, is very adroit at keeping a man dangling after her. A moment of time here, a glance there, then just a hint of the next time before she is gone again, leaving thirsty victims dying for another drop. Oh yes, that part is quite true. Is it being said that I am pursuing her?"

Miserably, Angela nodded, and Kit's sardonic smile deepened. "How droll. Perhaps I should have introduced you to her this evening. If I had known you were spying on me from the shadows, I would have done just that."

Recalling the beautiful woman in the carriage, Angela knew the answer even before she asked, "That was the contessa in the carriage?"

"Yes. Lovely, isn't she? Doesn't look anywhere near her age until one gets quite close. Then there are only a few signs of the years she has spent flitting about—a line or two, just the tiniest bit of sagging skin—but I should not bore you with the details."

"No," Angela whispered. She fumbled blindly for the edges of her cloak and pulled it around her as if for protection against the knife-edged slashes of pain that raked her. "I must . . . go."

Somehow, she was never quite certain how, Dylan was there, and it was his voice that directed her from Kit's cabin to the top deck, and his words that finally stilled her almost uncontrollable shivers. She recalled little of the carriage ride home, nor did she remember Emily putting her to bed. Everything was a blur, everything but Kit's relentless voice as he shattered any hope she had left.

Twenty-three

"Is it any coincidence," Charles Sheridan asked idly, "that Angela Lindell bears a striking resemblance to Elaine?"

Stiffening, Kit growled, "What the devil do you mean by that?"

The duke shrugged, and moved to stand facing the windows of his study, his hands clasped behind him. "Only," he said, his voice muffled by heavy draperies and thickly leaded glass, "that part of your resentment of the situation may stem from some misguided notion that Angela is just as treacherous as Elaine. That, my son, is doubtful. Only Vivian comes close to Elaine in duplicity, but she so far outdistances any other mortal woman that I think not even your misconception could make that vast leap."

After a moment, Kit said, "It amazes me that you married two such devious women. I have often wondered at the courage or stupidity of a man who would undertake such a venture."

The duke turned, smiling. "Do you? Love of a challenge, I suspect. Vivian St. Genevieve was only fourteen when we wed, and I had never laid eyes upon her until the day before the ceremony." He paused in reflection, a faint smile still curling his mouth. "Though you may not believe this, it was love at first sight for me. Of course, I was only seventeen at the time, and not exactly overjoyed at the prospect of a wife from the French countryside. Vivian changed that. As she changed every other aspect of my life in a very short time."

"She seems to have that ability."

Sheridan's ironic glance spoke volumes. "Indeed. When I discovered that I was soon to have an heir, I was thrilled for more than one reason. It would, I mistakenly thought, inhibit some of her more . . . reckless . . . qualities. Alas, she proved me quite wrong. Your birth only freed her from the duty of providing an heir, and set into motion an entirely new vista for her. She began to dabble in politics, still bearing a fervent loyalty to her own country, and I was beset at all sides with problems. How to keep my wife from endangering not only her head, but mine? I tell you, it was enough to drive even a less imaginative man quite mad."

Kit's smile was grudgingly sympathetic. Though lately he had formed a precarious truce with his father, it wasn't even close to anything resembling friendship. Conversations such as the one they were engaged in were infrequent and usually awkward. Perhaps it was the copious amount of brandy Kit had consumed after dinner that made the difference now. He wasn't certain.

Lifting his tumbler, Kit said, "She still drives men mad."

Sheridan turned. "Doesn't she? So tell me—how do you find her after all these years? Is she the devoted mother that you had always remembered?" His chair squeaked slightly as he sat down behind his desk and studied his son.

Wryly, Kit murmured, "Hardly. My memories are those of a six-year-old. Viewed from the illuminating distance of twenty-four years later, I have found vast discrepancies in my perceptions of what happened, and what I now believe to be the truth."

"I always thought you would, once you sifted through fantasy and fact. Of course, it took me years to differentiate between truth and bitter speculations. Even when I found you again, I believed that Vivian had committed the most heinous of crimes against a child. I was relieved to discover that to be untrue. It restored some of my faith in maternal affection."

When Kit remained silent, his father swiveled in his chair to look at him. "Christian," he said softly, earning Kit's upward glance, "your mother was careless, yes, but never callous. She loved you in her way, but she was very young and headstrong and totally committed to patriotism with a zeal few can ever realize. Do not judge her too harshly. She is what she is."

"As are we all." Kit took another sip of brandy, lowering the glass to study the slow drizzle of potent liqueur coating the sides. It felt as thick and syrupy on his tongue; he mentally blessed the Benedictine monks who had first distilled it. Brandy eased a multitude of worries if taken in small, isolated amounts. He heartily endorsed its medicinal properties in the treating of the human spirit. There were even times when brandy could erase the final images of Angela that had been seared into his brain.

He closed his eyes against that painful memory and

asked blindly, "How do you explain your marriage to Elaine?"

The duke's shrug was a thing felt, if not seen. "She was the antithesis of Vivian. Instead of a volatile temperament, she was always cool and collected, mindful of proprieties. I knew she would never risk my head or hers with impetuous behavior. Alas, it took me a shade too long to discover that her cool demeanor encased an even colder nature. Her treatment of you was my first indication."

Opening his eyes, Kit nodded. "She hated me. Never lost an opportunity to let me know it, either. I think I was a threat in some way. Her failure to provide another heir only made things worse. I can recall bitter arguments between the two of you over that."

"Yes. There were times I think she wished you would meet with an unfortunate accident."

Kit smiled grimly. He did not bother informing the Duke of several occasions he had narrowly escaped being killed. At the time, he'd not thought his father would believe him, or even care. It had only embittered him more over the years.

God, was his entire life to be a series of narrow escapes? He was beginning to realize that his control over his own destiny was still nebulous. Who could explain Angela's sudden appearance in his life except for an act of fate? Or perhaps, the whimsy of some laughing god.

"Perhaps," Sheridan mused, "I should not have divorced Vivian as I did. It was a precipitate act, fueled by jealousy, anger, and hurt at her leaving me and taking you with her. I viewed it as the highest betrayal. My acts, however, began a chain reaction that still has repercussions."

Looking up at the duke, he fumbled for the thread of their conversation, found it, and said, "If Vivian will only explain her reasons to me, perhaps I can forget her abandonment."

"I doubt it. One never forgets something like that. But you can accept it, even without an explanation that you are very unlikely to get. Perhaps it has escaped your notice that Vivian is adept at avoiding questions. That is what makes her so ideal at her profession."

Kit grimaced. "I find it abhorrent. How do I deal with the situation without betraying my own mother?"

Silence fell; a log in the fire popped and sent out a shower of sparks onto the hearth mat that quickly burned out. Finally the duke said slowly, "I don't know. Confront her, perhaps. But do not trust her enough to tell her of the proposition put forth to you by Mr. Pitt. That could be suicide. Concoct a plausible explanation, then allow her to make her own decision. After that, anything that happens will be of her own volition." He paused, then said, "I have my own doubts about the scheme Pitt proposes. Are you certain you wish to take such risks?"

Shrugging, Kit said, "There are no more risks involved than the ones I've taken for the past ten years. At least this time I will be working under the sanction of the king."

Sheridan's smile was cynical. "The treaty signed at Amiens will not last another six months. Napoleon will not stop until he is forced to stop. Even with a pardon for you and your crew, if the French take you . . ."

His voice trailed into silence. Kit needed no words to

tell him how quickly they would be executed if captured. He had committed too many crimes against the French to be given mercy if caught. It was understood, and the crew had heard the offer and voted to accept it, knowing what could happen. Only two men had declined, not being English. No one had blamed them. It was a dangerous proposal to undertake.

"We leave before dawn," he said into the heavy silence, and his father nodded.

"Do you intend to wish Angela farewell?"

The subject was still touchy between them, though Kit had slowly come to the conclusion that his father, true to character, had used Angela as a means to an end; in this case, to lure his son to London. Being an astute entrepreneur, John Lindell had been easily convinced to enter into a business venture with the duke. That had given Sheridan justifiable reason to invite the Lindells to social functions, and also gave him easy access to Angela. Mystified as to how his father had known about her at first—and why he thought she would matter to him—Kit was too stubborn to ask.

It had been Turk who had informed Kit that the spy they had employed was also employed by none other than the duke. "Gabriel is a multifaceted individual," Turk had observed with his usual understatement; only his logical assertion that it was hardly likely one could trust a man trafficking in deception for financial gain had defused Kit's first rush of anger. It also explained why Kit had so frequently been frustrated by near misses in his pursuit of Vivian St. Genevieve.

Now, he was just as frustrated though he had finally achieved his objective—another correct prediction Turk had made. It was infuriating that the giant could be so right so many times. And it gave him pause when he recalled Turk's insistence that Kit make amends with Angela.

God, he wanted to. How many nights had he lain in his bed and thought of her? Wondered where she was and if she thought of him at all. Most likely, he had mused, if she did think of him, it was with anything but charity. Still stinging from his mother's refusal to talk to him, he had been deliberately cruel to Angela, knowing it would drive her away from him. And it had worked only too well. The past month, both notes he had sent her had been returned unopened. He had only himself to blame, but his determination to dismiss her from his mind and life had wavered several times.

Looking up at his father, Kit said, "Perhaps I shall say my farewells to Angela before I leave. It should delight her to know that I am leaving London."

The duke smiled. "Filbert will have the carriage brought 'round for you."

A cold October wind pushed out the draperies in a bell shape and chilled the room. Flames danced like frenzied demons in the grate, sending sparks shooting up the chimney. Rising from her chair near the fire, Angela moved to the window and leaned out to pull it shut.

Dusky shadows shrouded the garden below, and the wind clacked through bare limbs as trees shed crimson and gold leaves into sodden piles on the ground. A sudden gust swept up a few of the drier leaves and whirled them in a spinning eddy; there was the smell of frost in the air, melding with the sharp scent of wood smoke.

Hesitating, Angela gazed into the garden, letting the damp air mist her skin. She thought of sea winds stirring up waves in lacy froths against the sides of a ship, wetting her toes and her dress. There was nothing outside to remind her of the sea, nothing but her own memories that never seemed to fade. Random events triggered the memories, sometimes nothing more than the warble of a sparrow to remind her of the exotic birds on St. Thomas.

Still leaning out the window, one arm outstretched as she gripped the latch to pull it closed, Angela shut her eyes and let the rain drizzle over her face and wet her hair. The wind chuckled around tall chimneystacks and building corners, tugging at her hair and seeming to whisper of far-off places. She shivered, then gave a start when a hand touched her shoulder.

"Miss Angela," Emily was saying, and with a final glance at the shifting shadows beyond the garden wall, Angela regretfully pulled the windows shut and turned.

"I was just . . . getting some fresh air," she explained lamely, and looked away from the sympathy in Emily's eyes. She could not bear that. No more sympathy. Even her mother had ceased to badger her into accepting social invitations; she suspected her father was behind that, but she did not care to explore the reasons for it.

"Miss Angela," Emily repeated, and there was a strange note in her voice that made Angela look up with a frown.

"Yes?"

"I . . . I came to tell you that I am leaving your employ."

Angela stared at her uncomprehendingly. Finally she asked in a shaky voice, "Why?"

"I can't tell you." Emily looked down at her clasped hands. Coaxing would not lift her head, and finally Angela reached out to grasp her chin.

"Tell me," she insisted, gazing into Emily's brown eyes. Color flushed the girl's face, and her mop of brown curls rioted over her forehead from beneath the neat white cap she always wore.

"Dylan," she blurted, and Angela understood.

Releasing Emily's chin, she nodded. "I see. You are going to stay with him, I imagine."

"Sort of."

"Sort of?" Angela eyed her speculatively. "What do you mean?"

"I have passage on a ship leaving London tomorrow tonight. I am to . . . to meet him in a month's time."

"The *Sea Tiger* is leaving?"

"Yes. Captain Saber is taking to the seas again. I was not supposed to tell you, but . . . but I couldn't just leave without telling you why."

Reeling from the emotional impact of knowing that Kit would be leaving London behind, Angela reached out blindly for a support. It was Emily's quickly proffered hand that gave it to her, and she stumbled to her chair and sank down into the cushions. She had somehow known that this day might come again, and thought herself prepared for it.

Was that what his unread notes had said? That he would soon be leaving? Perhaps she should have opened them, after all. It was just that she had hoped that he would come to her, not send her a formal, stiff note of explanation. Written sentiments had long ago left her skeptical, and surely he would know that. Why, then, had he not come to her? Why was he leaving without telling her farewell?

"Miss Angela," Emily said hesitantly, "maybe this is forward of me, but I think you should come along, too."

Angela stared at her blankly. What was the girl talking about? Why should she go to stay with Dylan?

"If nothing else," Emily said, "you'd be with me and Dylan. You're miserable here. Even your parents know it. Everyone knows it. If you came with me, you'd be bound to see Captain Saber again. He'd have to talk to you. Maybe then you could work things out. Oh, Miss Angela, it's worth a try. Do you intend to let him just walk away without taking responsibility for his actions?"

Angela smiled faintly. "That last bit of rhetoric sounds suspiciously like Turk."

Emily flushed. "Well, yes, he did say it first. It was his suggestion that you join me." Digging into her apron pocket, she brought out a thick envelope. "I already have our passage here."

Shaking her head, Angela murmured, "No, I shan't chase after a man. If he wants me—"

"Poppycock. You went after your fussy Frenchman and he wasn't worth two pence. Captain Saber loves you. If he didn't, he wouldn't have sent you two notes that you would not even read. He's been hurt bad in the past, and he's too proud to risk it again. Please. You must know deep in your heart how he feels. Don't you care enough to fight for what you want?"

Staring at her, Angela had the wild, crazy thought that Emily was right. It was insane, and she knew it, but something inside her urged her to do it. She had before, hadn't she? And even if it had turned out badly with Philippe, this time was different. Kit had let her into parts of his soul that no other woman had seen; she knew that instinctively. If she gave up now, she might lose it all. Yes. Emily was right. So was Turk. It was worth fighting for, even if she lost in the end.

"What's the name of this island?" Angela murmured, shutting her eyes and letting the sun warm her face. Emily stirred groggily beside her. It was late afternoon, and shadows had lengthened and deepened along the garden's stucco walls.

"I'm not certain. I just know it's near Crete. Safe, Dylan says, from Napoleon, because it's not important. Just a dot in the Aegean, he said."

After sailing along the coast of Spain and around through the straits of Gibraltar into the Mediterranean, their ship had finally docked on the large island of Crete. From there, they had taken another ship to a tiny jot of land in the Dodecanese Islands. It was warm here, with a temperate climate, though they were told it was the rainy season.

For the first time in months, Angela felt a sense of peace. On the voyage she had agonized over whether or not she was doing the right thing. Somewhere along the way, she had come to terms with her emotions and her motives. It had been very difficult trying to explain to her parents why she was leaving, but finally she had convinced them that she had to try. Even if Kit did not want her with him, she would be fine. Perhaps all she had needed was distance in order to put things in their proper perspective. Or maybe it was the reminder that the world was much larger than just London. How quickly one could forget and tend to judge events by a small, narrow point of view. Yes, no matter what happened when Kit arrived, she would be fine.

But when he came, the ship gliding in under cover of night and a light fog lying like clouds atop the surface of the tiny bay, Angela almost forgot her resolve. Nervous flutters of her heart were so distracting that she could barely keep her teeth from chattering. Emily gave her a concerned look.

"Are you sure you're all right, Miss Angela?"

"Quite s-s-sure." She clenched her teeth tightly together and grimaced. They were standing on the sandy beach near the quay. It had rained earlier, and the air was sticky with moist residue. "Just nervous," she added unnecessarily, and saw Emily smile.

Shreds of moonlight filtered through scudding clouds, bright and silvery, painting mundane surroundings with iridescent color. As the *Sea Tiger*'s sails caught the wind and tatters of fog, it turned in a slow, graceful half-circle and coasted into the harbor. There was the sound of lines humming through pulleys, creaking chains, and furling sails, canvas snapping as it was lowered. She could see the ship rocking gently in the bay, the sleek lines familiar and heart-stopping at the same time.

What would he say when he saw her?

She didn't have to wait long. A boat was lowered almost at once, and she saw the dark shapes of several people nestled in the tiny craft as it moved toward shore with a dipping of oars and splashing of water.

When the boat neared the end of the quay, she recognized Dylan in the prow. He leaped nimbly onto the stone dock, looping the anchoring line around a thick bollard.

Emily had already begun to run toward Dylan, her steps light and eager. Her heart in her throat, Angela held back, her eyes searching the gloom for Kit's familiar frame. Then she saw him stand, saw him leap up onto the dock with the same agility as Dylan, and as her pulses quickened and her mouth went dry, she saw him turn back to offer his hand to someone in the boat.

Hesitating, Angela strained to see through the shadows. Then she heard a feminine voice lifted in laughter, heard accents that she had heard before as the woman said, "Do not allow me to fall, or I shall be most angry with you, *mon chou.*"

Too paralyzed by shock and horror to move, Angela stood in anguished misery when Kit lifted up Contessa Villiers to stand beside him. How could he? Oh, she had been a fool to come, but she had never thought he would bring a woman along with him. And especially not this woman. Whatever was she thinking of to allow Emily to persuade her to come? Her first instincts had been correct. She should have remained in England.

It wasn't until Kit slid a steadying arm around the contessa's waist that Angela was able to break free from her daze and turn away. She fled back up the terraced hillside to the small, walled inn where she and Emily had a room.

Once again, she had sailed to meet a man who no longer wanted her.

Twenty-four

"I don't have to look far to find the culprit behind this scheme," Kit said shortly, his gaze shifting from Dylan to Turk and back. "Or perhaps I should use the plural tense instead of singular."

"It would be more appropriate," Turk murmured without a shred of remorse in his dark gaze. He met Kit's eyes without flinching. "I thought it a smashing notion."

"No doubt." Drawing in a deep breath, Kit glanced at the contessa, who seemed bored by the exchange. Lying gracefully upon a small sofa, she evinced more interest in her jeweled hands than she did the conversation. He was not, of course, fooled for a moment. She had heard every word. It was one of the traits that made her so successful.

Beckoning to Turk to join him, he left Dylan with the contessa and moved out onto the veranda of the small inn. When they were beyond earshot of the room they had just left, Kit asked tersely, "Where is she?"

"Presumably, in her lodgings. Emily informed me that she fled the beach. Contessa Villiers was not expected to be among the ship's passengers."

Kit shot him an ironic glance. "No doubt. It seemed the most expedient method of removing her from harm's way, however. Should I have conferred with you before bringing her aboard?"

"It would have saved a great deal of unnecessary trouble. I would have solved the quandary in an instant. And without undue stress."

"I'm most gratified to hear it. You were not present when the decision needed to be made, however, and I took the liberty of arranging my own life."

His sarcasm was not lost on Turk, who gave an eloquent shrug of his shoulders. "You're doing so well at it. I should never have suggested I could do a superior job."

Folding his arms over his chest, Kit said, "You couldn't. Your emotions aren't involved. Has it ever occurred to you that if they were, you might not react so logically at times?"

For a moment, Turk was silent. Then he said solemnly, "You are correct, of course. In times of deep emotional stress, I have been known to act very unwisely. It is much easier for one to remain detached and impart sensible advice, than it is to be involved and heed it."

Several moments passed before Kit said, "I'm going to talk to her. I should have before I left London." He waited for Turk to agree, and when no response was forthcoming, he muttered, "Hell, I actually stood in the rain outside her house for an hour. She came to the window and looked out. Her hair was all loose and flowing, and the rain misted her face—I could never dredge up the moral courage to face her after some of the things I led her to believe."

Shifting position, Turk turned to face him. "Perhaps it is not too late to make amends. If she came all this way just for you, it would be a shame for her to leave here as she did New Orleans."

Kit flinched at the comparison. He remembered only too well Angela's anguish after finding her betrothed. At the time, he had condemned Philippe du Plessis for betraying her. But hadn't he done the same thing in word, if not deed? Angela was right. There came a time in every person's life to take the risk of trusting someone. He was not a boy anymore, but a man who had experienced much of life. If he didn't trust himself not to choose a partner worthy of his love, how could he ever expect Angela to trust him? It was a fitting paradox, he thought grimly.

But it was much easier in theory, he found, than in actuality, to convince her. Angela refused to open the door. It was Emily who finally let him in, slipping past him and closing the door behind her. He stood awkwardly in the center of the room for several long moments. Angela would not even look at him. She kept her face averted as if it was too painful to see him.

Throwing himself into the hard comfort of a cane chair, he stared at her in growing frustration. "Angela," he said for what seemed like the tenth time, "look at me."

Still not looking at him, she said to a spot on the floor, "I was wrong to come here, Kit. Forgive me. Blame it on English weather in October. Sunny climes were too tempting."

"Bloody hell," he said, losing his temper and rising to his feet in a swift motion that drew a startled gasp from her. This time she looked at him, her green eyes wide with trepidation. He lowered his voice with an effort and said more calmly, "I had almost forgotten your eyes were that particular shade of green. Like the water in the bay at St. Thomas. Remember? It changed from blue to green, sometimes so clear we could see the fish darting around on the bottom."

A faint smile curved her mouth as she nodded. "Yes, I can remember that."

He couldn't help the almost painful rasp in his voice when he said, "Angela, there are so many things I remember about you. I admit, there was a time I didn't want to think about you, didn't want to love you. It was too risky. But now—"

"Don't," she gasped in a half-sob. Tears welled in her eyes and he reached out to her, but she avoided his touch. "No. Kit, I saw you earlier. I know that you are with . . . with the contessa."

"The contessa. I can explain that."

She interrupted him before he could form his thoughts. "There is no need to offer an explanation. You're free to be with whomever you wish. I should never have come here—"

"Dammit, Angela, will you listen?" He moved toward her, ignoring her efforts to avoid him as he took her by the arms. He held her tightly and gave her a small, frustrated shake. "Contessa Villiers is with me because I had to get her out of England. Did you hear the rumors about La Diabolique?" When she nodded, her head bent so that he had to stare at the curls atop her crown, he said through clenched teeth, "If I did not give her passage, she might have been arrested for espionage. There was an incident with a Colonel Despard that came to my attention . . ."

After a moment, Angela looked up and asked stiffly, "I can understand your wanting to keep her safe. But have you stopped to think that perhaps *you* might be tainted by the same charge? Unless, of course, you are willingly involved in treason." Her eyes widened, and she said with a catch in her voice, "Oh Kit, you—you aren't, are you?"

Amused in spite of the inference, Kit said, "No, angel. And you are wrong about my motives for helping the contessa. She is not my mistress, but my mother."

For a long moment, Angela only looked at him. Then she said haltingly, "Your . . . mother?"

Releasing her arms, Kit raked a hand through his hair and began to pace the floor of her small room. "Yes. Contessa Villiers is Vivian St. Genevieve, formally the Duchess of Tremayne. It's taken me years to catch up to her, years I wasted chasing her halfway around the globe and back—and when at last she decided to allow me to intercept her, it was in London."

A heavy silence fell, and he turned to watch Angela absorb the information. There was a puzzled frown on her face, and he knew she wondered—as he always had—why a mother would avoid her only son. It was a question that had haunted him for years, so he could not expect her to understand quickly.

"On the voyage here," he said, looking past Angela and into the dark night, "I asked the contessa why she had abandoned me. When I was very small, she left my father and took me with her. I won't go into details now, but on the voyage, she had arranged to have the ship intercepted so our trail would be covered. But the man who agreed to help her escape London did not want a small child. He concocted a drama that ended with my mother thinking I had fallen overboard and drowned. Frightened to face my father with my fate, she spent the next few years in hiding. By the time she discovered I was still alive, I had been captured by pirates· and was spending my youth in lively debauchery up and down the length of the Spanish Main. During this time, my father was also actively searching for me, having heard that she had abandoned me to my fate with pirates. After the first two years aboard a pirate ship, I knew no other life. I can recall being terrified at first, but being large for my age and agile, I learned quickly enough to keep from being abused. In time, I was comfortable with the pirates."

When he paused, Angela asked timidly, "But didn't you want to go home?"

"No." Kit shrugged. "What boy would? I did what I pleased, as long as I followed the same rules as the others. I was well versed in corruption, remember."

"But after you were returned to your father, surely you realized that you were suited for another life." Her brow furrowed in a delicate frown, and he resisted the temptation to kiss the tiny crease between her knit brows. She looked up at him, her eyes troubled beneath the long sweep of her lashes. "Kit, I am certain the duke wanted you to conform to a more appropriate position in life. I know you attended Oxford."

"Do you." Amused, he fought against the growing desire to kiss her. It amazed him that he had been foolish enough to leave her behind. Dylan and Turk should be rewarded for their meddling, however angry it had made him at first. "I wasn't a very good student," he explained.

"Too rowdy, they told me. I was constantly being caned for some infraction of the rules, and I was not very well liked by my contemporaries either."

"But Turk liked you."

"Ah, Turk was an outcast, too. Imagine, with his intellect, they had him cleaning out grates, carrying coal, and polishing fire dogs. I was appalled." He rested his hands on her shoulders, relieved that she allowed his touch. "I would never have suspected his intelligence if I had not accidentally discovered him reading one of my most difficult lessons on chemistry. Before I knew it, he was making suggestions about my solutions and formulas, and to my immense surprise, my tutors complimented me on my ingenious ideas." Laughing, he shook his head. "They were frankly disbelieving when I informed them who had really done the work. That is one time when my father supported me with great enthusiasm. I always wondered if it was because he believed in Turk, or was just grateful that I had found an interest that did not require vast sums of money to rescue me. Whatever, he sponsored Turk, and he was one of the most brilliant students there. Until we quit, anyway."

"Turk quit because you did."

"Yes. I tried to convince him to stay, but he was stubborn. You know how he can get."

"Yes." She fell silent a moment, a small smile hovering at the corners of her mouth. "I know very well how stubborn he can be when he believes in something."

"Angela." Kit took her hands in his, holding them. "Give me another chance. I know I've made mistakes. I'll probably make more. It won't be easy to change, but I'm willing to give it a try."

He looked down at her small, delicate hands, rubbing the backs of them with his thumbs. His hands were so large and brown, with scars and calluses . . . her outer fragility humbled him in the face of her inner strength. Hardly realizing he was speaking aloud, he lifted his head and stared down into her upturned face.

"I guess I've been a coward. It didn't seem like it. I thought I was just smart enough to keep a wall around me. But I've been running for most of my life. Here, I thought I could do anything, take ships and cargo, all for vengeance against my father. Against everyone who had ever betrayed me. But life isn't that simple. You can't hurt other people without hurting yourself. I should have seen that, should have understood. Or just listened to Turk. He loves to expound upon his rhetoric, but I dismissed him. He's a lot smarter than I am. God. I'm standing here admitting that Turk is right and I'm wrong. He should be here. He would love this. Before you know it, he'll have me eating his bloody macrobiotic diet."

He drew in a deep, aching breath, and saw with a faint spurt of surprise that Angela was laughing and crying at the same time. Tears silvered her cheeks, and he put up a hand to track a drop as it slipped down her face.

"Don't cry, angel," he murmured, folding her into his arms. "Please don't cry. I can't bear it when you do. It tears my heart out."

"Kit," she said against his shirt, her voice muffled by the bunched linen, "I'm not certain what you want me to say."

His embrace tightened. "Say what you feel. Anything but the truth would be unjust." Feeling open and vulnerable, he realized that he was quivering inside. What if she refused him? What if it was too late? He'd opened himself for her, laid bare his heart and his secrets—God, what would he do if he had already ruined it all?

Curling his hand in her loose hair where it tumbled down her back, he slowly drew her head back so that she looked up at him. Her eyes were still silvered with tears, but she was smiling.

"I love you," she whispered, and the world reeled abruptly before righting again.

"God," he said fervently, "I love you, too. Angela—will you marry me?"

"That depends," she said, tilting her head to one side. "Will I be the wife of a lord, or a pirate?"

"Which do you prefer?"

She thought a moment, then said so earnestly he knew she was telling the truth, "A pirate, I think."

Laughing, he pulled her up to her toes and kissed her, the deep, satisfying kiss of a man long-starved. "Why," he finally whispered when he broke the kiss, his breathing harsh and irregular, "do you prefer a pirate?"

Lightly touching his ear with one finger, exploring it with deliciously slow circles, she drew her fingertip down his jaw line in a leisurely glide as she murmured, "It has something to do with the way you wield your sword, I think."

"Ah." He took another hard breath as her hand moved to caress his throat. "My sword. I see. Do you mind? It's hard to concentrate with your hands . . . *Jesus*." The last was heartfelt as her hand dipped to the buckle of his belt. His stomach muscles contracted violently beneath the feathery pressure of her fingers. "Angela. . . ." This time his voice was a hoarse croak, embarrassing him.

She gave him an arch glance. "You have had things your way much too long, sir. I'm familiar with pirates, and the way they ravish their victims. Now you," she said, quickly drawing the dagger he always had tucked into his belt, "are my captive."

Rather edgy about the dagger, but willing to take chances, he slowly held out his arms to the sides. "I am at your mercy," he said, and Angela laughed.

"I'll be gentle. . . ."

"Love, be anything you like. Just be mine."

As his shirt cascaded to the floor in a white drift, she looked up at him with love shining from her eyes. "Always, Kit. Always and forever."

They were, he thought hazily as he followed her to the bed, the sweetest words he'd ever heard uttered.

Epilogue

The Caribbean, 1803

A warm, tropical breeze drifted through palm fronds and blew sand in tiny eddies across the beach. Angela shifted and put a hand over her eyes, shading them as she scanned the shoreline for Kit. He was due back any day now. With rumbles of war again in Europe—the duke, as usual, had been right about Napoleon and the treaty—Kit was being called upon much more frequently. Under the guise of piracy, he had managed to gather a great deal of information.

A faint smile curved her mouth. It was still amusing to recall her parents' shock when she'd returned home and informed them that she was now a countess. She had married Kit in a tiny Greek fishing village, with Emily as her best maid and Turk and Dylan and a host of pirates attending. Even Kit's mother had participated, with a languid indifference that characterized most of her reactions.

Unless it pertained to her beloved France.

While they were still in Greece, word had come that Colonel Despard and three dozen of his confederates had been arrested for a plot to kill the king. The colonel had been executed, and his followers imprisoned. Soon after, Contessa Villiers departed the island with a careless farewell.

"Does it bother you for your mother to be so indifferent?" Angela had asked Kit, and he'd shrugged.

"At times. It might be nice to have a mother who doted on me." Grinning, he'd added, "But I have a wife who dotes on me enough to satisfy me."

It was true. She doted. Grimacing at the word, Angela went back into the whitewashed stone house that nestled in pristine comfort on the side of a hill. Rollo scuttled across the floor, a scarlet arrow of noisy complaints.

"Bloody hell!" the bird screeched, and fluttered indignantly when Angela shooed him from her path. During a bad storm, he had broken a wing, and Kit had left him behind for Angela to nurse. Despite his bad habits and vulgar language, Rollo was a reminder of Kit and a comfort to her. The lory had even taken to riding on her shoulder at times, though he had a tendency to break into ribald songs and shock the occasional visitor.

Emily claimed that she and Dylan could hear the bird's high-pitched chatter in their cozy house a half-mile away when the wind was just right. Swelling with Dylan's child, Emily had blossomed into a beautiful woman, serene and confident and very much in love with her pirate husband. Even Turk had found a form of domesticity to his liking, though he had yet to wed the lovely native girl who shared his home.

"I find the notion of familial subsistence faintly abhorrent, though I admit it does have its rewards," Turk had observed one evening when they were all gathered around a fire on the beach. His devoted companion only smiled shyly up at him, her black eyes holding secrets that Turk seemed not to see. It was evident to everyone else that he was in love, proving, Kit had said with a sardonic smile, that Turk was not infallible after all.

Life on the dot of land in the Caribbean had been idyllic and lazy, and Angela's life in England remote. She didn't miss it at all.

It was Rollo that heralded Kit's return. Night shadows blanketed the island in velvet-soft shrouds and familiar sounds. Angela was lying in her bed when she heard the bird shriek, "Heave to, mates! Ship to starboard!"

Sitting up, she just had time to gasp before a shadow was at her side. "It's me, angel. Sorry about Rollo." Silently, she wrapped her arms around his neck and held him, her cheek against his shoulder. He was home. God, it felt so right to have him hold her again; the fresh scent of wind and sea clung to him in tantalizing familiarity.

"Angel," he murmured, nuzzling her cheek. "I brought you a surprise."

She smiled into the soft shadows. "You being here is gift enough."

Laughter rumbled in his chest, and he squeezed her gently before pulling away. "I'm certain it is. This gift, however, is multipurposeful."

"So are you." She drew her hand down his bare chest. He wore only a supple leather vest, trousers, and knee-high boots. Her hand bumped against the hilt of his dagger as she slid her fingers around the corded muscles of his stomach to the belt buckle. He caught her hand in his and lifted it to his mouth.

"Are you sure," he asked in a husky murmur, "that you don't want to see your surprise now?"

"Quite sure." Her mouth found his in the dark and clung, her lips moving softly against his, tasting sea tang and traces of wine. Beard stubble scratched lightly against her cheek as she brushed against his jaw. She had to gasp a little when his hand cupped the swell of her breast, his thumb raking in erotic circles around her nipple. Arching her back into his hand, she shivered.

It was several minutes before Kit's attention strayed to another area, and Angela was flushed and aching, her entire body aflame with need. Somehow—it always amazed her how he could manage it so skillfully—they were both naked, bare skin sliding in delicious glides of muscle and bone and sensitive nerve endings.

Holding him, Angela knew that nothing was as important as the man in her arms. He was all that mattered. In the past nine months, their love had grown strong and deep, and all the past secrets had been explored and reconciled. Oh, life was not perfect by any means. Napoleon was still a threat and Kit was committed to doing his patriotic best for England. There were times she was terrified that she would lose him. But she had faith in him, in his ability to survive. He'd conquered overwhelming odds to become the man he was now, and all the past adversity had been met with a courage and determination that had forged him into the man she loved.

"I love you," she whispered in his ear as he slipped inside her, and she felt him shiver beneath her palms.

"Angel," he muttered thickly, lifting his head to stare down at her, cupping her face between his palms, "I love you more than I ever thought it possible to love anyone."

It was much later before Angela remembered drowsily that she had not discovered Kit's surprise. He laughed in sleepy satisfaction when she asked him and tightened his arm around her.

"I brought home a duke as your new pet. He's eager to show you how to organize your household . . . as if he doesn't have enough to do in England tending both our business holdings while I'm off playing patriot."

Twisting, she asked, "You brought your father?"

"And Filbert. He insisted." Kit nuzzled the curve of her shoulder. "You know how insistent he can be."

"Like father," she murmured, "like son."

"Something like that."

Silent, Angela wondered if it was the right time to tell Kit that she had a surprise of her own. Should she tell him now that he would soon have a son or daughter of his own? No, he was tired from his journey and their lovemaking. It could wait until the morning. After all, they had the rest of their life together.

WHAT'S LOVE GOT TO DO WITH IT?

Everything . . . Just ask Kathleen Drymon . . . and Zebra Books

CASTAWAY ANGEL	*(3569-1, $4.50/$5.50)*
GENTLE SAVAGE	*(3888-7, $4.50/$5.50)*
MIDNIGHT BRIDE	*(3265-X, $4.50/$5.50)*
VELVET SAVAGE	*(3886-0, $4.50/$5.50)*
TEXAS BLOSSOM	*(3887-9, $4.50/$5.50)*
WARRIOR OF THE SUN	*(3924-7, $4.99/$5.99)*

Available wherever paperbacks are sold, or order direct from the Publisher. Send cover price plus 50¢ per copy for mailing and handling to Penguin USA, P.O. Box 999, c/o Dept. 17109, Bergenfield, NJ 07621. Residents of New York and Tennessee must include sales tax. DO NOT SEND CASH.